Ann Granger has lived in cities in various parts of the world, since for many years she worked for the Foreign Office and received postings to British embassies as far apart as Munich and Lusaka. She is married, with two sons, and she and her husband, who also worked for the Foreign Office, are now permanently based in Oxfordshire.

Shades of Murder

Ann Granger

HEADLINE

First published in 2000
by HEADLINE BOOK PUBLISHING

First published in paperback in 2001
by HEADLINE BOOK PUBLISHING

10 9 8 7 6 5 4

ISBN 0 7472 6803 7

Printed and bound in Great Britain by
Clays Ltd, St Ives plc

Typeset by CBS, Martlesham Heath, Ipswich, Suffolk

HEADLINE BOOK PUBLISHING
A division of Hodder Headline
338 Euston Road
London NW1 3BH

www.headline.co.uk
www.hodderheadline.com

ACKNOWLEDGEMENTS

There are many people I have to thank for their advice, help and encouragement during the writing of this book. So a big Thank-You to Professor Bernard Knight CBE, distinguished pathologist and fellow crimewriter, for his advice on the procedure regarding exhumations. To the Museum of the Royal Pharmaceutical Society for information on laudanum. To fellow crimewriter Dr Stella Shepherd and her husband John Martin, for their knowledge on matters medical generously made available to me on this and other occasions. To the Oxford Coroner's Office. To the staff of the Centre for Oxfordshire Studies at the Westgate Library, Oxford. To David Dancer of Oxford County Hall who showed me round Oxford's 'old' court and its atmospheric subterranean tunnel. To my agent Carole Blake, my editor Marion Donaldson, my long-suffering family and friends and above all, my husband, John Hulme.

A.G.

LIST OF CHARACTERS

The First Shade, Bamford 1889–90

William Oakley, of Fourways House
Cora, his wife
Mrs Martha Button, housekeeper
Watchett, gardener
Daisy Joss, nursemaid
Inspector Jonathan Wood, Bamford Police
Emily, his daughter
Sergeant Patterson, Bamford Police
Stanley Huxtable, reporter on the *Bamford Gazette*
Mr Taylor, prosecuting counsel at the trial of Wm Oakley
Mr Green, defending counsel at the trial

The Second Shade, Bamford 1999

Damaris Oakley   }
Florence Oakley   }   grand-daughters of Wm Oakley
Jan Oakley, great-grandson of Wm Oakley
Ron Gladstone, gardener
Superintendent Alan Markby, Regional Serious Crimes Squad
Inspector Dave Pearce, as above
Meredith Mitchell, Foreign Office employee
Dr Geoffrey Painter, poisons expert
Pamela, his wife
Juliet, his sister
Reverend James Holland, Vicar of Bamford
Superintendent Doug Minchin, Metropolitan Police
Inspector Mickey Hayes, as above
Dolores Forbes, landlady of The Feathers
Kenny Joss, taxi-driver
Dr Fuller, pathologist
Harrington Winsley, Chief Constable
Dudley Newman, builder

PART ONE

The First Shade

Murder most foul, as in the best it is,
But this most foul, strange, and unnatural.

Shakespeare, *Hamlet*, Act I, Scene 5

Chapter One

1889

Cora Oakley leaned against the lace-trimmed pillows. Sweat trickled from her hairline down her forehead, along her nose, across her upper lip and formed a salty pool in the puckered skin at the corner of her mouth. She was hardly aware of it. Tentacles of pain stretched from her throbbing jaw down her neck to her shoulder. The whole right side of her face felt afire. It had been three days since the tooth had been drawn and the dentist had promised the wound would soon settle.

Why must men always lie about everything? thought Cora. She touched the swollen flesh and winced.

The turret room had been hers since she'd come to Fourways. Most of it was in a velvet semi-darkness but she lay on the edge of a pool of light cast by a lamp on the bedside cabinet. The china base of the lamp was painted with violets. Inside the bulbous glass shade the flame, fed by the fuel store inside the base, twisted and jumped angrily like an imprisoned imp wanting to be free to create mischief.

I'm going to change my room, Cora decided. I don't like this room. I've never liked it.

William had said this was to be her room. His room was

at the other side of the house. That was hardly the normal arrangement for married couples but William wanted it that way and she knew why.

As if thought of her husband had called him up, the door opened and he came in, carrying a small tray.

'Here we are,' he said. He put the tray down on the table, by the lamp. 'I handed over Perkins's prescription. Baxter gave me this.'

Cora turned her head so that she could see the familiar little bottle with its handwritten label *Laudanum*, and beneath this, in brackets, *Tincture of Opium*.

'Baxter tells me there are new things coming along now for pain such as toothache. I told him you preferred to stick with what you knew.' He paused as if expecting she would say something. When she didn't, he went on briskly. 'Well, there's a jug of water, a glass and a teaspoon. Do you want to take it now?' He stretched out his hand to the bottle.

Cora rolled her head from side to side on the pillow in negation. She just wished he'd go away. She knew how to dose herself. The laudanum had been a friend for a long time now, one she could turn to in the depths of the black depression which haunted her. She would sleep undisturbed by the raging inflamed gum around the empty socket where the tooth had been. Yet even the prospect of sleep filled her with a prickle of apprehension. Recently, her sleep had been beset with nightmares. In despair, she asked herself if, awake or asleep, she was never to have peace?

'Very well, then,' William said. He stooped and planted a passionless kiss on her damp forehead. 'Goodnight.'

As he walked to the door, she found her voice and called, 'William!'

He turned, his hand on the doorknob, his dark eyebrows raised. Even in her present distress, she thought how handsome he was. She understood bitterly how a feather-headed seventeen-year-old such as she had been when they'd met, could have fallen in love with him. Fallen so completely for a man who was completely rotten, through and through.

She said, as clearly as she could through the swelling and pain, 'I intend to dismiss Daisy in the morning.'

'Doesn't she care for the boy properly?' His voice was cold.

'I don't like her attitude.'

'In what way?' Even though he stood in the shadows, she could see the contempt on his face, hear it in his voice.

He must think I'm stupid, she thought. But she was in too much pain to argue. Instead, she said, 'You have made me an object of pity and ridicule in the eyes of everyone who knows us.'

'You're talking nonsense,' he said briefly. He opened the door.

'It's too much,' Cora said, her tongue moving with difficulty in her mouth. 'Not again, William. I won't stand for it again.'

He didn't answer and as he moved through the open door she called, 'There must be an end to it, William!'

She had dared to use the word he couldn't abide. He swung back. 'Must?'

Driven by her pain and despair, she retorted, 'I shall seek a separation.'

She saw the corner of his mouth twitch, as if he was going to smile. But all he said was, 'Perhaps in the morning you'll make more sense.' And then he was gone.

* * *

'Goodnight, then, Mr Watchett,' said Martha Button.

She closed the kitchen door on the gardener and locked it. For good measure she then shot the bolts top and bottom and having done this, checked the window. Having satisfied herself that none but the most determined intruder could get into the kitchen, she cast a look of satisfaction around the room.

The kitchen range needed a good going over with blacklead but Lucy could do that in the morning. Keep the girl occupied. Mrs Button's eagle eye fell on the two glasses on the table and the sherry bottle. She put the bottle away in the cupboard and rinsed the sherry glasses, dried them and put them away, too. After a moment's hesitation, she gathered up the small plate on the table and rinsed that. All these things could also have been left for Lucy to do but there were some things, unlike the tiresome and messy job of blackleading the range, to which it was better not to draw a housemaid's attention. Not that Mrs Button and Mr Watchett weren't entitled to a glass of sherry and a gossip of an evening, but it was always important to keep the respect of one's underlings and not give them any cause to laugh at you behind your back.

It was getting late. Watchett had stayed longer than usual. Mrs Button went out into the main hall. A single gasmantle still glimmered there, hissing softly, though the other downstairs rooms were in darkness. The atmosphere was heavy with unseen presences as a house is at night. The grandfather clock marked the time as almost eleven. She went to check that the bolts on the front door were in place. Of course, Mr Oakley checked the door last thing, but tonight her employer had seemed absent in his manner. He'd retired early, before ten. She'd heard him go upstairs. Well, as she'd said to Watchett, it wasn't surprising he'd got things on his mind.

'I could see it coming, Mr Watchett. As soon as that girl Daisy Joss set foot in this house. Far too pretty for her own good.'

'Ah,' said Watchett. 'Never no good came from hiring any Joss.'

'And poor Mrs Oakley in the state she's in from her tooth. Having it pulled out, I mean. I really don't know why she didn't go up to London to a dentist used to dealing with gentlefolk. As it is, she's been in a terrible state ever since that local fellow yanked it out.'

'Doorknob and a piece of string,' said Watchett. 'Best way to get a tooth out.'

'It couldn't have done more harm!' sniffed Mrs Button.

The front door was bolted. She nodded and went to turn off the gasjet. In doing so, she caught sight of herself in the mirror and paused to pat her hair which was a curious mahogany colour. Then she made her way back to the kitchen and stepped through into the adjacent lobby from which the backstairs ran up to the upper floors. All alone as she was down here, she could've gone up the main staircase, but habit died hard. Backstairs were for servants, and though she was definitely an upper servant of the very best kind, she took herself to her bed by this route, through the darkened house, candlestick in hand.

Around her the house creaked and groaned in the falling temperature. On the first floor, the backstairs came out at the end of the corridor, right by the door to the turret room where Mrs Oakley slept. As Mrs Button turned to go up the next flight to the rooms under the eaves where she had both her own sleeping quarters and a little room designated her sitting room, she heard a sudden crash.

It was followed immediately by a cry. A cry so strange, so unearthly, she couldn't believe it was human. If it came from anything in this world at all, it seemed a tortured squeal issued by some animal in agony. Her heart leapt painfully and with her free hand she sketched the sign of the cross. She was a cradle Catholic, though her observance of any religion had been noticeable by its absence for many years. Now, sensing she was to be tested in some way in which she couldn't cope without divine help, she sought the comforting token of her childhood faith.

There was no doubt both sounds had come from behind Mrs Oakley's door. Fearfully, the housekeeper approached and after a moment's hesitation, tapped. 'Mrs Oakley, ma'am?'

There was no reply and yet, her ear pressed to the door panel, she thought she heard movement, a rushing sound, a strange rasping breath. Then, quite clearly, a strangled gurgle and another squeal, cut off midway as if the air supply to it had been interrupted.

Not knowing what she would see, and filled now with sheer panic, Mrs Button seized the knob and threw the door open.

'Oh, my God, my God!' The housekeeper clasped her throat with her free hand.

An infernal scene met her eyes, a medieval hell in which a figure lying on the carpet twisted and turned surrounded by flames and a dancing red and yellow light. The air was foul with a pungent stench, making Mrs Button retch and cough. It was compounded of burning wool, lamp oil, scorched flesh and an overpowering odour which struck her as familiar though for the moment, she didn't identify it. The bedside lamp lay in broken fragments on the blackened and smouldering carpet. Amongst the shards was something which struck her as odd but all this was noticed in the split second before her whole attention focused on *it*.

The creature, that burning thing, jerked and twitched on the floor uttering sobbing breaths as if it would scream but could not. The housekeeper tremblingly set down her candlestick and took a step forward and then, seized with terror and revulsion, stepped back again. To her horrified gaze, the creature raised itself by some superhuman effort amid the bonfire and reached out one blackened, peeling talon in mute supplication. As it did so, its long hair caught the flame and burst into a dreadful halo. The creature squealed on a high, thin inhuman note which died away as if the lungs had been squeezed empty of air and then fell back.

Mrs Button gasped, 'Mrs Oakley! Oh, Mrs Oakley!'

Chapter Two

1999

'Mr Gladstone,' said Damaris Oakley as firmly as she could, 'we've been through all this before. Neither my sister nor I have the slightest desire to have a water feature in the garden.'

'Why not?' he asked.

They stared hard at one another, presenting an incongruous contrast of styles. Damaris wore a very old tweed skirt, the lining drooping below the hem. This was teamed with an even older hand-knitted jumper in a strange bobbly pattern and a cardigan. In front, the cardigan's ribbing, to which the buttons were sewn, had stretched to hang below the waist. At the back, the cardigan had shrunk and ridden halfway up the wearer's spine. On her head Miss Oakley wore a venerable soft tweed hat which had belonged to her father and even had the remains of one of his fishing flies stuck in it.

Ron Gladstone, on the other hand, was a picture of respectable neatness even in his gardening attire. His cardigan was clean, buttoned up and covered a shirt and tie. His fading ginger hair was trimmed to military shortness. His small bristling moustache had kept its red hue and made him look like a combative cockerel. As a concession to being outdoors he wore stout footwear, but even that had clearly been polished before he left home and the few smears of mud and a smattering of grass clippings didn't really spoil the effect.

Damaris reflected, not for the first time, that helpful arrangements were all very well but they often carried hidden disadvantages with them. There was no way they could afford a gardener or even pay for regular visits from one of those garden maintenance firms. She and Florence had got quite beyond being able to cope themselves with rampant greenery and in despair they'd sought help.

Ron Gladstone hadn't been the first attempt to solve the problem. There had been a young man sent to them by Social Services. Damaris recalled him with a shudder. He'd worn an earring and had a spider's web tattooed on his shaven skull. He'd addressed both her and her sister as 'darling'. Being his darling hadn't prevented him from disappearing from their garden and their lives without warning, but with what remained of the family silver, including matching frames containing the only photographs they'd had of their brother Arthur in his RAF uniform. One of the photographs had been taken on his last visit home, just before the fatal sortie on which his plane had plunged into the Kent countryside.

Damaris had tried to explain what this had meant to the pretty young policewoman who'd come to take the details. 'We shouldn't have minded so much if he'd just taken the frames and left us the contents. After all, Arthur's picture couldn't possibly be of any interest to him, could it?'

She'd then fallen silent, embarrassed at finding herself speaking in this way to a stranger.

'Really rotten luck,' the policewoman had sympathised.

Yes, thought Damaris. Really rotten luck. Just what the Oakleys had always had. Her parents had never recovered from the loss of Arthur. She, in the old-fashioned way, had stayed at home to care for them as they aged and grew infirm until they'd died, by which time she was no longer of any interest to anyone else.

There had been a young man who'd wanted to marry Florence, but their parents had thought him unsuitable and in the end, Florence had bowed to their joint disapproval. The rejected young man had taken himself off to South Africa where he'd set up a winery in the Cape and done, they'd heard, rather well. Why didn't Florence fight for him? wondered Damaris. Why didn't she fight for herself? Easy to say now. So difficult to do then. Too late now, anyway.

'All dead and gone,' murmured Damaris to herself.

'What's that, Miss Oakley?' asked Ron, twitching his moustache.

'I'm sorry, Mr Gladstone. I was drifting.'

It was the vicar, James Holland, who'd suggested the present arrangement. At first, after their experience with the shaven-headed thief, it had appeared to be ideal. Ron had retired. He was living in a small neat flat with no garden. It left him nothing to do but walk down to the library every morning to read the newspapers and gardening magazines, and complain to the librarian about the noise made by visiting schoolchildren. The librarian then complained about *him* to Father Holland, who'd dropped in for a chat. That's when the vicar had his good idea and how Ron had finished up here, at Fourways, five days a week. On Saturdays he did his weekly shop and on Sundays he didn't work in the garden because it said in the Bible that you shouldn't, as he'd explained to Father Holland.

'But you'd know about that, Vicar!'

At first the arrangement had appeared ideal. The long grass was cut, the misshapen hedges trimmed. But gradually, Ron Gladstone began to get more grandiose ideas. The fact was, he'd begun to look upon the garden as 'his'. It was causing problems. They hadn't minded when he'd restored some of the overgrown flowerbeds near the house. The bright array of bedding plants had been cheerful. Doubt had set in when he'd cut the yew hedge along the drive to resemble castle battlements. Since then he'd had a host of other ideas, most of which the Oakleys found incomprehensible.

'I suspect, Mr Gladstone,' said Damaris, 'that you've been watching those gardening programmes on television again.'

'Never miss!' said Ron proudly. 'Get a lot of good ideas from them.'

'I dare say, but that doesn't mean my sister and I want an alpine garden, or a bog garden, or a patio with bar – bar-bee – oh, whatever it is. And we *don't* want a water feature!'

'I was thinking,' Ron told her, just, she thought crossly, as if she hadn't said a word, 'I was thinking of a small pond. Of course, if you'd agree to a pipe running from the house, I could make a little fountain.' He looked hopeful.

'We've got a fountain already,' she said promptly.

'You mean that chipped old stone basin stuck in the middle of the front drive? It don't work,' said Mr Gladstone.

'Does that matter?' asked Damaris. It hadn't worked, as far as she could remember, since she'd been a small child. The fat winged baby standing in the middle of the basin – no one knew whether he was a cherub or a Cupid who'd lost his bow – had long been covered in yellow and grey lichen which made him look as if he was suffering from some unpleasant skin disease.

'How can it be a fountain without any water? I'll fix you up one which does work.'

'We don't want a fountain, Mr Gladstone!' Damaris knew she sounded exasperated.

Some of her exasperation percolated through to Ron. 'Just a small pond, then, without a fountain – not but what it seems a pity to me, to only do half the job.'

Damaris was struck by a bright idea. 'We couldn't have a pond, Mr Gladstone. They encourage frogs.'

'What's wrong with frogs?' He looked surprised. 'They eat insects. They clean up your garden.'

'They croak,' said Damaris. 'They get under your feet and car wheels and get squashed. No pond, Mr Gladstone! Can we leave the subject for the moment? I wanted to have a word with you. You do know, don't you, that we're contemplating selling the house?'

Ron looked glum. 'I did hear it. What do you want to do that for?'

'We can't manage it, it's as simple as that. Mrs Daley comes in and puts a duster round three times a week but she's getting on and her legs are bad. She would have to give up at Christmas, she's told us. So that rather settled matters. Florence and I mean to look for a convenient flat with a modern kitchen.'

An image of the antiquated kitchen fixtures at Fourways swam before Damaris's inner eye, particularly the cold stone floor.

'Proper central heating,' she added wistfully.

Ron's moustache bristled. 'I have a flat!' he announced, as Martin Luther King once declared he had a dream. 'And very convenient I dare say it is. But it's – not – like – this!' He accompanied the last words by stabbing around him in various directions with the trowel he held.

'No,' said Damaris in a bleak voice. 'No. We shall naturally be sorry to leave. This was our childhood home. All our memories . . . But Florence and I have decided we're entitled to a little comfort at the end of our lives. And we mean to have it!' she concluded briskly.

'Then my advice to you,' said Ron earnestly, 'is to let me put in a small ornamental pond. Just over there, by the magnolia tree.'

This seemed such a complete non-sequitur that she could only gaze at him.

'You've got to make a place look a bit special if you want to sell,' he explained, seeing her bewilderment. 'A garden with a nice little water feature, that could tip the balance. People often buy a house because they've fallen for the garden.'

It was with great relief that Damaris saw her sister approach from the direction of the house.

She abandoned the fray with, 'You'll have to excuse me, Mr Gladstone!' and hastened away to meet Florence.

As she got closer, her feeling of relief faded. Florence's slight form, dressed in much the same sort of clothes as Damaris wore, looked as if a breath of wind would blow it away. She is younger than I am, thought Damaris, but she'll go first, I suppose, and I shall be left quite alone. We must get away from here. We mustn't spend another winter without proper central heating . . . we must get that flat!

She looked beyond Florence towards the house with its Victorian Gothic features which, set in the mould of the local stone, did make Fourways look like a castle or at least a baronial hall. I wasn't honest with Ron Gladstone just now, thought Damaris. I wasn't being honest with myself. It's true I've lived here all my life, and I ought to be deeply attached to the place. Yet really, I do believe I hate it. I feel as though, somehow, it's eaten me up. Even when I was young and had my job in Bamford, I cycled back home here directly work was finished because my parents expected to see me on the dot, for dinner. Others went off to parties and dances and met young men and got married. But not me, oh no! I was needed here. I shan't be a bit sorry to leave. I don't care who buys it. I don't care if they knock the whole wretched pile down. It never brought any Oakley any luck.

To Florence she said, 'Mr Gladstone is still going on about a water feature. I've done my best to dissuade him. We're fortunate to have him, I suppose. The garden was such a wilderness before he took it on. Do you remember Evans who was gardener when we were children?'

'Yes,' said Florence. 'He showed us how to plant runner beans in pots. We put them on the shelf in the old potting shed, labelled with our names. Your beans always grew better than mine and Arthur's grew best of all.'

Despite this happy reminiscence, it struck Damaris that there was tension in her sister's manner. Concerned, she asked, 'What is it, dear?'

'The post has come,' said Florence Oakley. The wind caught at her silver hair and tugged strands from the rolled sausage at the nape of her neck.

There was a silence. Damaris looked at her, waiting, her

heart heavy. She didn't ask what the post had brought. She knew what it would be and she didn't want to hear it. Every few seconds gained before the words were spoken were precious, because after they were spoken, nothing would ever be the same again.

Florence straightened up slightly with an effort, preparing herself to break unwelcome news.

'There is a letter,' she said. 'It's definite. He's coming.'

'Poison,' said Geoffrey Painter, 'was once a great deal more popular as a weapon than it is today. Ah, sausage rolls! Have you had one of these, Meredith?'

'Watch out!' whispered Alan Markby in her ear. 'It may be spiked.'

'Is Geoff bending your ear about poisons again?' asked the bearer of the sausage-roll tray, Pam Painter. 'Honestly, he's obsessed.'

Markby smiled at her. 'Speaking as a humble copper, I for one have often had reason to be thankful for Geoff's knowledge of poisons. It's been a great help to us.'

'That's no reason to encourage him to go on about them now,' said Pam briskly. 'Geoff! It's an off-limits topic, right?'

'You can imagine what she's like at county council meetings, can't you?' said Geoff, unperturbed at receiving this order. 'Alan and Meredith are interested, Pam.'

'It's a house-warming party,' argued his wife. 'The atmosphere's supposed to be cheerful!'

She bore her sausage-roll tray onwards to other guests packed in the rather small drawing room of the Painters' brand-new house. Meredith thought it was useless asking Geoff not to talk about poisons. He was one of those people who have managed to make a profession match a hobby. He loved his work and he loved talking about it. Standing in the middle of a packed room, his balding head flushed with the heat and his own enthusiasm, he had at his command a whole new audience. How could he ignore it?

'How do you like the new house now you're settled in?' she asked, deflecting him.

Geoff looked round the room as if seeing it for the first time. 'Fine. It's what Pam wanted. I find it a bit cramped myself but that's modern housing for you.'

Pam, passing by with an empty tray, caught the last words. 'We needed somewhere smaller. The children are at college. The other house was a rambling place and made a lot of work. Some people don't like these new estate houses but I haven't got the time to renovate an old place. I know you've done up your cottage, Meredith, and very nice it is too, lots of character and all the rest of it. Or it was nice before that unfortunate business which left it vandalised. But I've got plenty of other things I want to do outside the home. It's no use asking Geoff to decorate or fix anything, he was never a handyman. I wanted just to move in, unpack my stuff, and get on with living. Time to move, now or never, that's what I told Geoff.'

Geoff was nodding at all of this but still had objections up his sleeve. 'She said she wanted smaller, but now we haven't got room for everything and Pam won't throw anything away!'

'I can't throw away things the children might want one day,' said his wife vigorously. 'And you won't part with a single one of your books!'

To Meredith, she added, 'I admit the rooms did look so

much bigger when we saw them empty – but we'll settle ourselves, given time.'

She vanished into the kitchen with her tray. Meredith, looking round the room, thought how obvious the newness of it all was. It hung in the air in the whiff of wood and fresh paintwork. Even above the smell of food and drink, it was possible to discern that particular odour which clings to new carpets and curtains with its hint of chemicals. Not only had the owners to settle into the house, time would be needed for the house to settle about them.

'Arsenic!' said Geoff with a melodramatic leer. Now his wife was out of the way, he'd returned to his pet topic with boomerang inevitability. 'The great poison of the Victorian age. It was so handy for them. Nearly every household kept a preparation containing arsenic to keep down the vermin which infested even the best houses.'

'Surely,' said Meredith, 'that made it rather obvious?'

'Not all doctors recognised it,' said Geoff. 'Quite a few deaths probably slipped through the net confused with symptoms of medical ailments. Even if the law thought they had a case, proving it was the difficulty.'

'Nothing changes, then,' said Alan Markby ruefully.

Geoff seemed not to hear this. 'As recently as the early 1960s, the notorious Black Widow of Loudun walked free from a French court largely because doubt was thrown on the forensic evidence – and she was accused of having wiped out half her family and a few of her neighbours!'

James Holland's substantial frame loomed up beside them. 'Perhaps,' he said tolerantly, 'she was innocent.'

'Perhaps she was,' Geoff agreed. 'But a number of people who were hanged for arsenic murders in Victorian times could

20

have been innocent. Arsenic was also commonly used in such things as green dye. If you have a very old book with a green cover, wash your hands after handling it. There is a theory that Napoleon, on St Helena, was slowly poisoned by his green wallpaper.'

This appeared to appeal to Father Holland. 'Candlelight,' he said fondly. 'Gaslight. Hackney carriages. Women in those thumping great crinolines.'

The others stared at him.

'Victorian melodrama,' he explained. 'I love it. All those fog-filled London streets and great gloomy mansions. Throw in a bit of poisoning and I'm hooked.'

'That's not what I'd expect from someone in holy orders!' Markby grinned at him.

'I like a rattling good yarn,' said James complacently.

'Mushroom vol-au-vents? Oh no, Geoff, you're not still going on about poisons?' Pam had reappeared with a fresh tray.

'Books, said Markby quickly. 'We were discussing our favourite reading.' He looked past her to a young woman standing just behind her. 'What about you, Juliet? What do you like by way of light reading?'

The woman addressed moved into their circle. A stranger glancing at her for the first time would probably have judged her much younger than she was. The long braid of fair hair hanging down her back, the round schoolgirl glasses and fresh-complexioned skin embellished with very little make-up all suggested twenty. Only when she spoke and the listener paid closer attention, would he have increased his estimate to thirty. Juliet Painter was, in fact, thirty-four. She wore a three-piece outfit, straight but loose in shades of chestnut brown. The design was simple but, Meredith judged, expensive. The cost lay in the cut and in the material.

'Don't read much,' she said carelessly. 'Don't have the time. I wouldn't read the sort of thing James is talking about, anyhow.'

'Then you don't know what you're missing,' said James Holland, unperturbed by this put-down. They exchanged grins in the way old friends and sparring partners do.

'You estate agents too busy to open a book?' asked Geoffrey, fixing her with a mocking look.

They saw her flush and the snap of anger behind the round lenses. It was echoed in her voice as she replied, 'I'm not an estate agent, Geoff! I don't know how many times I've told you. Though I shouldn't need to remind you, you know it perfectly well. I'm a property consultant. I advise people and go house-hunting for them. I have got a talent, if I say so myself, for running down suitable properties, I sometimes go to house auctions and bid on clients' behalf. I enjoy doing it. I don't actually flog the houses myself,' she concluded sharply.

'Never had a kick-back from an estate agency with a mansion on its hands?' Geoffrey drained the last of his wine and looked round for somewhere to stand his empty glass.

'Shut up, Geoff!' said his wife with even more force than usual.

'That's damn near actionable,' Juliet said savagely, 'as well as stupid. How could I afford to risk my reputation by recommending an obvious dud? If anyone else had said that to me, I'd sue. Just because you're my brother, don't think you'll always get away with it, Geoff. One of these days you'll go too far. You always had a weird sense of humour.'

'And you, little sister, always rose beautifully to the bait.'

'Geoff,' said his wife firmly, 'people are running out of drinks. It's time for you to see to the booze.'

Geoff gave them an apologetic look and took himself off to open bottles, his wife in close pursuit.

James Holland chuckled in the depths of his bushy black beard. 'Something tells me poor old Geoff is getting an earful in the kitchen at this moment.'

'Poor old Geoff, nothing,' Juliet Painter retorted. 'He's had too much to drink. I wish he wouldn't keep on about his poisons. It unsettles people – haven't you noticed? I think Pam has. I always think . . .' She hesitated. 'I always think one oughtn't to talk too much about bad things in case they happen.'

'Speak of the devil,' murmured James Holland, 'and he'll appear.'

'That's right. I expect I sound superstitious, but I'm not.' Juliet tossed her long fair braid so that it swung to and fro like a horse's tail flicking away flies.

'It's not superstition,' Alan Markby said. 'It's the human subconscious at work, picking up the vibes that tell a person there's danger ahead. A legacy of our primitive past. Now, where have you been lately, Juliet, or who have you been talking to, that's resulted in your cavewoman instincts being reawakened?'

'Don't,' she said uneasily.

The door swung open and Geoff reappeared, brandishing a bottle in either hand. 'Top up? Red or white? I've promised to behave myself. Sorry if I upset you, Sis.'

'You're an idiot,' said his sister by way of accepting his apology.

23

'You don't know of someone who wants to rent a house, do you?' Meredith asked her.

Juliet looked surprised. 'I always know of people who want to rent. Where's the house?'

'Here in Bamford. It's my place in Station Road – just an end of terrace early Victorian cottage. It's not the sort of splendid place you usually deal with, but it's just been completely redecorated and refurnished.'

'Such a dreadful experience to find your place vandalised like that, as Pam was saying.' Geoff shook his head in commiseration.

'Yes, it was.' Meredith couldn't keep the revulsion from her voice.

Juliet, only an occasional visitor to the town, asked, 'What happened? I didn't hear about this.'

'Someone didn't like me,' Meredith said. 'She thought I'd done her a bad turn. So she did me a bad turn back.'

'Scary,' said Juliet in sympathy.

'You better believe it. She daubed red paint all over the place and chopped up my clothes. Anyway, since then I've been sharing Alan's place. At first I planned to move straight back in once my house was fit for habitation again, but somehow I don't fancy it and Alan I have been thinking . . .' She glanced at Markby.

'That we might look for somewhere together,' he said. 'My place was all right for me on my own. It doesn't really suit the two of us.'

Meredith thought he sounded just a little defiant, as if people might not believe what he'd said. Those who knew them well had said things like, 'Thought you two were each too independent,' or even, 'It's taken the pair of you long

24

enough'. With the defiance there was just a touch of satisfaction. He'd got what he wanted. She still didn't know if it was what she wanted, too.

Juliet eyed them both, business acumen written all over her. 'What sort of place do you want?'

'Hang on,' he protested mildly. 'Can't afford your fees.'

'I wasn't proposing to charge you a fee. I agree, you probably wouldn't want to pay me what I'd ask. But I hear of things on the market, you know, surplus to my requirements, or my clients' requirements. I could drop you the word.'

'That's very decent of you,' he said.

Juliet was staring thoughtfully at Meredith. 'I'll let you know about your house. I'd need to have a look at it.'

'With pleasure. Let me know when you want the key. It's near the station if anyone wanted to commute, like me, to the Great Wen every day.'

'Still at the Foreign Office, then?' asked Juliet.

'Still stuck there at a desk.' She was aware of an apprehensive glance from Alan. She wondered if he was still afraid, after all this time, that should some mandarin relent and offer her an overseas posting, she'd take it like a shot, be off.

Would I? she wondered. Is that why I've been so unwilling to tie myself into any permanent relationship, even with Alan? He knows, even though we're at last sharing a roof, that what finally made me move in was my place being rendered temporarily uninhabitable.

Beside her, Alan was fidgeting. He was backed against a bookcase and wedged there by Meredith on one side and James Holland's bulky frame on the other. 'Nice to see you down here from the big city,' he said to Juliet, easing his elbows free.

'I couldn't miss the grand house-warming!' A little ruefully, she added, 'I also had a business visit to make – to Fourways House.'

'The Misses Oakley?' Geoff exclaimed. 'Don't tell me one of your wealthy Middle-Easterners wants to live at Fourways and is ready to buy out the Oakley ladies with wads of cash?'

'No – A Middle-Eastern client wouldn't look at the place. It's far too dilapidated. The reason I went there was because Damaris Oakley wrote to me and asked me to call.'

She hesitated. 'It's hardly a secret that both Damaris and her sister have been struggling for years. They've decided to sell up for whatever they can get and move to a suitable retirement flat, preferably on the ground floor and by the seaside. I admit I did look the place over pretty thoroughly while I was there. Partly to give myself an idea of the sort of money they'd be able to spend on a flat if they sold up, and partly because I did think at first it might suit a client. But not after I'd looked at it.' She pursed her lips. 'Frankly, the property is going to be difficult to shift in its present state but they need to sell because it's the only capital they have.'

'I expect the gardens are in a mess, too,' observed Alan Markby, seizing on the aspect of the situation which interested him.

'Actually, they're in rather better state than the house. They've got an old boy who does the garden for them, *gratis*. It's his hobby.'

'Ron Gladstone,' nodded James Holland. 'I was

responsible for that arrangement. It seems to have worked out well, apart from the odd squabble about whether to put down crazy paving.'

Juliet turned to her brother. 'The Oakley sisters are an excellent example of the sort of people I can help, Geoff. They don't own a car, and they wouldn't have the physical strength to go haring around the country looking at flats. Damaris asked if I would do it for them. I said I would.'

'No offence,' said Geoff, who'd learned his lesson at least for the time being, 'but don't they need to sell at a reasonable price if they're to pay your exorbitant fee?'

This time she didn't react badly. 'As it happens, I'm not charging them a fee. I've known the old ducks all my life, for goodness sake! I ought to be able to fit in looking out for a retirement flat for them with tracking down property for other clients.'

'You're a dear girl,' said James Holland. 'It's very kind of you to give your time to help out the Oakleys.'

'I am not,' she said militantly, 'your dear girl. Or *anyone's* dear girl! Don't patronise me, James.'

'Would I ever?'

'If you're interested in Victorian poisonings, James . . .' Geoff began.

'You're going to tell them about the Oakley case, aren't you?' Juliet interrupted him. 'Don't you think it's best forgotten?'

'Ah, the mysterious death of Cora Oakley,' said Alan Markby. 'I'm familiar with that one. But I won't spoil your fun if you want to tell it again.'

'I don't know it,' said James Holland.

'Nor I,' added Meredith promptly.

27

'It's a horrible story,' objected Juliet. 'Don't tell it, Geoff, please.'

'James and Meredith would both be interested,' said Geoff obstinately. 'Well, if I can't tell it, I've got copious notes on it, if either of you would like to borrow them. You probably know I plan to write a book on controversial trials one day? When I get the time, if ever. Mind you, I got no help from the family. They let me know in no uncertain terms they didn't intend to rattle the bones of the family skeleton for me. But it just so happens I unpacked the Oakley research only yesterday. It's on the desk in the study. Would one of you like to take it with you when you go? I have it all saved on disk.'

Meredith and James Holland looked at one another.

'Ladies first,' said James gallantly. 'Pass it on to me when you've finished, Meredith.'

Geoff beamed at them. 'William Oakley was charged with the murder of his wife, Cora. He got off and was damn lucky to do so. Many a man went to the scaffold on flimsier evidence.'

'I've seen a portrait of William, tucked away in disgrace in a dusty back bedroom at Fourways,' said Juliet unexpectedly. 'I came across it when I was being shown round by Damaris. She was very embarrassed. She just said "That's my grandfather!" in a starchy voice before hurrying me on. I nipped back for a look when her back was turned. In the portrait William looks the sort of chap who passed for handsome in those days. Lots of curling black hair and flourishing moustachio with a touch of a tippler's complexion!' Juliet illustrated her words with a mime of her right hand and pulled a wry face. She then blushed bright red and they all looked at her. 'All right,' she said, 'I was interested! I didn't say it wasn't an *interesting* story, just that it was horrible. Anyway, you only have to look at William to see he's the sort of man who'd murder his wife.'

'The criminal countenance,' Markby mused. 'A very popular theory once, but generally dismissed now. What happened to William after the trial, I wonder? He'd hardly have been welcome in local society after a scandal like that.'

Geoff shrugged. 'I'd like to be able to tell you that he came to a sticky end, but the truth is, nobody knows what became of him. Inevitably there was gossip. People shunned him. So, with his reputation shot to pieces, both sides of the family made it clear to him that he should go away and stay away. He went abroad and was never heard of again. It was the way they dealt with family scandal then. The boy grew up in the care of relatives. When he reached twenty-one, he applied to the courts to have his father legally declared dead. My guess is the move was intended to clear title to the house and its then considerable estate. Extensive enquiries failed to turn up any trace of the fellow. No letters had been received from him. The bulk of his late wife's substantial fortune had passed to the boy under her will and William had little cash. His wealth lay in the bricks and mortar of Fourways, yet he hadn't approached anyone for financial help. He'd apparently vanished off the face of the earth, so he *was* declared dead.

'The son, thank goodness, didn't turn out a chip off the old block. He lived happily with his wife and family at Fourways, though they say he never recovered from the loss of his only son, Arthur. Neither of the girls married. Now, as Juliet said, they're old and not in very good health. I'm not surprised they want to move to more suitable surroundings.

But all the same, it's sad to think of the last of the Oakleys leaving Fourways after more than, what? At least a hundred and thirty years the family's been in residence there. And honestly, I find it hard to imagine them being happy in a small modern flat with neighbours under their noses.'

Meredith had been mulling over the facts. 'It's a sad story, but perhaps not that unusual. I don't mean the murder, I mean families dying out, money running out, big old houses falling into disrepair. Who can afford to live in them now but pop stars, rich Arabs and a handful of successful business types?'

'Successful crooks.' Markby sounded resigned. 'They like to splash their money about and live in style.'

'Not in Fourways, they wouldn't,' said Juliet in the voice of one who knew – which gained her a curious look from Markby. 'Or I suppose not,' she added hastily. 'Don't look at me like that, Alan. All my clients are ace respectable. I told you, Fourways is a crumbling dump.'

Pam Painter surged up again, flushed and breathless. 'Don't tell me! I know what you've all been talking about.' She turned to Markby. 'Do you know, Alan, you bring out the worst in Geoff. Whenever you come here, we seem to end up discussing violent death.'

'Don't blame the poor chap,' said Geoff. 'He gives me the opportunity to indulge my hobby. But as it happens, we were discussing the sale of Fourways. Nothing to do with murder at all.' To Meredith he whispered, 'I'll give you the box of papers when you leave. Keep 'em out of sight of Pam!'

Chapter Three

1889

On the horizon the darkness was edged with a pale streak. The two men who stood, side by side, well muffled up against the bitter wind, eyed it with unease and impatience. They had spent the past hour in this churchyard and the only shelter was in the lee of a small mausoleum. From this doleful vantage point they watched proceedings a few yards off. Several men were busy around a gaping hole in the earth. Two of them were still industriously deepening it, shovelling out yet more soil. Another couple held lanterns. They didn't speak. The tools scratched and chinked against small stones and grit. Occasionally, a rustle in untrimmed grass a little way off announced some small creature scuttling about its business, alarmed by the unexpected human presence at this hour.

Just a foot or two away from the hole a constable in a waterproof cape watched in gloomy silence. At his feet stood an open box containing glass jars. From time to time the constable looked down at these as if ensuring that no one had managed to spirit them away.

The remaining person in this group was a bespectacled

31

little man who scrambled around the diggers with a trowel in one hand and a glass jar like those in the box in the other. In contrast to the dour silence of the diggers, he uttered bursts of protest along the lines of, 'Just a minute, I've got to take a sample here. I say, hold on there!'

'Look here, Wood!' exclaimed the larger of the two men by the mausoleum. His size was exaggerated by his full cape and the tall silk hat he wore incongruously in this setting. 'Can't those fellows hurry it along? Soon people will be on their way to work, the sun will be up, and we'll collect a gawping crowd.'

'Yes, Sir Herbert,' said his companion, who was more prosaically clad in an ulster topcoat and a bowler hat jammed well over his ears. He'd taken the further precaution of wrapping a woollen muffler several times round his neck and over his chin. His voice, as a result, came indistinctly from somewhere within its folds. Wood added mildly, 'The scientific gentleman is holding things up.'

Sir Herbert muttered. He took the point being gently made. Responsibility for the delay rested not on the local men but on the soil analyst who'd travelled with Sir Herbert from London.

At that moment the church clock struck the quarter hour. 'You see?' said Sir Herbert peevishly, 'It's a quarter to six.'

Wood was spared having to find a reply by a burst of coughing from their right.

'And that fellow is getting on my nerves!' added Sir Herbert irritably.

Both turned in the direction of the coughing and stared hard at a black-clad gentleman who called out defensively, 'I've got a cold!' Unfortunately his affliction made this come out as, 'I've dot a dold.' As if to prove it further, he drew out a large white handkerchief and trumpeted into it.

Sir Herbert muttered his disgust. Wood said in his mild voice, 'Got to have the undertaker here. He'll identify the coffin – when we get to it.' He gave an apprehensive glance at the diggers who had again been held up by the scientist intent on filling his glass jars with soil.

'I know why the fellow is here,' snapped Sir Herbert, 'but from the sound of him, someone will be burying *him* soon!'

At this perceived insult, the undertaker moved further off, quivering with indignation. It was now perceptibly lighter. All around them, shapes emerged from the gloom giving the impression that the crowd of onlookers Sir Herbert feared, had arrived in the shape of stone cherubs and angels. Marble hands clasped in horror, they fixed the desecration, and the living who'd wrought it, with pupil-less eyes. The pale streak on the horizon had become a pinkish haze.

Wood thought, Red sky at night, shepherds' delight. Red sky in the morning, shepherds' warning. He hoped it wasn't a bad omen. He was as keen as the Home Office man to be out of here. He didn't like churchyards and he particularly didn't like the ostentatious sculpture all around. He'd once told his daughter Emily, only half joking, that when the time came to bury him, he wanted only a simple headstone bearing the legend,

> *Here lies Jonathan Wood.*
> *If he did any harm,*
> *He did some good.*

Emily hadn't been amused. In fact, she'd been so distressed he'd found himself apologising profusely and insisting he was very well, thank you. Yes, honestly, never better. No, not even an ache or two.

Sir Herbert said in a low voice, 'I can tell you, Wood, the Home Office isn't at all happy about this one. Dash it all, we have nothing but the statements of a dismissed housekeeper and a lot of local gossip. My belief is that, should it come to a trial, defence would have a field day. If it weren't for the fact that the dead woman's father has a friend in the cabinet, this exhumation wouldn't be taking place!'

'We've got a classic set of circumstances,' said Wood, easing his chin out of his muffler. 'Mr Oakley has had a reputation of being a man about town for a long time. He'd pretty well run through his own money even before he married a wealthy wife. If he'd had a grain of sense he'd have stopped chasing petticoats, but there, it'd got a habit with him, I dare say. His wife was threatening separation. So,' concluded Wood, lapsing into the vernacular, 'he done her in.'

This brought forth the tetchy reply, 'Circumstances is all you have! The Crown has to prove it, dammit! If he did it, then the fellow was confounded ingenious. No one at the original inquest doubted the death was anything but a dreadful accident. And another thing. That scientific chap has taken samples from all over this churchyard. If arsenic is found anywhere else, the Crown's case will fly out of the window. It's happened before and it'll happen again.'

Wood thought gloomily, yes, it had. And if it did happen again, he knew who'd get the blame. Bamford wasn't a big town, but it was an important market centre for the surrounding countryside, and its police station was expected to maintain law and order over a generous domain. For that reason, it warranted an inspector in charge where other small towns had to make do with no one more senior than a sergeant.

Not, of course, that a really top-notch inspector had been sent to this rural backwater. No, they'd handed it to Wood. He even suspected he'd got his promotion just so that they could kill two birds with one stone. He'd worked hard and had some success in his career but he wasn't the sort of man who made a good impression in social circles outside his own. Grudgingly, they'd made him inspector and rubbing their hands, he was sure, they'd put him here in Bamford. He'd saved them having to take a more dashing figure from duties elsewhere.

He didn't mind. He liked it here. He felt at ease among its people both in the town and the surrounding country. He liked being in charge of his own little kingdom. To help him he had a sergeant and two constables, one of them over there by the grave. Like him, the sergeant and the constables were solid, dependable men, but not destined for greater glory.

But now, unexpectedly, a chance of glory had come along. Not that he liked to think he saw it that way. Still, if he put a hand on the collar of a gent like William Oakley . . .

A sudden cessation of work at the graveside took his attention. The constable came scrambling towards them over hummocks and kerbstones. He saluted.

'We've reached the coffin, Mr Wood, sir.'

'Right!' said Wood with relief. 'Won't be long now, Sir Herbert. Constable, get that undertaker over there sharpish.'

But the undertaker chose to take his revenge by proceeding at a stately pace towards the spot. One of the lantern-bearers lowered his light into the pit. The undertaker leant over at a perilous angle and took so long before he pronounced judgement Wood feared Sir Herbert would deluge him with strongly worded advice. In the nick of time, the undertaker turned from the grave and was coming back, still at that same stately pace. Perhaps he couldn't walk any other way.

'Yes,' he said, his consonants still distorted, 'that's the coffin, gentlemen. The nameplate is quite clear.' He whipped out the handkerchief and blew his nose again.

'Then let's get out of here with it!' growled Sir Herbert.

The undertaker stuffed his handkerchief into a pocket and offered, 'You may wish, gentlemen, to open the lid briefly first, while we're out here in the fresh air.'

At that moment, the church clock struck six.

'No time!' snapped Sir Herbert.

Wood said in his mild voice, 'For all our comfort . . .'

'Oh, all right, then,' agreed Sir Herbert. 'But make it quick, can't you?'

'Jenkins!' called Wood to the constable. 'Once the coffin is up and – er – ventilated, make sure they board over the hole securely. We don't want anyone falling in. And you had better stay here to guard it. We don't want trophy-hunters, either.'

'Yes, sir,' said Constable Jenkins glumly.

'Don't worry,' Wood told him. 'I'll send Bishop to relieve you as soon as I get to the station.'

Constable Jenkins's expression, visible now in the pale early morning light, showed that he interpreted this last statement as meaning, 'When I've had a good stiff drink!'

Chapter Four

'You're very quiet,' Alan observed as they drove home through the darkness. 'It's no use trying to read that box of papers Geoff gave you in this light.'

'I couldn't resist taking a quick look.' Meredith regretfully closed the box on her knees. The car's headlights played off shopfront windows and made lights dance across the puddles a rainshower had left on the pavements. After the claustrophobic heat of the Painters' party it was blessedly cool.

'I found it very warm in there, didn't you?' She turned her head to study her companion's profile. 'I thought Dr Fuller was your pathologist. I didn't know you used Geoff's services.'

'Fuller is our regular pathologist and a very good one, but he's not a poisons expert. So when we, or when Fuller on our behalf, has something in that line, we send it off to Geoff's poisons unit. Mind you, he's right in saying deliberate poisoning is far less common today than it once was.'

A group of young people had spilled out of a pub and were milling about on the pavement. Alan slowed the car as he passed them. An argument was in process between three youths, and others were being drawn to the scene as iron filings to a magnet. Fortunately, at that moment, a marked police car arrived on the scene and parked conveniently for the occupants to watch. Markby pressed his foot on the accelerator and moved on again.

Meredith heaved a sigh of relief and he glanced at her.

'Sorry,' he said. 'It's the policeman in me. Can't leave a possible trouble scene until I'm sure everything is under control.'

'I was afraid,' she said with same asperity, 'you were proposing to deal with it yourself.'

'If necessary. A police officer is obliged to do something if he sees an offence being committed, whether he's on duty or not.'

'So call up help. You don't have to rush in like Superman and take them all on single-handed.'

He was silent and she knew her criticism had angered him. But she was entitled to a viewpoint and, for goodness sake, as she was with him there had been a likelihood she might have been drawn in too. The yobs could have set about the car.

All the same, after the silence threatened to become the obstinate kind which neither wanted to break, she took the step of saying, 'I was scared, that's all. I don't want to squabble over it.'

She sensed that he relaxed. 'I wouldn't have let you come to any harm.'

How would you have protected me? she wanted to ask. Against a drunken mob? She didn't ask. Instead she thought, I'm used to looking after myself, that's the trouble. If I'd been alone, I'd have assessed the situation and avoided it. Put my foot down, if I'd been driving, and raced straight past. But I'm not alone these days, not since I moved in with Alan. I can't get used to it. We're starting to squabble. We didn't do that before. We argued, yes, but we didn't snipe at one another. And he didn't talk about protecting me, for crying out loud! What am I – a half-wit?

As a lateral extension of this thought, she heard herself saying, 'Geoff and his sister squabble – have you noticed? He's in his forties, like you. She's in her thirties, like me. Put them together and they seem to regress to a pair of four-year-olds.'

'So what? It's not serious,' he said aggravatingly. 'Laura is my sister and we wrangle.'

They had reached the house as he spoke and the car rolled to a halt.

'Yes, you do.' Meredith conceded the point unwillingly. 'But you and Laura aren't competitive like the Painter siblings. I would have thought they'd have outgrown it by now, that's all.' Lest this turn into another disagreement, she added crisply, 'But then, I was an only child – what would I know?'

They had progressed into the house on this last statement. Alan threw the switch which lit up the entrance hall. Chucking his car keys on the telephone table, he asked, 'You do still really want to go ahead with looking for a new house together?'

He had that look in his blue eyes which always made her feel she'd been put on the spot. She was annoyed by it because she wasn't a suspect in a case. She didn't have to come up with excuses and alibis. He wanted the truth but she couldn't give it because she didn't know it. Yet she felt she had to answer.

'What makes you think I don't?' she prevaricated, setting down the box of papers with unnecessary care and moving past him into the kitchen.

'I didn't say I doubted you. I did wonder why you asked Juliet to find you a tenant and not a buyer for your place.'

So that was it. 'Oh, I see!' She turned from the sink. 'Look, I'm practical, OK? This house of yours, it isn't suitable and if we're to live together, we need somewhere else.'

'I know that. I never thought I'd ever be sharing this place with someone. It was only ever bought as a place to keep my stuff and sleep.'

'But suppose things don't work out, Alan? I don't like burning my boats. It's a sort of comfort to me, I suppose, to think I have got my own place – if I should ever need it again. If I can rent it out, that will cover my mortgage. I can always sell later when we've seen how things go.' She turned her back to him and twisted the cold tap. Water splashed down into the kettle. 'It doesn't mean I don't love you. It's more a doubt I've got about myself. I've tried to explain that to you before.'

He came up behind her, put his arms round her waist and kissed the back of her neck. 'I do understand. But it took me so long to lure you in here, I can't really believe my good luck.'

'Don't count your chickens! You might yet live to rue the day I crossed your threshold.'

'I won't do that,' he said. 'I'll never do that.'

She twisted her head to smile up at him. Peace had been made. He didn't want to squabble any more than she did.

Yet, when he'd taken away his arm, he asked, 'You're not

really going to wade through that box of Geoff's research material?'

Something about his voice sounded censorious to her ear. She bridled.

'Of course I am. I'm interested in local history.' The kettle had boiled. 'Tea or instant coffee?' she asked. 'I could, I suppose, make cocoa.'

'Spare me the cocoa,' he grumbled. 'I'm saving that for my dotage. And local history, my foot! It's ghoulish curiosity.'

'It is not! Why do you object?' That was a way of saying, 'What business is it of yours?' Surely they weren't going to fall out over the history of the Oakley family? 'I'm interested in it as a human situation,' she said carefully. 'This was a man accused of murdering his wife, a woman he must once have loved.'

'Must he?' Alan asked drily. 'Cora Oakley was very wealthy. William had nothing but an estate encumbered with debt.'

'Then she at least must have loved *him*.'

Markby was watching her as she spoke, her flushed face, the way she avoided his gaze. Something was worrying her. Something to do with them. Please God, he found himself asking, not again. Not like it was with Rachel. Rachel and I were happy when we first married. We were young, of course, and naive. We should have known we could never make a go of it. Rachel hated the police work. She never wanted to be a copper's wife. She always treated my job as something like a mild illness that I'd get over, in time. Then I'd go and find myself a job she liked better. Something with lots of corporate entertainment and travel attached to it. Dinner parties and dressing up.

His failure to answer had attracted Meredith's attention as his remarks hadn't. She looked up and fixed her large hazel eyes on him. He noticed her mascara had smudged. The observation triggered an upsurge of emotion in him so strong it caused pain. This is love, he thought. It's such a powerful thing, no wonder people are afraid of it. She's afraid of it. Am I the proverbial fool who rushes in where angels fear to tread?

More harshly than he intended, he asked, 'Does love solve everything? I've known men and women who've killed for love. It doesn't have to be for greed or hate.'

She looked startled at the emotion in his voice. There was another awkward silence.

Markby hunched his shoulders. 'It takes more than motive to convict a murderer, in any case. I've met men with motive a-plenty and opportunity, sometimes with a track record of violence. There's been no doubt in my mind they were killers. They've known I've known it. But they've looked me in the eye and told me they didn't do it, and I couldn't prove they did – and they were right. I haven't been able to prove it, just as no one back then could prove William Oakley murdered his wife. He *could have* done it, yes. But you have to show he *did do* it. Quite a different kettle of fish.'

His gaze became that of a man looking back into the past. 'All police officers,' he said, 'hate cases like that. Some become obsessed with them. They worry away at them for years hoping some new bit of evidence will turn up, or Chummy will get over-confident and betray himself. Sometimes it happens and we get him in the end, although not, of course, if he's already stood trial and been acquitted. Then he's laughing at you. But I've known officers who've still gone on searching because they've wanted to know that they were right, even if the villain is beyond the law.'

In a sober voice Meredith said, 'How implacable you are. You never give up.'

'No,' he agreed. 'I never give up.'

'Geoff?' Pamela whispered loudly in the darkness.

In the adjoining bed, her husband stirred and muttered, 'What?'

'How do you think things went this evening?'

She saw the humped shape move as he turned over. 'Everything was fine. What's the worry?'

'I'm not worried about the party, for crying out loud! I meant Juliet – and James Holland.'

The springs of the other bed creaked alarmingly as Geoff Painter sat up with a start. 'Good God, Pam, leave well alone. I know my sister. She'd hit the roof if she thought you were match-making.'

'I'm not match-making!' she said indignantly. 'They've known each other for years. They're friends. They're both on their own . . .'

'That's lousy logic. It's like saying kippers are nice. Meringue is nice. Kippers topped with meringue must therefore be delicious!' he growled.

She flopped back onto her pillows with a sigh. 'I ought to have known better than to ask you.' After a moment she went on, 'What Juliet was saying about the Oakley sisters leaving that house, selling up, it'll be dreadfully stressful for them. They were both born in that house. Damaris must be eighty-two, Florence eighty, or so I'd estimate. What about the contents?'

'House contents sale. Local auctioneers would run it for them.'

'It's not as simple as that. What about family mementoes, things like that portrait of Wicked William Juliet told you about? Everything in that house must have memories for them. It'll be like selling off or giving away bits of themselves. Disposing of their lives.'

'I know what you mean,' he replied after a moment. 'You're probably right. But then, neither you nor I have yet reached that age. Perhaps they're ready to clear out the past. Perhaps they want to get rid of it all. It could be they see all that furniture and Victoriana not as memorabilia but a burden, a responsibility they want to get rid of. Have a word with Juliet, if you're worried. But she's probably thought about that side of it.'

Geoff thumped his pillows into shape and settled down again. 'My sister is nothing if not efficient. I think she could throw up a challenge to you in that department, Pam – although even she wouldn't try and arrange someone's love life. You're playing with fire!'

'Sometimes, Geoff,' said his wife crossly, 'you do talk nonsense. Oh, and by the way, I saw you giving that box to Meredith.'

'So? She's interested,' he returned defiantly.

'How,' she demanded, unconsciously echoing Alan Markby, 'can anyone be so obsessed as you are with something which happened so long ago and can't matter now?' Before he could present an argument for this, she snapped, 'Oh, go to sleep!'

'I *was* asleep . . .' mumbled the voice from the other bed.

* * *

Across town, Alan was already sleeping soundly. Meredith slipped out of bed and pulled on her dressing gown. Downstairs, she collected Geoff's box and took it to the kitchen. She felt like a child, raiding the fridge for a midnight feast. Settling herself at the table, she undid the string round the box with tingling anticipation. The lid removed, she found a jumble of papers inside: photocopied newspaper clippings and bundles of trial transcripts which someone had freely annotated in a flowing hand. At the bottom of the box, secured with an elastic band, lay a bundle of what looked like reporter's notebooks. The topmost one was inscribed in the same flowing copperplate script with the name *Stanley Huxtable*. 'What's this?' Meredith murmured. 'Geoff must have forgotten these were in here or he wouldn't have let them out of his grip.' More recent notes were in biro – in Geoff's handwriting. Meredith spread the whole lot out on the table before her and debated where to start.

Chapter Five

It wasn't to be expected that William Oakley would welcome the reopening of enquiries into his wife's death. Inspector Jonathan Wood, walking slowly up the drive towards Fourways House, reflected that he would no doubt like being questioned about it even less.

Beside Wood walked Sergeant Patterson, stout of build and red of face. Wood knew, even without looking at him, that Patterson was impressed by Fourways. Personally, Wood didn't care for the fashion for Gothic which had dominated his lifetime. He preferred the old Palladian style of his grandparents' day. It appealed to his sense of rightness, of balance. Look at this place, he thought in disgust. Those pointed windows might be all right in a church, but not in a private house. As for that turret thing up there – what had the architect been thinking of?

'Rapunzel, Rapunzel,' he said aloud unwisely, 'let down your golden hair.'

'I beg your pardon, Mr Wood?' asked Sergeant Patterson cautiously.

'Don't you remember your *Grimm's Fairytales*, Sergeant?'

'No, sir, can't say I do.' Patterson's brow creased in effort. 'Hansel and Gretel,' he said uncertainly.

Well, you couldn't have everything. Wood took pity on him and explained about the turret.

'Oh, that, sir,' said Patterson. 'Very fancy. The whole place is very fancy. Very nice indeed.'

Wood was suddenly irritated. 'Nice or not, we're not here to tug forelocks and bow and scrape, understand? Oakley might be a gentleman but he's a wrong'un, just the same.'

'Yes, sir,' said Patterson, still doubtful.

It might, thought Wood, have been better not to have brought him. Constable Bishop could've taken notes. Bishop was inclined to nicely-judged insubordination and unlikely to be impressed by a big house and the swell gent living in it.

The door was opened by a maid in a starched cap with streamers and an apron so pristine and crisp it might've been made out of icing sugar.

'Yes?' she asked pertly. A single glance at them had told her these were not gentlemen callers. Her expression suggested they should have gone round the back, to the tradesman's entrance.

Wood, aware that Patterson looked embarrassed beside him, said loudly, 'Inspector Wood from Bamford Police Station, come to see your master. He's here, I take it?'

The maid revised her attitude. For one thing, she was eaten up with curiosity now she knew the identity of the caller. 'He's here, sirs, but he's out at the stables. I believe his horse is lame. He's waiting for the veterinary surgeon.'

'Well, while he's waiting he can talk to us,' said Wood. 'Go and fetch him, there's a good girl.'

She tossed her streamered cap. 'Very well. Would you like to come in and wait?'

They stepped over the threshold, Patterson looking about

him for a mat on which to wipe his boots. Seeing only an expensive Turkey carpet, his visible unhappiness increased.

'I'll take your hats, sirs,' said the maid.

She received their bowlers as if they'd been contagious, set them on a hall table, and showed them into a small sitting room. Wood suspected there was a larger, plusher drawing room somewhere, but they weren't deemed worthy of it.

Patterson was by now so overwhelmed he'd broken out in a sweat.

Wood asked unkindly, 'Got your notebook, Sergeant? Then get ready to write it all down. And try to get the spelling right this time.'

They waited eight minutes by the ormolu clock on the mantelshelf before Oakley appeared. He threw open the door and marched in, his manner aggressive, and stared at them. He was dressed to ride out, in breeches and topboots, but was in his shirtsleeves and waistcoat above that. He must have taken off his jacket when examining the horse. Wood was interested that Oakley had left the stables so quickly on hearing who was in his back parlour, he'd omitted to put it on again first.

'I can guess why you're here,' Oakley said pugnaciously. 'It's as a result of the slanderous gossip put about by that woman Button.'

He was a good-looking fellow, thought Wood. Dark curly hair and a luxuriant moustache of the kind Wood had once tried to grow but abandoned in the face of his daughter's mirth. Oakley's complexion was at present flushed. He was well-built, muscular thighs stretching the material of the breeches, and tall. Oh, yes. The ladies would like Mr Oakley.

'Perhaps you wouldn't mind if I asked a few questions, sir?' he said mildly.

'Of course I damn well mind! But I suppose we'd better get it over with. Sit down, man. And you,' he added to Patterson, 'going to write down what I say, are you?'

'Yes, sir,' gasped poor Patterson. 'If it's all right.'

Wood glared at him.

Oakley didn't bother to reply. He threw himself into a nearby chair and said, 'Go on, then. Fire away. I've nothing to hide.'

'Perhaps we could begin with the day your wife died?' Wood put a hand to his mouth and cleared his throat. 'A painful subject and I'm sorry I have to bring it up.'

'Are you?' Oakley gave a short laugh. 'You could have fooled me. What about it? And she died during the night, after eleven.'

'Yes, sir. I realise that, sir. But I was referring to the afternoon. I believe you rode into Bamford and visited the pharmacy of Mr Baxter.'

'So? All this was gone into at the inquest following my wife's death. She was in great pain from a drawn tooth. Dr Perkins had prescribed laudanum as a remedy and he testified to that at the inquest. I fetched it from Baxter's pharmacy.'

Patterson was scribbling industriously and breathing heavily through his mouth at the same time as he always did when concentrating.

'Were you and your wife on good terms, sir?'

Wood saw the glitter in the man's eyes. 'That's a damn impudent question. As it happens, yes, we were on excellent terms, thank you.' Oakley paused, then shrugged. 'We had some little differences from time to time as married couples

50

do, but they were trivial in nature.' He fixed Wood with a sudden direct stare. 'I had no reason to wish my wife dead. Apart from anything else, we had – *have* – a young son. Would I seek to deprive my son of his mother?'

Wood didn't answer this. Instead he asked in his inoffensive voice, 'Your wife was a wealthy woman, as I understand it.'

'She had some fortune, yes.'

Wood pursed his mouth. 'As I heard it, she had considerable fortune, sir. Quite a bit of income deriving from interests in manufacturing companies, factories of one kind and another, some up North, woollen trade. Also, I believe, a London company – London Chemicals, I believe it's called.'

Oakley said sarcastically, 'Don't play the fool, Inspector. You know perfectly well what the place is called. You've been there – they told me. You were asking questions about my last visit there.'

'Which took place a month before your wife died,' Wood said. 'You administered your wife's business affairs.' It wasn't really a question, but Oakley answered it, even so.

'Of course I did. My wife was a married lady with a household to supervise. You don't expect her to have run round factory floors asking questions about profit and loss? Besides, when we married she was only eighteen. For your information, I visited all the enterprises in which she had a financial interest on a regular basis. If no one keeps an eye on things, that's where problems start.'

Too true, thought Wood, and I've got my eye on you. Aloud he said, 'You're well-known in gambling circles, Mr Oakley.'

'I don't know who told you that.' Oakley paused as if he

expected to be told who. When Wood remained silent, he added, 'So?'

'You have debts?'

There was a silence. Oakley said evenly, 'You are an impertinent fellow. However, I suppose you're doing your job. I have, Inspector, such debts as a gentleman normally has. I am scrupulous in settling them. You may ask around. Anyone will confirm that.' He leaned forward so suddenly that Patterson jumped and nearly dropped his pencil. 'I know what you're suggesting and I can tell you, I take a damn poor view of it. I've never misused my wife's money in any way.' He sat back again and added more calmly, 'Nor can you prove that I did.'

No, I can't, thought Wood and felt a brief apprehension. The Home Office hadn't wanted this case reopened. Without Oakley's father-in-law's friends in high places, it wouldn't have been.

Seeking surer ground, Wood went on, 'If we could return to your visit to the London Chemicals factory. You're quite right, I've been there. They make all kinds of products. I was impressed. Domestic, horticultural, agricultural . . . Rat poisons, too.'

Oakley said drily, 'They're much in demand.'

'Most of them arsenic-based,' Wood went on in a conversational tone. 'I've always bought the arsenic direct myself from Baxter's, signed the Poisons Book, and put the stuff down. Not that we've got rats in the house these days. Get the occasional mouse. I find a trap set with a bit of cheese works well for them.'

Oakley looked as if he'd like to kick Wood down the front steps. His hands, resting on the carved oak arm of his chair, twitched. Perhaps it'd been a good idea to bring Patterson, after all. Oakley would think twice before tackling the sergeant's burly frame.

'Are you aware, sir, that during the process which produces the arsenic in commercial form, a highly toxic vapour is also produced?'

'So I believe. I am not a chemist.' Oakley was keeping a tight rein on his emotions, but his voice crackled with tension.

'But you must have seen the process at work? During your visits to the factory?' Wood raised his eyebrows.

'Possibly. I can't recall a precise occasion.'

'You'll know, then, that this vapour has a strong smell, very like garlic. Not a flavouring I'm fond of,' added Wood. 'I'm not one for foreign food.'

Oakley said in a dry voice, 'You're not suggesting that on my visits to the factory I was exposed to this toxic vapour? I have no idea what it smells like. Or I didn't until you told me.'

'Really?' asked Wood. 'To return to the night of your wife's death. Could you run through the sequence of events for me?'

'I can't think why you should need me to. All this came out at the original inquest. Well, let's see.' Oakley frowned and steepled his fingers. 'I took the laudanum and a water jug to my wife's room. I offered to mix a dose but she indicated she would do it herself. A lamp was left burning by her bedside to give her light. I bade her goodnight. I dined alone downstairs. I smoked a cigar in the library and read the newspapers. Then I went up to bed myself.'

Wood asked curiously, 'Did you look in on Mrs Oakley, to see how she did?'

Very quietly, Oakley said, 'No. Do you think I don't regret it? I presumed she'd be sleeping. I didn't wish to disturb her. I didn't have any idea anything was wrong until Button awoke me, some time between eleven-fifteen and midnight. Don't ask me to be more precise since I wasn't interested in looking at clocks at the time. Button was in a very distressed state and told me there'd been a dreadful accident. I ran to my wife's room at once. I found that she'd fallen while attempting to get out of bed and her nightgown had caught alight. She had suffered severe burns. I sent the groom at once for the doctor but he was unable to help her. She was dead by the time he got here.'

In the following silence, the ormolu clock ticked softly. Patterson rustled the pages of his notebook.

Oakley said very slowly and clearly, 'I believe the tragedy occurred because my wife was drugged with laudanum and not able to control her movements. That was also the opinion of Dr Perkins and of the coroner. Those who have spread malicious rumours suggesting otherwise have much to answer for.'

Wood replied, just as evenly, 'The housekeeper, Mrs Button, behaved with great courage and initiative on that night. She smothered the flames with a coverlet from the bed. Yet you dismissed her from your employ only two weeks later.'

'Yes.' Oakley's voice was cold. When he saw that Wood meant to wait for an explanation, he went on reluctantly, 'It upset me to see her about the place. It – reminded me. I felt I couldn't bear to have her continue under this roof. I gave her an excellent reference and a month's wages. She has repaid me with vile lies.'

Oakley got to his feet. 'Now I'd be obliged if you'd leave my house. I'm expecting the veterinary at any moment. I don't intend to answer another one of your tomfool questions.'

There was nothing more to be gained here today. Wood and Patterson left, the Sergeant clearly only too pleased to be out of the house.

As they walked back down the drive they heard a child's laughter. A little boy, perhaps four years old, ran out from a small shrubbery towards them. Seeing strangers, he stopped.

'Master Edward, just you come back here!'

A girl burst out of the shrubbery. Her uniform proclaimed her a nursemaid. She was remarkably pretty, her cheeks flushed rosy red, lips parted to reveal perfect teeth. She stopped short, just as the child had done, on seeing Wood and Patterson, but like her charge, showed more curiosity than alarm. Despite this, Wood was sure she had no trouble identifying what business the gentlemen were on. He noted wrily that it didn't ruffle her composure beyond a momentary blink of her bright eyes. He thought to himself that here was a pert little madam and no two ways about it!

'Good afternoon, gentlemen,' she said, favouring them with a pleasant smile. She walked to the child and picked him up. 'Excuse me, won't you? It's time for his tea.'

She bore the boy away towards the house. Slipped the net before he could ask her a single question, Wood felt a mixture of annoyance and admiration.

Patterson, who'd straightened up when bathed in that smile, now relaxed again and looked a trifle wistful.

'Daisy Joss,' murmured Wood.

'What, that nice little girl?' asked a shocked Patterson.

'Yes, that nice little girl!' snapped Wood. 'It might've been a bit more clever of Mr William Oakley to have dismissed *her*!'

Chapter Six

The following Monday evening Meredith stood on the Paddington concourse, waiting for the train home. It had been a stressful day and the main cause of her annoyance was called Adrian.

Her office was large but she was obliged to share it. There was plenty of room and the desks were at opposite ends. Up till now the arrangement had worked fairly well. The other desk had been occupied by Gerald. But Gerald had moved on and Adrian had come in his place.

Meredith had never thought she'd miss Gerald so much, his love of gossip, his devotion to the tabloid press, his drawer full of Mars bars and other sweet and savoury snacks. Adrian was in a different mould altogether. On the plus side, he was young, tall, well-built and possessed of a first-class university degree. On the minus side, he had a complexion as pink as boiled shrimp, gingery-fair hair, a receding chin and a fondness for bright blue shirts and Italian suits.

In Roman times, certain categories of convicted criminal had the nature of their offence branded on their foreheads as a warning to others. It was Meredith's opinion that Adrian might profitably have had 'ambition' tattooed on his brow. She had established quickly that he was an eavesdropper, a toady, a man who 'ran with the hare and the hounds' as the saying went. He sought the acquaintance of those who might be of help to him in his career and was careless of those who wouldn't be. Meredith, he'd obviously decided, was of no use in aiding him to scale the heights of success. As a result, his manner towards her veered between the off-hand and the downright rude. She also had reason to think that when she was out of the room, he rifled through the contents of her in- and out-trays. Gerald's curiosity had been insatiable but of the harmless kind. Adrian's was to a purpose. He wanted to get something on her, something he might use in future if need be. It was in the nature of the beast. He had the instincts of a blackmailer and was the type to rejoice in the discomfiture of others. She had to watch out.

The usual home-going commuter crowd milled about the station. They stood singly and in small groups, polystyrene cups of hot drinks in their hands, their eyes fixed on the departures board. At this time of the evening the trains filled quickly and if you didn't want to stand up for half your journey, then the moment the platform number flickered up there on the screen, you were off like a greyhound from the traps.

What makes you pick out just one man in the crowd in those circumstances? Meredith never knew what made her do it. He was standing quite close, only a few feet away. Although his back was towards her, she guessed he was young. In build he was compact and muscular. He wore jeans and a tight grey T-shirt marked with darker patches of sweat at the armpits. A large rucksack lay at his feet, an airline's luggage receipt attached to it. She noticed that he kept his face turned up towards the departures board, as if he was not just unsure of the platform number, but uncertain about the very existence of the train. How far had he travelled, she wondered. Was this his outward or inward journey? As if aware of her scrutiny, as we can be when someone is staring at us, the man glanced back and she felt his gaze scan her before she could look quickly away and pretend to be concentrating on something else. She had the impression of features which were unusual but attractive, extraordinary large dark eyes and a small mouth with curving lips. She was filled with a sense of unease which she put down to guilt at being caught spying.

Then the platform number had flashed up on the screen and the crowd moved like a herd of spooked cattle, stampeding for the gates. Meredith ran with the rest, clearing the way with a well-wielded briefcase and finally collapsing panting and triumphant into a window seat. The other passengers shoved and squeezed until all seats were taken and the losers stood resentfully at the end of the carriage, waiting for the first people to reach their destinations to vacate their places. It was only then that she realised that the young man was seated opposite her.

He'd stashed his rucksack between the seats and as the train drew out, he looked eagerly from the window, clearly seeing it all for the first time. Meredith, as curious about him as he was about the world through which the train gently rocked, made the most of her chance to assess him further, instead of concentrating on the *Evening Standard* crossword as she usually did.

She judged him in his late twenties or early thirties; it was hard to tell. His skin was very sunburned as if he spent a lot of time out of doors, his hair dark and curling and faintly touched at the temples with early grey. His bare forearms were dusted with fine black hairs as were the backs of his loosely clasped hands. His face was oval. He had a long straight large nose and those huge dark eyes. A medieval face, she thought, stepped from a church fresco, but whether belonging to saint or sinner it was impossible to say.

Then, without warning, he turned his head to look straight at her. He smiled.

'There are a lot of people on this train,' he said. His accent was marked, but his voice was pleasant and easy. Any concern he'd had about his journey had vanished. He reclined in the seat in a relaxed way, apparently unbothered by the lack of room which resulted in other passengers being huddled like sardines in a tin, stiffly conscious that elbows clashed and feet became entangled. It occurred to Meredith that even though he appeared so relaxed, it disguised an underlying energy, ready to be switched on in an instant. She was reminded of a big cat, sunning itself on the savannah, yet watchful and always ready to spring.

In reply to his comment, she said rather more brusquely than she intended, 'There always are. It's the rush-hour.'

'Yes? I'm not used to big cities.' He smiled again in a confiding, disarming manner and revealed a gold tooth, the left canine. Somehow this touch of continental dentalwork added to the air of harmlessness and Meredith felt her earlier misgivings fade. 'I'm a countryman, isn't that what you say?'

'Which country?' she asked, before she could stop herself.

'I'm from Poland.'

Now was the moment to mumble, 'Oh, really?' and stop the conversation right there or she'd be stuck with his chat-up line for the rest of the journey – depending how far he was going. She wondered where he was going and, just as if he'd read her mind, he said, 'I'm going to a town called Bamford. Do you know it?'

She couldn't deny it and at once he became eagerly attentive, leaning forward and asking, 'What is it like? Do you know it very well, the people there very well? I've never been there.'

There was a kind of childish urgency in his request for information. Far too late now to hide behind the *Evening Standard*. Other passengers had opened paperback novels, fished office work from their briefcases, were muttering into mobile phones or had fallen asleep. She was on her own. She did her best to give a thumbnail sketch of Bamford.

'It's only a small place, some nice old buildings, but it's a workaday town, not on the tourist circuit. There are a lot more picturesque places not far away, like Bourton-on-the-Water, Chipping Camden. You'll find it all in tourist literature or guidebooks. Bamford hasn't really got much to offer in that line.'

He listened to all this, nodding, and when she stopped speaking, he asked, 'You appear to know it very well – you live there perhaps?' His voice expressed only a conversational curiosity, yet it struck her that his dark eyes had become just a little speculative. Saint or sinner? she found herself wondering again.

'Yes, with my partner.' That was to let him know their acquaintanceship was going to end at Bamford station. But as soon as the words left her mouth she realised, with a jolt, that this was the first time she'd ever referred openly to Alan as her partner. Their relationship had moved on, she thought. They were partners, he wholeheartedly, she as ever ravaged by secret – or not so secret – doubts. Suddenly she felt ashamed at her quibbling attitude. She had either to show equal commitment to the partnership or walk away from it, and she didn't want to walk away from it. She *would* put her house on the market, she decided. Not for renting out but for sale. Unless she took that necessary first step, there could be no progress along their road. She must phone Juliet and let her know.

Her travelling companion was still looking thoughtful, pursing his mouth and tapping his fingers on the little shelf under the train window. It surprised her to see that his hands, albeit strong and tanned, were quite small and as well-formed as a woman's.

'Perhaps I'll visit these other towns.' His tone dismissed the whole lot. He wasn't interested in touristic details. 'I really want to know about Bamford, you see . . .' Without warning he leaned forward, smiling conspiratorially, and she realised with some alarm that she was about to become the recipient of a confidence. 'I'm not here just as a tourist. I'm here to visit my family.' He sat back and his smile widened, the gold tooth flashing.

'Oh, right.' Meredith was reluctant to go on with the conversation and did her best to speak in a way which would close it off without being impolite. She wondered afterwards if this was because she'd sensed somehow that she was about to be told something which would disturb her.

'I disengaged mentally,' she explained to Alan when she was telling him all about this later. 'And that was my mistake because I was totally unprepared for what was coming. I thought he meant he had relatives descended from Polish émigrés, but it wasn't that at all. I nearly fell off my seat when he asked if I knew the Oakleys.'

'The Oakleys?' She'd gaped at him. Cautiously, she began, 'I don't know a family, I mean a big family . . .'

He was shaking his head. 'It's not a big family. There are just two ladies, quite old, sisters.'

The train had drawn into one of the stations along the line and the carriage had largely emptied. When it drew out again, Meredith and the stranger had no one seated near them.

'We can't,' Meredith said firmly, 'be thinking of the same people.' It seemed impossible.

'They live at a house called Fourways.' He pronounced the name of the house as if it were written as two words. Four Ways.

Meredith gasped, still unable to believe it, 'You're talking of Damaris and Florence Oakley.'

The gold tooth flashed. 'Yes. They're my cousins. You know them? This is wonderful!' He looked her full in the face and she saw the spontaneous pleasure in his dark eyes turn to something very like triumph. 'I'm Jan Oakley,' he said simply, as if this must explain everything. He pronounced his name in Polish fashion, 'Yan'.

It wasn't often Meredith found herself struck dumb but this was one of those rare occasions. She realised she had her mouth open and closed it. 'Oh,' she managed feebly.

She still hadn't really recovered her composure when they reached Bamford. Her companion retrieved his rucksack and walked briskly beside her along the platform. Meredith was five foot ten in height and took a perverse pleasure in noting that her companion was slightly shorter. But he had the musculature of a gymnast and strode out with a bounce in his step. To her annoyance, his attitude seemed to suggest they were now old friends. She knew she had to get rid of him sharpish, but at the same time, her mind was buzzing furiously. Was he expected at Fourways? Cautiously, she asked.

'Oh yes, I've been in correspondence with my cousins. They know I'm coming today.'

'Are you – is someone meeting you?'

He frowned. 'No, but I can I find a taxi, can't I? Is the house very far away?'

'It's on the outskirts of town, near a crossroads. That's how it got its name.' They'd reached the exit at the front of the station. 'It isn't very far,' Meredith told him. 'The taxi fare shouldn't be very much.'

'It has been very nice to meet you,' he said, very politely, and held out a hand. Unthinkingly, Meredith put out her own hand to shake his, but he seized her fingers and raised them gallantly to his lips, accompanying this with a formal bow. 'We shall meet again, I hope?'

Not if I can avoid it, thought Meredith, making for her car in the busy car park. However, as things turned out, she hadn't seen the last of him that evening. As she drove slowly along the station approach, she saw Jan Oakley making a lonely figure, his rucksack at his feet, by the deserted taxi rank. She slowed.

He had recognised her and came towards the car, his expression hopeful. 'All the taxis have been taken. I have to wait perhaps twenty minutes until one comes back.'

'I'll run you out there,' said Meredith resignedly. 'Put your pack on the back seat.'

He tossed it in immediately and slid into the passenger

seat beside her. 'This is very kind of you,' he said, it seemed to her complacently.

Meredith made no reply to this, but concentrated on weaving her way out of the station car park through the other cars all driven by impatient commuters, anxious to be home.

As they drove through town, Jan remarked, 'It looks a nice place. Why did you say it wasn't interesting?'

'Because I live here, I suppose. I mean, yes, it's all right. Are you thinking of staying long?' Meredith tried to suppress the tone in her voice which said, 'I hope not!'

'It depends,' he said vaguely. 'Perhaps two weeks, or three?' He was slouched in the seat, his eyes fixed on the windscreen, his hands resting on his knees. A small gold crucifix had escaped from beneath the T-shirt.

'What sort of work do you do in Poland?' she asked, probing for more information about him. So far, he seemed to be making all the running. She felt as if she'd been caught off-balance and didn't like it. That kiss-hand business, for instance – she'd never liked that. But if he had a regular job, he would have to get back to it eventually. He couldn't prolong his stay indefinitely.

He raised his hands and spread them out, palms facing. The crucifix wasn't the only jewellery he wore. His wristwatch looked expensive and she wondered if it were a fake – and just how much of a fake its owner was. 'I look after horses,' he said.

'Horses?' She hadn't expected that.

'Yes, thoroughbred horses – on a stud farm. We breed fine horses in Poland. They're a valuable export for our economy.'

That explained the outdoor appearance and his claim to be a 'countryman'. Horse-breeding was big business in

Poland, Meredith recalled from an article on international showjumping. Jan's English was good; he obviously fancied himself a bit. He might, despite his casual appearance, have quite an important job on that stud farm, wherever it was.

For the second time in their brief acquaintance, he spoke as if he'd followed her thoughts. 'I'm what you call a veterinarian.'

'That's an American term,' she told him. 'In this country we say veterinary surgeon, or vet, for short. Oh, here's Fourways!'

They'd reached the house almost before she'd realised it. The sun was sinking in the sky, streaking it with cyclamen pink on turquoise. Against the paintbox colours the house looked of a piece, part of the backdrop to a stage production – *Lucia di Lammermoor*, perhaps. Built at the height of the Victorian Gothic revival, its windows were tall and thin, pointed and filled with arched tracery. Meredith knew from past visits that they didn't let in very much light. There were gargoyles under the eaves masking waterspouts and at one corner of the upper floor was a funny little pepperpot turret sticking out as if it had been a last-minute burst of inspiration on the part of the architect.

Jan Oakley leaned forward, his hands resting on the dashboard above the glove compartment, staring through the windscreen at the house. There was an extraordinary tension about him; electricity crackled in the air between them. His face held an exalted look as if he gazed on some holy relic. Meredith found herself unable to speak and could only sit and wait.

After a minute or two he turned to her and said quietly, 'You can't understand what this means to me. I've dreamed

66

of this place. Actually to see it, to be here, not just for myself but for my father and grandfather, who never saw it – even my great-grandfather who left this house to come to Poland.'

'Your great-grandfather?' It all fell into place. 'You're William Oakley's great-grandson!' she gasped. 'You're Wicked William's descendant!'

He turned to her and she realised she'd made a bad mistake. Hostility glittered in the dark eyes and something more. It was as if she'd attacked her companion personally. For a second she panicked, thinking he would physically strike back. But then the hostility faded. His tongue flicked across his lower lip as if, for him, this had some calming effect. Certainly, he relaxed. The dark eyes held nothing worse now than a mild reproach.

'Why do you call him that – Wicked William? Was he a bad man?'

Even that softly-phrased question set alarm bells going in Meredith's head. How much should she explain? Should she tell him that she was even now working her way through Geoff's research material? No. She didn't want to cause another upsurge of that anger. 'He left home under a cloud,' she said. In case he didn't know this expression, she added, 'There was an unfortunate incident.'

Jan was shaking his head. 'I know what you're talking about. He was accused unjustly of having murdered his wife. He didn't do it. She was addicted to laudanum and while under the influence of the drug, suffered a tragic accident. He told my great-grandmother, his second wife, all about it before they married. She told their son, my grandfather, he told my father and my father told me. You see, I know all about it. My grandfather told me when I was a child that his

67

mother had been a woman of great good sense. She would never have married a murderer. She knew her husband was an English gentleman. He wouldn't have lied to her.'

Somehow Meredith found the strength to say, though she knew her voice trembled, 'He stood trial.'

'He was accused by a servant who had some grudge against him, but a jury – a *British* jury –' Did she only imagine something mocking in his tone? '– found him Innocent. So, he was.' He spoke the last words as simple fact, a matter of logic, which couldn't be gainsaid.

Alan would have something to say about the difference between being found Innocent and being innocent. But Meredith was momentarily shaken. Unconsciously, she'd accepted Geoff Painter's claim that Oakley had been 'lucky to get off' and assumed Oakley's guilt. At least she ought to finish working her way through Geoff's notes before coming to a conclusion. In any case, she knew she'd be unwise to trespass further on a forbidden subject.

She found herself saying weakly, 'Well, this is quite a moment for you, then. I do understand that.'

Privately, she was thinking, Perhaps *he* feels that way about it. I wonder how Damaris and Florence feel about *him*?

'Well, said Alan Markby, 'that's what you might term a turn-up for the books!'

'Not half. I still can't take it in.'

He poured them both another glass of wine. 'No wonder you came in declaring that I'd never guess whom you'd met and where you'd been. I certainly *couldn't* have guessed. He's genuine, I suppose?'

'That's what's worrying me,' Meredith confessed. 'No one

has ever mentioned any Polish Oakleys before. I admit I don't know Damaris and Florence all that well, but I've always understood they were the last of the line. On Saturday evening at the Painters' we were talking about them, about the family, for goodness sake! Geoff said then that the sisters would be the last Oakleys at Fourways, and Juliet, who has been seeing them recently, didn't suddenly say, "Hang on, Geoff, there's a Polish horse doctor and he's hotfooting his way over here, about to land on the doorstep." Yet this Jan told me he'd been in correspondence with them. He definitely reckons he's expected. I just don't see how it's possible.'

'Well, I've known them all my life and I've never heard of a Polish branch of the family,' Alan agreed. 'But that doesn't mean the Oakley sisters have been unaware of it.'

'And never said a word to *anyone*?' Meredith sat back in her chair and pushed a hank of dark brown hair out of her eyes. 'In all these years?'

'Think about it from their point of view,' Alan said. 'Their father was Wicked William's and Cora's son. As they grew up, William's name would never have been mentioned; it would've been the family skeleton-in-the-cupboard, a dreadful blot on their honour. Anything they later found out about him would have been veiled in the same secrecy. It was a scandal. Don't underestimate the fear of scandal, especially in someone of that generation.'

Meredith was mulling it over. 'I suppose so,' she said unwillingly. 'This Jan's an odd sort of chap. One minute he appears harmless and the next – oh, I don't know! He was so excited when he saw the house, his face lit up, really shone. I found it unnerving. I kept thinking of those paintings of saints with their eyes fixed on glory. And then I thought how

Lucifer means "light-bearer", and I didn't know whether I had a saint or a devil with me in the car.' She looked embarrassed. 'Sorry if I sound way over the top. He was just – different. We like to pigeon-hole new acquaintances, I suppose. But I couldn't slot him under any heading.'

Alan was looking thoughtful. 'I think you might be right to feel some concern. The Oakleys are planning to sell up, move to a retirement flat, spend the rest of their days in peace and comfort. It's such a big undertaking for them it must fill their minds every minute of the day. All the planning, even with Juliet's help, must be a nightmare. I doubt they can really be doing with long-lost relatives at this time, even if he is completely harmless despite your fears. In fact, it's the last thing they need. On the other hand, I don't see what we can do about it. It's a family matter, isn't it?'

'What about Interpol?'

He twitched his eyebrows, startled. 'Isn't that making a big jump in reasoning? We've no reason to believe he's a crook. The Polish authorities could confirm whether or not he's for real or a fake, but there again, we've no excuse for contacting them. Presumably his travel documents are in order or he wouldn't have got through immigration at Heathrow.'

'There is one thing I can do,' Meredith told him. 'I can phone Juliet Painter and warn her. She's got an excuse to visit Fourways and check things out. I'll do it tonight.'

She paused. 'I was going to phone her anyway. I've changed my mind, about my house.'

She saw the alarm flood into his eyes. 'You've moving out? Going back to your place?'

'No. I have decided to sell my place.' She waited.

He said quietly, 'I don't want you to do this just to please me.'

'That's not why I'm doing it. I'm doing it because I want to show you I care. That I'm not half-hearted about us looking for a new home together. That I want – that I want this new stage in our relationship to work and I'm prepared to do my bit towards it.'

Later, she moved her head on his shoulder and said, 'Today, for the first time, I told someone you were my partner.'

'That's nice.' He smoothed her hair. 'Whom did you tell?'

'How grammatical you are. I told Jan Oakley.'

'Ah? In self-defence?' He was smiling, but the smile didn't reach his blue eyes.

'Perhaps it was, but it won't be in future.' She said softly, 'I mean it, Alan.'

He reached out and took her hand. 'I do know what a big step this is for you.'

She squeezed his fingers. 'Funnily enough, it's not as difficult to make as I thought it would be. Dithering never helps, does it? It's always best to make up one's mind.'

'For better or worse?' he asked quietly.

'Getting married is a bigger step.' Meredith drew a deep breath. 'I'm making progress, Alan, but I need to do it in my own time.'

So they left it at that, for the time being.

Damaris Oakley toiled slowly up the winding staircase, steadying herself with a hand on the banister. The oak was worn as smooth as silk by the touch of countless other hands. Behind her came their visitor, his clumsy backpack bumping against the treads. She could hear his breath, was conscious of the scratching of the rucksack against the woodwork and the rustle of his clothing, the heat of his body and the smell of male sweat. It was as if some large wild beast crept up the staircase behind her. She had to fight back terror, an old, old terror which had resurfaced.

When she and Florence had been small, a nursemaid had frightened them with stories of the bogeyman who lived in dark corners and jumped out at passing children. As a result, she and Florence and even Arthur, although he was a boy and knew he ought to be brave, would only go up and down the stairs together. Hands gripped for mutual reassurance, they'd peer fearfully into each shadowy corner, uttering squeals of dismay at each creak of the woodwork. At last their father had found out how terrified his children were and had conducted an elaborate ceremony, involving raiding the dressing-up box, to banish the fiend.

And now he was back. Perhaps, thought Damaris, he'd never really gone away at all. He hadn't been fooled by Papa in an Oriental dressing gown and a turban. He'd just been biding his time and here he was. No longer a shadow, but flesh and blood. Our flesh, she thought, and our blood. At the other end of a long life, she had to deal with him again. The bogeyman had become reality. He was there now, following her up the staircase as he'd followed two scared little girls nearly eighty years ago.

They'd reached the corridor. She led him along it and opened the door. 'I've put you in the turret room. I hope you'll be comfortable. There is a bathroom just along there. The hot water is a little erratic. If you want to take a bath, let me know and I'll light the geyser for you. I wouldn't like to let anyone do it who wasn't used to it. It's got a mind of its own.'

'I expect I'll be able to manage it, dear cousin, if you'll just show me once how it's done.'

The large dark eyes were fixed on her with a kind of gentle mockery. But Damaris was less affronted by that than by being hailed as his dear cousin. She didn't care if he blew himself sky-high with the geyser. But she wasn't his 'dear'. She could hardly bring herself to believe she was any sort of cousin.

She knew he'd seen her wince and that it amused him. He wouldn't laugh aloud, he was too clever for that. She knew she was in the presence of someone who was very clever. She was aghast at the helplessness which swept over her at the realisation. How well equipped was she for the battle of minds which lay ahead? Although her own mental powers were in good shape, she knew that the brain of a woman of eighty-two must soon lag behind in a race with that of a man of whatever he was – twenty-nine, thirty? To her it seemed incredibly young. Yet there was about this young man something which was old. She couldn't quite be clear about what it was until she thought, Young in years and old in sin, and the expression seemed to explain it all.

Am I being unfair? she asked herself with a pang of conscience. Am I blaming this person about whom I know nothing for something which happened a hundred years ago and which ought, in reality, to have been relegated to history long since. But how can you relegate something to the 'dustbin of history' when here it is, large as life, smiling at you from those luminous dark eyes?

Clinging to everyday detail as if to a lifebelt, she said

73

carefully, 'I ought to explain about meals. You'll take breakfast with us, of course, and perhaps lunch if you are here. But my sister and I don't eat an evening meal as such. We find we don't need it. We make ourselves something light, often just toast or a sandwich. So I've arranged for you to dine at The Feathers. It's a pub, two minutes' walk down the road. They know all about you. Just go in and tell the landlady, Mrs Forbes, who you are.'

There was no way, she and Florence had decided immediately they knew he was coming, that they could cook for a man. Not with the old gas cooker playing up the way it did and the work and shopping involved. Mrs Forbes had been very understanding and helpful. She was a businesswoman, of course, and some hard bargaining had followed. Damaris's intuition told her that the cost of feeding Jan would fall on his hostesses. The same thinking had prevented her from booking Jan into The Feathers on a full bed and board basis. He was going to cost them money, but Damaris was determined it would be as little as possible. Jan would be provided with the cheapest thing on the bar menu for the evening (usually sausage and mash or a burger and chips). Damaris would be billed by Mrs Forbes when Jan left. If he wanted anything more elaborate, it would be made clear to him by Mrs Forbes there was an extra cost, to be paid from his own pocket, on the spot.

'Dear Cousin Damaris—'

He's doing it on purpose! thought Damaris. He's doing it because he knows I don't like it.

'You'll find I won't be the slightest trouble to you. In fact, while I'm here, I can help you. Anything you need done, I'll be very happy to do it. I'm quite a handyman.'

74

'We've got one,' said Damaris unkindly. 'We've got Ron Gladstone.' Jan was leaning towards her, his face now expressing only anxiety to please. She had an impulse, subdued with difficulty, physically to push him away.

If Jan had heard her words, he gave no sign. He'd walked into the room. There was a gasp. He'd stopped in his tracks, struck by the sight before him. Damaris smiled slightly to herself, a dry, bitter little smile.

'The portrait!' The young man turned to her, eyes shining. 'I recognise him. I have an old photograph. It's—'

'William Oakley,' said Damaris. She looked across the room at it. The sun had set almost completely and just a last ray of light touched the gilt frame with a pink finger. The frock-coated sitter stared out at them, handsome, unreliable, his dark gaze mocking, his red lips upturned in a half-smile without warmth. One hand was tucked inside his breast lapel in Napoleonic style, the other rested on a book.

'My grandfather, but your great-grandfather. I remembered that portrait was stored somewhere about the house. I looked it out and dusted it off and put it in your room. I thought,' Damaris added, 'it seemed apt.'

She left him to unpack and made her way downstairs to the kitchen. Florence was there, cutting thin slices of bread in preparation for their supper that evening which was to be Marmite sandwiches.

'Everything all right?' Florence asked, setting down the breadknife which was so old and much-used that its blade had worn to something resembling a rapier.

'All right' wasn't the phrase, thought Damaris. Everything was all wrong. The Oakley bad luck working its baneful effects to the last.

'I've told him he's got to go to The Feathers if he wants any dinner.' Damaris picked up the butterknife and prepared to set to work on the bread slices.

'Perhaps he'll get fed up and leave soon,' said Florence optimistically. 'He'll be very bored. The food at The Feathers can't be good for the digestion, it all seems to be fried. As for the turret room, it's very cold even in the middle of summer.'

'Let's hope so,' said Damaris grimly. 'Or something will have to be done.'

Chapter Seven

The case against William Price Oakley, accused of the murder of his wife, Cora, last year, opened today amid scenes of great excitement. The public benches were crowded, those hopeful of attending queuing outside since daybreak. The press box was also well filled, some of the gentlemen of that calling having travelled from London. One even represented the international news agency founded by Baron von Reuter and sat ready with pen and paper to set down the details and send them around the world. Such is the morbid interest aroused by murder trials in all parts of the globe.

Stanley Huxtable, a red-haired, stocky young man and the *Bamford Gazette*'s regular court reporter, was rather pleased with this piece of copy. Stanley sat through trials of all sorts on behalf of his employer. Usually it was smalltime stuff and the miscreant was up before the magistrates. Bamford wasn't a hotbed of crime, not unless you counted petty theft and the usual drunk and disorderly on a pay-day. It wasn't often he got anything as good as a murder and the chance to attend the assizes in Oxford in his professional capacity. A journalist could let himself go on a murder. To the citizens of Bamford, Oakley was a local boy. They wanted to know every detail and it was up to Stanley to supply it, hurrying back at the end of the day with material for the special late editions being put out to cover the trial.

The nation shared their curiosity. You only had to look at this, admittedly rather small, press box, filled to overflowing with sweating hacks. Seated next to Stanley, the Reuter's man was mopping his brow and the nape of his neck with a spotted handkerchief.

Stanley settled his bowler hat on his knees and licked the tip of his pencil. When he'd been a cub reporter he'd been taught to write everything down. 'You think you'll remember, my boy, but believe me, you won't!' his mentor had intoned. So Stanley had already written, *Court very warm.*

It was likely to get warmer. The room was not large. The press box was a narrow single bench shielded by a low wooden wall, fixed to the side of the room at right angles to the rest of the benches which ran across the room side to side. It faced the jury benches across the room in a similar situation against the far wall. The witness box was to Stanley's left. In front and to the right of him, on the benches set across the room, facing the judge, sat counsel. Behind them was an empty row, half of which was partitioned off to form the dock. Behind this rose the grey-painted public benches in ascending ranks. They were rapidly being filled by said public, which was jostling its way through the entrance at the top of the room. *Packed like sardines*, jotted Stanley, *and nearly as smelly*.

The public was at last seated, waiting, holding its breath in anticipation for the moment of drama. It came. Like the devil in a stage play popping up through a trapdoor, the defendant, William Oakley and his escort appeared, first their heads, then their bodies, up the narrow stair that gave access to the subterranean tunnel running between the prison and the courtroom. Oakley was led to his place in the dock, the heads of those seated above craning to look down on him. This was the man they'd come to see. This was the murderer! The escort took its seat on the remaining half of the row, forming a stiffly uncomfortable red-faced mass of heavy wool uniforms.

Preliminaries were briskly completed, the defendant entering a plea of Not Guilty in ringing tones. There was undisguised satisfaction on the public benches. A plea of Guilty would have seen the whole proceedings despatched in minutes and everyone sent home, other than the condemned man and those who would escort him back through the tunnel to prison, and ultimately to his appointment with the hangman.

Counsel for the prosecution, Mr Taylor, tall, thin, with an elongated neck, rose to his feet and clasped the front edges of his robes in either hand.

'We're off!' murmured the Reuter's man.

The courtroom held its collective breath.

'Gentlemen of the jury,' Taylor began, 'we are here in the presence of a dreadful crime, dreadful in its concept and execution, and rendered more dreadful by the hand of Fate.'

Good start, thought Stanley, scribbling. The old boy's got a nice turn of phrase.

'The accused, William Oakley,' Taylor was saying, 'married a rich wife and during their marriage administered her money and kept an eye on her business interests. This was convenient for him, because he's a man who needs money, a gambler, a follower of the turf and a womaniser. Mrs Oakley had been very young, only eighteen, at the time of the marriage and was accustomed to defer to her husband's judgement. However, as the years went by, Mrs Oakley became aware of her husband's incessant philandering and, being now a mature lady in her thirties and not a girl of twenty, was resolved to do something about it. The final straw which broke the proverbial camel's back was an affair begun between the accused and the nursemaid, Daisy Joss.

'Mrs Oakley made it clear she was prepared to indulge her husband no longer. Not only would she cease to make money available to pay his debts, she might even have come to consider a legal separation. It was then that William Oakley hatched a scheme to rid himself of his wife. It probably came to him during a routine visit to London Chemicals, a factory in which his wife had interests. Arsenic, that well-known and readily available poison, was used at the factory in the manufacture of rat poisons. Secretly to procure a small amount would be easy. But to poison his wife by the usual method, that is introducing it into her food, presented difficulties. He had no reason to visit the kitchen where the food was prepared. They shared the same meals, served by one of the maids. But at London Chemicals he was able to observe the way in which arsenic crystals are obtained from the ore, and was told that in the process, a highly toxic gas is produced. William Oakley, gentlemen, had found his means.

'Having abstracted a small amount of arsenic ore from the factory, William Oakley now had to await his opportunity. It came soon enough. Following a painful dental extraction, his wife had asked him to bring laudanum from the pharmacy in Bamford. She would be taking it that night and under its influence first become drowsy and then sleep heavily. Oakley's plan was that his wife should die in that sleep and that the death would be attributed to another cause – namely, over-indulgence in the laudanum. Oakley's plan was as follows: once he was satisfied that his wife was in a drug-induced slumber, he would creep into her room and construct a primitive but working apparatus, using the heat from the bedside lamp to vaporise the arsenic. He would then leave the room, making sure windows and door were shut. His intention was to return later, his nose and mouth well muffled, throw open the windows to let out the smell of garlic caused by the vapour, remove the evidence, pour away much of the laudanum and then return to his own room and await the morning. By then, the tell-tale garlic odour would have disappeared, Mrs Oakley would be dead in her bed and the large amount of laudanum missing from a full bottle, purchased only that day, would indicate she had overdosed herself with the drug.'

Taylor paused at this point. *Checking the jury's reactions!* thought Stanley. Taylor need not have worried. The whole courtroom hung on his every word.

'Things didn't go to plan. Mrs Oakley had not taken so much laudanum that she was unaware of the odour of garlic filling the room. Or possibly, her husband, on closing the door as he left after setting up his dastardly apparatus, had disturbed her. She awoke, saw that something very strange was happening, and attempted to get out of bed. Alas, she was overcome by the vapour and fell, bringing down the lamp. That set alight her nightgown and, dying as she was from the effects of the toxic vapour, she could do nothing to save herself.

'At this point, another thing unforeseen by William Oakley happened. The housekeeper Mrs Button arrived on the scene. She was unable to save her mistress but she did notice the smell of garlic, so typical of the process, and threw open a window to let it out. Had she not opened that window, gentlemen of the jury, it is possible the housekeeper might also have died from inhaling the dreadful vapour. You will also hear that she noticed foreign items amid the wreckage of the shattered lamp, although she had no way of knowing what their presence meant. We shall show that what Mrs Button saw was the remains of the apparatus set up by Oakley, also brought down in Mrs Oakley's fall.

'The inquest on the death concluded that Cora Oakley had fallen while drugged and brought down the lamp, dying of burns and shock. Defence will doubtless seek to make much of the fact that Mrs Button said nothing to contradict this at the time, only later when she had been dismissed from Mr Oakley's service. Mr Oakley must indeed have disliked seeing daily a woman who had witnessed incriminating evidence of his crime. He may have suspected the housekeeper had noticed the smell and seen the remains of his devilish device and was puzzling over them. Mrs Button had indeed been worried; once dismissed, and feeling herself released from any obligation to her former employer, she went to Mrs Oakley's parents. They had never been satisfied with the manner of their daughter's death and set in train the events which brought William Oakley to be in the dock today.'

Neat! scribbled Stanley. *But you've got to prove it, old son*!

Chapter Eight

Ron Gladstone stood in front of the dilapidated stone building, sucking his front teeth. His whole attitude was one of deep disapproval.

'Shocking,' he said aloud. 'And I dare say worse inside.'

The building in question had been put up more years ago than anyone could remember. It stood in the far corner of the grounds, away from the house, and was hidden by a tangle of shrubbery. When Ron had started working in Fourways gardens, he'd been there a week before he'd realised this place even existed. Ramshackle and overgrown as it was, he'd seen no reason to do anything about it right away. He'd put it low on his list of priorities for the garden and it was only today that he'd made up his mind to tackle it.

The building's solid stone block walls had withstood the ravages of time fairly well, but its corrugated iron roof had rusted, warped and collapsed entirely in the centre, leaving a hole through which years of rain must have entered. Not surprisingly he discovered, as he checked methodically, that all the woodwork was rotten. Ron's screwdriver sank in like cheese, as he muttered and prodded at window and doorframes. 'Blimey! Rough bit of workmanship, this,' he observed of the door itself. 'And dropped.'

By this Ron meant that the door no longer sat square within its frame. Though held in place by rusted hinges on the one side, it had been dragged askew over the years by its own weight and the bottom corner on the handle side rested on the ground. It was locked by means of a hasp and padlock and it was to tackle this obstacle that Ron had brought along the screwdriver. He set to work on the aged fixtures. The screws resisted surprisingly but he got them loosened in the end and was able to wrench off the whole locking device. With the padlock circumvented in this way, he put it, the hasp and the screwdriver on the ground. His next task was to oil the hinges. He then seized the door handle in both hands and hauled on it. It took him several minutes and he risked splinters in his fingers before the oil worked into the metal joints and they groaningly obliged. At last he was able to drag it open sufficiently to allow him to squeeze through.

'Phew!' he muttered, taking out a handkerchief to mop his brow. 'Wonder when that was last opened!'

He edged through the gap. It took a few moments for his eyes to become accustomed to the gloom. The air was stale and damp, smelling of earth and decay. There were windows all along one wall. They were hung with cobwebs so thick and huge they might have been heavy lace curtains. The cracked and broken panes were encrusted with dirt. The shrubs outside had grown up hard against them, poking twig fingers through gaps and invading the shed with greenery. As a result, next to no daylight seeped through by this route. The main source of light was the hole in the roof. It revealed to Ron's bemused gaze a time capsule of long-ago gardening activities and all of it covered with a layer of thick dust and more strings of cobweb. The floor was of beaten earth, muddy in the centre beneath the gap in the roof. Utensils were propped against the walls or were stacked in corners. Beneath the windows ran a long bench covered with broken earthenware flowerpots, seedtrays, yellowed seedpackets, dried out scraps of vegetable matter. A collection of what looked at first glance like pebbles turned out, on inspection, to be the dried speckled remains of runner bean seeds. Ron picked up one of the flowerpots and a trickle of earth, dried to the consistency of finest dust, ran out. He felt as though he'd broken open a tomb. Unlike Howard Carter, however, he wasn't faced with 'wonderful things' but only junk.

'Been a potting shed,' he observed again aloud to himself.

He turned round. Against the back wall stood an extraordinary-looking mechanical contraption, rusted into immobility, a cross between a dogcart and a lawnroller and he realised that was exactly what it was – a roller designed to be drawn by a pony.

'A museum would like that,' said Ron.

He transferred his attention to the shelves around the walls, stacked with tins, jars, packets, all rusted, grimy, discoloured. Most of the labels were illegible. Ron scratched his chin. Getting rid of that sort of stuff, if you didn't know for sure what it was, could be tricky. You couldn't just abandon a pile of old fertilizers and weed-killers on the local dump and leave the whole lot to leach into the soil. The council were fussy about that sort of thing these days. The council, in fact, might have to be contacted about the disposal of all this. He would have a word with Miss Oakley.

In a way Jane Austen would have recognised, Ron always referred to Damaris as Miss Oakley and to her younger sister as Miss Florence.

'Better see what we've got here,' he muttered. He reached up and took down a packet, opening the top flaps and sniffing suspiciously before poking it with his finger. Potassium permanganate crystals. The old gardeners used to make a solution of it. Ron remembered vaguely, from his youth, the buckets of purplish coloured liquid and of being told, by his father, to pour it round the tomatoes and be careful how he did it. And this? Bonemeal, solidified into a cake. More crystals. Dried blood, he guessed.

In taking down the last item, he had uncovered a dark bottle, pushed to the back of the shelf. He lifted it down. Protected by the items which had been stored around it, its label had survived in a more legible state than most. Ron carried it to the best of the light, under the self-made skylight, wiped the dust from its glass shoulders and rusty cap, settled his spectacles on the bridge of his nose and peered at the lettering. He gave a low whistle. 'Crikey!' His voice held awe.

At that moment, he heard the sound of footsteps approaching. Someone walked briskly and with heavy echoing tread across the grass. Neither of the Oakley ladies. Who the devil? Ron replaced the bottle on the shelf and hurried to the door. He poked out his head and got, as he put it afterwards, quite a shock.

A youngish man had arrived outside and Ron hadn't the foggiest idea who he might be, where he might have come from or what he might be doing there. He was what Ron called sloppily dressed, by which he meant jeans and one of those upper garments which looked like underwear and were inexplicably topwear. But the image which leapt into Ron's mind was that of a spaniel he'd once owned. It was something about the newcomer's large dark eyes and anxious-to-please expression.

Nevertheless, Ron was deeply suspicious. It might be a burglar, casing the joint. Ron was an *aficionado* of the police procedural form of crime fiction. It was a basic belief of his that any male between sixteen and forty, wandering around without obvious cause, was up to no good. Moreover, this young fellow looked distinctly tough, for all his innocent expression. Ron emerged fully from the shed and prepared to see off this intruder.

'Looking for someone?' he asked with dangerous civility.

'No, only looking at the gardens.' The voice was foreign. Ron thought he might've guessed as much. Blooming tourist of some sort, just walked in.

'These are private grounds,' he barked.

'I know.' The young man put his hands in his pockets and eyed Ron up and down.

The spaniel image faded. Ron had a feeling that the young man's previous anxiety had been connected with his not knowing who was in the potting shed. Having seen Ron, he had decided this was no threat. Which, thought Ron grimly, is where you're wrong, my son!

'You're the gardener here?' There was casualness, even a touch of insolence in his voice, or so Ron fancied.

Ron bristled. 'I keep the gardens tidy for Miss Oakley and her sister. Entirely voluntarily. Just to help them out.'

'Ah?' The young man seemed to make a decision to revise his approach. He became less off-hand and more affable. 'I'm a relative of the family, visiting them. My name is Jan Oakley.'

'And mine's Cary Grant,' said Ron sarcastically.

'I am pleased to meet you, Mr Grant.' The young man extended a hand.

'Gladstone!' snarled Ron. 'My name is Gladstone!'

The young man looked wary, as if the elderly gentleman was proving to be a little confused about his own identity. He withdrew his hand.

'Miss Oakley,' challenged Ron, 'said nothing to me about expecting visitors.'

'Only one visitor, only me. Why should she tell *you*?' The dark gaze was now frankly insolent.

Still, though the question wasn't polite, Ron had to admit it was justified. Why should they tell him?

'What are you doing in this barn?' asked Jan.

Ron bristled again. Cheeky young blighter, he thought. I'd like to knock his block off. What does he think I'm doing in there? Brewing moonshine? But of course he couldn't tackle the intruder physically. The other was young and strong.

As if to demonstrate his disdain for Ron's opposition, the newcomer had strolled past him and, uninvited, had pushed his head through the opened doorway while, at the same time, grasping the lintel with his raised right hand, as if to claim some right of possession. 'It's very untidy. It's your shed?' The criticism and the question were both put without the speaker turning.

'No, it flipping isn't my shed!' snapped Ron. 'I wouldn't let any shed of mine get into that state!' He fought for self-control. 'I was inspecting it. Never been in it before – had to unscrew the padlock.' He indicated his screwdriver, the padlock and the hasp on the ground. 'I guessed it might have been used to store things and it has been. It'll have to be cleared out now the ladies are going to sell up.'

He felt a pang of sadness at the thought that he wouldn't now ever have the chance to restore the old potting shed to useful life.

The young man, who had still been peering into the shed, seemed to freeze. He released the lintel, turning slowly and suspiciously. 'Sell? Sell what?'

'The house, of course,' said Ron, adding with a return of his suspicion, 'thought you'd know that, seeing as you're family, or so you say.'

'I am family!' The young man's voice and manner were suddenly so pugnacious, Ron stepped back. Then the other added more calmly, 'But I didn't know the house was to be sold. Thank you, Mr Gladstone. It affects what I've come to tell my cousins. I must go and find them at once!'

He turned and made off rapidly across the lawn. Ron watched him go. When the stranger had disappeared, he looked back at the shed and heaved a sigh. Once you'd been disturbed, you could never get back to a job, it was a fact. There was more to it than that. The encounter had left him deeply unhappy. For the first time since coming to Fourways, Ron felt no pleasure at the thought of any of the garden tasks he'd carried out so contentedly until now. The cluttered old potting shed, previously a challenge, had turned into a wearying chore-in-waiting. He'd have a go at clearing out this place another day. He pushed the door back into place, but lacked the energy to replace the rusty hasp. He picked it up, together with his screwdriver, and set off in the wake of the visitor. He had a feeling he ought to find work nearer to the house today, just so as he could keep an eye on things. Ron recognised a tricky customer when one hove into view and Jan Oakley – if that was indeed his name – struck Ron as very tricky indeed.

Juliet Painter returned to her London flat late that evening. It had been a tiring and futile day. Her latest client was a Texan oil multi-millionaire who'd decided he wanted an English country estate with opportunities for shooting, fishing and some corporate entertainment. She'd driven all the way up to Yorkshire to view a possible property only to find, to her surprise and some dismay, that the present owner was in dispute with a ramblers' club and the place was being picketed.

Shoulder to shoulder the objectors stood, dressed in a motley collection of anoraks, cagoules, Fair Isle sweaters, thick wool stockings and heavy boots. They bore placards proclaiming their right to roam and sang, not very tunefully, 'We shall not be moved!'

As she drew up and let down her window, the crowd surged forward alarmingly. A stout woman in corduroy trousers pushed her face hard against the opening and bellowed, 'Access for all!' A terrier she had by a leash, put its front paws against the car door and barked its support.

'Yes,' said Juliet pleasantly. 'I quite agree. Does that mean I can go through?'

The woman withdrew a few inches, looking a little disconcerted. She studied the young woman in the car, assessing the fresh complexion, braided hair, round glasses.

'Are you family?' she asked in the manner of an usher at a wedding.

'No,' said Juliet. 'Not even slightly.'

A bearded man with a worried frown, touched the woman's

arm. 'Peaceful protest, Mrs Smedley,' he chided.

She shook him off. 'I am peaceful!' she snapped. The terrier yapped.

'You can go through,' said the bearded man to Juliet, addressing his remark over Mrs Smedley's brawny shoulder. 'We only want our rights.'

'Fine by me,' said Juliet. 'I only want mine.'

The crowd had fallen quiet. Suddenly, a younger man wearing similar spectacles to Juliet's rushed forward and thrust a handful of leaflets at her through the open window.

'Thank you,' she said, and put them on the front passenger seat.

As if this had been the object of the whole exercise, the crowd now fell back and parted like the Red Sea to allow her through. She pressed the window button, just in case, as she rolled past them. Behind her they formed up again and as she reached the front door and parked, she heard, in getting out of her car, their discordant chants begin again, interspersed with shrill barks.

Her arrival had been noted within. The front door creaked open a few inches. Juliet approached and it was pulled open further, just enough to allow her to squeeze through the gap, which she did. It was immediately shut behind her. In the dark hallway, she found herself faced with a furious old man. Unsure whether this was the owner or some kind of butler, she hesitated and then solved the problem by introducing herself.

'Juliet Painter. I wrote.'

'You are expected, miss,' said the butler (as he must be). 'Kindly follow me.'

Through a maze of chilly corridors, he led her to his

employer whom she found staring from an upper window with an expression suggesting imminent apoplexy.

'You chose your day to come!' he greeted her. 'Look at 'em! It's like the blasted French Revolution – hordes of 'em bleating about their rights!' He turned a bloodshot eye on her. 'What about *my* bally rights, eh? What about them?' He breathed heavily for a moment or two before adding more mildly, 'Want to see over the place?'

She wasn't sure she did. However, she'd come this far and braved the mob of latterday *sans-culottes* outside. She might as well view the place though she was well aware by now what she'd find. As expected, it was a mausoleum of Edwardian furniture and grisly hunting trophies. Stag's antlers lined the corridors and a moth-eaten collection of stuffed birds and small mammals fixed her with beady eyes as she passed by. Disapproving family portraits sneered at her from smoke-blackened walls. Although the day was a mild early summer one, every corner of the house was icy cold.

After the tour of inspection, they sat down to a lunch served by the furious butler, and punctuated by bearded faces appearing at the windows. It hadn't been a very good meal, consisting of lumpy vegetable soup, tough cold cuts and a piece of cheese so dried out it had cracked into fissures like an Ice Age rock formation. Juliet suspected the elderly retainer was also the cook. The wine, on the other hand, was exceedingly good, the butler bringing to the table a dusty bottle which would have fetched a high price at auction. Though normally not a lunchtime drinker, especially when on business, Juliet was tempted to a couple of glasses. Partly this was because one didn't turn up one's nose at vintage wine and partly because she suspected what was to come that afternoon and felt in need of some Dutch courage.

They emerged afterwards to view the grounds. Juliet was now suffering severe indigestion from the cheese, which kept burping up reminders of its presence in her stomach in a way that would have been embarrassing if her host had appeared to notice. But his attention was taken elsewhere. All along their way they were severely hampered by woolly-hatted personages of either sex, and occasionally of unattributable sex, popping out from behind walls, bushes, out of ditches . . . the only thing they hadn't done was drop from the sky. They still brandished placards and in addition thrust forward ancient maps which showed, they claimed, rights of way. They were earnestly eager to engage her and the owner in conversation. All they wanted, they continued to insist, was freedom to roam.

As it was, Juliet's freedom to roam and inspect had been severely curtailed. But she was very glad indeed she'd witnessed all this. It made her decision straightforward. The place wouldn't do.

Rights of way, she'd found before, could cause a lot of trouble. Millionaires like privacy. They are also understandably nervous about their own security. The Texan oilman would not want his defences breached by anoraked and booted open-air enthusiasts. Nor would he wish to see them straggling across the landscape like a column of refugees when he was trying to entertain high-profile guests. The shooting might be thrown into question because the game birds had been disturbed. She struck this particular property from her list of possibles.

'Sorry,' she said to the present owner who stood by her in simmering resentment. 'I shall have to inform my client about this. I can tell you now, he won't—'

'I know,' interrupted the owner disconsolately. 'And I don't bally well blame your client!' He returned to gazing from the window across his moors, dotted with spots of moving colour marking the triumphant progress of the ramblers. 'You know what I'd like to do? he added wistfully. 'I'd like to bloody shoot them.'

Driving back to London, Juliet thought about the owner with sympathy. Although she wasn't unappreciative of the ramblers' argument, and didn't really approve of breeding birds simply to shoot them, she was annoyed with the demonstrators. They were the cause of an entire day wasted. There was no question of the Texan oilman taking on the dispute over access. Not that he couldn't get his lawyers on to it and probably get some decision in his favour, but ill-will would result locally and that sort of thing was best avoided.

Still, thought Juliet recalling the present owner, poor old chap. There he is rattling round in that gloomy great house. Presumably he has no family anxious to live in it. He probably couldn't afford staff even if staff could be found. That funny old butler is probably all that's left and the two of them are growing old together in cold and discomfort. There may be death duties and the place would have to be sold probably, when he dies. He wants to sell now, of course he does, and spend some of the cash before the taxman gets it. He could move to a comfortable cottage. He's in the same situation as Damaris and Florence really, only Fourways is a much smaller house and hasn't got acres of moorland all round it. Thank goodness the Oakleys don't have a human problem, like ramblers, gumming up the sale process!

It was late when she got in and the first thing she did was relax in a hot bath. Then she got herself some supper. After that awful lunch she needed decent nourishment. It was getting on for eleven and she was about to stumble off to bed, when she remembered the answering machine she'd left switched on that morning. Better check and see if there were any messages.

There were three. The first two were routine. The third drove sleep from Juliet's brain at once.

A quavering voice, filled with shock and alarm, which she barely recognised as that of Damaris Oakley, pleaded, 'Juliet? I realise you may not be there but if you are, please pick up the phone. I don't get on very well with these message machines . . . Juliet? Oh, you aren't there . . . Please get in touch as soon as you can. We need your advice. Something dreadful has happened!'

Chapter Nine

Inspector Jonathan Wood made his way home from a day in court. He felt weary, not just because it had been a long day, but because he anticipated the strain the days ahead would bring. Not that he expected to be called again to testify. His part was over, his role played. He would go about his daily business, here in Bamford, ostensibly occupied, secretly wondering what was going on in that courtroom. He'd find out like anyone else. One evening he'd buy a copy of the *Gazette* on his way home and there it would be. A verdict of Guilty or one of Not Guilty. If he were sensible, he'd put it out of his mind till then. But commonsense and emotion are old enemies.

Normally he never allowed himself to dwell on the outcome of a trial because that wasn't his business. His business was to lay hands on the culprit and deliver him up to due process of law. What the law then did was its business.

But in this case he couldn't allow himself the luxury of standing back, congratulating himself on having done his bit. He'd seized the opportunity offered to enquire further into a death he had felt, from the first, had been far too convenient, given Oakley's circumstances. A second chance. Policework so seldom offered that. No wonder he'd grabbed it with both hands.

Now, in a burst of self-criticism, Wood asked himself if he'd become obsessed, convinced in his own mind of Oakley's guilt, allowing personal dislike of the man to muddle cool assessment of the facts.

If he had, and he was wrong, it would be a black mark on his record not easily erased. The Home Office, he knew, continued to be unhappy about the whole thing. At least they were fortunate in having the prosecution conducted by a distinguished barrister in Taylor, whose angular figure and long neck put Wood in mind of a heron patiently fishing among the weeds and stones, waiting for that telltale flash of silver.

So far things were evenly balanced. Wood had lingered in court to hear the evidence following his own brief appearance on the stand. The jury had heard that the exhumed body had indeed revealed traces of arsenic. However, as Sir Herbert had feared, the jury was also informed that arsenic had been found elsewhere in the soil of the churchyard, and contamination of the remains from this source was not impossible.

The manager of London Chemicals had been an interesting fellow, well aware which side his bread was buttered. His testimony had been a model of sitting on the fence. Yes, he remembered Mr Oakley's visit. Yes, Mr Oakley had asked a lot of questions about the processing of arsenic ore. Mr Oakley was a gentleman who had always taken a very active interest in what went on in the factory. It made a great deal of difference to the manager's life, dealing with someone who understood. They were always pleased to see Mr Oakley at London Chemicals. Were exact records kept of the amount of ore in stock? Yes, of course they were. Ah, well, it would depend how much went missing. A very small amount might not be missed. It was difficult to check now after so many months, if not impossible, as he'd told the police.

And then there was Martha Button. Please God Martha Button stuck to her story . . .

When the principal witness for the prosecution, Mrs Martha Button, was called to take the stand, it is fair to say the atmosphere reached fever pitch. One would have been forgiven for thinking oneself at a major sporting event.

Stanley Huxtable squinted at the woman who was squeezing her bulk into the narrow confines of the witness box. To the crafted piece of copy above he had added the jotted notes: *Martha Button a stout person not above eight and forty. Decently dressed in brown. Hair a bit odd. Suspect henna or a wig.*

He glanced across at the prisoner's handsome profile. His weeks in a cell awaiting this trial had not harmed his physical well-being, other than a touch of prison pallor. He'd probably been paying from his own pocket for meals to be sent in from a nearby cookshop. The man looked impassive, staring at the witness as if she were of no more importance than the sad little mouse that had found its way into the holding cells below into the courtroom, and now crouched bewildered by the closed door to the tunnel, unable to return.

Did Oakley give any thought to his own return through that nightmare-inducing tunnel at the end of the day? What had been in his mind as he'd walked the short underground distance today? Had he been afraid? Not, it seemed, of anything Martha Button might say. What, then, confident? Why? Justice is notoriously blind. Did he trust in a clear conscience? Or in his own audacity to save his guilty neck?

Either way, he'd made an impression on the public benches, all right, especially on the fair sex represented there. Stanley transferred his gaze to Inspector Wood who'd taken the stand earlier. Wood was scowling at the witness. He's worried, thought Stanley, tapping the pencil on his notepad. He's depending on her.

The witness was taking the oath in a nervous but clear voice. Mr Taylor's opening questions were clearly designed to put her at ease and she had visibly relaxed by the time she'd begun to describe the events of the fatal evening.

'Poor Mrs Oakley had had a tooth pulled and was in terrible pain. It upset me just to see her suffer. Of course, it wasn't the only thing upsetting her.'

Mr Taylor leaned forward, his voice soft and coaxing. 'What do you mean by that?'

The witness responded in kind, tipping her upper half over the edge of the witness stand. She said in a hoarse whisper, 'There was Mr Oakley's behaviour.'

'You must speak up,' said the judge.

'What about his behaviour?' asked Taylor. 'You mean his behaviour that evening?'

'Oh no, sir. That evening he was all kindness. He rode to Bamford and fetched laudanum for her. He took it up to her himself on a tray. It was the least he could do, seeing as he'd been carrying on with that flighty girl, Daisy Joss—'

At this, counsel for the defence bounced to his feet. It was perhaps a pity that he was as small and round as his prosecuting confrère was tall and lean. 'Objection! This is not evidence, this is below stairs gossip!'

The witness took offence and retorted robustly, 'I don't gossip, sirs! It's plain fact and what's more, she wasn't the first.'

One or two on the public benches sniggered.

'I shall over-rule the objection in this instance,' said the judge. 'You may continue, Mr Taylor. But the witness will remember she is giving evidence and must only tell us facts of which she is sure.'

'That's what I'm doing, isn't it?' demanded the witness, nettled.

'Please go on, Mrs Button,' said Taylor hastily, obviously worried his prize witness was going to upset the judge.

Mrs Button regained composure and took up her tale. 'Mr Oakley ate alone in the dining room. Roast chicken,' she added, 'and a tapioca pudding.'

'I don't think we need to know what he ate, Mrs Button,' said the judge wearily. He'd met witnesses like this one before. First all nerves, then, when they got talking, you couldn't stop them and half of it was inadmissible or irrelevant. He glanced at the clock on the wall above the jury. He was to dine with the Lord Lieutenant that evening, and did not intend to let matters drift on. Garrulous servants were the very devil.

'Well, I'm telling you anyway,' countered Mrs Button, 'so you can see I remember the evening. It's not gone fuzzy in my memory. It never will. I'll remember every detail of that night to my dying day! After his dinner, he went off to the library to smoke his cigar. That was his habit. I supervised the skivvy as she washed the dishes, then I sent her off home. She lived nearby.'

'So who was in the house that night, after the skivvy left?' enquired Mr Taylor.

The mouse had disappeared. Stanley drew his feet up under his seat apprehensively.

Mrs Button was reeling off names. 'Mr and Mrs Oakley, sir. Myself. Lucy, one of the maids. I sent her up to bed straight after she'd cleared the dinner table because she'd been sniffling. She'd a bit of a cold. Jenny, the other maid, wasn't there because she'd been given permission to attend a family funeral and wasn't coming back till the next morning. Mr Hawkins, Mr Oakley's man, wasn't there that night either, because the master had sent him off to London on some business or other. The nursemaid, Daisy Joss, was up in the nursery with her charge. Watchett, the gardener, looked in during the evening to discuss vegetables and fruit. He told me what he'd got at its best in the garden and I told him what I should need in the morning. Then he left to go to his cottage. I locked up the back door and I set off to my own bed after I'd checked the downstairs doors and windows. It was about eleven o'clock.'

The public benches were silent, hanging on every word. *Could hear a pin drop*! wrote Stanley in his notebook.

Taylor was asking, 'And had you seen any more of Mr Oakley?'

Mrs Button shook her head. 'No, I hadn't seen him but I had heard him in the hall and going up the main stairs. I supposed he was going to bed. That would've been a little before ten.'

'You are sure of the time? Take care. This is important.'

'Oh, I'm sure, sir,' replied the witness. 'I took notice of it by the kitchen clock because he didn't usually go up so early.'

'Did he not, indeed?' asked Taylor rhetorically for the sake of the jury. To Mrs Button, he said, 'I see. So you set off to bed? By what route?'

'I went up the backstairs, sir. On the first floor, the stairs come out by Mrs Oakley's room. It's what we called the turret room.' At this point the witness began to show signs of distress. 'As I was just turning to go up the next flight to the top floor, where I had my room – oh, I can hardly speak of it. It brings it all back! I heard a dreadful noise. It curdled my blood and that's a fact. I'll never forget it, never!'

'Compose yourself, Mrs Button,' urged Mr Taylor. 'Can you describe this noise?'

Mrs Button knew her moment had come. She drew herself up. 'It was a shriek, sir, like a soul damned!'

There were gasps of horror and anticipation from the public. The Reuter's man was scribbling furiously. Prosecution, thought Stanley, looked like the cat that had got the canary. Defence was fidgeting with his papers. Inspector Wood was watching intently. Only the accused man sat impassive, as disdainful as ever.

'And what,' purred Mr Taylor, 'did you do next, Mrs Button? After you had heard a shriek?'

'Why, sir, I ran to Mrs Oakley's door. I could hear her making a strange gurgling and gasping. I threw open the door and then, sir, I saw a dreadful sight. I pray I never see another such. The mistress lay on the floor in her nightgown and it was all ablaze! She was twisting and writhing on the carpet, the flames were crackling . . . She held out her hand towards me, poor soul, as if she couldn't speak. She couldn't seem to draw breath. I saw the lamp lay on the floor broken. She must have fallen and brought it down. And her hair, sirs, her hair. It just burst into flame and fizzed and was gone like a firework.'

Mrs Button began to cry and several ladies among the public joined in.

The judge picked up his gavel and struck the bench. 'The court understands your distress, Mrs Button, but you must pull yourself together. Please go on.'

Subdued, the witness told them how she had seized the coverlet from the bed and thrown it over the burning woman to quench the flames. 'She was in dreadful pain, the skin peeling from her arms. But she couldn't speak. I believe she would've done if she could. She hadn't the breath left. I wasn't surprised. There was a dreadful smell in the room, burnt flesh and hair and something like garlic, really strong.'

'You are familiar with the smell of garlic?' interposed Mr Taylor.

Mrs Button assured him she was. She had once had a place where the lady of the house had been French and insisted she, Mrs Button, use the stuff to spoil her good English cooking. 'I went to throw open the window. I could hardly breathe myself for the nasty smell of it and my head was beginning to ache just by being there.'

Mr Taylor, his manner nicely balanced between satisfaction and decent horror, turned towards the jury. 'You could hardly breathe yourself. I beg the gentlemen of the jury will note these words.'

The jury tried to look like men noting important evidence. Some managed it better than others. One of them, Stanley recognised him as a local grocer, was looking a little sick.

'What else did you notice, Mrs Button?'

The witness raised a gloved hand and jabbed her forefinger at the court in emphasis. 'Now, that was an odd thing. There was a sort of pot lying on the floor by the mistress, a common thing, and some bits of metal, metal rods. Not the sort of things you'd expect to see in a lady's bedroom. Nor was any of it there normally – *that* I can tell you!'

Mrs Button announced the last words defiantly and paused as if waiting to see if anyone would take up the challenge. When no one did, she continued on a slightly disappointed note, 'Anyhow, I hadn't got time to worry about any of that then. I hurried to fetch the master. He made like he was very upset, of course, when he saw her lying there. He told me to run down to the stables and tell Riley, that's the groom, to ride for Dr Perkins. So that's what I did. When I came back, Mr Oakley said Mrs Oakley was dead and I do believe she was. He asked me to sit with her while he went to get dressed, before the doctor came. So he went out and I sat there. It was then I saw the pot and metal rods had gone. It's my belief he slipped it all into the pockets of his dressing gown. It had big pockets, plenty of room.'

Little defence counsel rocketed to his feet. 'Oh, objection, m'lud! This is a conclusion drawn by the witness and surely inadmissible!'

The witness didn't wait for the judge's ruling on the point. Combatively she snapped, 'Well, all I know is, it was all there when Mr Oakley came in and it wasn't when he left, and *I* didn't take it!'

* * *

Now, on his way home, Wood recalled his second visit to Fourways House with Sergeant Patterson, when they'd gone there to arrest Oakley. The expression on the man's face when he'd realised what was happening to him, was etched into Wood's memory. Disbelief, anger and then – scorn. Yes, scorn. Perhaps it was the memory of those scornful dark eyes which worried Wood most of all.

It had grown dark because it was still early in the year. The gaslighter was making his rounds, leaving a trail of bright lights in his wake. The air was heavy with the sulphurous tang of smoke, the warm odour of horse manure and the clammy touch of evening mist. Yet there were still plenty of people in the streets. Grocers and butchers had kept their shops open, hoping to lure in the last-minute shoppers, the returning office-worker, the improvident housewife.

Newsboys ran about with the evening editions. The *Bamford Gazette* had brought out a special. Wood bought one, scanned the trial report briefly, and stuck it in his pocket to read at leisure later. It had been written by that chap Huxtable. The reporter was by way of being a regular obstacle in Wood's path, hopping out in front of him to ask for comments on every subject under the sun. Tomorrow the nationals would carry the story and he'd have to worry about more than Huxtable.

He put the key in the door of his modest end-of-terrace home in Station Road and tried, as always, to turn it quietly. But Emily heard him. Before he had the door fully open, she'd darted from the kitchen where she was busy preparing his supper, ready to help him off with his coat and exclaim over damp rainspots on the nap of his bowler hat.

'I knew you would be late,' she said, cutting short his apology.

'Has the supper spoiled?' asked Wood, sniffing the enticing scents from the kitchen.

'No, I made a steak pie because I could keep it warm.' She was divesting him of his ulster as she spoke and bore it away to hang it up in the hall where warm air wafting from the kitchen would dry it.

'Steak pie,' said Wood, unwinding his muffler. 'My favourite.'

They both smiled. Whatever she cooked for him, he always claimed it was his favourite dish. It was a private joke between them. She was twenty-three and had cared for him for six years now, since the death of his wife. She should by rights be in her own home, looking after husband and children, not here with him. But it wasn't just filial loyalty which kept her here and the smile reminded him.

One half of her face lit up, the pretty half. The scarred half grimaced. She'd been the prettiest of children until the dreadful day when her full skirts had swung into the flames of the open fire. There were other scars on her body but no one could see those.

The facial scars couldn't be hidden. So Emily hid. She hid here in this house and had her whole life here. In vain he assured her there would be someone out there, beyond the front door, who would see behind the scars to the loving and capable person whose heart was unscarred. But Emily hadn't the courage to risk rejection. She stayed here, sallying forth once a week to do the shopping, and once on a Sunday morning to attend the local Wesleyan chapel, on both occasions veiled like a widow.

As a result, she'd become an object of curiosity and mystery in the neighbourhood, and accounts of her disfigurement were exaggerated.

They always ate in the kitchen at Wood's insistence. He saw no reason for untidying the tiny dining room and giving her the work of tidying it up again. He was allowed to do nothing. He would happily have lent a hand around the house, unlike most men, but she was adamant. This house was her domain, her life. Outside it, he was in his world. Inside it, he was in hers.

When they were seated at the kitchen table, she asked, as she doled out his portion of pie, 'How did it go today, Father?'

She knew about the Oakley case because he was accustomed to discuss things with his daughter. Usually he toned down the violence and unpleasant detail. This time that had been difficult.

'As well as could be expected,' he answered. 'The woman Button gave her evidence confidently enough and it is no longer my concern, my dear!' He immediately destroyed this fine statement with, 'I watched Oakley. He sits there with a superior look on his face. He's going to make a fool of the lot of us. I feel it in my bones.'

'This isn't like you,' she chided.

'No, it isn't. I'm well aware that the matter is in the hands of the lawyers. But it happens to a policeman, my dear, that every so often he comes across a villain he particularly wants to nail. I want William Oakley. I've wrestled with my conscience over this sincerely enough even to satisfy that minister of yours. But the truth is, I believe him a devious, clever, calculating, cold-blooded killer. I want to hear that

Guilty verdict, of course I do. I admit it. There!'

Afraid he sounded too ferocious, he stopped and smiled apologetically. 'Listen to me, I sound a monster myself. Take no notice of me, Emily.'

She had stopped eating and was pushing a piece of piecrust round the plate with her fork. Her eyes fixed on it, she said, 'It's because of me, isn't it? It's because of this.' She touched the scarred side of her face. 'It's because Mrs Oakley burned that you want him so much.' She looked up as she finished speaking and her candid blue eyes stared into his.

For a moment he was silent with shock. Was she right? It seemed so obvious when she said it, and yet he wasn't aware of that being his reason. Did she understand him so much better than he understood himself?

After a moment he managed to say, 'No, Emmy, it's not personal. Not in that way. I feel it here,' he tapped his chest, 'and here,' he tapped his head. 'But in court it'll come down to whether the jury believes the testimony of that housekeeper. Either way, I can contribute no more to the matter.'

Stanley Huxtable lived in lodgings. His landlady was a woman of strong teetotal principles and an uncanny ability to detect even a single bottle of porter brought into the house. She allowed no card games, no music (other than communal hymn-singing), and no visitors. It was Stanley's habit, therefore, to spend his evening in the public houses of the town. Not to get drunk, that would have put at risk not only his lodging but his place on the *Gazette*. Just, he told anyone interested, to see a jolly face or two and have a bit of cheery conversation.

Tonight he was settled in the corner of The George with a pint of porter, a pork pie and a pickled egg. No journalist he'd ever come across ate sensible meals. They never had the time or opportunity.

He was just tucking into the pork pie when he heard a voice.

'Mind if I do?'

It was the Reuter's man. Without waiting for Stanley's reply, he seated himself at the table and set down his own pork pie and whisky and water.

They ate and drank in companionable silence for a while. Then the Reuter's man observed, 'That woman, Button, she did pretty well for the Crown. If she goes on like that, she'll hang him.'

'See what Defence makes of his cross-examination,' said Stanley. 'Bet you a pint here tomorrow night, she comes apart at the seams.'

'You're on,' said the Reuter's man.

Stanley wiped his lips with the back of his hand. 'I'd have thought you'd have been putting up in Oxford.'

The Reuter's man chuckled and shook his head. 'Nobody knows the fellow in Oxford, do they, eh? That's why they're hearing the case there. Won't pick up any titbits about his private life, see. This is his stamping ground here in Bamford. I expect you know a tale or two about him, eh?'

'Not really,' said Stanley. It wasn't altogether true, but if the man from the international press agency wanted information, let him wear out his boot leather like everyone else.

'Bit of a swell,' opined the Reuter's man.

Stanley was prepared to agree: William Oakley was a real

toff. But even toffs had been known to murder the missus, he pointed out.

As men of the world, who'd seen it all, the two journalists nodded sagely.

Chapter Ten

'Naturally I drove down there straight away the next morning, that's to say, yesterday.'

Juliet Painter and Meredith Mitchell had wedged themselves uncomfortably at a corner table in a busy burger bar. It wouldn't have been the choice of meeting place for either of them, but neither had much time to spare at lunchtime and this place was convenient. Meredith had coffee and a packet of fries, Juliet coffee and a doughnut.

Juliet leaned across the table to avoid having to raise her voice above the surrounding racket. 'I had intended to go down anyway, after you phoned and told me about Jan so-called bloody Oakley the night he arrived. But I had to go up to Yorkshire the next day. It was all arranged. So I had to put off going to Fourways. It's a real pity because it let that creepy yobbo put his plan of action into effect first. If I'd gone there at once, I'd have spotted what he was up to and turfed him out.'

'You don't like him.' Meredith smiled at the ferocity in Juliet's voice. Then she shook her head, frowning. 'I couldn't make up my mind. On the one hand I didn't like him, either. On the other, there was something quite touching in his emotion at seeing the house for the first time.'

Juliet snorted. 'Don't you believe it. It's an act.'

'He is a member of the family,' Meredith pointed out. 'Or if he isn't he's mugged up the family history and it's difficult to see how he could have done that over there in Poland unless there was an oral tradition he'd inherited. He sounded as though he really believed in his great-grandfather's innocence. If Fourways had become a sort of legend in his family, talked about and imagined . . . well, it must have been exciting to see it there before him in bricks and mortar. He spoke as if he'd made some sort of pilgrimage to the house.'

'The Holy Grail was sought by the pure in heart,' said Juliet. 'There's nothing pure about Jan Oakley. He's a conceited blighter, too. When he was first introduced to me he rolled his eyes like a silent movie star and gave me a sickly leer I suppose was meant to be seductive. Twit. At least, after you warned me, I made sure he didn't get to kiss my hand. Yuk!'

Listening to her as she spoke, Meredith was suddenly visited by one of those irrelevant thoughts which pop into one's head at all the wrong moments. She found herself wondering how long Juliet's schoolgirl looks would last and how she'd age. She couldn't keep that braided hairstyle for ever. She was blessed with a beautiful complexion and that always helped. Somehow, it was impossible to imagine Juliet old. Meredith dragged her mind back to the topic in hand.

'It's up to them, the sisters, to turf him out. Whatever he claims, it's their house and he's their guest.'

'Don't they just wish they could? They didn't want him there in the first place. He invited himself. But they accept he's family and they felt obliged to let him come and to give him a bed now he's here . . .' Juliet hissed with annoyance and bit a lump out of her doughnut. 'Besides,' she added indistinctly, 'how can two elderly women, one of whom – Florence – is very frail, force their will on someone who's young, fit, determined and utterly without scruple. Because, believe me, he is unscrupulous.'

'Yes, somehow I can believe that,' Meredith nodded. After a moment, she asked, emphasising her question with a wave of a chip, 'We can be sure he is a real, genuine, on-the-level Oakley? After all, that's what it all rests on, isn't it? He could have heard about William Oakley in some way we don't know. There are lots of books about celebrated historical crime cases. Perhaps there's an obscure book somewhere which includes the Oakley case and this man, whoever he is, has got hold of a copy? Can we be sure of his identity?'

''Fraid so,' Juliet mumbled through a further mouthful of doughnut. She swallowed and added more clearly, 'Wish I could say he wasn't who he says. I asked to see his passport. There it was, Jan Oakley.'

'There are such things as false passports, you know.'

'Tempting thought. But even if he'd found an account of the trial somewhere, it's hard to believe he'd go to the lengths of getting a fake passport. Anyway, he's able to provide a lot more plausible detail and we can't say it's untrue because we have no record of what happened to William after he left the district following his acquittal. His own son had to go to the courts to get him declared dead, if you remember.'

'And this Jan is able to tell us what happened to William?'

'The whole thing,' said Juliet glumly. 'It seems Wicked William wandered around Europe for a while, travelling as fancy took him across the Austro-Hungarian empire.

Eventually he fetched up in Krakow which the Austrians controlled then. There he had a bit of luck. He found another wealthy woman to marry, this time a Polish merchant's widow with several business interests. Jan's even got a photograph, a sepia thing, showing William and his second wife. Where would he get that from if it wasn't in the family? I mean, I know there are any number of old portrait photos around, but this ties in with everything else he says. I tell you one thing, she must have had money because William certainly didn't marry her for her looks! In the photo, William himself looks much as he does in that portrait Damaris has got, and thoroughly pleased with himself as well. So, William ran the businesses, used his wife's money to make more, managed to keep his hands off the maidservants, and prospered. Who says crime doesn't pay?'

'Not Alan. He says crime pays too many people too well. Not the yobs who end up in gaol. The big boys, who don't.'

'Jan's a yob,' said Juliet fiercely. 'I'd love to see him in gaol. Tell Alan I'm working on it and actually, I'd like some help. That's why I'm here, talking to you.'

Meredith sipped her coffee and winced. 'I've already tried that on Alan. He says we don't have anything against Jan. Just being who he is and being here when he isn't wanted, isn't a criminal offence.'

'Extorting money is,' retorted Juliet.

Startled, Meredith put down her cup. A group of teenagers laden with trays pushed their way past the table. When she could speak again, Meredith said, 'Are you sure about this, Juliet? I thought the Oakleys didn't have any money. They're selling the house to realise some capital.'

'Hoping to sell the house,' corrected Juliet. 'That's what

gave Jan his chance. You'd better hear the rest of it. This is Jan's version, by the way. Naturally we've not had a chance to check out any of it yet. Here goes. William's Polish wife died first and left everything to him. When William died, his will left all his property to his children equally.'

Juliet held up a slender forefinger tipped, perhaps surprisingly, with a magenta-painted nail. 'OK, he had two children in Poland, a boy and a girl. But he also had a child in England, remember, whom he didn't see fit to mention by name. It's clear he wanted to keep his Polish property out of the hands of his English son. William was, without a doubt, a double-dyed stinker of the first degree.

'But, and here's the rub, what did he mean by "all his property"? Did he mean his English property, too? His daughter died of diphtheria before the First World War. His Polish son inherited all the Polish property and business interests. After the First World War, Krakow became part of Poland again, but nothing changed for the Oakleys. The present Jan's grandfather carried on running the businesses. We'd know nothing about them if it wasn't for the fact that they lost everything under the Communists. Our Jan's own father inherited nothing. The Polish family fell into poverty and its only surviving member is the Jan we've got here. With the change of regime in Poland, a lot of people are trying to get back sequestrated property. Our Jan – I call him that for want of anything better – started going through the family papers. Originally he wanted to get together a case to put to the present Polish government for restitution of interests lost under Communism. But hey! What does he find? A copy of the will of his English great-grandfather. To sum up, he says he has a claim on a share of William's English estate, represented now by Fourways. Because, you see, though Cora had the money, the house, Fourways, belonged to William. If the sisters now sell it, he wants half the money. His argument is that, under the will, his grandfather should have inherited half William's English estate, and that's the half Jan is claiming now. Damaris and Florence have been knocked completely all of a heap.'

'You need legal advice,' said Meredith promptly. 'I'm not the one you should be talking to. Try Laura, Alan's sister. She's a solicitor.'

'I know that. As it happens, she acts for the Oakley sisters. I went with them to see her, and she told us that she's never had a case like it. She needs time to look it up, but her first reaction was that Jan hasn't a leg to stand on. We don't know that the will he's talking of is genuine. We haven't seen it, only a certified translation Jan brandished under Laura's nose. Even if it is on the level, and even given that Continental family law is different from English family law, we're talking here of a will drawn up before the First World War, in a foreign city under the control of an empire which no longer exists. All independent records have long been lost. Plus, says Laura, William was declared dead legally here and his estate disposed of quite properly at the time.'

'So,' said Meredith, biting off the end of a chip, 'tell Jan to buzz off back to Poland.'

'I did, and he said he will take the matter to an English court. Appeal to the famous British justice and fair play, as he put it.' Juliet uttered a sound which could only be described as a growl. 'And, as Laura says, if he does that, it could drag on, whatever the outcome. The law is slow. It could hold up the sale of Fourways. It would cost the sisters both money and time. But time, you see, is what they don't have. We're talking here of women in their eighties who want to be settled in a new home before the coming winter. They only have a few months, it comes down to weeks, to sell, buy anew and move. Jan knows that. That's where he's being clever.'

'I see . . .' Meredith said slowly. 'So you think he's trying to force an out-of-court settlement from them?'

'I'm positive of it. From his viewpoint, the beauty of the case is that he doesn't have to *win*. He only has to cause delay. He wants them to agree, in writing, to pay him a large sum of money out of the proceeds of the sale of the house. Pay him, in other words, to go away and let them get on with the sale.'

'They mustn't agree to do any such thing!' said Meredith vigorously.

'I've told them that; Laura's told them. But they're old, they're confused, frightened. He's sitting there under Fourways roof and possession is nine-tenths of the law. He keeps telling them how impoverished he is, how he's their kith and kin. He's an Oakley.'

Juliet allowed herself a dry smile. 'There, I agree with him. He's an Oakley all right. He's William Oakley reincarnated.'

She sighed again. 'The sisters are in a terrible state. He's made them feel under an obligation towards him. He's told them how the family suffered under Communism, was reduced to poverty. He's putting on the moral pressure. He keeps reminding them that he's the sole surviving Oakley apart from themselves, and how the whole future of the family lies in their hands. Between that and the veiled threat of protracted legal quibblings, Damaris and Florence are being put under intolerable pressure. They can't afford to give him half the money from the sale of Fourways, but they're beginning to see themselves pushed into doing it. If that's not extortion, I'd like to know what is.'

'I'll tell Alan,' said Meredith. 'There must be something we can do.'

'I told Pam and Geoff about it and they're horrified. Pam being a county councillor and everything, she doesn't let things rest. She went straight over there to Fourways and instructed the sisters not to do a thing until we'd all had a chance to put our heads together and sort this out.'

'Was Jan there when she went to Fourways?' asked Meredith curiously. 'Did Pam meet him?'

'He wasn't there, as bad luck would have it, at least not in the house. Pam was all geared up to make mincemeat of him. She went looking for him in the gardens, breathing fire and vengeance, but the only person she found was Ron Gladstone, the gardener. He recognised her – he voted for her, it seems, at the last county elections. Anyway, he promptly buttonholed her and asked her to do something about Jan. She had to tell him it wasn't a council matter. It was, however, a matter of personal interest and she assured him she'd leave no stone unturned and all the rest of it. Pam has a lot of experience of calming agitated council-tax payers.'

'This chap Gladstone was upset, then?'

'Distraught, according to Pam. He's very fond of the ladies, as he calls the Oakleys, and he took an instant dislike to Jan.' Juliet glared at a youth in a reversed baseball cap who had spilled coffee perilously near her as he pushed his way to a table. 'Pam does get things done. She's pretty good, although she does go over the top sometimes. For instance, she keeps trying to bring me and James together.'

'James Holland – the vicar?' Meredith was startled. 'Well, he's a very nice person, I suppose.'

'He's great. I love him to bits as a friend. But as a husband? I ask you,' said Juliet, 'what kind of vicar's wife would I make? Visiting the sick and getting up the noses of the poor? It's not my scene.'

'Vicars' wives are different now. They have careers.'

'Well, my career requires me to be in London, not stuck in a draughty vicarage in Bamford. James and I are old mates, but I doubt he wants to marry me any more than I him. Still,' Juliet dismissed the digression, 'that's got nothing to do with Damaris and Florence.'

'I'm sure Alan can help,' Meredith said optimistically. 'Perhaps if Jan thinks the police are watching his activities, it might frighten him into behaving himself.'

Juliet's gaze had grown absent. She was staring across the restaurant. 'You know, on my visit to Yorkshire I met an old gentleman who told me he wanted to shoot some people who were making trouble for him. I understand exactly what he meant. I could, without the slightest compunction, murder Jan Oakley. It wouldn't be a crime or a sin or anything.' Juliet's gaze returned to Meredith. 'It would be putting things right.'

Meredith made her way back to her office deep in thought. She pushed open the door and was jolted back into the present.

Adrian was stooped over her desk and as the door opened he leapt back as though someone had set fire to the soles of his feet.

'Oh, Meredith . . .' he said sheepishly and took off his

gold-rimmed spectacles. 'Thought you'd gone to lunch with a chum.'

'Just a working lunch,' said Meredith grimly. 'Something you need on my desk?'

'Ah, the corrector fluid – if you've got some. I've made a bit of a mess of some notes.'

Meredith walked across and picked up the little white bottle. Silently she held it out to him.

He'd had time to rally. 'Well, well,' he said jovially, 'under my nose, wouldn't you guess?'

'Adrian,' Meredith said calmly, taking her seat, 'I'm not stupid. And when you've finished with the corrector, screw the top on properly or it dries out.'

He edged his way back to his end of the room where he busied himself shuffling papers about and liberally daubing corrector fluid over everything.

Twerp! thought Meredith unkindly, but she was more than just annoyed. She was determined. Like Jan Oakley, Adrian had to go. She wasn't sure yet how to bring this about. But there had to be a way.

Unknown to Meredith, others had already been urging Alan Markby to action in the matter of removing Jan. His first caller was his sister, Laura.

'He may not have broken the law technically, but the fact is he's a rogue. He's trying to get money out of those two old women. I'm their solicitor. I can advise them – I can urge them to wait until his story's been checked and his identity verified, but they say he knows far too much about the family to be a fake. All they want is for him to go away, and if money will do the trick, they may offer it to him. In the end, if they decide to give him the money, it's their decision and I can't stop them. By the way, I'm not breaking any client confidences. I told them I thought I ought to speak to you. They were all for that. Can you go and call on them? They know you. They remember our family from years back, even barmy old Uncle Henry. I'm sure they'd listen to anything you told them.'

Fifteen minutes later, he received a call from Pamela Painter. 'I dare say you don't like being disturbed at work, Alan. Geoff doesn't,' she began in her brisk voice. 'But this is quasi-official. You know about this fellow who calls himself Jan Oakley?'

Markby said he did know. Yes, he also knew about the will and Jan's claims. No, he didn't like the sound of Jan at all.

'Well, then,' said Pamela vigorously, 'you've got to do something.'

'It's not a police matter, Pam.'

'Neither is it a council one. But it *is* our responsibility, Alan! It's our responsibility as human beings.'

Markby was inspired by this stirring appeal to ask, 'Have you been in touch with James Holland? Perhaps if Jan Oakley was approached by a priest . . .'

'That's a good idea, Alan. I'll get on to James straight away. But we've all got to do our bit. *All* of us, Alan. This Jan person isn't going to be allowed to get away with it!'

As a result of this, when Meredith walked through the door that evening, she found Alan waiting for her.

'We're going out for a meal,' he told her.

'Great.' She dropped her briefcase on to a chair and kicked off her shoes. 'Give me time to shower and change . . .' It occurred to her that Alan had an enigmatic look on his face. Suspicion seized her. 'Why and where?'

'I thought we might try The Feathers.'

'That pub near Fourways? The food's only pretty average as far as I've heard.'

'Jan Oakley takes his evening meal there.'

'Oh,' said Meredith. 'I was going to talk to you about him. Juliet and I had lunch together.'

'Laura's been on the phone to me. Ditto Pam Painter.'

'It's all about this will, then? This ploy Jan's got to force some money out of the sisters?'

'He hasn't broken the law,' Alan warned her. 'We have to go carefully. But there's no reason why we can't apply a little pressure of our own.'

'Pretty average' Meredith decided, as they entered the pub, was a fair description of The Feathers all round. It was principally an old stone building under a slate roof. At some time, probably around the middle of the last century, it had been extended without sympathy for the original style, leaving an ugly hotchpotch. Inside, a similar lack of taste reigned. Old anaglypta wallpaper, though freshly painted cream, was already turning brown from cigarette smoke, coming away from the wall and parting company at the seams where the rolls joined. Framed sepia photographs of a historic nature added to the general air of brown-ness. The photographs, while genuine, were not particularly interesting. The best of them showed the staff of The Feathers circa 1900, posed in front of the inn. All the men wore bowler hats except for a youth who wore a tam-o-shanter. The landlady was dressed apparently, in mourning.

The Feathers, Meredith decided, had never been a jolly place. A scowling bull terrier positioned at the landlady's feet in the picture seemed to be making the fact clear to anyone who hadn't already got the message.

Despite this, the L-shaped bar was half-full. Meredith touched Alan's arm. 'That's him.'

Jan was seated in the far corner in the short leg of the L. He was just finishing his meal, and as they watched, put knife and fork down and pushed the plate to one side. She thought he cut, as he'd done at the taxi rank, a lonely figure, a young man without companions eating a solitary pub meal. She felt a twinge of sympathy.

'Why don't you go and chat him up?' Alan murmured. 'I'll get some drinks.'

'OK. Half of cider, please.'

As Alan went up to the bar, Meredith walked across the room and fetched up before Jan. Realising someone was there, he looked up warily. But then he recognised her and to her dismay his whole face lit up with delight and his dark eyes glowed in that exalted way which disturbed her so.

'It's my kind friend from the train!' He leapt to his feet, jolting the table and causing the beer in the glass on it to slop dangerously. 'The very first person who made me feel welcome in England and here you are again! Well, this is great, just great!' He held out a hand towards her in greeting.

'Please don't get up,' said Meredith, gripping the back of a free chair with both hands to brace herself against this overwhelming enthusiasm, and also so that she wouldn't be trapped in that kiss-hands routine again. 'I just came over to say hello and ask how you're liking England.'

'You've got to believe me, it's all just wonderful,' Jan

assured her, gesturing urgently towards the chair she held. 'Please, please sit down. You know, I really wanted to meet you again. I've told my cousins, Miss Painter, everyone, how kind you were to me.'

'My companion's just getting us some drinks,' Meredith interrupted this fulsome speech but pulled out the chair. She sat down. 'Did you enjoy the meal here? We're thinking of eating here tonight.'

Jan contemplated his emptied plate, shrugged and said, 'It was hot and not unpleasant, a meat pie of some kind.'

A shadow fell across them. They looked up to see Markby, holding a glass in each hand.

'Oh, Alan,' said Meredith duplicitously, 'let me introduce you. This is Jan Oakley. I did mention to you we'd met on the train.'

Oakley thrust out his small, strong sunburned hand eagerly. Meredith felt a pang of conscience. Markby, drawn into the company at the table, sat down.

Now that he had someone to talk to, Jan's whole manner brightened. Once again, Meredith found herself filled with unwished sympathy for him. Eating alone in the corner of a dingy pub every evening wasn't something she'd want to do herself. She wished he hadn't cast her in the role of his 'kind friend'. She was neither kindly disposed towards him nor prepared to be his friend. She sat at this table under false colours. But then, she'd known that would be the situation when she set out to introduce Alan to him.

'How are the Oakley sisters?' she asked, when Jan had told them how he'd visited Bamford and found it enchanting and walked in the countryside and found it beautiful, just like pictures he'd seen.

'My cousins are very well,' said Jan promptly. 'And, as you can imagine, they are delighted to see me.'

This was said in such a complacent tone that Meredith was startled. Did he really have no idea how much distress he was causing by his presence and his extraordinary claims?

She ventured. 'It must have been a bit of a shock to them, finding they had a relative of whom they knew nothing.'

Jan conceded that it had been a surprise. 'It was a surprise for me, too, when I discovered they existed,' he pointed out.

'How did you find out?' Markby asked mildly. Jan blinked and stared at him, his features frozen. 'How did you find out the sisters existed?' Markby asked again.

As if a switch had been pressed, Jan became animated again. 'A Polish friend was travelling to England, on holiday. I told him about the house, all I knew from family stories. I asked him, if he was in the area, to check it out. I didn't know if it was still there but I thought there was a chance. Well, he did and came back and told me not only was it still there, but members of the family still lived in it. So then I wrote a letter to them . . . and it went from there. Now we're all getting along like a house on fire.' Jan appeared pleased at being able to produce this expression. He drained his beer. 'I can buy you both a drink?'

'Oh, no, thank you all the same,' Markby declined. 'We're going to take a look at the menu in a minute. Will you be staying much longer?'

'At The Feathers?' Jan looked puzzled.

'No, at Fourways,' said Alan in a gentle way which caused Jan to flush.

'Well, I've only just got here, you know.' He managed, thought Meredith irritably, to sound quite coy. Juliet was right.

The man was an actor. Meredith's sympathy for him faded.

'I've known the Oakley sisters all my life,' Markby was saying. 'When I was a small boy, my mother used to take me over to Fourways sometimes, visiting. Old Mr Edward Oakley, their father, was still alive then. He was in a wheelchair. I found it rather a forbidding place but the women made such a fuss of me, it more than compensated for it.'

Jan's expression had become cautious. Now he was eyeing Alan in the speculative manner Meredith remembered he'd had when quizzing her in the train about Bamford.

'I'm sure they did,' he said. 'They're very hospitable.'

'Still,' said Markby, 'I expect you have to get back to your job in Poland. I understand you're a vet?'

'Yes, yes. A veterinary surgeon.' Jan had grown restless, his strong brown hands moving back and forth along the table rim. 'And you, Alan? You work in London as does Meredith?'

'Good Lord, no. Thank goodness. Not for me that journey up to Town and back every day. I work locally, or fairly locally. Over at Police Regional HQ.'

Jan's hands were stilled. 'Indeed? In what capacity?' His question also seemed to hang motionless in the air.

'I'm a Police Superintendent, CID,' said Markby cheerfully. 'A detective.'

Jan blinked slowly, reminding Meredith as he'd done on the train journey, of a large cat. For a moment he sat motionless then he gathered himself together and stood up.

'Well, it's been a real pleasure to see you again, Meredith, and to meet you, Superintendent. But you want to have your dinner and I have to get back to Fourways. My cousins will wonder where I am!' He edged out from behind the table and gave them his gold-toothed smile. 'I recommend the steak pie and chips.' He made a rapid exit.

'Well,' said Markby ruefully, 'that's what happens when people find out I'm a copper.'

'It's fired a warning shot,' said Meredith with satisfaction, 'and put the wind up him. He had guilt written all over him when he bolted just then. Still, now he is aware that you know the Oakleys and that you're interested. What did you think of him?'

Alan considered his reply. 'I found him a little pathetic, actually.'

'You shouldn't feel sympathy for him,' urged Meredith, overlooking her own momentary pity for Jan earlier that evening and her unease at the role she'd played here tonight. 'It's a sort of trick he's got. I fell for it for a while. Juliet didn't.'

'I didn't say I felt sorry for him.' Alan shook his head, his fair hair flopping forward over his forehead in the way it did. 'I'm a copper, remember? My feelings of sympathy are strictly limited to those I know for a fact are deserving of it, and I seem to meet fewer and fewer of them. You want my honest opinion? I agree with you and Juliet. He's certainly a con artist of sorts. But is he criminally so?' Without waiting for an answer, he added, 'He's no veterinary surgeon, I'd put my last penny on that. I'd say he works outdoors and with animals. A stableman, perhaps, on that stud farm he told you about? But definitely not a professional man.'

'So you think he's a liar?' Meredith pounced on this.

'I think he lied about his occupation. I suspect he's right in his claim to be an Oakley.'

'So why lie about his job?' she demanded.

Alan gave her a tolerant look. 'Oh, come on. Young men

lie for all kinds of reasons. In this case, to build up his image, impress a young woman he met on a train. All right, it's a silly thing to do, but it's understandable. Look at it from his point of view. He's turned up from nowhere. He wants to make a good impression on an attractive woman. He may be a scrounger, but he doesn't want to look like one. It's human.'

'Do you feel this way about all the crooks you deal with?' Meredith's hazel eyes blazed indignantly at him.

'Of course not. But I do meet a lot of crooks, some absolute villains, some pathetic little misfits. If Jan's a crook – and it's not established he is – he's in the latter class.'

'He is a crook,' Meredith insisted. 'He's trying to get money from the sisters.'

'Ye-es,' Alan looked thoughtful. 'Possibly he just hasn't understood the situation. He's arrived from Poland where I dare say he lives in a small flat. They live in a big house in extensive grounds, just the two of them. To his mind, that means they're rich. What's more, they're family. Why shouldn't they help out a poor relation? See it through his eyes.'

'The house is falling down,' Meredith argued. 'If he can't see that, he's blind. They wear old clothes and live on sandwiches.'

'So, they're rich but eccentric. It must be difficult for him to understand their exact circumstances. Genteel poverty is outside his experience. As for this business of his great-grandfather's will, he may well have persuaded himself he's entitled to a share in imagined Oakley wealth. He may have been indulging in some Walter Mitty daydream of being an English gentleman with a country house – you know the sort of thing.'

'Well, he'd better be disabused, pretty quick. I'll speak to Juliet again.'

A voice above their heads interrupted them. 'He's a smarmy little blighter, that one,' it said fiercely.

Startled, they looked up.

A large woman with white-blonde hair, wearing an orange sweater spangled with gold stars, had appeared. Juno-esque, she stood over them, hands on hips. Seeing she'd attracted their attention, she went on, 'I'm the landlady here, Dolores Forbes. And you,' she addressed Markby, 'are Superintendent Markby. I know you.'

'People do,' said Markby with resignation.

'Seen your picture in the paper,' Dolores informed him. 'And on the telly, local news. I've got a good memory for faces. You need that, in the pub business. I never forget a trouble-maker.'

Before Markby could enquire what kind of trouble he might innocently have caused Dolores Forbes, that lady had pointed to a notice pinned above the bar. 'See that? Barred from one, barred from all. All the publicans round here operate that system. I never have any trouble in my bar. As soon as I see one of those young hooligans come in, I send him packing with a flea in his ear and then I'm on the phone to all the other pubs in the area. They don't stand a chance.'

'I bet they don't,' said Markby with respect. 'I'm glad to hear it.'

Dolores leaned over the table, an alarming manoeuvre in which her large bosom shifted its centre of gravity and appeared about to topple her full length between them.

'Miss Oakley,' she said in what she probably fondly imagined was a whisper, 'came and asked me to feed him, that fellow. He's some sort of relative. Turned up like a bad penny. To my mind, he can get going back again to wherever he came from. Like I say, I've got a sixth sense for trouble-makers and he's one.'

Having delivered herself of this statement, she straightened up, much to her listeners' relief, and asked mildly, 'Do you want to see the menu?'

She grabbed Jan's dirty plate and swept it off. Moments later the menu was plonked down in front of them.

Meredith looked round the bar which was marginally fuller but just as subdued. It struck her that the clientèle looked cowed. Dolores did not stand any nonsense, and it seemed wasn't one for boisterous fun and jollity, either.

'Do you really want to eat here? Can't we go somewhere else?' she asked with a furtive eye on the splendid figure of the landlady behind the bar, informing some other hapless customer of her strongly held opinions about something.

'No, but how do we get out? She'll see us.' Markby grimaced. 'We'll be marked down as backsliders.'

'We can creep out now – look, she's gone.'

'Quick, before she comes back!'

They scuttled out like a pair of children who know they've done something for which, later, there will be retribution.

'Right!' Juliet's voice came wrathfully down the phone line. 'I'm sorry Alan's taking that attitude and I'm surprised. I'd have expected him to tell Jan to scram.'

'Alan's done all he can – shown an interest in the Oakleys and let it be known they're old friends. Jan knows he's a policeman. It should have some effect.' Meredith defended Alan's position.

A snort came from the other end of the connection. 'Well, if Alan won't do anything, it's up to you and me.'

'Why me?' asked Meredith promptly. 'I've done my bit.'

She wasn't allowed to get away with that. 'Now you can do a bit more. Listen, Jan thinks you're the bee's knees. He talks about you all the time. He calls you the kind person who first befriended him in England. Believe me, you made an impression! He won't listen to anything I say because I'm involved with the Oakleys in a business way: I have an interest in the sale of the house. He's more than hinted to me that he thinks I'm trying to cut myself in on any deal he makes. Dirty little trickster that he is, he's judging me by his standards! But you don't have any interest in Fourways. I want you to get him on his own, when Alan's not around. You're the one person who can get him to listen.'

'Oh, no!' returned Meredith vigorously. 'I want nothing to do with him. Alan can think up something. Give him time.'

'We haven't got time to wait for Alan to do something. You've got to help, Meredith. We have to meet guile with guile. Don't refuse, please. You can't. Ask him over, chat to him nicely and persuade him to drop this claim.'

'You overestimate my powers of persuasion.'

'Nonsense. He respects you. You're probably the only person he does respect. He wants you to think well of him. Anyway, you're a professional diplomat. It ought to be child's play for you.'

'I am – or was – a professional consular officer. I dealt with lost passports and British citizens who got themselves into various forms of trouble. I've had to talk myself into a few foreign gaols before now to see banged-up Brits, but that's it.'

'It sounds a very good basis to me,' said Juliet. 'Come on, Meredith, don't let the side down.'

Meredith reflected that it was difficult to refuse this kind of appeal, something which made her resent it all the more.

'When am I going to do this? I work in London all week.'

'So ask him over on Saturday.'

'It's not so easy now I share a roof with Alan.' Meredith paused to reflect that a lot of things weren't going to be so easy, now she was sharing a roof with Alan. She'd have to account for herself in a way she'd never done before.

'Meredith? You still there? You've gone quiet,' demanded Juliet's voice.

'Yes, I'm still here. I've just remembered Alan's going to a football match on Saturday afternoon with Paul, his brother-in-law. All right, it's madness, but I'll write Jan a note and ask him to drop by if he's free. But I've got really deep misgivings about this, Juliet.'

'I haven't,' said her friend. 'I'm counting on you.' She hung up before Meredith could change her mind.

PART TWO

The Second Shade

Diseases desperate grown,
By desperate appliances are reliev'd . . .

Hamlet, Act III, Scene 9

Chapter Eleven

Ron Gladstone had broken the habit he'd observed since starting to work in the gardens and turned up on a Saturday. He didn't like the idea that the Oakley sisters would be left all weekend with Jan and no outsider on hand to keep an eye on things. A lot could happen in twenty-four hours, he told himself.

The morning passed fairly uneventfully with nothing more than another fruitless discussion about a water feature. In the early afternoon he prepared to tidy the yew hedge he'd cut into battlements. He was proud of this work of topiary art. It lined the right-hand side of the drive leading from the main entrance to the circular gravelled area before the front door, dominated by Ron's bugbear, the lichen-encrusted cherub. To guide his eye today he'd driven in a cane at either end of the hedge and stretched a length of garden twine between the two.

Ron thought the hedge made quite an impression on anyone turning in the gateway. He'd been more than a little upset that Damaris Oakley hadn't received his skilful shaping of the yew with more admiration and delight. But it was like her refusal to consider a water feature, preferring, for reasons unfathomable, that fat stone baby sitting in a bowl. It hadn't worked in donkey's years and acted as a receptacle for every bit of garden debris to float that way. Ron had early realised, with regret, that both the Oakley sisters were extremely conservative where gardening was concerned. Ron itched to be creative in twig and flower. His original dream, when he'd started to work here, had been to recreate the gardens as they might once have been in their Victorian heyday. Like those gardens down in Cornwall, thought Ron, that everyone makes such a fuss about.

Sadly, he hadn't received the support he'd hoped for and now, even more sadly, he wasn't to have the time or opportunity. Fourways was to be sold. If he'd been the sort of gardener who was paid wages, he might have hoped the next owner would keep him on. But as a volunteer, a man pursuing his own hobby on someone else's land, well, that was something else. And who knew what would happen to Fourways? The whole place could be demolished, given over to developers. That's what usually happened these days.

However, come what may, Ron would stay at his post. He would garden on to the end. It was additional reason to give up his Saturday. 'Make hay while the sun shines!' said Ron to himself. He grasped the shears and was about to start when a taxi turned in the gateway. The gates themselves had fallen down years ago and rusted somewhere in the undergrowth. The tyres crunched the gravel chips as the taxi drew up, engine throbbing, and its driver got out to exchange a brief word.

'What you doing here, then, Ron?' he greeted him. 'Don't usually see you here of a Saturday.'

'Hullo, Kenny,' Ron returned. 'Come to take the ladies shopping?'

This was a regular weekly fixture. Ron guessed, but would never have said it, that the sisters liked to visit the local supermarket on a Saturday afternoon because often fresh goods were reduced in price. Bamford's stores didn't go in for Sunday trading. They knew that any citizens determined to spend money on the Lord's day of rest would be heading for distant superstores and retail outlets. However, by asking a question of his own, Ron had neatly avoided answering Kenny's.

'Yeah.' Kenny Joss propped himself against his taxi, arms folded. His forearms were heavily tattooed. 'Here, is it right, what I heard, that the old girls have got a visitor? Some long-lost relative or other?'

Ron snorted in disapproval, partly because he thought the Oakleys should be referred to more respectfully and partly at the mention of Jan.

'You heard right enough,' he conceded. 'He reckons he's some sort of relative, but he's a foreigner, so I don't see how he can be, myself.'

'I've got family in Australia,' argued Kenny. 'Lots of people have got family living all over the place.'

'Australia is all right,' retorted Ron. 'They speak English.'

'What, don't this fellow speak any English?'

'Oh, he speaks it.' Ron grew more irritated. 'He's always coming and bothering me with his questions. I'm keeping an eye on him, I am!'

'So that's what you're doing here on a Saturday afternoon,' said Kenny, preparing to get back in his taxi. 'Snooping.'

Ron's moustache fairly crackled with ire. 'Keeping observation, Kenny.'

'Good luck to you. I'd better go and get the old dears. I'll leave you to it, the observation. You made a neat job of that hedge, Ron.'

'Thank you.' Ron cheered up.

'Bit thin over there?' Kenny pointed to the patch of hedge in question.

'Give it time,' said Ron and realised, even as the words left his mouth, that time was what neither the hedge nor he nor anyone had.

About ten minutes later the taxi rolled past again, this time with Florence and Damaris seated together in the back. Damaris wore a flat-topped felt hat which suggested 'good works' and held a large basket perched on her lap. Florence wore a jersey-knit helmet with side flaps which tied beneath the chin. Two padded jersey circles encircled her brow in the manner of a medieval chaplet or an Arab *keffiyeh*. Ron waved at them as they made their stately progress by him and they waved back, like royalty, with a single raised motion of the hand and a gracious inclination of their heads.

Ron worked at the hedge for some minutes but the shears were stiff and needed a drop of oil. He set off with them in the direction of the dilapidated stableblock. It was to one side of the house, shielded from sight by trees. Ron stored his tools and other necessities in what had once been a tackroom. As he passed by the house, veiled in shadows thrown by the trees, he glimpsed a movement inside through one of the windows. Ron immediately stopped, retreated a few steps and by a circuitous route crept up on the window and peeped in.

He recognised the room as being the one the Oakleys always referred to as the study. It was full of heavy furniture, leather armchairs and a chesterfield. Bookshelves groaned with dusty tomes no one had opened for years. Through the uncleaned panes Ron was able to make out the figure of Jan. He was stooped over a large Victorian roll-top desk and appeared to be fiddling, as far as Ron could make out, with the lock. Suddenly Jan straightened, then gripped the edge of the roll-top and pushed it up. His movements were those of a man pleased with himself.

'Picked the bloody lock, I bet!' muttered Ron from his post at the window. 'Miss Oakley keeps the key on her key-ring, I know that.'

Now that the desk was open, the interior pigeonholes could be seen to be filled with all kinds of papers. Jan looked round, causing Ron to dodge back, fearing he'd betrayed his presence. But when he ventured to look again, it was to see that Jan had found himself a chair which he'd pulled up to the desk and now sat, carefully going through the documents, odd letters and bills with which the desk was stuffed.

Ron moved away from the window and stood unhappily with the shears forgotten in his hand. What to do? Tap on the window and give the fellow the fright of his life? Wait until the Oakleys returned from the shopping expedition and drop a word in their ears? Keep watch and see what else Jan might do? Then, when all the evidence was assembled, present the Oakleys with it at some later date?

He returned to the window. Jan appeared to have found what he was looking for and was eagerly scanning a large stiff sheet of paper. Another such lay by his hand. As Ron watched, Jan nodded, folded up both papers and returned them to envelopes which he put back in the pigeonhole from which he'd taken them. He pulled down the roll-top and satisfied himself the lock had clicked into place. He then walked out of the study.

Ron remembered he was on his way to the old tackroom. He set off there, deep in thought and very dissatisfied.

The tackroom had been swept out and rearranged by Ron, but signs of its original use remained in poignant reminder of a lost heyday. Wooden pegs protruded from the walls where once harness had been stored. There was, even now, a very faint smell of saddlesoap, tobacco, hoof oil and the acrid odour of horses. Ron sat on a bench to attend to his shears. His whole figure and attitude were no different, had he been aware of it, from that of the stablemen who'd once sat here to buff up leather and polish brass.

Ron worked automatically, his mind busy. The visitor had been poking about in things which were none of his business, he had no doubt about that. Ron was beginning to regret that, through his hesitation, he'd missed the chance to tap at the window and let Jan know he'd been seen. On the other hand, if he'd accused Jan, the man need only reply that he was acting with his cousins' permission. He could tell Miss Oakley when she returned, but the point was, *should* he? Jan would deny it, if taxed. There would be a nasty family row and it wasn't after all, Ron's family. He decided to think about it. He couldn't let it go. Jan had to be dealt with and stopped from snooping like that but in a way which would cause the ladies minimum distress. Ron bent his mind to the problem.

About half an hour after this, as Ron was back clipping the yew with his newly-oiled shears, he was surprised and disconcerted to see Jan himself emerge from the house. He walked towards Ron with his springy athletic stride. He wasn't wearing jeans today but fawn slacks and a patterned sweater. Going to a party? thought Ron grimly.

Jan had drawn level and stopped. 'You're hard at work, Mr Gladstone.'

He looked so thoroughly pleased with himself that Ron had to bite back a snappy response. He had made up his mind to speak to Jan himself about the incident in the study and say nothing to the sisters. They'd only be upset. But Ron hadn't yet worked out just what he was going to say to make it clear that whatever game the visitor was up to, Ron had rumbled it. It would take careful wording and Jan had caught him on the hop. Ron had to content himself with a nod and a muffled, 'Yes!'

Jan didn't take the hint. 'I'm going to walk into Bamford. It's a pity there's no bus service out here. I could have gone with my cousins in their taxi but it would have been a squash.'

And you wanted the house to yourself, thought Ron, so you could pry into things undisturbed. 'Off you go, then!' he said to Jan, wishing that Jan's departure could be made permanent. 'I've got work to do. Can't stand here chatting to you.'

But the fellow still stood there and had a funny smug look on his face. He was obviously keen to impart some piece of information.

'I'm going to see a girl,' Jan said. 'She's invited me to tea.'

With that he marched away, leaving the astounded Ron staring after him.

'Well!' exclaimed the gardener. 'I don't know who that might be, but whoever she is, she wants her head seen to.'

Meredith would have agreed with him. She should never

have let Juliet talk her into this. So ashamed of her weakness was she that she hadn't told Alan anything of Jan's proposed visit. She watched him drive away with Paul, waving them off with a nonchalance she didn't feel.

Back in the kitchen she prepared to entertain Jan. Meredith picked up a packet of chocolate sponge mix and read through the instructions with deepening gloom. She could, of course, nip out and buy a cake but she felt that if you invited someone, you ought at least to give them some homemade food. The trouble was, cooking wasn't her strong point. But the instructions seemed simple enough. Add an egg. Add so much water. Beat it all up and put it in the oven.

Meredith did all this but the mixture didn't look right. She poured it into a tin (ought it to be that runny?) and shoved it into the oven. As she washed up the mixing bowl she composed a speech which would persuade Jan to abandon his harassment of the Oakleys. She lined up the points in her argument. The sisters were old. Despite what Jan may have thought when he arrived, he must be able to see for himself they were poor. William Oakley, the mutual ancestor, was viewed by them with abhorrence. This bit was going to be difficult. Jan didn't like any reference to William being a murderer. Meredith would have to say the sisters had been told a quite different version of the story Jan had been told. As a result, his relationship to them was something which they found embarrassing. He must realise that to use it to try and extract money was dishonourable. What's more, it was useless. They didn't have any.

The timer on the oven buzzed. Meredith took out the cake. It didn't exactly look like the picture on the packet, but much smaller and oddly shaped, rising to a point. The appearance wasn't improved when she iced it. The icing kept running off. She scooped it up and put it back until most of it adhered, then put the cake in the fridge to set the icing quickly before it all ran off again.

She had just completed this manoeuvre when the doorbell rang.

Jan was on the step. To her horror, he was holding out a large bouquet of brightly coloured blooms.

'Thank you,' she said weakly, taking it. 'Do come in.'

But he'd already walked past her into the house and was appraising his surroundings. He looked unimpressed.

'It's my partner's house,' said Meredith hastily. 'We're going to sell it and buy another.'

'Ah, the policeman. He isn't here?' Jan looked around him enquiringly and, Meredith fancied, with just a touch of apprehension.

'He's gone to a football match. He'll be along later.' Quite a bit later. He'd probably go for a pint with Paul after the match or go back to visit his sister and her children. She didn't expect Alan to turn up before some time this evening, but it was better that Jan thought he might walk through the door at any minute.

'This is really kind of you, to invite me like this.' He was smiling at her.

Meredith reminded herself the plan was to persuade Jan to do as they all wished, and this involved being nice to him. 'I know what it's like to be a stranger,' she told him as she urged him towards the sitting room. 'Do go and make yourself comfortable. I'll make the tea.'

In the kitchen, she quickly rehearsed her lines. Provided she could keep the conversation going as she intended it to, there shouldn't be a problem getting Jan to listen. Whether she'd get him to agree to abandon his plans was another thing. She feared Juliet had overestimated her powers of persuasion.

Jan was relaxed on the sofa, one arm stretched along the back, when she brought the teatray in. He was slightly flushed and she suspected he'd been investigating the room and had hurriedly sat down when he heard her approach. She handed him some tea and, although he'd looked a little startled at the sight of it, a slice of the cake.

'Very nice,' he said politely but with some difficulty as the mixture seemed to be sticking to his teeth.

Meredith thought it a good moment, while he was occupied, to begin her prepared speech.

'Look, Jan, I want to be frank with you,' she said. 'I did think you might be at a loose end today and would like to share a cup of tea, but I do have another reason for asking you to come along this afternoon.'

If she'd thought he'd be surprised at this, she was wrong. He was nodding, as if she'd spoken as he'd expected, smiling at her almost as if they shared some secret. He'd managed to swallow the cake and now set down his cup. 'Sure, I understand. I've been thinking about it, too.'

'About your cousins? About the sale of the house?' She was taken aback, not thinking he'd be the first to broach the subject.

But he was shaking his head. 'My cousins? Why do you want to talk about them? I came here to see you. You wanted to see me. That's what it's all about, isn't it? Clever of you to get rid of the policeman. We certainly don't need him!'

'Now look here,' Meredith said quickly, 'let's get this straight. I asked you here to talk about your cousins. Alan's my partner. He and I are thinking of selling this house. Selling a house is a major project. It's a very stressful time for anyone.'

Jan was nodding as she spoke. He eyed the cake, but thought better of requesting another piece. 'OK, you don't have to tell me that. I know. So what? I'm here to help them.' He said this with that familiar complacency which again stopped Meredith briefly in her tracks. Did he really believe this? Clearly subtlety would be lost on him. She wasted no time on it.

'I'm sure you want to help them, but so far, you only seem to have alarmed them. I understand you've made some claim on the property.'

Jan dusted off his fingers and shook his head. 'You've been speaking to Miss Painter. She's a very fierce lady!' He chuckled. 'Unfortunately, she's quite misunderstood my interest. I could, of course, make a claim on the property under the terms of my great-grandfather's will. But I've no intention of doing so. My cousins need to sell the house. I understand that perfectly. It's in a very bad state of repair and all the rooms – ' he grimaced ' – are very cold. There's no proper heating, only a gasfire in each room, quite inadequate. To be honest with you, Meredith, it's made me very sad to see the dear old house in such a sorry state. However . . .' he shrugged. 'It can't he helped. What can't be cured must be endured – isn't that an English saying?'

'Yes,' said Meredith faintly.

'I'm all for them selling it,' he said. 'May I have another cup of tea?' He held out his cup.

Meredith poured his tea rather absently, splashing it into the saucer. 'When you say you're not intending to make a claim on the property, does that mean you don't expect to get some share of the money from the sale?'

He smiled, the gold tooth flashing. 'Well, it would be very nice if my cousins felt they could be generous. I don't say I don't need the money – but I don't expect it. I understand their situation. They're in sadly reduced circumstances.'

'You don't?' This was contrary to everything Juliet had claimed.

'No. And now, we don't have to talk about this any more, do we?' he leaned forward. 'After all, it's not the real reason you've asked me here, is it? I've also been trying to think of a way in which we might meet again.'

'I'm sorry, but you've got this all wrong!' Meredith began in alarm.

Jan ignored her protest. 'Pretty clever of you to send your policeman to a football match.' He patted the sofa. 'Come and sit here by me.'

'Of course I'm not going to sit by you! Are you deaf? Listen, I'm not interested in you! I asked you here to talk—'

'Don't give me that.' There was an odd flicker in the depth of his dark eyes. It gave her a split-second warning of what was coming.

As he dived towards her, Meredith snatched up the teapot and threw it in his face.

It was only half-full, not as hot as it had been, and most of it went down his shirt, but he let out a wild yell and swore, or she presumed it was swearing, in Polish. He gasped, 'You English bitch! You can't do that to me. I'll show you—'

Meredith snatched up the cake-knife. It was an old-fashioned one she'd found lying about in a kitchen drawer.

The edge was serrated but the tip came to a sharp point.

Jan froze, staring at the knife. For a brief moment his reaction hung in the balance. She held her breath, but didn't flinch. She mustn't look afraid, she knew that. But she *was* afraid, not just of what he might do, but of what she might have to do to stop him.

Then, with one of those sudden changes of mood of which he was capable, Jan shrugged. 'Frigid Englishwomen,' he sneered at her. 'Everything they say is true.'

'Out!' she ordered crisply.

'All right, all right. It wasn't going to be anything worth staying for, anyway, was it?'

He walked to the door in his jaunty way. She heard the front door slam and from the window, saw Jan striding off down the street. Only then did she begin to shake uncontrollably.

Snatching up the knife had been a purely reflex action. She'd been threatened and she'd grabbed a weapon. Suppose he'd called her bluff? Would she have used it? This, she thought, is how murder is done, that easily. What would she have pleaded? Self-defence? One thing was certain: Alan must never know. She didn't think Jan would tell anyone he'd been routed by a cake-knife. Not that he really had been. Rather, he'd seen she was really angry and it formed no part of his plans to find himself locked in a local cell. Meredith took the remaining cake back to the kitchen and put it in a tin. There it would probably sit until she remembered it and threw it out. Then she drew a deep breath and rang Juliet.

'He's been and before you say anything,' she began immediately, 'it didn't work.'

'Why not?' came Juliet's truculent response.

'Why? For Pete's sake, what am I? A miracle-worker? It didn't work because he's too smart. He doesn't deny that it would be nice, in his words, if his cousins gave him some money, but he can see their circumstances and so he doesn't expect it. Not a penny.'

'*What*?' came in a howl down the phone line.

'Of course,' Meredith tried to be fair, 'it could be he's realised we're all ganged up against him and he's backing down.'

A snort. 'Don't you believe it! He's got another trick up his sleeve.' Juliet's voice was incredulous.

'I don't know what to believe. All I know is, after that, he tried his luck with me and I threw him out. Juliet, you are not to tell a soul about that. Alan would flip if he knew.'

'So would Damaris and Florence. Meredith, when you say he tried his luck, how, um, insistent was he?'

'Not as much as he might have been. His brain clicked in in time. Jan's not one to spoil any plans he's got by needless rough stuff. He's a thinker, our boy. Still, the sooner he's on the plane back to Poland the better.'

'Now what?' asked a glum Juliet.

'Perhaps we should talk to Laura again? Get her to tackle him. All I know is, I've done absolutely all I can do. Someone else is going to have to settle Jan's hash.'

Damaris and Florence had spent a long afternoon in Bamford. Apart from the supermarket, Florence had visited the hairdresser to have a biannual trim and Damaris had set out to purchase underwear. There was, fortunately, still a small shop in Bamford which sold proper vests and knickers.

While waiting to be served Damaris studied with

fascinated bewilderment a mannequin decked in the briefest scrap of material to preserve decency below the waist and a sort of wired effort to support the bust. The plaster figure wore sheer black stockings which stayed up without suspenders.

'Here you are, Miss Oakley,' said the elderly shop assistant, displaying a pair of capacious lock-knit bloomers on the glass counter top. They were in a style called, inexplicably, after a period of French history, *directoire*.

'What?' said Damaris. 'Oh, I'm sorry. Yes, those will do very well.'

The assistant's gaze flickered scornfully at the mannequin in its diaphanous scanties.

'Silly thing, that,' she said, 'but we've got to keep all the modern stuff in stock. The girls don't wear anything else these days.'

'None of it can keep them very warm,' observed Damaris, thinking, But you don't feel the cold when you're young. Your blood is warm. Your skin tingles. You are alive.

'They'll pay for it later in rheumatism,' said the assistant comfortably.

Outside the shop two young girls stood gossiping on the pavement. She supposed them sixteen or seventeen. One wore jeans and what appeared to be a man's tweed jacket, rather old and probably bought at a jumble sale. She had long dark hair twisted in many narrow ringlets, rather like a Restoration beau. The other girl, in contrast, had short flame-red hair sticking up in spikes and wore a flowing black skirt patterned with scarlet poppies, over heavy boots. The pair of them giggled hilariously over something.

Damaris thought with shock, I don't believe I was ever

young. Oh, young in years, but never in behaviour. We Oakley girls were well brought up. We Oakleys must never give cause for scandal or gossip. We Oakleys must never show lack of moral fibre.

It was only as she grew older, really quite a bit older, well into middle-age, that Damaris had understood her parents' obsessive need for respectability, for decorum, for dependability. It was a necessary veil to obscure the truth, that over Fourways and the Oakley family stretched the skeletal hand of a cruel, foul crime. They lived in the shadow of a murder. They must pay the price, all of them and for ever, for William Oakley's sin.

So they were taught that frivolity showed weakness of moral will. It was dinned into them that as long as they behaved properly and did their duty, they need never be ashamed of anything.

It was rubbish! She felt as if scales had fallen from her eyes and, now far too late, she'd seen the reality of this doctrine. She and her sister had been the victims of an underhand deception, designed to control them.

It certainly worked on me! thought Damaris in helpless fury. I never did anything rash. Never took any risks. Never flouted the rules of good behaviour. I always did my duty and cared for others and now what? It's my turn and who's going to care for me or do their duty by me? No one. It's *my* turn, but I've got to look out for myself and for Florence.

Once again she and her sister were picked out to be victims, to be manipulated and controlled. This time by a young man of whom they knew virtually nothing and whose grip over them came entirely from a distant blood-tie and his unscrupulous determination. Laura Danby, their solicitor, had told them a court would almost certainly find against Jan and they were not to worry. She would do, wouldn't she? thought Damaris grimly. Secure with a loving husband, four healthy children and a flourishing career, Laura could urge them to take a serene and carefree attitude. But this wasn't about the law. This was about the power games played by people trapped under one roof and Damaris knew all about them!

Aloud, she murmured, 'This time I won't be cheated, I absolutely will not! I'll do whatever's necessary to protect myself and Florence.'

It was five o'clock by the time Kenny deposited them at their front door. Ron Gladstone had left. Kenny carried their shopping through into the kitchen for them while they took off their hats and coats and made themselves tidy, peering into the spotted hall mirror, tucking stray hairs into place and putting each other's collars straight.

They had just finished this when Kenny came back. 'All ready to go on parade, then?' he asked cheerily.

They laughed politely at this joke and offered to make him tea, which he declined.

'Put most of your stuff on the table in the kitchen, except for the eggs and cheese. I put them in your fridge. You ought to get yourselves a proper freezer. Save money.'

'What should we put in it?' asked Florence.

Kenny considered this and said, 'Fair enough.'

Damaris carried her purchases upstairs. She could hear Kenny chatting to Florence in the hall below but not what he said. She heard him leave, whistling.

When she came downstairs again, Florence was in the kitchen holding a jar of savoury spread. 'Kenny's very obliging,' she said, as Damaris entered. 'Despite those awful tattoos.' Florence's cheeks were pink. She'd been a pretty girl and men had always liked her.

'His mother was a Joss,' said Damaris crisply. 'Britannia Joss. The Josses were always rough diamonds.'

The Joss family were a numerous and close-knit tribe, regarded with suspicion by the whole town. Various members appeared regularly before the local magistrates and any petty crime was generally attributed to them. However, their lack of social standing didn't appear to bother them in the least.

'Oh, I remember Britannia,' said Florence significantly. She paused. 'There are still Josses living down in that terrace of cottages before the garage, aren't there?'

'Yes.' Damaris added wrily, 'The Josses and the Oakleys must be among the oldest of Bamford's families.'

'There used to be Markbys,' mused Florence, 'but now there's only young Alan and dear Laura who went off and studied law. I believe Alan's a policeman. I remember when their mother brought them here as children.'

'He'll be forty or so, Alan,' said Damaris. 'Time flies. Yes, he is a policeman.' She picked up some remaining groceries and began to put them in the cupboards. Then she broke off and turned her head. Footsteps clattered on the kitchen flags and Jan appeared unexpectedly from the kitchen lobby. He must have come down the backstairs which they never used.

'So, you're home again, safe and sound!' he declared, rubbing his hands together.

Both Oakleys stared at him in silence, neither able to think of a suitable response.

'How was your afternoon?' he went on.

Damaris managed to say, 'It was fine, thank you.'

Jan was smiling at her. 'Well, it's been a lovely afternoon, hasn't it? Mr Gladstone's gone home. I don't think he approves of me, I don't know why.'

This observation didn't prevent him looking pleased with himself and Damaris wondered what lay behind it. He'd seated himself at the kitchen table as if settling in for a chat.

'I've spent a very nice afternoon.' He leaned forward in a confiding manner and both women drew back. 'I've been to tea with a charming young woman.' He shook a finger at them. 'I think you know her.'

When they didn't respond but continued to gaze at him blankly, he added with a note of triumph, 'Meredith. Meredith Mitchell.'

The Oakleys exchanged glances. Florence looked bewildered and Damaris said quickly to her, 'It's all right, dear.'

To Jan, she said, 'Really? That must have been very nice for you. Perhaps you'd like to go and watch the television?'

He beamed at them and jumped up, putting her in mind of a jack-in-the-box she'd possessed as a child. She recalled it as an unpleasant toy, leaping out at one with a shrill squeak, decorated in garish colours and bobbing its foolish grinning face from side to side. She had let her distaste show. Jan's smile faded.

'Yes, I'd like to catch the early evening news,' he said stiffly.

Damaris watched him hurry out of the kitchen, pushed the jack-in-the-box image away and turned to her sister.

'Right! What shall we have? I thought cheese on toast –

oh, you've already got out the Marmite.' She indicated the jar in her sister's hand.

'I think I'd prefer it, if it's all the same to you,' said Florence. 'We could have it on toast.'

They set about preparing this simple snack in silence. Florence broke it by asking anxiously, 'Oh, Damaris, what's going on? What was he doing, having tea with Meredith? Or rather, what was *she* doing? She's always seemed such a nice, sensible person to me.'

'I'm sure there's a perfectly good explanation,' Damaris answered robustly.

Florence, still speaking in a whisper and glancing nervously at the door, went on, 'He is a good-looking young man. He isn't going to – to make trouble, is he? Laura told me Meredith is Alan's friend.'

'No,' Damaris said slowly. 'He isn't going to make any more trouble. I won't allow it.'

They sat in the kitchen until Jan went off to have his evening meal at The Feathers. When he returned, still in an insufferably good mood, they made an excuse and vacated the sitting room to go to bed early, leaving Jan before the TV watching a game show. He seemed to take great pleasure in this, applauding whenever the contestant won another prize.

Damaris fell into a fitful sleep. She woke with a start. The room was in darkness but the phosphorescent numbers on the dial of her old-fashioned alarm clock showed it was only just after ten. She felt strange, tense, her senses heightened. She swung her feet over the side of the bed, her toes searching for her slippers. Pulling on her threadbare dressing gown she went to the door and opened it. Damaris put her head into the corridor and listened.

There it was, a cry, a fearful sound, not loud but hoarse, despairing, filled with pain and terror. Possibly she'd heard a previous one in her sleep and it had wakened her. It was followed by the crash of a heavy object falling and a drumming noise.

Damaris reached for the light switch and cautiously made her way downstairs. The sitting-room door was open and she could see the television screen still flickering inanely. The hallway was further illuminated by light streaming through the open kitchen door at the far end. Just inside the hall, by the kitchen door, lay a broken glass tumbler and a spreading water stain. As for the crash she'd heard, that had been caused by the fall of a telephone table which lay on its side. The telephone itself lay on the floor, the receiver at the end of its twisted cord upturned and silent. By it was Jan's twitching body.

He sprawled on his back, his protruding eyes fixed on her in a horrid stare. He had vomited and a blood-stained scum dribbled from his parted lips, drawn back like a wild animal's. His expression was one of pain and of deep disbelieving shock. His hands clutched at the worn carpet, his knees were drawn up and she realised that the drumming sound she'd heard had been that of his heels on the wooden floorboards. He seemed to recognise her as she bent over him in horror. He tried to form some words but his tongue would not oblige.

'Damaris?'

It was her sister's voice from above. Damaris hurried back down the hall and up the stairs. Florence must not see this.

'Go back to bed dear. You'll catch a chill. Jan isn't very

well. I'm going to call an ambulance.'

'What's the matter?' Florence's grey hair was braided into a thin plait which lay over her shoulder. She clutched at the bodice of her nightgown.

'I don't know, but the ambulance men will take care of it. Do go back to bed, promise me!'

Damaris pushed Florence gently ahead of her as she spoke, back into her bedroom. She closed the door on her still protesting sister. She thought Florence would stay there. She had always been a biddable person.

Damaris made her way back to Jan and picked up the two halves of the telephone. It occurred to her that the receiver ought to be issuing a buzzing noise. She replaced it on the base and lifted it again but there was still no dialling tone. Damaris looked at it perplexed. Then her gaze travelled down the cord and she saw that it was unplugged. Jan, in his fall, had disconnected the instrument. She pushed the jack back into place and to her relief, got a dialling tone at last. She dialled 999 and asked for an ambulance. She was promised one would be with her within a quarter of an hour. In the meantime, she was advised to put the patient in the recovery position.

Damaris replaced the receiver and, as the table still lay on the floor on its side, she pushed the telephone through a gap in the banisters and rested it on a stair tread. Fighting back revulsion, she forced herself to pull and push Jan's prostrate form until she managed to get him on his side. The unaided effort left her panting and exhausted but she wouldn't call Florence. She propped him in position with the two telephone directories and hauled herself to her feet by gripping the banister above her. For an instant she felt quite pleased with herself at having managed it but then, with dismay, saw the movement had caused more disgusting liquid to drain from his open mouth. His face had a strange lividity, bluish in tinge and mottled with brown stains. Damaris gave an exclamation of disgust and backed, stumbling, away.

The ambulance arrived soon after. The paramedics, though startled at the sight which met them, were quick, efficient and – as far as they could be – reassuring. Jan was driven away into the night.

Damaris reclimbed the stairs wearily and went to Florence's room to tell her it was all right; Jan had been taken to hospital. More likely the hospital morgue, she thought. She didn't doubt for a moment she'd witnessed death throes.

She told Florence she would make some tea. She didn't really want any but felt she had to do something. On her way to the kitchen, she collected the shards of broken tumbler. She imagined Jan had gone to the kitchen to fetch water but before he could drink it, his illness had overcome him; he'd let the glass slip and stumbled towards the telephone in a vain attempt to seek help. It wouldn't do to leave broken glass about.

The kitchen looked large, chilly and unfriendly. Damaris pulled her dressing gown more tightly about her and found a paper bag in a drawer. She wrapped the broken glass in it and put it carefully in the waste bin. Then she padded to the sink to fill the kettle.

'How did that get there?' she murmured to herself.

Lying in the bottom of the sink was an ordinary knife smeared with some brown sticky substance. Marmite! thought Damaris and was puzzled that this knife could have been overlooked when she and Florence had washed up their few supper dishes.

While the kettle boiled, she fetched pan and brush and swept up any tiny remaining fragments of glass on the hall runner.

This done, she took the tea up to Florence and did her best to allay her concerns for Jan. She couldn't dismiss the man so easily from her own mind. Leaving her sister's room, she paused and turned her steps in the direction of the turret bedroom which had been his during his stay and to which he would almost certainly never return.

On the threshold Damaris hesitated, then walked in and looked around her. William Oakley's painted sardonic gaze met hers. He seemed to be sneering at her in a triumphant way. Damaris felt a flush of anger. She went to the dressing table, pushed aside Jan's hairbrush and men's toiletries – of which he seemed to have a great many – and yanked off the embroidered cotton runner.

She took it to the portrait and with an effort, managed to throw it up and over the top edge of the frame so that it hung down, concealing the picture.

'There,' said Damaris with satisfaction. 'That's taken care of *you*!'

Chapter Twelve

Stanley Huxtable met up with the Reuter's man again on the platform at Bamford Station the next morning. Together, they pushed their way on to the crowded early Oxford train.

The short journey to the city passed without conversation. Stanley had passed a restless night and was regretting the pork pie he'd had for his supper. He was sure it had been off. Neither did the Reuter's man seem disposed to be chatty. From time to time he belched discreetly into his spotted handkerchief.

Back in their places in the press box, however, both put aside their digestive problems and concentrated on the matter in hand. Mr Green, the plump little defence counsel, was preparing to cross-examine Mrs Martha Button.

Mrs Button took the stand with aplomb, an old hand now. Stanley wondered whether it was his imagination or if the auburn wig was tipped a little further over her forehead this morning. She certainly presented a more beetle-browed appearance than the day before. Little things like that, in Stanley's experience, could make a lot of difference to how a jury received things.

He glanced at the defendant, William Oakley. His air was as it had been since the beginning of the trial, that of the supercilious observer of a vulgar spectacle. The blighter is confident, thought Stanley.

'Now then, Mrs Button,' began Mr Green cheerily, 'are you still employed in Mr Oakley's household?'

Mrs Button managed to look both annoyed and wronged. 'No, sir. Mr Oakley turned me away just two weeks after the poor lady died.'

'Oh,' said Mr Green significantly, 'you were dismissed. Did Mr Oakley say why?'

Mrs Button's huffy air increased. 'No, he didn't. He just said I should have a month's wages and to pack my bags. He was very nasty about it. I was surprised. I believed I'd always given satisfaction. No one had ever said so if I hadn't!' Mrs Button leaned over the edge of the witness box and said hoarsely, 'It's my belief it was his guilty conscience. Every time he set eyes on me he was reminded of his poor dying wife.'

'I dare say he was,' said Mr Green. 'But surely that signifies a natural grief, not a guilty conscience?'

'He never grieved for her, or I never saw any sign of it!' snapped Mrs Button. The auburn wig was now definitely working its way down her forehead. Pretty soon, Stanley decided, she'd look like a guardsman wearing a busby.

Mr Green pressed his plump paws together. 'You know that Dr Perkins has said that when he attended the sad scene, he saw nothing which he could not explain?'

Mrs Button looked uneasy. 'Dr Perkins hadn't seen what I'd seen, had he? He hadn't seen that pot and the other bits. He hadn't smelled that nasty smell.'

She had walked nicely into Mr Green's lair. 'Ah, yes,' he purred. 'The pot, metal rods and garlic odour. You didn't mention those things at the time of the inquest, Mrs Button.'

Mrs Button looked confused and for once had no ready reply.

The judge ordered, 'The witness must answer.'

Mrs Button rallied. 'I was in a state of shock myself. I'd seen a horrible sight, hadn't I? My wits was all over the place. It wasn't till later I got to thinking and remembering.'

Mr Green pounced. 'Yes, very much later. Not until you had been dismissed from Mr Oakley's employment! Only then did you go to Mrs Oakley's parents and make these allegations concerning a garlic odour noticed by no one but you and some debris which you alone saw.'

The witness began to look tearful. 'I did see it, sir.'

'But you said nothing about it,' insisted Mr Green. 'I put it to you, Mrs Button, that you were resentful at being dismissed and went to Mrs Oakley's parents to vent your spite against your former employer by making entirely false allegations.'

The tears vanished before Mrs Button's anger. 'That's not true! I'm an honest woman, as anyone will tell you. I've stood here and sworn to tell the truth!'

'Indeed you are upon oath, Mrs Button,' riposted Mr Green. 'I put it to you again, you waited an inexplicable two weeks before making these unsubstantiated claims.'

'I don't know what that word means,' said the witness sullenly.

'Unsubstantiated? It means no other person than yourself has claimed to have witnessed these things or been able to show that they existed.'

'How can there be another witness if I was the only one there?' burst out the goaded Mrs Button, her wig now slipping to one side. At least one juror, a younger one, had noticed and was hiding a grin.

'Ask him!' She flung out a hand and pointed at William Oakley. 'Ask him about his behaviour. I saw him carrying on with Daisy Joss with my own eyes and I spoke very sharply to the girl about it. There were others knew about it, too. Poor Mrs Oakley told me herself, the day she died, that she intended to dismiss Daisy the very next morning.'

Mr Green knew he held the whip hand. 'Mrs Button, you are free with your claims that others knew. But no one but yourself has actually made such claims public.'

Mrs Button, despite her emotion, had become aware of the displaced wig. She raised a hand and pushed it back into place. 'Other servants knew, but they'll be afraid for their situations and not want to speak up!' She spat the words defiantly. 'And as for gentlemen, they don't go telling tales on one another, do they? It doesn't mean they haven't got tales they could tell.'

The public liked that. Several jury members smiled. But Stanley wrote on the notepad, *I said she'd go to pieces*. He pushed the pad towards the Reuter's man so that he could read it.

'Calm yourself, Mrs Button,' urged Mr Green duplicitously. He was clearly delighted. 'Let us return to the evening in question. You have said you heard your employer go up to bed shortly before ten o'clock.'

The witness confirmed this warily.

'But you yourself didn't go up until eleven. What were you doing during that hour?'

'My duties,' said Mrs Button loftily. 'I had to check that the skivvy had washed the dishes properly and not broken anything. I mixed up a hot drink for the girl who had a cold. It was lemon juice and honey. I stood over her while she drank it. Then Mr Watchett, the gardener, came in about vegetables. I sat for a while drawing up plans for meals the next day and writing a note for the washerwoman. Then I went up to bed myself, or I started to—'

Mr Green interrupted. 'Yes, quite. Let us stay in the kitchen for a while, if we may. What time did Watchett the gardener arrive?'

Mrs Button looked uncertain and said she couldn't rightly say. Possibly half-past nine.

'This seems to me very late,' said Mr Green. 'How long did he remain?'

'Half an hour, perhaps a bit longer,' confessed Mrs Button.

Mr Green smiled at her, something which appeared to fill her with alarm. 'To discuss vegetables? A fascinating subject indeed to have taken you both so long. Did you discuss anything else?'

Mrs Button was belatedly learning to be careful. 'I asked after Mrs Watchett. She has trouble with her legs. They swell up something dreadful, full of water, and the doctor was to draw it off.'

'So you discussed Mrs Watchett's legs and vegetables. You also discussed the family which employed you both, perhaps?'

Mrs Button rightly divining which way the wind was blowing, said promptly, 'No, sir. I don't gossip.'

But she was in Mr Green's toils.

'But if Watchett arrived at half-past nine, as you've told this court, and remained over half an hour, he was presumably there when you heard Mr Oakley go up to bed? Something which happened, you said, shortly before ten o'clock.'

Mrs Button said she supposed so.

'You suppose so?' Mr Green would let nothing escape him. 'But it must have been so. I find it strange, Mrs Button, that in the middle of this animated conversation about vegetables and Mrs Watchett's infirmity, you heard Mr Oakley go upstairs.'

'Well, I did,' said Mrs Button sourly.

'And remarked upon it to Watchett?'

'I may have done so, sir.'

'And did you,' asked Mr Green, 'also remark that it was an early hour for your master to retire?'

Mrs Button repeated that she may have done.

Mr Green hovered, a small furry predator about to sink sharp teeth into its prey. 'Did you tell Watchett about Mrs Oakley's pain from her drawn tooth? That she, too, had retired early because of it?'

'Yes, I believe I did,' said Mrs Button cautiously. But it was clear she knew her caution came too late. 'But only to say the poor lady was suffering greatly.'

'And you still claim,' Mr Green asked silkily, 'that you did not discuss the family?'

Distressed, Mrs Button protested, 'That is not fair, sir.'

'We are not concerned with fairness but with fact,' she was told. 'Now then, while Watchett—'

Taylor, the prosecution counsel, was also well aware that things weren't going his way. He uttered a dignified protest. 'My lord, the defence is seeking to confuse the witness and trail red herrings of the most blatant kind.'

The judge had his own doubts. 'Is all this business about the gardener relevant, Mr Green?'

'It is, indeed!' said Mr Green firmly. 'As I shall demonstrate.'

'Well, demonstrate it quickly,' ordered the judge.

Mr Green, suitably chastened, hurried to make his point. 'Mrs Button, we've established that you and the gardener were together in the kitchen for much of the evening, after you'd sent the skivvy home and the sick housemaid to bed. Did you offer your visitor any form of sustenance?'

'He had a piece of my Madeira cake,' said Mrs Button with a slight air of pride.

It came before the proverbial fall.

'Very nice,' said Mr Green. 'And perhaps a glass of Madeira wine to go with it?'

'No, sir, it was sherry,' Mrs Button was betrayed into saying.

Mr Taylor had closed his eyes and appeared to be praying. He could see his case beginning to crumble as when the first incoming waves lap at a child's sandcastle on the shore.

'Sherry?' cried Mr Green, bouncing up and down on the balls of his feet. 'Aha! You and Watchett were sampling your master's sherry while you were discussing vegetables and Mrs Watchett's legs!'

'It was the kitchen sherry,' argued Mrs Button. 'I keep it for the trifle.'

But Mr Green rolled merrily onward. 'So after some time gossiping with Watchett and drinking sherry, the gardener went home to his long-suffering wife and you went up to bed. I put it to you, Mrs Button, that your wits were sadly fuddled by then.'

'If you mean I was drunk,' cried Mrs Button, 'you're wrong! I only had the one glass.'

Stanley Huxtable wrote, *Laughter in court*. As order was being restored, he leaned towards the Reuter's man and whispered, 'That's it – you owe me a pint.'

Chapter Thirteen

When Markby had returned from the football match on Saturday evening, after a detour via his sister's home, he'd found Meredith sitting in the kitchen, a glass of wine before her. Her expression was unusually closed and angry, her mouth set, her eyes imperfectly shuttering inner turmoil. His first impulse was to wonder whether this had anything to do with him. He glanced at his wristwatch. Was he late? Had he promised to take her out somewhere this evening? Good God, why was he thinking like this? This was how it had been when he'd been married to Rachel, evening after evening coming home to find storm cones hoisted.

'What's up?' he asked cautiously.

'Nothing,' she said automatically.

'Why do women always say that when it's obviously not true? Here you are, hunched over a bottle, drowning your sorrows—'

'One glass!' she protested indignantly. 'I was just having one glass to help me think.' She tossed back her fringe of dark brown hair and made an obvious effort to sound normal. 'Good game?'

'Middling,' he replied. 'Paul was happy enough. His team won. Mind if I join you?' He fetched himself a glass and poured wine into it. 'Cheers!' He saluted her. 'Now tell me.'

'Don't want to,' she mumbled, avoiding his gaze.

'Confession is good for the soul. It can't be that bad, surely?'

'Don't you believe it. I made a complete idiot of myself this afternoon.'

'Went shopping and bought the wrong dress?' He expected these words to be received as an insult but if he couldn't get her talking by just asking, he had to resort to trickery.

As anticipated, she snapped out of her introverted cocoon. 'Do me a favour, Alan! I've done that often enough but I wouldn't brood over it for the rest of the day. I'd stick it at the back of the wardrobe with all the other bad buys. I meant what I said. I made a fool of myself. I screwed up good and proper. I was so stupid! I should never have let Juliet talk me into it.'

'Right.' Markby set down his wine. 'And what did Juliet talk you into exactly?'

Colour entered her pale cheeks. 'She persuaded me to ask Jan Oakley here to tea so that I could talk sweet reason to him. As if anyone could do that!' Meredith said wrathfully. 'I didn't tell you about it, Alan, because I had misgivings about the whole idea and I thought you'd say I was crazy – and you'd have been right. Although you did say yourself, in The Feathers, that perhaps Jan hadn't understood the situation. So I thought I'd just explain it to him.'

'So what happened?' Markby asked patiently.

She scowled. 'None of it went according to plan. I asked him about his claim on Fourways and he blithely dismissed it! Said he had no intention of pursuing it. So then I asked whether he still wanted a share in the sale price and again, he dismissed that. Said it would be nice if his cousins were generous but he quite understood their situation.'

'It sounds,' Markby said, 'as if he was already very reasonable and you had nothing to do.'

'He was crafty, not reasonable. He took the wind out of my sails and left me nothing to talk to him about.' Morosely she added, 'I can't really blame Juliet. I knew it was a bad idea from the start. I should've had the strength of my own convictions and refused point blank.' She fell silent.

Markby eyed her thoughtfully. It was unlike her to let anger simmer on like this. He asked, as casually as he could, refilling her glass as he spoke, 'Anything else happen?'

She gave a little jump and the wine splashed. 'No. What else could happen? I just felt a fool. I don't like that. No one does.'

'True,' he agreed. 'I just wondered whether Oakley might have introduced some other subject.'

'No, he didn't – because I threw him out!' There was manifest satisfaction in the way she expressed the last words.

'Wasn't that a bit drastic? If he was being as co-operative as you say, agreeing to everything?'

She flushed again. 'I meant, I showed him out. He didn't stay long. I realised he was too devious to have any sensible discussion with him, so I got rid of him.'

She was a rotten liar, Markby reflected. He could make a pretty good guess at what had happened. Oakley had made a pass at her. If she didn't want to tell him about it, she wouldn't. He was angered, not by her failure to confide in him, but by the combination of elements which had led up to the present situation: Juliet's original request, Meredith's agreement, and finally, Oakley's behaviour.

When he next saw Oakley he'd have a few straight words to say to him. In the meantime . . .

'For goodness sake,' he said, 'stay clear of Juliet Painter. She's got Jan Oakley on the brain.'

Meredith's look changed to one of some embarrassment. 'I did ring her – I had to. She was expecting me to report. I told her what he said. She thinks . . .'

'Go on,' Markby sighed. 'What does Juliet think now?'

'She thinks Jan's got some other plan up his sleeve. That's why he's no longer making an *open* claim on Fourways or the money from the sale. He's realised it's counter-productive. She doesn't think for one minute he's given up.'

'Whatever Jan is up to, we'll find out about it in due course,' Markby told her. 'Now then, let's go out somewhere and enjoy the rest of the evening. Forget Oakley. He really isn't worth worrying about.'

Sometimes our words come back to haunt us. It was certainly Markby's experience on the following Monday when he arrived in his office. He was a little later than usual. He'd stopped off to make a couple of out-of-office calls and it was almost eleven. Every officer he passed on his way to his office appeared to be holding a cup of coffee.

'Anything of interest happen over the weekend?' he asked Inspector Pearce who'd appeared and was hovering in the doorway. A stain on his shirt indicated Pearce had already had his coffee.

'Coroner's office rang,' said Dave Pearce diffidently. 'They reckon they might have a suspicious death. The chap died in the hospital on Saturday night, apparently of some form of poisoning. Dr Fuller conducted the postmortem at eight this morning. You know how he likes to make an early start.'

Pearce spoke with the voice of one who'd been called out at this unreasonable hour more than once and required to stand by while Fuller made his dissection. 'Get 'em on the slab, get 'em opened up and get 'em out of the way!' was Fuller's motto. Markby, who'd also suffered from Fuller's addiction to crack-of-dawn autopsies in his time, nodded in sympathy.

'Dr Fuller confirms poison though he's not sure yet what it is. He's told the coroner's office that though he wants confirmation, he thinks it's one for us. He's sent samples for analysis to Dr Painter.'

'That'll keep Geoff Painter happy,' commented Markby. He hung up his Barbour and turned round. 'Poison makes a change. Funnily enough, we were discussing the subject at Painter's house recently. We commented that poison has got rarer as a weapon. Do we have a name for the victim?'

Pearce consulted a scrap of paper in his hand. 'Chap called Jan Oakley.'

'*What*?'

At the tone of the superintendent's voice, Pearce looked up in alarm. 'Oakley, sir. He was a Polish national here on a visit, which may complicate things. He was staying with relatives near Bamford, at a house called Fourways.'

'I know it,' Markby said bleakly. 'I also knew – I met this fellow Oakley.'

'Oh, crikey,' said Pearce.

'To put it mildly, Dave. What happened?'

Pearce set the piece of paper down on the desk in a tentative way. 'We've only got the bare essentials, sir, as I said. It started with a 999 call late on Saturday night, asking for an ambulance to go to the house. The caller was a Miss Damaris Oakley, an elderly woman. She said a guest in the house had been taken ill. When the paramedics got there they saw the chap was in a bad state, but they didn't want to alarm the old girl. He was taken straight to hospital but pronounced dead ten minutes after arrival. Postmortem's routine in that case but the hospital thought it might be poison of some sort. Sorry, that's all I've got from the coroner's office at the moment. I don't suppose they know any more. We're all waiting on Fuller and Dr Painter.'

Markby scowled at the scrap of paper bearing this meagre information. 'Has anyone been out to Fourways?'

'I believe the coroner's officer may have gone out there to let the people there – a couple of elderly sisters – know that the police have been called in. I was going to go myself some time today.'

Markby got to his feet and retrieved the Barbour. Struggling into it, he said, 'I'd better go out there myself, Dave. I know the Oakley sisters. They're very old and likely to be very distressed. Get on to the Polish Embassy in London, will you, consular department. They ought to be informed that one of their nationals has died. Ask them if they can tell us anything about Oakley. His behaviour after arriving in the country wasn't all that could be desired and his background may be a little dodgy, too. We're going to have to check into it all and it isn't going to be easy.'

'Right-o,' said Pearce. 'It's going to be a bit awkward for you too, sir, isn't it?'

'Dave,' Markby informed him, 'you're proving a master of understatement this morning!'

* * *

The Oakleys had gone into a semblance of mourning when Markby found them. Damaris wore a charcoal-grey skirt and a pale grey jumper. Florence had found a rusty black skirt and teamed it with a purple jumper. They sat side by side on a worn velvet sofa which had once been bright green but had faded now to a golden mossy colour. As a piece of furniture, Markby judged it nearly a hundred years old.

But everything else in the room – apart from a television set which looked out of place – appeared in a time warp. The electric-light fittings seemed to date from the 1930s, to judge by the Bakelite wall switches shaped like plum puddings. There were even the gasmantles from an earlier form of lighting still protruding from the walls. The Oakleys had simply gone on living in the home their parents had bequeathed to them, dusting the same ornaments, taking the time from that same loudly-ticking ormulu clock on the mantelpiece, drawing the faded velvet curtains with tattered linings at night and opening them in the morning.

All this struck Markby with a sharp pang of remembered discomfort. When, as a child, he'd been brought to Fourways, the visits had taken place in this room. He'd found it intimidating, not least because old Mr Oakley had still been alive and present. To the child Alan, the old fellow had appeared a veritable Methuselah. He must, adult Markby made a rapid calculation, have been at least the age his daughters were now, probably well into his eighties. He'd been an invalid and confined to a chair which was placed near the old-fashioned gasfire for warmth. That fire was lit now, but only glimmered at the lowest possible level. All the rooms, Markby knew, had similar gasfires. It was the only form of heating. The fires were lit when a room was occupied and switched off the moment it was left empty. This piecemeal heating did nothing to dispel the clammy atmosphere of the house. He remembered that so well, too.

Old Mr Oakley, despite hogging the fire, always had a brightly-coloured crocheted blanket over his knees. His spine had been bowed so that the first glimpse one had of him was the pink bald top of his head. His hands rested immobile on the arms of the invalid chair, thin, speckled with brown spots, like bird's talons. As soon as anyone approached him, he would look up from beneath shaggy white brows and that was what Markby remembered most. He remembered, too, the fear that ancient, piercing stare had evoked. There had never been any vestige of warmth in it. No welcome, no humour, no kindliness for a child, only a sullen range at life's treachery. The personality of the old man had filled this room. Even as a child, Markby had realised that the old man's will ruled this house. He fancied there was an oppressive trace of it about the place, even now.

The two women received his condolences without apparent emotion. He went on to explain that at the moment he had taken charge of the inevitable enquiries. At this news, they did show some reaction. They visibly relaxed. Markby's heart sank. If they thought they were in for an easy time because of this, they were wrong.

'I should warn you,' he said, 'that I may not remain in charge. I, ah, I met your cousin and Meredith met him several times. It puts me in a rather difficult situation.'

'Oh, I see,' said Damaris. 'We should naturally like you to be in charge, Alan. We would feel so much more at ease, wouldn't we, Florence?'

'Oh, yes,' said Florence. 'I didn't see him, you know, before he went to hospital. Damaris told me about it. I'm rather glad I didn't see him in – in that state. But it meant my sister had to cope alone so, in another way, I wish she'd let me come downstairs.'

'There was absolutely nothing you could have done, dear,' her sister comforted her.

Markby cleared his throat. 'I'm afraid I need to ask you some questions. Other police officers will come and ask you the same ones and a lot more. I expect you think it's not the moment for me to bother you, but unfortunately policework takes no heed of people's feelings.'

Damaris spoke, her voice firm. 'We quite understand. You have a job to do and it's our job to help you. Ask away, Alan.'

'When did you first learn of the existence of Jan Oakley?'

'About six months ago,' Damaris confessed. She glanced at her sister who nodded. 'We said nothing to anyone. That may seem odd to you but I can explain. You see, he was Grandfather William's descendant.'

Florence joined the conversation unexpectedly. 'Our grandfather was a dreadful man, many believed him a murderer. He was charged with the murder of his wife but acquitted.' Her voice was high and nervous. She leaned forward to emphasise her words and then sat back abruptly, pink-faced, as if she'd been caught in some misdemeanour.

Markby thought sympathetically that to her mind, she had indeed trespassed. She'd spoken to him, an outsider, of the family skeleton in the cupboard. Damaris confirmed this impression.

'That's right,' the elder sister said calmly. 'It's hard for anyone nowadays to understand. Grandfather William was expunged from family memory. Nowadays it would be different. I believe the modern expression is to *let it all hang out*. These days, someone like our grandfather would sell his story to the tabloid press. Well, in our day it was called washing your dirty linen in public and you didn't do it. Our grandfather was never mentioned in this house. His portrait was hidden away in a box room. We wouldn't have dared ask about him.'

'In that case,' Markby asked them curiously, 'how did you know about him and his alleged crime?'

'Other people, not our parents, told us,' said Damaris simply. 'Sooner or later someone will always tell you bad news.'

That was true enough, thought Markby. Bad news always travels faster than good. 'Did Jan invite himself or did you invite him to come?'

'We certainly didn't invite him!' they chimed in indignant unison.

Damaris continued, 'He simply wrote and said he would come. We wrote back and explained we were both getting on in years. Our household wasn't arranged to accommodate a young man. We feared it would be inconvenient for all concerned. He took not a bit of notice. He had no manners at all, no consideration for anyone. He just wrote again and said not to worry, he wouldn't be in the way. Huh!'

'There was a lot more,' said Florence, 'about his roots, whatever he thought they might be, and wanting to see the family home! It wasn't his family home. It was ours.'

'So he came here,' Damaris continued. 'We had to put him up. We didn't wish to look prejudiced. Anyway, it was pretty obvious he'd have very little money and we couldn't afford to pay his hotel bill. It was bad enough having to pay Mrs Forbes for his evening meal. We crossed our fingers and hoped he'd turn out rather better than we feared. Needless to say, our hopes were vain. He turned out to be a thoroughly vulgar sort of person, quite ghastly. Always calling me his dear cousin and talking about seeing the old home. Then there was this business of the will he claimed our grandfather had made. I know Laura has told you about that. He wanted half any money we might get from the house. He had absolutely no right to anything!' Her eyes flashed with anger.

'So you didn't like him and he caused trouble,' Markby said, heavy-hearted. 'He was a threat.'

'We disliked him intensely and he was trouble from the moment we first heard about him. However,' Damaris added with an unexpected note of humour in her voice, 'we didn't bump him off.'

Markby passed over this and said, 'The cause of death appears to be poisoning. At the moment, no one is suggesting it was anything other than accidental. Still, we need to find the source of it. Probably we'll have to search the house.'

Both his listeners looked stunned.

It was Florence who asked in a shaky voice, 'What sort of poison, Alan?'

'We don't know yet. Dr Painter is still conducting tests. So we ask you not to broadcast the fact for now.'

'We're hardly likely to!' riposted Damaris drily, rallying.

'Would it be possible to see his room?' Markby asked her.

'Of course. I'll take you up there. It's the turret room.'

'I'll stay here,' said Florence. 'I don't like that room. I

never go in there. It's where our grandmother, poor Cora, died, you know.'

Markby, who'd started to walk to the door, turned in surprise. 'Cora Oakley? That was her room?'

'Yes. Some say it's haunted. It's certainly always very cold in there. We've never seen anything, of course.'

'Right . . .' said Markby faintly.

He followed Damaris up the creaking old staircase, taking a good look around him as he did. Juliet Painter had made a shrewd judgement on the saleability of Fourways. It was in a dismal state. Apart from the electrical wiring which would want replacing, he was sure the roof must leak. He sniffed. There might be dry rot. Dust, dampness, decay. He wondered what Jan had thought when he first saw it.

'Here!' said Damaris baldly, throwing open a door.

Markby stepped inside. Florence had been right. It was cold in here despite the sunshine outside. A scattering of spent matches in the grate by the gasfire testified to Jan's efforts to warm the place up. In the centre of the floor was a blue and red Turkey carpet. In the gap between carpet and walls the floor was covered with ancient cracked linoleum. There was a brass bedstead neatly made up, presumably, by Jan himself. There was a chest of drawers, an old-fashioned marble-topped washstand, but no jug or basin, a chair and a large wardrobe designed to house the voluminous garments of another age. A dressing table didn't match the rest. It was kidney shaped with a cretonne frill in front of it and a 1940s' Utility look to it. He suspected it had been brought in here from elsewhere in the house for Jan's benefit. On it, some of the bottles lying on their sides, was a jumble of men's toiletries. He picked one up and saw it was an expensive brand. Perhaps, after all,

Jan had been into black-marketeering in Poland.

Markby turned round. Damaris was standing patiently in the doorway. He gave her an apologetic smile and went to the wardrobe. Inside hung a meagre collection of clothes. He searched briefly through pockets. He found a Polish passport, an identity card, one of those cheaply printed little paper slips showing a luridly coloured picture of the Virgin and a few lines of prayer in Polish, some loose change and a wallet with English paper money, amounting in all to about sixty pounds. It seemed likely it was all Jan had.

'Do you mind?' he asked Damaris. 'I need to take all this away. I'll give you a receipt and in due course, you'll get it back.'

'We don't want it. We don't want any of it,' she said stonily.

Markby tried the drawers of the chest. In the top left-hand one was Jan's return air ticket to Poland. Jan had given himself a month to achieve his aims. He probably reckoned that was as long as the sisters would allow him to impose on them. In a stiffened envelope of the sort used to send photographs by mail, he found a sepia portrait of a handsome, moustached gentleman standing with his hand on the shoulder of a well-corseted female whose silk dress couldn't disguise her peasant ancestry. Her features were coarse, her gaze sharp and bigoted. The man's gaze both mocked and challenged the photographer. 'I know what you are thinking,' it said. 'But I care nothing for you. I have what I want.' His stance, hand on shoulder of the woman, held no affection only triumphant possession. Across the corner of the stiff card was stamped, in letters once gilded but now dull brown, *Photographien Hable, Krakau*. Otherwise the drawers held a few items of underclothing and socks. Jan had travelled light. Markby glanced round and located the rucksack described by Meredith, poking out above the carved wooden pediment of the wardrobe. He pulled it down, dislodging a good deal of dust. It was empty but for one of those sealed packets of scented wipes airlines hand out to passengers to clean themselves up.

All in all, these were the belongings of a poor man, yet a man vain enough to want luxury toiletries and spending more on them than he could afford. The whole confirmed what Markby already suspected. Jan hadn't been any kind of mafioso. Jan had been a man seeking his fortune, a poor man persuaded that he might obtain riches. Or at least, enough money to enable him to return to Poland a good deal better off than when he left it.

Only one thing remained unexplored in the room. That was a curious item. It was a picture, hanging on the wall above the fireplace but covered with an embroidered strip of cloth.

Markby looked at Damaris. 'May I?'

She nodded. He went to it and pulled the cloth away. The face in the oil painting leapt to view, larger, in full colour, but essentially the same as the face in the photograph. A sardonic painted gaze met his, set in a handsome, untrustworthy face. The mouth and chin, he thought, were cruel. The sitter could only be one person.

'Is this a portrait of William Oakley?'

'That's him,' said Damaris. 'I put it there for Jan. I thought they ought to be together.' Again an unexpected flicker of amusement. 'It was the one thing in the entire house which I might have given him. He could have had that, taken it back to Poland, with pleasure.'

Markby peered closely at the portrait. William's left hand lay on a book. He hoped it wasn't the Bible, which would have been a detail of high hypocrisy. It wasn't a Bible. Whatever it was, the title was painted in brief strokes on the spine. Markby squinted and distinguished, through the varnish, BR-D---W.

'Bradshaw!' he exclaimed. 'Did you realise that?' he asked Damaris. 'Your grandfather's hand is resting on a compendium of railway timetables.'

'Is it, indeed?' returned Damaris. 'I hope William took it with him when he left here. He'll have needed it.'

Markby stepped outside the house and breathed in deeply. He felt chilled and was grateful for the midday sun playing on his face. The interior of Fourways was as oppressive as it had ever been, or perhaps it had been the turret room which had affected him like this. He didn't believe in ghosts but there had been a definite feeling of unhappiness in that room. He looked around him.

As Juliet had told them, the garden was in a better state of upkeep than the interior of the house. The lawns were mown, hedges clipped. Flowerbeds near the house were in good order. Markby's gardener's soul appreciated all of this. One day, he thought wistfully, he'd have a garden like this. At the moment he was restricted to a patio and a greenhouse and had little enough time to attend to those. He set off on a voyage of exploration. Turning the corner of a yew hedge clipped into castellations – a labour of love if ever there was one – he found himself face to face with a neat oldish man wearing a cardigan, well-pressed trousers and, incongruously, gumboots.

For a moment they stared at one another. Then the man announced, 'Gladstone!'

'Victorian Prime Minister,' said Markby promptly.

'No, *I'm* Gladstone!' snapped the other. 'Ron Gladstone. I take care of the garden.'

'Ah yes, of course. I congratulate you. It looks splendid.'

Gladstone looked mollified but still asked sharply, 'Who are you?'

'Superintendent Markby,' Alan obligingly fished out his warrant card and passed it over.

The gardener took it and inspected it closely before returning it. 'I have to ask who strangers are,' he said. 'We get all sorts wandering in and out here, you know.'

'Do you, indeed?' said Markby, showing interest. 'What do they want?'

'Half of them are just curious. The other half are up to no good, I dare say. I've caught that fellow Newman prowling round here a few times.'

'Dudley Newman?' Markby asked in surprise. The man was a well-known local builder.

'I could guess his game,' said Ron sourly.

So could Markby. He looked round him and felt a spurt of anger. Was it necessary to build over everything? No doubt Newman had got wind of the impending sale and scented profit. If he could buy the land cheap, he could cover it with little brick boxes.

'There are no gates, you see,' Ron was saying. 'Some people seem to think this is a public park. I've had people in here walking their dogs!' The gardener's face grew red at the memory. 'I caught a woman here only the other day with a poodle. It was fouling the grass. I had a few words with her,

184

you can believe! I told her to be off and take the dog's mess with her. I gave her a paper bag and my trowel and made her scrape it up. Sometimes, you know,' Ron went on confidentially, 'they're abusive, are dog owners. But I don't stand no nonsense.'

'Quite right, too. I'd like to see the garden, if you don't mind.'

Ron was only too pleased to show him around and they set off across the lower lawn.

'There's a lot I could do here, but well, the ladies won't have it. They're very conservative in gardening matters. You'll have noticed that eyesore in front of the house? That stone basin with a statue in it?'

'The fountain? Yes.'

'It's not a fountain if it doesn't work,' argued Ron. 'And it doesn't work. I said to them, "I'll make you a nice new water feature. A nice little pond with an electric pump sending up a jet." If they wanted a fat baby in the middle of it, they could have one. You can get them in plaster or even better, in fibreglass. You can clean up that easier. But they won't hear of it.' He shook his head sadly.

Markby murmured sympathetically and they walked on for a moment or two in silence. Eventually Ron cleared his throat.

'I can't say I'm surprised to see you. The police, I mean.'

'Oh? Why is that?'

'It'll be to do with that fellow who called himself Jan Oakley, won't it? Something funny about his death, I dare say. It wouldn't surprise me. He was up to no good, I saw that the minute I set eyes on him. Strange sort of chap. Bit dotty, if you ask me.'

Markby did ask him.

'Why?' Ron snorted. 'Because he kept saying he owned the house or part of the house. How could he?'

'And what makes you so certain he was up to no good?'

Ron hesitated. 'Because he snooped. As a matter of fact, I'd like to tell you about it. It's been on my mind. I don't like to mention it to the ladies, you see. Upset them.'

'Tell me,' Markby invited.

They had stopped near a ramshackle stone building, apparently some kind of potting shed or garden store. Ron cleared his throat and took a moment to sort out his words. 'It was the day he was took sick and carted off to hospital. It was Saturday and normally I don't come at the weekend but since he turned up I've been uneasy in my mind about those two women here on their own with him. In the early afternoon, the ladies went shopping. Kenny Joss came and fetched them in his taxi. He comes once a week regularly and takes them into town. Off they went and I was here in the garden. As it happens, I was tidying up the yew hedge by the gate where I met you just now. I needed to oil my shears . . .' Ron told Markby how he had spied Jan, through the study window, tinkering with the roll-top desk and searching through its contents.

'I didn't want to upset the ladies so I thought I'd have a strong word with the fellow myself when I got the chance. You might say I had the chance almost at once because he came down the drive not long after. He'd smartened himself up, not before time. He said he was going out to tea with some woman. He was probably making that up. Anyhow, I hadn't worked out what I wanted to say to him so I let him go on by. Never saw him alive again, of course, so I was saved the trouble.'

'So you weren't here when he returned?'

Ron blinked and shook his head vigorously. 'What did he die of?' he asked. 'Drink and drugs, was it?'

'We haven't released the details yet. Why do you think drink and drugs?'

'That's what it always seems to be these days, in my newspaper, anyway.'

Markby knew he'd have to go back to the house and tell the sisters straight away of Jan's interest in the study. He was sorry for it because he knew Ron was right in saying it would upset them. But it couldn't be helped. He had to know what Jan was after – supposing that he was looking for something in particular and not just being nosy. Perhaps he'd been searching for something which might support his extraordinary claim to a share in the house? At least the sisters' opinion of Jan wouldn't suffer. He was already as low in their estimation as he could sink.

'However he died, he's no loss!' said Ron Gladstone briskly, summing up the general view.

Markby thanked him for his information and the tour of the garden and set off back towards the house.

He thought, as he approached, that the best way to come upon it was from the garden. Seen like this, it had a quaint, theatrical air to it with its Gothic windows and carved waterspouts. The Oakleys were surprised to see him again so soon and took his explanation with some dismay but otherwise stoically. Damaris took him to the study without delay.

Markby, as Damaris searched through her keyring, inspected the dusty shelves. Leather-bound copies of the classics jostled county histories, once-popular novels by writers long forgotten, tales of travel throughout the world and adventures in the British Empire, bound copies of the *Strand* magazine and *Punch* together with other, defunct magazines. No one had arranged or, presumably, catalogued the books. Amongst them might lurk a few treasures. Diffidently, he mentioned this to Damaris.

As he'd expected, she showed little interest. 'I doubt it, Alan. Most of it is old stuff belonging to my father. He was a great reader, especially after he became wheelchair-bound.'

She'd found the key she needed and pushed it into the lock of the roll-top desk. 'This was my grandfather's desk, William – the cause of all our troubles! His initials are on it here, see? In gilt, a bit knocked about, but you can just make out WPO – *William Price Oakley*. It doesn't surprise me to learn that Jan was prying into things in here. It is the sort of behaviour I'd have expected of him. I doubt he could have found anything of interest, though, unless he wanted to read old letters or check old household bills.'

The top rolled back with a protesting squeak. 'It's typical of Ron Gladstone to keep it to himself in case we were upset,' Damaris went on. 'He's a kind man even if he does have wild ideas about the garden. We have to keep him in check or I don't know what he'd create out there. Has he told you about the water feature he wants to install?'

Markby admitted this.

'He tells everyone!' said Damaris. 'Well, there you are.'

Markby gazed at the higgledy-piggledy contents revealed. 'Is this as it was when you last saw it?'

'More or less,' Damaris said. 'Half of this stuff could be thrown out but you know how it is, one just goes on stuffing things in.' She reached out and picked up a package of tattered envelopes tied together with red ribbon. 'These are my brother Arthur's last letters. My parents kept them and so we kept them. But no one will be interested after we're gone. Perhaps I should burn them.'

'Don't be hasty,' Markby urged her. 'Sometimes old letters are of interest to a museum.'

He had said the wrong thing. Damaris stiffened. 'I don't think I'd care to have our family's private correspondence read by all and sundry, thank you!'

He didn't point out that Jan might have read them. Instead, Markby said, 'Perhaps you could check through and see if anything is missing or shows signs of being tampered with.'

Damaris pulled out the chair and gazed baffled at the assortment of papers.

'Take your time,' he urged her. 'I'll just sit over here, if I may, and wait.'

He settled on the chesterfield as Damaris began to work methodically through the pigeonholes, pausing now and then to peer at something or occasionally just lose herself in thought as some old memory was prompted. Eventually she had finished. She had put aside two long envelopes and now turned to him with these in her hand.

'I think he may have looked at these. The envelopes were unsealed, but now they're sealed. He probably read the contents and then stuck the flaps down so that if he were tackled, he could deny it.'

'May I ask what they contain?' Markby got up and came to join her. 'Just generally.'

'I've no objection to your knowing and I dare say Florence won't have, either. They contain our wills. Your sister drew them up for us a few years ago. They're very simple, nothing to interest Jan. We each leave everything to the surviving one. If I go first, Florence has it all. If Florence predeceases me, then her share becomes mine. We have no one else.' She looked up, doubt in her face. 'That would have been of very little interest to Jan, wouldn't it? After all, he surely didn't think we would change our wills to accommodate him?'

'He may have been planning to try and persuade you . . . yes, I think it very likely. He would first need to find out exactly what the present provisions were – whether anyone else were a beneficiary and likely to protest if the wills were changed. I dare say he was satisfied to find out there was no one else in his way.' Markby felt a pang of contrition. 'I'm sorry to speak about your relative like this. It can't make things any easier for you.'

'Speak away,' said Damaris. She returned the envelopes to their pigeonhole. 'I don't doubt for a minute he was self-seeking and treacherous. He wouldn't have got us to change our wills, though!' She smiled at him, a wide charming smile that suddenly revealed what an attractive young woman she must once have been. 'Florence and I,' she said, 'can be very stubborn.'

Chapter Fourteen

Inspector Jonathan Wood of Bamford Police had managed to occupy himself with his normal work during the remainder of the week, blessing the fact that he was a simple guardian of the law and not a lawyer. Every evening he bought the *Gazette* and read the report of the trial penned by Stanley Huxtable. Matters had recently got bogged down on points of law, exacerbated by the difficulty of making Watchett, the Fourways gardener, understand the meaning of hearsay. Watchett, frustrated, had finally become abusive in the witness box and had to be removed. That would've done the prosecution case no good.

Policework seemed by comparison so simple. You got together enough evidence to arrest the villain and then you handed him over to justice. But then, ah, then, what a business was set in hand. A microscope was taken to the evidence, a fine-tooth comb passed through the technicalities. Then, as a policeman, you spent your nights asking yourself, Is there anything else I could have done? What did I miss?

Emily opened the door as he approached it. She must have been watching from the window. She took his coat as usual but instead of going to hang it up, stood with it bundled in her arms. She scrutinised his face and he responded with a happy mask.

'Well,' he asked cheerfully, 'and what am I to have tonight?'

'Pork chops,' his daughter told him. 'And a steamed pudding.'

'Chops, my favourite. And a pudding, too? You spoil me, my dear.'

He wasn't fooling her. He never could fool her. But she said nothing for the moment.

'And have you been out today?' asked Wood.

'To the grocer's,' she told him. 'For some tea.'

That meant only to the corner shop but it was better than nothing. It wasn't right for her to be locked up like some kind of prisoner in the house. It was unhealthy; it could affect the mind. Wood was haunted by a report he'd once investigated. Neighbours claimed a woman was held prisoner. When they'd looked into it, it had been a quite different and much sadder case. The poor creature had been a victim of a mental disorder which made her afraid to go out. It had reached a point where she would not leave her room in which she lived like an anchorite. The smell in that room had been dreadful. At the suggestion she walk out of it, escorted by Wood, she had set up such a screaming. Of course Emily wasn't like that. She wasn't mad. But these things started somewhere.

'I'm glad you went out, my dear,' he said. 'You should have the exercise.'

They'd reached the pudding, a splendid creation, light as a feather and stuffed with currants. Emily placed it on the table with pride. Wood beamed at it and reached for the treacle.

'I hoped it would make you feel better,' said Emily. 'You've been working too hard.'

'And so it does. It'd make a dying man sit up and think twice about shuffling off the mortal coil. There is nothing,' said Wood, tipping treacle generously over the double helping of pudding she'd served him, 'like a steamed pudding for putting the world to rights.'

Emily said calmly, 'I thought I might go to the courthouse on Monday.'

Wood was dumbfounded. He sat back, resting the handle of his spoon on the tablecloth. 'Travel to Oxford, my dear?' It was unheard of. 'How? Alone?'

'I've spoken to Mrs Holdsworth. She would like to go as well and would accompany me. You wouldn't object? I think I might like the train journey. We could sit in the public area, could we not?'

'Yes, yes, of course you could, my dear.' Mrs Holdsworth was their next-door neighbour, a bustling practical widow who took a motherly interest in Emily and an interest of quite another type in Wood himself. He had become adept at fending off Mrs Holdsworth.

'But . . .' Wood floundered. He had longed to hear her say she would enlarge her world, go out somewhere away from these few streets around the house. But to the Oakley trial?

He fell back on saying pettishly, 'I didn't know Mrs Holdsworth had an interest in notorious cases.'

Looking down at her plate, Emily said quietly, 'Whatever her reason, on my part it isn't vulgar curiosity. It's something else which I can't explain. I want to see him. I want to see William Oakley.'

The pudding had lost its savour. Was Oakley's fascination

so great that even at a distance, at second-hand, Emily felt its lure?

'You may find some of the testimony distressing. It's all very unpleasant, you know.' Wood was silently damning Mrs Holdsworth. He was sure this idea had originated with her.

'Shall I hear something you haven't already told me?'

He was caught.

'Very well,' Wood said heavily. 'Then go, by all means.'

Chapter Fifteen

Most people have mixed feelings about Monday mornings. Usually Meredith didn't mind the weekly return to work, but that had changed since Monday meant sharing the working day with Adrian. It didn't help that he was looking especially pleased with himself this particular Monday. She couldn't help but be reminded of Jan's misplaced confidence in his own charm. Adrian was even, in a patronising sort of way, polite. He may have hoped Meredith would enquire what had put him in such a good mood but she wasn't going to oblige him with her curiosity. She did her best to ignore him but it was difficult. His indigo-shirted presence at the far end of the room was like an ever-present duenna: she couldn't do a thing but he knew about it. She could feel her stress levels rising. Just after twelve, as she was debating whether to take her lunch break early, her phone rang.

'Meredith? Alan here.'

'Oh, Alan!' She greeted him with relief, but then it struck her that his voice was as tense as she felt. Her heart sank. She cut short her greeting to ask, 'Is something wrong?'

Adrian began an elaborate pantomime of paper-shifting which was meant to convey to her that he wasn't listening. Marcel Marceau would have looked more natural.

Quietly, in her ear, Alan's voice said, 'This is just a quick call to give you some news you won't be expecting. I'm afraid it's not good.' A moment's pause. 'Jan Oakley's dead.'

'Dead?' Meredith exclaimed. Adrian's head shot up. 'But – but he can't be!' She stared at the receiver in her hand in disbelief. An image of Jan appeared before her mental gaze, as she'd last seen him. His curved lips twisted in a sneer and his dark eyes glowing with spite as rejected, he'd taken his leave of her. What could possibly have happened to the man? It had to be a mistake.

'Unfortunately he can be and is. I'll tell you more about it this evening. In the meantime, should Juliet Painter get in touch with you, fend her off. She may want to meet you and talk about it – if she's heard, and I dare say she has, as Geoff's involved with the postmortem tests. I don't think it would be a good idea for you to be talking it over with her today, not until we know a bit more.'

'How is Geoff involved?' Meredith managed to ask in a reasonably normal voice. She'd turned her back on Adrian but was unhappily aware of him hanging on to her every word.

'It looks like poison.'

This was a nightmare. Meredith swallowed but her throat was dry and the veneer of normality had left her voice. She could hear herself croaking. 'You know he came to tea on Saturday. I made some cake.'

'Doubt it was your cooking,' Alan consoled her. 'We'll talk it over tonight.'

Meredith put down the phone and turned back to find Adrian had left his desk and was hovering over hers.

'Bad news?' he enquired, a gleam in his eyes.

'Bit of a surprise, but nothing to worry about,' she said briskly.

'Family?' Adrian's pink face expressed only decent commiseration but the air around him shimmered with excitement.

'No, nothing like that. It's all right, Adrian. Nothing for you to bother yourself about.' Meredith picked up her bag. 'I'm going to lunch.' She left him staring discontentedly after her.

The canteen was by no means full. Meredith looked around and spotted a familiar face from the consular department. She carried her tray to that table and asked, 'May I join you?'

'Sure,' said the solitary diner already there. He pointed at the facing empty chair with his knife. 'Park yourself down.'

Meredith settled herself and cut into her poached eggs on toast. 'Mike, you're on the East European desk, aren't you? You deal with Poland. I wonder if you'd check something out for me?'

'No problem. What is it?' Mike continued munching as he spoke.

'I would like to know what, if anything, our embassy in Warsaw has on Jan Oakley, spelled O-A-K-L-E-Y. He's a Polish citizen of British descent.'

'I'll check it out after lunch. What's your interest?'

'I – I met him in Bamford. I'm curious about him.'

Mike held her gaze. 'Just curious? Or do you think he's dodgy?'

'Whatever he was, it's in the past. He's dead.'

'Blimey, not another of your murders?' Mike managed to combine amazement with a good deal of curiosity of his own.

'You don't have to make me sound like a serial killer. I

just happen to get involved in these things because – Look, I don't know whether he was murdered or not, and that's the truth. He's only just died. What I do want is to be forearmed or forewarned, I'm not sure which. I don't like nasty surprises and I've just had one.'

Mike grunted. 'Talking of which, how're you getting along with that chap in your office?' When she admitted, not very well, he went on, 'I was talking to someone who knew him a couple of years ago in the Middle East. He didn't endear himself to his colleagues. You want to watch yourself. Word has it, he's not a man to confide in.'

'Believe me, Mike, I'm not likely to!' was her heartfelt reply.

'He's been asking around about you, you know.'

'*What*? I didn't know.'

'He's heard about your Sherlockian escapades. If you're about to get involved in anything else, for God's sake, don't let him know.'

Juliet rang, as Alan had suggested she might, early in the afternoon. She suggested they meet after work for a drink and to talk over the news.

'I really have to get off home,' Meredith told her. 'Can't we make it another day?'

'Jan's dead now, today!' snapped Juliet. 'We've got to get it sorted out fast. Can you imagine what this is doing to Damaris and Florence?'

'It's a police matter.' Meredith took refuge in procedure. 'They'll want to interview us all and I don't think we ought to be discussing it ahead of that.'

'Rubbish. This is exactly the moment we ought to be

discussing it. Look, I'm only asking you to find half an hour. Has someone told you not to talk about it? Was it Alan? He can give orders to his underlings but he can't give them to civilians. You're perfectly free to talk to me.'

The suggestion that she might be thought to be taking orders nettled Meredith. Half an hour couldn't hurt; she'd watch her words. 'There's a pub near the station – The Duke of Wellington. I'll see you there.'

'What's going on, then?' Adrian's voice came from the other desk as she put down the phone. 'Got mixed up in something nasty?'

She froze him out with a look but it was going to take more than that to keep his nose out of her business.

Unfortunately, just as she was packing up to leave later that afternoon, Mike appeared in the doorway. Even more unfortunately, Adrian was at a filing cabinet behind the opened door so Mike couldn't see him.

'This chap Oakley you were asking about . . .' Mike began.

Damn! thought Meredith. I should've warned Mike to let me know privately. She jumped up to push him back out into the corridor but wasn't quick enough.

'About eighteen months ago he made enquiries about getting himself a British passport, but it turned out he wasn't eligible. Then he came in with some story about a will and a fortune which would be his if he went to England and claimed it. He was told to go and get himself a lawyer. The impression he gave was that he had a few screws loose. That the sort of thing you wanted to know?'

'Thanks, Mike. Just my personal curiosity, you know.' She rolled her eyes towards the unseen Adrian. Mike looked contrite and mimed, 'Sorry!'

'Who's Oakley?' Adrian emerged from concealment the moment Mike had left.

'Nobody important. Adrian, do you think you could possibly mind your own business?'

He gave her a look which was surprisingly vicious. 'Not pulling chestnuts out of the fire for that copper boyfriend of yours, I hope?'

The malice in his voice rang a dozen warning bells, but Meredith managed to fake reasonable surprise. 'Good Lord, no!'

His mouth twisted unpleasantly and just for a moment, he really did look extraordinarily like the late Jan Oakley.

Juliet was at the pub ahead of her, sipping gin and tonic in a corner. A city type leaning on the bar was watching her, clearly planning his move. When he saw Meredith coming in to join Juliet, however, he changed his mind and turned his attention to the barmaid. Meredith dumped her briefcase on the mock leather-covered banquette and at the same time managed to set down a glass of white wine without spilling it. The minor achievement pleased her. She took a seat.

'I'm here, as requested. But you probably know more about all this than I do, Juliet. All I know is he's dead, suspected poisoning.'

The pub was filling up with people stopping off for a quick half pint before setting off home. At least, with so many talking all at once, no one could eavesdrop on their conversation here.

'Have the police found that will of William Oakley's?' Juliet demanded.

'How should I know?' Alan had been right. This meeting

wasn't a good idea. People always imagined Meredith had as much information as the police had. What's more, they were always sure they could persuade her to divulge it. No one ever wanted to believe she didn't know and wouldn't tell if she did.

Juliet was tapping her magenta nails impatiently on the table top. 'Perhaps it doesn't exist. Perhaps it never did. Perhaps the whole thing was an elaborate scam.' She sounded hopeful. 'Anyone could see he was a crook. You do agree with that, don't you?'

Meredith bit her lip. If Mike was right in his information, Jan had claimed the existence of William Oakley's Polish last will and testament long before he arrived in England. That might, of course, have been part of his plans.

Nevertheless, she eyed Juliet with some curiosity. 'You've not seen it?'

Juliet shook her head. 'Not the original. He showed us something he claimed was a certified translation. Laura took a copy of it but said without the original to check it against, we couldn't be sure of it. I asked Jan to produce the original of course, but he said it was in Poland with his lawyers. If you ask me, he was either frightened to let it out of his hands or he didn't want anyone here looking too closely at it. Always supposing there is an original. He insisted he would produce it when the time came – his words.' She stopped the irritating rat-tat of nail on wood and said abruptly, 'He was murdered. No one's said so, no one's used that word yet – but he was, you'll see.'

Meredith said cautiously, 'If he was murdered because of that will, then it really doesn't matter whether it exists or not. It's enough that someone believed it to exist.'

'You mean Damaris, Florence and me, don't you? We're the ones involved with the sale of Fourways. Well, I didn't poison the little rat and I'm as sure as I can be of anything in this world that neither of the Oakley sisters did!'

'It needn't involve the will at all,' Meredith pointed out. 'We don't know what else Jan was involved in.'

'I'm prepared to believe he was up to his neck in skulduggery,' was Juliet's reply. 'But how do we find out? For all we know, he's been rubbed out by the Mafia.'

'I imagine they shoot people. More direct than poison and you get an instant result. I wonder what he was poisoned with?' Meredith mused.

'And how someone slipped it to him. Geoff's working on it at his lab.'

It was ridiculous to feel so guilty about the cake. She'd eaten some. She hadn't even felt sick. Meredith picked up her briefcase. 'I really do have to go or I won't get a seat on the train.' She stared into middle distance, for a moment reminiscent. 'That's where I met Jan, on the train. I can't help but feel a bit sorry for him now when I think about him. He was so – so happy to be here and to see the house.'

'How can you be sorry for someone who not only caused trouble when he was alive, but who's causing even more now he's dead? You will tell me if Alan comes up with anything?'

'If you want to know what progress the police are making, read the newspapers or ask Alan yourself,' Meredith told her.

'I shall,' Juliet said confidently.

Markby didn't know that Meredith was sitting in a pub with Juliet Painter; he had other things to worry about. At about the same time as they were meeting he had just arrived at the morgue.

The call had come in late that afternoon. Dr Fuller's assistant asked whether it would be possible for Superintendent Markby to drop by. She managed to make it sound quite a jolly little invitation. He knew better.

'Now?' Markby asked, glancing at the clock. Fuller was known to be a man with many family commitments centring round his three talented and formidable daughters. He was invariably dashing off to school concerts or rehearsals in church halls and most people had learned from experience that to contact Fuller any time after four in the afternoon was to receive a very tetchy response. Fuller arranged his early start to his day so that he could get off early at the end of it. So, what was so urgent it came between Fuller and the latest string trio recital?

'He'll wait for you,' said the assistant. She seemed to realise that this was an unheard-of arrangement and added on a note of apology, 'It is very important. Dr Painter is here as well.'

Markby told her he'd be there shortly and replaced the receiver. It had to be about Jan Oakley. But why was he not to receive a written report as usual? What could be the urgency?

With foreboding, he set out. If there was an aspect to his job which he disliked more than any other, it was visiting the morgue. In the days when he'd been obliged to attend autopsies, that had been understandable. Now he'd handed that unenviable task on to others. But he still didn't like going anywhere near the place. He knew he ought, by now, to have become hardened to the sight of mangled bodies and to unpleasant things pickled in jars. But he never had and he never would. He couldn't prevent himself from thinking of the sad human remains as individuals. He hoped he never did. Once they ceased to be real people to him, he knew it would be time to retire.

Fuller was far from his usual cheery self and as for Geoff Painter, Markby had never seen him so awkward. The man seemed positively embarrassed.

'Good of you to come, Alan,' he said, shaking his hand. 'Could've waited until tomorrow, but thought it best – in the circumstances.'

Markby raised his eyebrows.

'Coffee!' announced Fuller in a breezy voice which rang distinctly hollow. 'I'll get someone to bring us some. I don't think the girl's gone home.' He reached for his phone.

'Thank you.'

There was an awkward silence until the coffee arrived. When Fuller's assistant had left them, Markby set the ball rolling with a brisk, 'Well, what can I do for you both, now I'm here? This is about Oakley, I take it?'

Fuller said in some relief, 'You know about it already, of course.' He was a small plump man with sandy hair and round dark eyes. Markby was always put in mind of a hamster especially when, as now, Fuller was watching him with a mixture of wariness and interest, his podgy hands clasped in front of his stomach.

'I know what's on the file and that's not much as yet. We're waiting for the PM report from you.'

'I had to call in a colleague,' said Fuller quickly, bobbing his head in the direction of Geoff Painter. 'I'm not a poisons expert. I recognised the outward signs, naturally. There was discoloration of the skin, pre-death muscular spasm and vomiting, and when I opened him up, damage to the stomach lining. I sent samples over to Painter pdq.'

Fuller sat back, his body language indicating he had said his piece and would say no more.

'When I heard who the deceased was,' Geoff took up the narrative, 'I dropped everything else and concentrated on the analysis of the samples Fuller sent over. In fact, it didn't take me very long. I checked and re-checked, of course, because I couldn't believe my eyes at first.' He drew a deep breath. 'Arsenic.'

'Arsenic!' Markby almost shouted. 'Are you sure?'

'Out of the Ark,' commented Fuller and snapped his lips shut again.

'Of course I'm bloody sure.' Geoff didn't sound so much angry as despairing. 'I suppose my analysis was made quicker by the fact that we'd been talking of it only the other evening at my place, at our housewarming. That's what makes all this so damn difficult, Alan! There we all were, talking not only about arsenic but about the Oakley sisters. My sister had been engaged by them to help them sell their house and buy a flat. Along comes this Jan out of the blue the following week and is delivered to Fourways by Meredith, I might remind you. He throws a spanner in the works regarding the house sale. Everyone's furious. Juliet's spitting mad. The Oakley sisters are devastated. My wife goes rushing over there to tackle Jan but fortunately didn't find him. You and Meredith sought him out in some local pub to explain the error of his ways to him. Meredith, I've been given to understand by my sister, invited Jan to tea on Saturday. Now there's the wretched fellow –' Geoff flung out a hand to indicate the morgue's refrigerated bodystore, '– dead as mutton. Can't you see? It leaves all of us in a damn awkward situation. We've all of us been buzzing around the man like moths round a flame since he set foot in England.'

Markby held up both hands to calm the speaker. Geoff looked about ready to lose all control. Fuller, having passed the buck successfully, observed them both with clinical detachment.

'Take it easy, Geoff,' Markby urged. 'I'm sorry if I appear to question your findings, but didn't you tell us, on the occasion of our conversation at your party, about the Black Widow of Loudun who walked free because the forensic evidence was unclear?'

'Oh, come on!' burst out Geoff heatedly. 'That was forty years ago! Techniques are more sophisticated now and anyway, I assure you, none of the mistakes was made by either me or Fuller here –' Fuller looked startled at being dragged back into the thick of things '– which was made in the laboratories back then.'

'Certainly not,' said Fuller firmly. 'I can't speak for Painter, but I can speak for myself. Deceased showed every physical sign of poisoning.'

'All right,' said Markby, trying to cling to method amongst apparent increasing madness all around. 'If it's arsenic, did he ingest it?'

'Oh, almost certainly,' said Fuller. 'Judging by the state of the stomach lining and gullet,'

'I didn't carry out the post mortem,' said Geoff, 'but I did analyse some of the stomach contents and I agree. In principle, arsenic doesn't have to be ingested. It could be applied to the skin in some preparation over a long period.

206

The ancient Egyptians used it in face paint and it probably killed a few of 'em.'

'We are, therefore, talking about murder,' Markby insisted.

Painter said almost wistfully, 'He could have taken it himself, I suppose.'

'Suicide?' Markby nodded. 'We'll have to consider that. But I'd have thought arsenic as a means of suicide went out with Madame Bovary.'

Geoff reddened and twisted on his chair. 'Ah, well, there's an outside possibility – just a theory – I believe that in certain rural areas of Central Europe it's still believed that dosing oneself with controlled amounts of arsenic does you good. The locals start by taking just a little and increase it. Incredibly, they survive. Yet a hundred milligrams is normally lethal.'

Geoff sighed and went on in a tone of deep regret, 'I have to say, in this case, I've got to rule it out. It isn't a case of slow accumulative poisoning. He took a massive dose, more than enough to do the trick. You understand my tests aren't complete, but I don't anticipate any change to my basic findings.'

'All right, Geoff. You'll write all this up, both of you, as soon as you can?'

Fuller nodded. Geoff Painter looked, if anything, more miserable. 'I have to mention this, Alan, in case you've forgotten. Also at our house-warming party, I mentioned the murder of Cora Oakley which occurred at Fourways back in the 1880s. I lent Meredith my collection of research papers on the case.'

'Yes, she's reading through them. It keeps her quiet in the evening, I must say,' Markby remarked.

'I know Juliet wouldn't let me tell the whole story, but you already knew it, didn't you?' Geoff said piteously. 'And I dare say Fuller here does?'

'Oh yes,' said Fuller, perking up. 'Quite a *cause célèbre*, that one. The husband was charged but got away with it. He used arsenic.'

'I know,' Meredith said that evening, 'that at a time like this everyone says they can't believe what's happened. But truly, I can't.'

'Then you'd better start believing it,' said Alan grumpily.

'I do! It's just, he was so – so alive on Saturday afternoon, objectionable and smarmy by turns, just his usual dodgy self. Now I feel guilty.'

'What on earth for? You were all set to have me contact Interpol the moment you met him,' Alan pointed out.

No one likes to be reminded of inconsistencies in their attitude. Meredith was obliged to say unwillingly, 'Perhaps we didn't give him a chance. Perhaps he was telling the truth when he said he would make no further claims on Fourways or the Oakleys.'

'You didn't believe him when he told you that, so why start believing him now? It's too late for you to start changing your mind, anyway. The man's dead. Someone, somehow, fed him arsenic. Half a dozen people wanted him out of the way, including a pair of elderly sisters and possibly the sister and wife of the poisons expert. All of us were aware of the trouble he was causing. You and I made a special expedition to The Feathers the other evening to warn off Jan. We've all of us, in short, had a finger in that particular pie.'

The evening was cool rather than chill, but they had set a

small log ablaze in the hearth, seeking, Meredith thought, warm and comfort in the aftermath of a shock. The wood crackled and spat. She wondered whether to tell Alan she had spoken to Juliet Painter, despite his advice not to. She decided against it. He was already out of sorts and I do not, she thought, have to account to him for every minute of my day!

'Neither you nor I had a motive to kill Jan,' she said firmly. 'Nor, come to that, the means. I didn't want him dead. I just wanted him to go back to Poland and stop pestering the Oakleys and making Juliet's life difficult so that she'd stop making *my* life difficult! We knew him and we didn't like what he was doing, but as for our involvement, both you and I were just trying to help.'

'Something I'll have to explain to the chief constable tomorrow. He's requested my presence at nine sharp.'

She twisted in the crook of his arm. 'Surely they wouldn't take you off the case?'

'They might. I'll argue that they shouldn't. I've known the Oakleys since I was a nipper and I'd like to be the one dealing with them. On the other hand, it's a good reason why I shouldn't.'

'If it's any consolation,' said Meredith gloomily, 'you're not the only one compromised. I asked a colleague in the consular department if the Warsaw Embassy had anything on Jan.' She summed up Mike's information. 'Adrian was eavesdropping. You're going to have to cover my enquiry. Can you put in an official request for information first thing tomorrow, before you go off to the Chief Constable? I thought it was interesting that Jan had been talking about a will eighteen months ago. It indicates it really does exist.'

She shook off the gloom and became animated. 'For my money, that will not only exists but it's hidden somewhere. I don't believe it was left behind in Poland with some lawyer. Jan would have brought it with him. He saw it as his passport to a fortune.'

'I didn't see it when I checked his room. Since then SOCO have been in and gone over the place and they've not found it either.' Alan shrugged. 'But you've seen Fourways. There must be more hiding places there than you could winkle out in a month of Sundays. We could tear the place apart and not find it.'

He cleared his throat and asked in an embarrassed way, 'Got any of that cake left?'

'Sure. Out in the kitchen. I'll cut you a slice.' She got up.

His embarrassment increased. 'No thank you, though I'm sure it's delicious. I – I'd like to hand it over to forensics.'

He saw her face redden, eyes gleam with outrage. 'You're not suggesting –? I hadn't got any reason to spike the wretched thing. As if I would! Anyway Jan only ate one piece and I ate some, too.'

He warded her off. 'We're going to have to account for every minute of Jan's last day. We have to track down everything he ate, starting with breakfast. He'll have had that at Fourways. I don't know what he did about lunch. He had tea with you. He ate, I suppose, at The Feathers in the evening. All that can be checked. After that, we're up against the unknown. Where else did he go that day? What else did he eat?' Markby paused and added, 'Did he know anyone else in England? Had he threatened or been threatened by anyone else?'

Meredith said very quietly, 'If he only knew the Oakleys

210

and threatened to make trouble for them, then Damaris and Florence are the obvious suspects. But that's ridiculous! Those two old women?'

'I agree it seems unlikely, to say the least.' He recalled his visit. 'Juliet is right about the state of that house. The land is worth more and at least one developer has shown interest in that. You remember Dudley Newman? I suppose the house might make a hotel. Someone could paint a stain on the floor of the room Cora died in and tell the story of the murder. The punters like that kind of thing.'

'Don't be so gruesome.' She sounded shocked.

'Gallows humour, a copper's speciality. It's a shame about the house. It was in the back of my mind when I went there that it might suit you and me.'

'In the state both you and Juliet say it's in?' Meredith shook her head in disbelief.

'So it'll be going cheap. We could do it up. No, we couldn't, actually. It's got past that stage. I'm really sorry. The press will like it when the story gets about. Can you imagine it? A crumbling mansion, a couple of sisters they'll probably describe as being recluses, to say nothing of a mysterious death in the same family and same place in years gone by. There will be pictures in all the papers, you bet. The Oakley sisters are in for a lot of unwanted attention. I don't know how they're going to cope with it. They mightn't be reclusive but they are intensively private.'

His tone became brisker. 'What we need to do is trace the source of the arsenic. The likelihood is that if we can find where it came from, we'll have our murderer. It's not something you can buy over the counter these days or pinch from some processing plant without it being realised. A

211

modern murderer can't get hold of it as easily as William Oakley did.'

He got no answer to this and looked up curiously.

Meredith had paled. '*Déjà vu* . . .' she said soberly. 'It's creepy, really. Two murders at Fourways, both using arsenic, separated by a century. In the first William was accused of being the murderer, but escaped justice. In the second his great-grandson is the victim. It's almost as if someone has been waiting all that time to mete out a sort of warped revenge.'

Chapter Sixteen

Stanley Huxtable set off for court on Monday morning anticipating plenty of lively copy as Mr Green was due to begin his defence. Rubbing his hands together briskly as he waited for the Oxford train at Bamford Station he looked about him for the Reuter's man and was both relieved and suspicious not to see him. The man from the international press agency had been assiduous in attaching himself to the local man and Stanley knew it wasn't for the pleasure of a fellow hack's company. But now that Stanley couldn't see him, he began to worry where he was. Had he overslept? Had he stumbled on some story and beaten Stanley to it?

At that moment, all thought of the absent Reuter's man was pushed from Stanley's mind. A pair of women had arrived on the platform. One was middle-aged and respectable in appearance. The other, Stanley presumed by her figure and the way she moved, was young. He couldn't be sure because her face was obscured by a heavy veil as though she were in deepest mourning. The older woman was fussing round the younger one who seemed very nervous.

Now, what's all this? wondered Stanley. Is the young one a widow? Is the older one her mother?

At that moment, the breeze caught the veil and for the

barest second it flicked aside. He caught a glimpse of her left profile, and a very pretty profile it was. But he was more intrigued by her reaction to the movement of the veil. Her hand shot up to drag it back into place, after which she looked round as if to check no one had noticed. If she'd seen Stanley at all at that moment, she'd have seen a young man intent on studying the railway tracks.

The train was approaching. It drew in with a groan of its mighty wheels and a hiss of expelled steam which enveloped the platform and waiting passengers in a cloud of thick smelly fog. When it had cleared, the two women were nowhere to be seen. Stanley shrugged and climbed aboard.

The Reuter's man had travelled ahead of him and was sitting in the press box by the time Stanley arrived. He'd pinched Stanley's place nearest the witness box. What's more, he'd already come by some information.

'He's going to put that nursemaid on the stand,' said the Reuter's man.

'What – old Green?' asked Stanley disbelievingly. 'He never is.'

'That's what I've learned. It might be clever at that. If she comes over well, as an honest girl and all that, it scuttles that housekeeper's testimony well and truly.'

'He's taking a blooming big risk,' said Stanley, adding, 'Well, I'm damned!'

The Reuter's man nodded in agreement but he had mistaken the reason for Stanley's last words. Surprised as he'd been to hear of defence's intentions, he was even more surprised to see, entering the court through the public gallery, the two women he'd last seen on Bamford Station.

They appeared to be debating where to take their seats. The older woman seemed to be for sitting in the lower rows to have a good view. Her young companion appeared reluctant and eventually, had her way. The women found themselves seats on the highest tier, tucked into the far corner. Others soon put themselves between the women and Stanley's view of them. In no time, the seating was packed. He tapped his pencil thoughtfully on his notepad. The reporter in him sensed some kind of story but he couldn't see how it tied in with current proceedings.

The Reuter's man had heard correctly. Mr Green did indeed call Daisy Joss. All necks craned as she walked to the witness stand. Recalled to business, Stanley scribbled, *Daisy very pretty, pert girl, dark curls, fresh complexion.* Then to satisfy his female readers, he added, *Wearing black straw hat, boater-style, decorated with bunch of cherries.*

Mr Green, smiling benevolently upon her, established her identity and her position in the household at the time of Mrs Oakley's death. 'And were you happy in your situation?' he asked. 'Was Mrs Oakley kind to you?'

Daisy said Mrs Oakley had always been very kind and she Daisy, had been very happy. Asked whether Mr Oakley had also been kind, Daisy replied firmly that she had seen very little of Mr Oakley. He was a gentleman very much taken up with his horses and his dogs. He seldom came to the nursery.

In reply to further questions, she recounted how on the fatal evening she'd been awoken, in her room next to the nursery, by shouts from the garden and had recognised Mrs Button's voice. From her window, Daisy saw a bobbing lantern moving towards the stables. Some minutes later Mrs

Button came running back towards the house, lantern in hand; Daisy could see her clearly, what with the lantern and the moonlight. Shortly afterwards she heard hoofbeats.

Mr Green asked, 'You were not tempted to go down and find out what was going on?'

'No, sir, it was not my business. Anyway, the child had woken up and was fretful. I sat with him for some time until he went off to sleep again and then I went back to bed.' Daisy paused and added with a tremor in her voice, 'I found out the next morning that Mrs Oakley had died. I was terrible shook up. She was such a nice lady.'

'And are you still employed as nursemaid at Fourways?' asked Mr Green.

'Yes, sir. I was ready to leave at first, when I heard how Mrs Oakley had burned to death. But Mr Oakley said that the child had lost his mamma and what a bad thing it would be if he were to lose the nursemaid he knew and trusted at the same time. Mr Oakley was very worried about the little boy. So I agreed to stay.'

With a sorrowful air, Mr Green remarked, 'You have heard another witness suggest you had an improper relationship with your employer.'

At this Miss Joss snapped into life and retorted, 'That's not true. It's a wicked lie. I am a respectable girl. There is no one can say I have a bad character!'

'You have heard it said in this court,' pointed out Mr Green, still in sorrow.

'Only by Mrs Button,' returned Miss Joss, 'and she is a spiteful old woman. I am walking out with a decent young man. His name is Harry Biddle and he works for Mr Salter the tobacconist in Bamford. We are to be married when he

216

has saved some money and I am older.'

'And how old are you now?' asked Mr Green in kindly tones.

'I am seventeen, sir, but my father says I am to wait till I'm twenty to be married.'

'Thank you, Miss Joss,' said Mr Green, smiling upon the dutiful daughter.

To his description of the witness, Stanley added, *Clever as a cartload of monkeys*.

Mr Taylor was well aware of the threat to his case posed by the virtuous Miss Joss. He rose, long and lean in his black gown, and pushed forward his head at the end of his long neck.

The bird has spotted the fish! thought Stanley who, like Inspector Wood, had also been struck by Taylor's resemblance to a heron.

'Now, Daisy,' said Mr Taylor in a gentle tone, 'are you a truthful girl? Do you understand what it is to swear as you have done on the Good Book? Do you know what perjury is?'

The witness informed him she was extremely truthful. She had regularly attended Sunday School, passed the scripture examination and been awarded a prayer book.

'Well, that is very nice,' said Mr Taylor deflatingly. 'How long had you been employed at Fourways when the tragedy occurred?'

'Three months or thereabouts,' said Daisy.

'Only three months? I understood you to say Mr Oakley had persuaded you to stay on the grounds that the child was used to you, yet you had only been his nursemaid for some weeks.'

'Three months is a long time in the life of a little boy, sir,' Daisy told him reproachfully. 'The child likes me. I like him. I am very fond of children.'

'When Mr Oakley asked you to stay on, did he offer to increase your wages, as a reward for your loyalty?'

'Yes, he did,' said Miss Joss. 'Because he could see I was ever so upset and ready to go home.'

'Did Mr Oakley ever tell you you were a pretty girl?' asked Mr Taylor suddenly, dropping the pretence of gentleness.

'No!' declared Miss Joss. 'Whatever next?'

Mr Taylor said, 'I think most of us know what usually happens next.'

'Well, he never said anything like that!' snapped Daisy, her heart-shaped face turning a not-unattractive crimson. She gripped the edge of the stand in her gloved hands. She was very small and now appeared to be standing on tiptoe.

Stanley's gaze wandered to the public benches. From the expressions on the faces he could see, they were cheering her on. He tried to see the veiled woman, but too many people were in the way.

'He never teased you? Never stole a kiss?' demanded Mr Taylor.

'No, he never did and I think it's disgusting, what you're saying,' stormed Daisy.

Stanley looked this time at the jury. At least some of them seemed to be agreeing with her.

Mr Taylor wasn't ready to give up. 'Do you, indeed? Tell me, what do you do with your wages, Miss Joss?'

'Some I give to my mother,' said Daisy, 'and the rest I save. It's all for my bottom drawer.'

Mr Taylor leaned forward, his long neck craning, his thin

218

lips drawn back over his discoloured teeth. 'But you spend some of it, don't you? Is it not true that one week after the death of your mistress, you went into Bamford and bought a new hat and several pairs of silk hose?'

Mr Green looked up in alarm. He needn't have worried.

'Yes,' agreed Daisy. 'It's like I said: I'm hoping to be married. I buy things for my bottom drawer and for my honeymoon journey. We're planning on Torquay.' Her little face crumpled unexpectedly and a sob broke in her throat. 'You are making things sound as they're not, sir. I don't know why you are doing it.'

'You were also observed at church to be wearing coral earrings which had belonged to Mrs Oakley,' said Taylor, unmoved by the sob.

Miss Joss gazed at him in wide-eyed bewilderment. 'Yes, sir. But I came by them honestly and am not ashamed. Mr Oakley said he knew his wife had been fond of me and he wished me to have some little memento of her. So he gave me the earrings.'

'*Fond* of you?' snarled Mr Taylor. 'Mrs Button tells us Mrs Oakley had told her she meant to turn you away. Did you know your mistress intended to dismiss you?'

Miss Joss drew herself up to her full four feet ten inches and stared bravely at her tormentor. 'No, sir, because she didn't. That is just old Ma Button's lies. She never liked me because she caught me giggling about her once with Jenny, one of the maids. She didn't like any of the maids or me. You can ask the others. She gave the housemaids a terrible time and she would've done me if she'd been able and I hadn't been up in the nursery. It was because she couldn't get at me any other way that she's made up these nasty stories. None of what she's said is true, not one word.'

Stanley scribbled, *And the fish is too quick for him.*

Court adjourned for lunch.

'Pub?' asked the Reuter's man.

'See you there,' said Stanley. 'Got something I want to do first.'

At this, the Reuter's man's antennae quivered and he parted from Stanley with great reluctance.

For a moment the two women had appeared uncertain whether to leave their places, but eventually they rose and made their way towards the exit. As they left the courthouse, Stanley followed discreetly in their wake.

From time to time he glanced back to make sure his shadow, the Reuter's man, wasn't tagging along. But the lure of a pint of ale had been greater. No sign of the spy.

The women walked at a brisk pace. They wanted to take refreshment and then get back in good time so as not to lose their places. After considering and rejecting a couple of busy restaurants, they turned into some tearooms. Stanley followed.

It was the sort of place which, at this time of day, offered light lunches, mostly in the shape of cold meats and salad. The clientele was sparse and he wondered if this had been the deciding factor in their choice. The women had taken a seat in a dark far corner against the wall.

'Yes, sir?' asked a thin, harassed female in a rusty black dress and off-white pinafore.

Stanley glanced hastily at the menu and settled for a pair of poached eggs and a pot of tea. The women had also ordered. He waited. When the food came, she'd have to raise that veil.

She did so, but again, he could only see her left profile. She kept her head rigidly in position so that he got no glimpse of her full face or right profile. She ate quickly, as if afraid of some interruption.

She was right to fear it. Stanley dabbed his mouth with his napkin, rose from his table, and approached.

He was almost upon them when the older woman saw him and uttered an exclamation. In a flash, without waiting to see what was amiss, the young woman had pulled down the veil and he was confronted by a black curtain.

'Excuse me, ladies,' he began. 'Huxtable of the *Bamford Gazette*. My card.'

He held it out but neither moved to take it, so he was forced to place it on their table. The younger woman had frozen. The older one glanced disparagingly at the card.

'What do you want, young man?'

'Just a word. I noticed you in court. I'm covering the Oakley trial. There's a lot of public interest in it and I was wondering what aspect of it had attracted you ladies. Are you acquainted with Mr Oakley, or one of the witnesses, perhaps?'

'No!' snapped the older woman. 'Why we're there is our business, young man, and none of yours. If you intend to pester us, I shall call the manageress and request you are put out!' She picked up Stanley's card at last and thrust it into his pocket. 'And take that with you!'

He knew then it was no use persevering. This old dragon meant to guard the girl in her charge against all comers. Stanley withdrew, after a last look at the girl who sat, head bowed, features invisible.

* * *

'Well?' asked Wood that evening of his daughter. 'And what did you think?'

Owing to her absence that day, they were dining on cold ham pie from the grocer's and pickles. Emily had been apologetic about that but he'd assured her he'd always been partial to ham pie.

She rested her elbows on the table and her chin on her clasped hands. 'I think I am very lucky to have my life here in this house with you. Mrs Oakley was a rich woman with a big house and servants, but she couldn't have been happy and she died horribly however it came about. If she'd lived, after the burns, she'd have been like me, scarred and afraid to let folk see her.' After a moment, she added soberly, 'I didn't think people could be so wicked.'

'Well, they can,' said Wood sourly. 'And how did you think the defendant looked?'

Emily said thoughtfully, 'He reminded me of that stray dog which ran around the streets here last year and caused so much trouble. Do you remember it? It must have been a beautiful dog once. It wasn't a mongrel, it looked like some sort of carriage dog. But it had got so dirty and starved and wild. Some men decided to trap it with a net. They drove it into a doorway. It turned on them as they came up, snarling and snapping, but it seemed sure it must be caught. And then,' Emily hesitated and gave him a slightly nervous look, 'and then, at the very last minute, when it seemed impossible, it gave a great leap over them all and ran off. We didn't see it again.'

There was silence. Wood pulled himself together and asked as calmly as he could, 'And will you and Mrs Holdsworth be going again?'

'Oh no,' said Emily, reddening. 'I suppose I was curious, no matter what I said. But my curiosity's satisfied now and anyway, I couldn't give you another cold dinner this week.'

Chapter Seventeen

'This is a rum do, Superintendent,' said the chief constable, Harrington Winsley.

He was a small peppery man with a neatly trimmed moustache and a military manner. He had, at an earlier stage of his life, been a soldier and like many of those who pass through the armed services, tended to reach for Queen's Regulations or their equivalent whenever there was a problem.

'What's your version of all this?' Winsley folded his hands and rested on the top of the huge oak desk which dwarfed him. Had it not been for the force of his gaze a beholder might have been tempted to find the sight of the chief constable funny. Markby, who knew Winsley to be crotchety and at times unpredictable, knew his situation was anything but amusing. Nor did he particularly like being asked for his 'version' of events. However, he summed up what he knew of Jan.

Winsley received the information glowering. 'See here, Markby, there is something you should know. Last Friday I received a letter from this fellow Oakley.'

'What?' Markby exclaimed incredulously.

'I have it here.' Winsley indicated a crumpled sheet of

lined paper on his desk. 'I took no immediate action as I wanted to find out just who the fellow was first, and also, if possible, to have a word with you. Now any action I take is dictated by his death. Especially,' Winsley cleared his throat, 'if it turns out to be suicide. In his letter, Oakley complains of police harassment. Specifically, he mentions you.'

'This is nonsense!' Markby broke in angrily. 'I only met the fellow face to face once. I didn't harass him. I admit I thought him a wrong 'un, but I'd no reason to suppose him engaged in any criminal activity. I was anxious, yes, to protect the Oakley sisters who are elderly. I thought a word in his ear, just to let him know someone was watching, might do the trick.'

'And now he's dead,' said Winsley. 'Which is deuced awkward, you've got to admit.'

'I know he's dead! But why the dickens should he commit suicide – and with ruddy arsenic?' Markby fairly shouted. He made an effort to calm himself. 'I discussed this with Painter and Dr Fuller. We all thought it unlikely. Look, this was a man who had high hopes of some considerable financial gain—' He snapped his fingers. 'Got it. He saw I might be an obstacle and he wanted me warned off. So he wrote that letter. I've got to hand it to him, Jan Oakley had initiative.' He eyed the creased sheet of notepaper. 'May I see the letter, sir?'

Winsley hesitated, then reached it across his desk.

Markby took it, scanned it, and tossed it back. 'Not only initiative. He had a lot of imagination, too. It's a complete fabrication. He couldn't have proved any of this.' He reflected. 'For my money, he was playing the same trick as he was trying on the Oakley sisters with his story about a

226

will. He was playing for time, just trying to get me off his back for a week or two.'

'Nevertheless, I can't let it lie there in my in-tray and do nothing about it, not now.' Winsley shook his head. 'It must form part of the investigation into his death and be itself investigated.'

'*I* am to be investigated, you mean?' Markby said tightly.

'No use taking offence. But for his death, it'd be a routine thing, cleared up in no time at all, I don't doubt. But as it is, here's a man who, within days of penning a letter accusing you of harassment, is dead. Some of these foreigners,' added Winsley, 'can be deuced unstable. Think they're being persecuted, that sort of thing.'

Markby said angrily, 'I think we'll find he was murdered, though by whom and why is something I can't tell you now. We'll find out.'

'I should hope so,' Winsley growled. 'Confound it! Who in his right mind would choose arsenic? There are pills galore of all sorts around if you want to spike someone's food.'

'Much the opinion of Dr Fuller,' Markby agreed. 'Dr Painter thinks the same and has reason to wish it had been anything but arsenic. It was simply bad luck that we were all discussing the historical Oakley case and indeed, arsenic poisoning, at his house-warming party. Even worse luck that Painter's planning a book and lent papers on the case to Meredith.'

'Maybe,' said Winsley, 'and maybe not! You say there was a room full of people at the time of this conversation. Who knows who might have been listening?'

Goaded, Markby retorted, 'I don't think the vicar did it.'

Winsley's bloodshot pale blue eyes bored into him. 'Can't discount a chap just because he wears a dog-collar. I knew an army padre once who ran a gambling syndicate.'

'A far cry from murder,' Markby pointed out.

Winsley disliked opposition in whatever form it might come. He hit the desk with his fist. 'I didn't bring you in here to quibble, Superintendent!'

'Quite,' returned Markby. 'I'd like to suggest that if we can find out where the arsenic came from, we'd be well on the way to finding out who administered it. It's not something anyone can just lay a hand on. It should be traceable.'

'Motive?' demanded Winsley in a challenging tone.

This was the bit Markby had been dreading. 'That's the tricky part. The two people with the strongest motive for wanting him permanently out of the way are the Oakleys, two women aged eighty and eighty-two respectively. I've known them all my life and I'd be loath to believe it of them. He was living in their home and ate his breakfast with them. Lunch he ate there sometimes. Dinner he ate at a local pub. Inspector Pearce is checking out the pub this morning. It's called The Feathers, rather an indifferent place.' Markby cleared his throat. 'And on the afternoon of his death, he had tea at my house.'

'*What*?' Winsley appeared in danger of an apoplectic fit. 'What the devil was he doing there?'

'Meredith, my – the person who's sharing my home – invited him. She had hoped to talk him into going back to Poland. He was causing a lot of trouble.'

'So he wasn't in her best books, either? Were you all ganging up on him? No wonder he felt harassed. Did anyone have a good word to say for the fellow?'

Markby had to deny this. Jan hadn't had the gift of making himself popular.

Winsley sat back in his chair and smoothed his moustache as an aid to thought. 'You've informed the Polish Embassy, I take it? Fellow was a Polish citizen.'

'Yes. They're sending down someone from their consular department in London. I've given them Oakley's details and asked if they can help us by filling in any background on him. Just in case his death is as a result of something he was involved in at home and which followed him here.'

'Right!' Winsley grew excited, fairly bouncing on his chair. 'One of these East European gangster types. They've been causing trouble all over Europe. That would be a convenient explanation for us and it's more than likely. Those fellows could get hold of arsenic. They can get hold of any damn thing they want.'

'There is no evidence as yet . . .' murmured Markby.

His bubble of enthusiasm pricked, Winsley subsided. 'It would suit us very well,' he said wistfully. 'Now, look here, Markby, normally I'd consider you the ideal man to put in charge of this. We have to be very careful whenever there might be international repercussions, dealing with embassies, all that.' Winsley frowned. 'Isn't your young woman in the Diplomatic?'

'She's currently working at the Foreign Office in London,' said Markby mildly. 'I don't know that I'd call her my young woman. I don't think she'd fancy that.'

Winsley looked disconcerted for all of ten seconds. 'Harr-um! Quite so, yes. As I was saying, normally I'd say you were the ideal chap, but in view of the fact that not only you, but everyone you know seems to have been involved in this, to say nothing of your long acquaintance with the Oakley women and now this blasted letter, I can't let you have a free hand in this particular show.'

Markby said quietly, 'I have never been taken off a case in my entire career.'

'Dare say you haven't, but you must see how it looks. Don't take it personally, my dear chap. It's no reflection on you. But we have to be so damn careful these days. Frankly, I'd like you to handle it entirely. It's inconvenient to involve others and doesn't look good. But I'll have to bring in someone else, someone from outside the area, to relieve you of the responsibility of this investigation.'

This was going further than Markby had anticipated. The sub-text was clear. 'Is it being suggested I would seek to influence any officer at Regional HQ? Or that Inspector Pearce is incapable of independent judgement?' He could hear the anger welling up in his voice.

Winsley leaned as far across his over-size desk as his physical stature allowed. 'There's no question of taking your whole team off this. Only of replacing you as officer in charge. It's no use taking umbrage. If the press get hold of this, and I dare say they will, can you imagine what they'll make of it? Besides, Painter is also involved. The whole thing is virtually a family affair! It may be a little irregular, but I've decided I've no choice. My hand is forced. I've made a request to the Metropolitan Police.'

'The Met?' Markby almost leapt up in protest but managed to keep his seat. 'Surely you don't think some London man will be the best person to come down here and pick up the reins of a case in a rural backwater like Bamford?'

'Come now,' objected Winsley. 'Bamford is hardly a

backwater. I can remember when it was, not so many years ago, but with all those houses they've built there and the new roads, I don't think Superintendent Minchin will find it too strange. The problems of the countryside and those of the city are much the same these days.'

'Minchin?' asked Markby suspiciously.

'The chap who's coming. Didn't I mention his name?' Winsley's expression was suspiciously bland.

'No, you didn't,' Markby said. 'Look, sir, I must question the advisability of bringing in someone from London. There are forces nearer to us who could probably spare someone . . .'

'Alan –' Winsley's use of his first name grated, 'you must see how it is. Yes, a neighbouring force could send a team. But the chances are it would consist of officers known to you; you would be known to them. These would be men you'd sat by at dinners, shared Christmas drinks with, played golf with—'

Markby interrupted to say he didn't play golf and went out of his way to avoid police social functions.

'Nevertheless,' said Winsley, overruling his objections, 'it remains a matter of justice not only being done, but being seen to be done. Superintendent Minchin will be with you tomorrow, together with Inspector Hayes, first thing. Perhaps you could arrange somewhere for them to stay?'

Dave Pearce, unaware of the bombshell dropped on his boss, had arrived at The Feathers.

It was not a pub he knew well. He vaguely remembered having been there for a drink with Tessa, his wife, on one occasion. Tessa hadn't liked it there and they'd not returned. He stared at it without enthusiasm. Its tiny upper windows peeped out from beneath the eaves as if they resented being obliged to let in any light at all. Its sign showed the feathered crest of the Prince of Wales. The main door stood propped wide to the world although it was well before opening time. As Dave approached, a smell of beer, smoke and stale food drifted out, along with the sound of a vacuum cleaner. At this hour of the morning – it was half-past nine, any pub in the land would have presented the same welcome. Last night's fug and debris were being cleared out.

Pearce ducked his head under the low lintel and made his way towards the sound of domestic chores. He found himself in the main bar. The impression he got would have tallied well with Meredith's, and he remembered why he and Tessa hadn't returned. It was a gloomy old place. He stared at the dark walls, lined with oak-stained pine strips to the halfway point, and papered with nicotine-stained painted anaglypta from there to the ceiling. All the chairs had been upended on table tops to facilitate cleaning. A small man with receding collar-length fair hair and an earring, who might have been any age between thirty-five and fifty, pushed the vacuum cleaner back and forth with little enthusiasm and moderate efficiency. A Jack Russell terrier which had been wandering around, sniffing at the stained red carpet, ran towards the intruder uttering short sharp barks.

'Police!' called Pearce above the grind of the vacuum and the yapping of the dog. He held up his warrant card and edged his trouser-legs away from the Jack Russell's teeth.

The cleaner switched off his machine. 'He don't bite,' he said.

In fact, the Jack Russell had stopped barking as soon as

the vacuum's roar ceased. It now stood watching Pearce with bright-eyed interest, ears cocked. Its manner indicated it thought the visitor was about to do something exciting.

'I'd like to see the landlady, Mrs Forbes,' said Pearce.

'What's it about?' the cleaner demanded.

'Is she here?' asked Pearce in a tired voice. 'Just go and get her, will you?'

'She'll want to know why you're here,' retorted the cleaner, standing his ground. The Jack Russell uttered an impatient yelp.

'Enquiries,' snapped Pearce.

'It's not likely to affect our licence, is it?' persisted the cleaner. 'We haven't had any trouble here. Dolores won't allow it.'

'I'm making enquiries into the death of Mr Jan Oakley,' Pearce admitted at last. He could see himself standing here all day arguing with this pipsqueak. The information had the desired effect.

'Gawd,' said the cleaner in awe. 'I'll go and get Dolores.' As he hastened towards a door in the further wall, he turned his head and called back, 'She's not going to like this, you know.'

Pearce realised he was being given fair warning. He braced himself. Even so, he was almost bowled over by the force with which Mrs Forbes erupted through the door and into the bar. She presented a fearsome sight. Her blonde hair was tortured round large rollers which studded her head like some sort of helmet. She wore a tight black sweater and tighter black trousers and was balanced on four-inch heels. She looked like an avenging Valkyrie.

'What's all this?' she demanded, descending on Pearce

who managed, just, not to step back. 'Darren says you're asking about that fellow Oakley. I heard he'd died. What's it got to do with us?'

'I understand, Mrs Forbes,' Pearce quavered, 'that he ate here every evening.'

'So what?' snarled Mrs Forbes.

Pearce pulled himself together and tried to take charge of the conversation. 'We're trying to trace his last movements and we're particularly interested in what he ate during that day. He ate here every evening. So you can help us if you tell us what he had that Saturday, if you remember.'

''Course I remember! He had the cheapest thing on the menu. That was the arrangement I had with Miss Oakley. He had the pasta with basil, tomato and mozzarella. There was nothing wrong with that.' Her eyes narrowed. 'What did he die of?'

'We think he was poisoned,' admitted Pearce.

'Poisoned!' yelled Mrs Forbes into his face and this time Pearce did dodge back. The Jack Russell, which had retreated under the nearest table as the landlady approached, now scuttled out of the open front door. Pearce wished he could do the same.

'No one,' Mrs Forbes was breathing heavily, her splendid bosom bouncing up and down like a couple of marker buoys on a choppy sea, 'no one in my entire life has ever accused me of poisoning anyone with my cooking or with any food served in any establishment I've run. I've been in this business since I was nineteen! *Darren!*'

The cleaner rushed forward obediently. 'Yes, Dolores?'

'Tell this copper what you had for your supper last night,' she ordered.

'I had the pasta,' said Darren. 'It was very nice, too. I like pasta.'

'See?' demanded Mrs Forbes. 'How are you feeling today, Darren?'

'I'm fine,' he said.

'You've not got the guts-ache? Don't feel sick? Didn't have the runs during the night?'

Darren denied suffering any of these medical symptoms.

'Darren's got a delicate stomach,' said Mrs Forbes to Pearce. 'If there'd been anything wrong with the pasta, he'd have been the first to know it, wouldn't you, Darren?'

'Yes, Dolores. I can't touch a curry but pasta is all right.'

'I'm not interested in Darren's stomach!' shouted Pearce, overriding this united defence. 'I'm interested in Jan Oakley's! What else did he have? Just the pasta?'

'He had a couple of pints of lager. It was bottled lager, so you can't blame the pub for anything to do with that. Not that there's anything wrong with the draught lager here. All the pipes are washed out regular. Same goes for my kitchen. It's cleaned top to bottom every day, isn't it, Darren?'

Darren, who presumably did the cleaning, agreed gloomily that it was.

'Spotless!' snapped Mrs Forbes. 'You come and see for yourself.'

'I don't need—' began Pearce, but found himself propelled into a white-tiled kitchen which did, he agreed, look spotless.

'Fridge!' snapped Mrs Forbes. Pearce was hauled to the fridge which was thrown open and his head almost thrust inside to enable him to inspect it. 'Cupboards!' Doors flew open and clashed shut above his head. 'Floor!' Mrs Forbes pointed imperiously downwards.

Pearce wondered whether he was expected to kneel at her feet and beg forgiveness at having cast aspersions on the kitchen of The Feathers.

'I've had the environmental health bloke here, checking,' went on the landlady, still in full flow, 'and he said it was a shining example, didn't he, Darren? He said he wished all the kitchens he saw were like this one.'

'We got a certificate,' added Darren.

'And there it is, on the wall. See?' Mrs Forbes flung out a scarlet-tipped finger. 'We got an award from the council! And in case you're wondering,' she concluded, 'that dog never sets a paw in here, does he, Darren?'

'I bet he doesn't,' said Pearce, getting a word in edgeways at last. 'All right, your kitchen's a ruddy marvel. Wish my kitchen at home was the same.' (Good job Tessa couldn't hear him say that. He'd find himself in the divorce court before he knew it.) 'Can we get back to this fellow, Oakley?'

'What else do you want to know about him?' Dolores Forbes sniffed. 'Not that I can tell you anything, apart from the fact he wasn't my cup of tea. I felt sorry for those two old dears. She was paying the bill for all the food he ate here, you know, was Miss Oakley. A scandal, I call it. I don't suppose she's got anything much but the old age pension for all she and her sister live in that big house. It's in a terrible state inside and the garden only looks decent because Ron Gladstone comes over and keeps it nice, just out of the kindness of his heart.'

'Was Oakley always alone when he ate here?' Pearce refused to be sidetracked.

'He didn't know anyone,' Mrs Forbes pointed out. 'The only time I ever saw anyone sitting with him at his table was one evening when Superintendent Markby came in with a woman and they went and talked to that Oakley for a few minutes. Then Oakley got up and left.' She frowned in memory. 'And the superintendent and his lady friend left, too, just after. Don't think they ate here.'

'Why wasn't Jan Oakley your cup of tea?' Pearce thought that Markby and Miss Mitchell had probably got the same impression of this place that he and Tessa had received. It wasn't what you might call welcoming.

'I can tell 'em,' said Mrs Forbes darkly. 'Wouldn't have trusted him an inch. He was quite a nice-looking feller, I'll give you that, and always spoke very politely. But the old ladies didn't want him there, you know, at the house. He was sponging off them and they knew it. They didn't like him one bit.'

It now struck Pearce that Mrs Forbes seemed to know rather more about the internal affairs of Fourways House than might be expected.

'How do you know?' he asked. 'How do you know the house is in such a bad state of repair and they didn't want Oakley there?'

'Our Kenny told me all about it.' In explanation, she added, 'He runs a taxi service, see. He takes them shopping regular, every Saturday, and anywhere else they need to go during the week, as and when they need it. Kenny says the house fair gives him the creeps but he likes the old ladies. Anyhow, he could see they didn't care for that Jan. Ron Gladstone, he didn't like Jan neither.'

'Then perhaps I'd better speak to Kenny,' said Pearce. 'What's his other name?'

'Joss,' said the landlady. 'He's a cousin of mine.'

So the battling Dolores was a Joss. Pearce knew the Joss clan well, both from experience and by reputation. He eyed Darren. 'Is he a Joss, too?'

'Course he's not!' Mrs Forbes looked quite shocked. 'He's my partner, Darren Lee.' She paused and added more mildly, 'Charlie Forbes and I didn't last long. I was only twenty when I married him. You don't know what you're doing when you're twenty, do you?'

Charlie Forbes certainly hadn't.

Markby had left the chief constable on civil if frosty terms. He felt angry, perhaps unreasonably so. He knew Winsley was probably right. Jan's complaint of police harassment, even if proved unfounded, would cast a shadow over investigations. Add to that Markby's own long acquaintance with the Oakleys, plus Meredith's involvement with Jan, the additional ingredient of the Painters in the mix and yes, a fresh pair of eyes should be looking at this case. But cool logic didn't help, nor that the replacements were to come from London, of all places! The fact was, to outside eyes, Markby had been deemed unsuitable. It reflected upon him and would be remembered.

But Markby's team remained on the case. Minchin and Hayes wouldn't be able to investigate the case entirely on their own. They'd call on all the support and help within Regional HQ they could get. That meant Pearce in particular would have to act as their guide and interpreter. Markby used the last phrase advisedly. Not only would the newcomers need someone who knew the case and its background, but a more important aspect to the new arrangement was that it disregarded the personalities in the case. The Oakleys, for example: how would they react to the man from the Met? They'd hardly unburden themselves to him. He'd be a stranger and they didn't chat about personal affairs to strangers. That it was a police matter wouldn't make a jot of difference to this. And Meredith?

He drew into the entrance to a field and took out his mobile phone. She was at her desk.

'Listen,' he said, 'perhaps you should take a few days off. The CC has asked for a couple of heavies from the Met to come down and take over. They're bound to want to interview everyone at length. That's going to include you, I'm afraid.'

'They've taken you off the case, then?' She sounded depressed and furtive. That fellow Adrian was probably listening in. Another reason for her to stay out of her office.

'I've been left technically in overall charge. That's a sop to keep me quiet. But,' added Markby quietly, 'as long as I'm at Regional HQ I *am* in charge – and the CC and the pair of city slickers he's calling in will find that out!' More briskly, he went on, 'Superintendent Minchin and an Inspector Hayes are to arrive tomorrow. I'm to find them accommodation.' He paused. 'I thought they might have your place. It's empty.'

'My house?' She sounded startled.

'Why not? It's either that or The Crown. Your place has been fixed up. Everything's new in there, carpets, the lot. It's furnished. The Force will pay the usual rate for temporary renting. They'll be more comfortable and one of us will get something out of this.'

'This isn't like you, Alan,' came the surprised voice down the line.

'Let's say, I'm not my usual self. Shall I offer them your place, then – or just drop them off at The Crown?'

'They can have my place with pleasure. I'll leave the details to you, and I'll arrange time off. See you tonight.' A pause. 'Don't take it to heart, Alan. It's just a question of the circumstances and you knew it was a distinct possibility – you told the Oakleys so. I don't suppose Winsley really wants these London men down there. It makes it look as if we can't manage in the country. I'm sure he'd rather it was you. He's probably worried about publicity.'

'That's more or less what Winsley said.' Markby added, 'Knowing someone is right doesn't always make it easy to accept an unwelcome judgement.'

He returned to his car and drove slowly and thoughtfully back to his office. Pearce was there.

'I've been to The Feathers, sir,' he greeted Markby. 'What a place! I thought the landlady was going to run me out by the scruff of my neck. It seems unlikely Oakley was poisoned there, unless the atmosphere got him!'

Markby managed a faint grin. 'Yes, I've met Dolores. Well, Dave, you'll be making your report to someone else from tomorrow.' He explained about Minchin and Hayes.

Pearce looked glum. 'Bit off, that.'

'I can't comment. I'm sure Superintendent Minchin knows his stuff. You'll be the officer providing the necessary link between them and this office. I don't need to say that you should provide them with every assistance. They will depend on you to a great extent. Cheer up, Dave. There's no reason why things shouldn't run smoothly.'

Markby suspected he sounded less than convincing. Pearce certainly looked as if he feared the worst.

Detective Constable Ginny Holding put her head round the door. 'Sir? There's a chap here from the Polish Embassy.

His name's –' She glanced at a business card in her hand '– Landowski. Tadeusz Landowski.' She stumbled over the pronunciation.

'That was quick,' Markby observed. 'Well, show him in. I'm presumably to carry on until Minchin gets here.'

He wasn't sure what to expect from a Polish consular officer. Landowski, when he bounced in, proved to be a chunky, aggressive young man in a leather jacket, polo-neck sweater and chinos. He seized Markby's outstretched hand, pumped it furiously and then sat down abruptly in the chair indicated.

'I have come at once,' he said. 'As this is a matter of murder.'

'We appreciate it,' said Markby.

Landowski nodded acknowledgement of his gratitude. 'I have sent a report back to Poland by diplomatic bag. It should be there in the morning. We shall, naturally, pass on to you any information we can find concerning this man Oakley. But I have to say, not only is it not a Polish name, but the man does not appear to have made his mark, as you say, in any other way. We shall, of course, check police records.'

'His great-grandfather was an Englishman, William Oakley,' said Markby.

Landowski, after the first outburst of energy, had relaxed slightly. Ginny Holding appeared with coffee. She was an attractive girl. Landowski, sidetracked, gave her a seductive grin and thanked her in noticeably more mellow tones.

Wasting your time, chum! thought Markby with satisfaction. She's got a boyfriend and he's a copper.

Landowski set down his coffee on Markby's desk and leaned forward confidentially. 'I'm a fan, you know, of the

British whodunnit. It will be very interesting to see your police force at work in a murder enquiry. Real life, eh?'

'Enquiries,' said Markby, 'will be conducted by a Superintendent Minchin. He arrives tomorrow from London.'

'Scotland Yard!' cried Landowski in glee. 'It is like the good old John Dickson Carr, the much admired Ngaio Marsh!' He rubbed his hands together briskly.

'I think,' said Markby mildly, unwilling to dispel this innocent assumption, 'that you'll find we've moved on a bit since those days.'

Landowski contemplated him and then, with a sudden return to his businesslike manner, said, 'I understand he had English relatives, this Oakley.'

'Yes, two elderly women, sisters.'

'They will meet the funeral costs?'

Taken aback, Markby confessed he hadn't thought about Oakley's funeral.

'We must think about it,' said Landowski reproachfully. 'I should prefer it did not fall as a cost on the Polish state.'

'Perhaps,' ventured Markby, 'there is someone back home who'd like his body returned – when the time comes.'

Landowski was shaking his head. 'That will be unlikely. To return a body is a very expensive business and covered by many regulations. There must be a certain type of coffin. It must be conveyed in a refrigerated hold. It all adds to the cost.'

'The women in question,' Markby told him, 'are in their eighties and not very well off financially. The deceased was a thorough nuisance to them during his entire visit. They only discovered his existence recently. To pressurise them to find money they can ill-afford to pay for his funeral . . . Let's say, technically you might be able to do it. Decency, however . . .'

Landowski looked glum. 'I sympathise. But I am obliged to do my job, as you say. However, perhaps there is some closer relative in Poland? Although, frankly, they'd probably have no money, either.' He considered this and added hopefully, 'Or there is your social security?'

'He'd only been in the country a couple of weeks,' said Markby crossly. 'And to put it bluntly, he's one of yours.'

Landowski recognised an impasse. 'Well, when the body is released, we shall see what can be done. May I know the cause of death?'

'Certainly. He was poisoned with arsenic.'

Landowski's face lit up. 'Arsenic!' he breathed. 'Just like the good old days.'

Well, that was one way of putting it.

Chapter Eighteen

Rotund little Mr Green, for the defence, had slowly gained the serene look of a card-player who knows he holds a winning hand. And now he played his trump. He called to the stand Mr Joseph Baxter, pharmacist, of Bamford.

Baxter, in contrast to defence counsel, looked nervous. At his first attempt at speech, his voice stuck in his throat and he had to start again. He then agreed that on the fatal day, he had dispensed laudanum for Mrs Oakley and the drug had been collected and paid for by Mr Oakley.

'It was all according to prescription,' added Mr Baxter jumpily. 'Since the 1868 Pharmacy Act we've not been allowed to dispense large amounts of opium-based preparations unless a doctor has prescribed it. And Dr Perkins had prescribed it. The lady had toothache. It's still a very popular thing for toothache.'

'Quite,' said Mr Green gently. 'Had you dispensed laudanum to Mrs Oakley before?'

'Ye-es,' said Baxter, eyeing his questioner. 'She relied on it to kill any pain. Dr Perkins had prescribed it for her before.'

'And she had also come in and bought it herself, over the counter, without prescription?'

'Only pennyworth's!' burst out the pharmacist. 'We do

still dispense tiny amounts to people without prescription. It's something people know about and trust. Not everyone in Bamford can afford to visit a doctor. They dose themselves.'

'No one is suggesting you have done anything improper, Mr Baxter. Did Mrs Oakley, on these occasions when she bought small amounts over the counter, say why she wanted it?'

'Sometimes she said it was for some pain she was suffering and sometimes for one of the servants. Before she had that tooth pulled, she put up with the ache for over a month. She did come in on several occasions during that time. In the end, I said to her that she should get it seen to. "You are quite right, Mr Baxter," she said. Shortly after that, she did get a dentist to pull the tooth.'

'You recommended her to get the tooth pulled out,' Mr Green leaned forward. 'Why?'

'Why, sir, because she was in pain and a toothache like that, it doesn't go away!' Baxter exclaimed.

'And for no other reason?'

Baxter swallowed, his Adam's apple rising and falling in his throat. 'I didn't like her taking so much laudanum, and that's a fact. I've known people get dependent on it. Not so much now as in the old days, before the Act. Why, in my father's day – he was a pharmacist in Bamford before me – people did get addicted to it. Opium's like that and laudanum is, after all, a tincture of opium.'

'You feared the lady was becoming dependent?'

'To tell the truth, sir,' admitted the pharmacist, 'I did. Had it been anyone else, I'd have had a word with her husband, but I don't like to interfere in matters concerning gentlefolk.

I – well, I depend on their good will. Any tradesman does. Suppose I was wrong? How would Mr and Mrs Oakley take that?'

'So you dispensed regular small amounts of laudanum to this lady and you said nothing. Tell me, suppose a person became addicted in the way you have described, how would this manifest itself?'

'Difficult to tell, sir. But opium, it plays tricks on the mind. Sometimes people see things which aren't there. Or things which *are* there, look different to them. Sometimes the imagination is excited. I've heard of poets and such who've written wonderful lines under its influence. But sometimes, it's more in the nature of a nightmare. After a while, the person becomes listless, loses interest, can't organise himself.'

'And would such an addicted person be likely to misinterpret what he or she saw around him?'

'Very likely,' said Baxter, adding, 'but I don't know it was so in Mrs Oakley's case, sir.'

'No, you don't, but I'm asking you for your opinion in a general way. Would such a person be inclined to clumsiness?'

'They might be, sir. Of course, after they'd taken a dose, they'd be drowsy and not able to organise their movements, as you might say.'

'So, if a person who had taken laudanum on retiring, were then to attempt to get out of bed, what would happen?'

'They'd fall over,' said Mr Baxter simply.

'Thank you, Mr Baxter,' said Mr Green.

He looked rather as though he expected a round of applause and Stanley Huxtable was half surprised he didn't get it.

* * *

When he summed up his defence for the jury, Mr Green radiated even more confidence.

'Gentlemen of the jury, we are here in a British court of law. It is a basic rule of British justice that an accused person is judged not upon gossip or innuendo, but upon evidence, tested and found reliable.

'Let us consider the evidence in this case. It seems largely to consist of the testimony of a dismissed servant, Martha Button. Mrs Button has claimed that her employer was improperly involved with the nursemaid, Daisy Joss. But Daisy is walking out with a respectable young man and hoping to be married. She is saving for her bottom drawer. Is it likely she would jeopardise her future happiness? The prosecution has drawn attention to the fact that since Mrs Oakley's death, Daisy has remained employed at Fourways with an increase of wages. But surely it is right of Mr Oakley to minimise, as far as is possible, the upset to the daily routine of his son, a child who is now motherless? As for the gift of earrings, they were in the nature of a small memento and coral is hardly the most expensive substance used in jewellery. In fact, the earrings may more properly be described as a trinket.

'Moreover, the dead woman, Cora Oakley, had been taking laudanum on one pretext or another for some time, to the extent that it was beginning to worry the dispensing pharmacist, Mr Baxter. You have heard him describe how a person who had become so dependent, might become muddled and liable to imagine things. Might not Cora Oakley have taken morbid fancies into her head? Might she not have imagined that a kindly word from her husband to the nursemaid, a little joke perhaps, indicated some blameworthy activity? In such circumstances, I do not think we can read too much into anything she told Mrs Button, the housekeeper, about dismissing the nursemaid.

'Now we come to the manner in which the prosecution has claimed William Oakley sought to bring about his wife's death. He is said to have taken a small quantity of arsenic ore from a factory to which he was making a routine visit. Did anyone see him take it? Was it found in his possession? Did the factory report any substance to be missing? The reply to all three of these questions is a resounding NO! The existence of this sample of ore is entirely hypothetical – one might say fanciful. So, what of the items we have been told formed part of the apparatus set up by Mr Oakley? Items which, we're also told, so mysteriously disappeared? Who saw them? Only Mrs Button. Did Dr Perkins see them when he arrived that night? No, he did not. Who smelled the garlic odour in the room? Only Mrs Button. Did Dr Perkins smell it? No, he did not. Did Mrs Button mention either of these things at the original inquest? No, she did not. When did she mention them? After she had been dismissed from her place.

'Let us consider, on the other hand, what is positively known and agreed as fact. Had Mrs Oakley been taking laudanum for a painful condition of the mouth for over a month before the tooth was pulled? Yes, she had. Had she taken it that evening, after the extraction of the tooth? Yes, it had been prescribed by Dr Perkins. Mr Oakley himself purchased it and took it to her bedside, anxious to help his wife in her distress. Did Mrs Oakley later fall and bring down the lamp, setting alight her clothing? Yes, she did. Did Mrs Button herself see her unfortunate mistress in flames? Yes, she has given us a graphic account. Did Dr Perkins give his opinion at the time that death was due to burns and shock?

Yes, he did. Gentlemen of the jury, we have heard much ingenious conjecture in this court, but nothing established beyond reasonable doubt to show other than that Mrs Oakley died as a result of falling while in a laudanum-induced stupor and setting herself aflame. *That is what happened . . .*'

'Right,' said the Reuter's man, when the judge had concluded his directions to the jury. 'Jury's out. Time for a pint.' He gathered up his belongings and then stopped to ask his companion, 'Looking for someone?'

Stanley, whose gaze had been searching the public benches, said, 'No, no one in particular. Just looking to see who's turned up.'

'The verdict will pack 'em in!' prophesied the Reuter's man. 'Come on, they'll be three deep at the bar.'

That evening, in his cheerless lodgings, Stanley read through his notebook and on a clean page, sketched a slim figure in black. He sat staring at it for some time before writing beneath it, *If you live in Bamford, I'll find you.*

Chapter Nineteen

Meredith opened the door at ten the following morning to find Juliet Painter on the doorstep, round spectacles agleam.

'I thought I'd find you at home,' she said. 'I didn't think you'd be going up to London with all this going on down here.'

Meredith led her into the kitchen and switched on the kettle for coffee. 'Alan thought it best. That's to say, it *is* best. There's someone coming down from London to take over the case and he'll want to talk to me. Besides, I've got a spy in my office.'

'Literally?' asked Juliet, brightening. 'James Bond?'

'His name is Adrian and his spying activities are confined to snooping on his colleagues. He is definitely no James Bond. More like Pussy Galore.'

'I'm glad you're here,' Juliet accepted her coffee, 'because I'd like you to come with me to visit the Oakleys.'

'Juliet,' Meredith said as firmly as she could, 'I've already been drawn into this much further than I like or need. Why should the Oakleys want to see me?'

'Because they need friendly, supportive faces around them. Come on, Meredith. Besides, you're good at this sort of thing.'

'What sort of thing? Visiting the distressed elderly?'

'No, detecting.'

'Oh no!' Meredith flung up a warning hand. 'Alan would hit the roof.'

'Alan this, Alan that. Do you know, he's starting to run your life?'

'He is not!' The suggestion genuinely offended Meredith. It wasn't true nor was it about to become true. Besides, this morning Alan had shown little interest in what she was doing. He'd left for HQ grim-faced to welcome Minchin and Hayes who were driving down from London and due to arrive, traffic permitting, at around eleven. They had again discussed it and decided that Minchin and Hayes would be offered Meredith's cottage as a base. If they didn't want it, The Crown Hotel would have to be a substitute.

'Perhaps,' Markby had said, 'I ought to show them The Crown first. They'll jump at the cottage after that.'

Juliet wasn't accepting Meredith's denial. 'It certainly sounds like it. Anyway, you've just said he's not investigating this any more, so he can't object, can he?' Wheedling, she asked, 'You're home aren't you? What are you going to do all day?'

Meredith surrendered, less because of Juliet's argument than because of her own curiosity. 'All right, I'll come along. Though I can't think what we're going to find out.'

In fact, they found at once that they were not the first visitors to Fourways that morning. Parked before the front door was a shiny dark blue Jaguar. Juliet parked her Mini behind it and they both stared at the numberplate through the windscreen. It was personalised, just initials and a single digit.

'That,' said Juliet, 'doesn't look like any kind of squad car *I've* ever seen.'

'I've seen it,' said Meredith slowly. 'I mean, I haven't seen that car which is obviously brand new, but I've seen that plate or similar. It belongs to Dudley Newman.'

'The builder? Hell's teeth!' Juliet threw open her door. 'Let's get in there. It looks as if we've arrived not a moment too soon!'

It had been some time since Meredith had met Dudley Newman and she wondered whether he'd remember her, or if he'd want to. On the previous occasion there had been a death on a building site run by his firm. Generally people don't want unpleasant memories revived.

He rose from his chair as they entered, ushered in by Damaris. He looked much as she recalled him, well-built, running to a little extra weight now, in his early sixties, thinning hair. Florence looked relieved at the sight of Juliet. Meredith wondered what Newman had been saying.

'We've met before.' Newman cut through any possible embarrassment with minimum fuss. 'Markby investigating this one, too, is he?'

His tone was jovial but his eyes sharp. He shook Meredith's hand perfunctorily. He wasn't pleased to see her but he was assessing the situation, wondering if he could turn it somehow to his advantage. He knew of her friendship with Alan.

'No, I believe someone else is going to take charge of investigations.'

At this both Damaris and Florence looked alarmed. 'Not Alan?' Damaris asked.

'I don't think so, Miss Oakley. I don't know much about it, but I understand there will be someone else.'

Florence said in trembling tones, 'I know he warned us, but we had hoped it would be Alan. We know Alan.'

'Yes, I'm afraid that's the problem.'

'We've met as well, just the once,' said Juliet to Newman, entering the conversation.

Newman was nodding. 'You had a client might've been interested in that big place I renovated over Cherton way. He didn't take it.'

'He liked the house but then he found one he liked better,' Juliet said simply.

'Well, that's business.' Newman dismissed the topic and retook his chair.

'And are you interested in Fourways?' Juliet also saw no need for niceties.

Newman looked cautious. 'I might be, in a manner of speaking. Not to do it up. It's gone past that stage. Sorry, ladies.' This last was cast as an aside to the owners of the house he was disparaging.

'Mr Newman,' said Damaris, 'is interested in purchasing the property with a view to developing the land. We've told him, Juliet, that we shall be advised by you.'

Clearly Newman didn't like this arrangement. 'It'd be a good thing,' he said sulkily.

'And what,' asked Juliet, 'exactly do you have in mind, Mr Newman?'

'Five or six upmarket, four-bed, double-garage homes. Possibly built of local stone. There's a call for that kind of house around here. I'm fairly sure I can get planning permission.'

'Including demolishing the present house?' Juliet asked.

'It's not going to attract English Heritage, is it?' Newman said coarsely. 'I could, of course, turn it into flats but the cost'd be prohibitive.'

'So,' Juliet said smoothly, 'it's a question of what you'd be prepared to pay for the land.'

He returned her stare. 'Naturally, I'd have to go to the banks to fund a big development. That means I've got to think about interest payments. So, while I pay a fair price for anything I buy, I've also got my costs to think about, too. So I can't be paying over the odds.'

Meredith saw this kind of conversation distressed both sisters. This was why they'd asked Juliet to handle the sale of Fourways. This kind of business deal wasn't their world. They had no idea how to go about it. They flinched from it as from some gruesome sight.

'Perhaps I could come to your office and talk it over,' Juliet suggested.

Still unwilling to admit the necessity of including her, Newman mumbled, 'If you want. Give my secretary a call.'

He'd clambered awkwardly to his feet. 'Well, I'd better be getting along. Nice to see you again – er – Meredith.'

'My regards to your wife,' said Meredith politely.

'What? Oh, yes, I'll tell her.'

'He is a graceless sort of man, isn't he?' said Damaris when she returned from seeing the visitor out. 'I am so glad you came, Juliet.'

'Was he trying to get you to agree to something?' Juliet demanded, instantly combative.

'No, not exactly. I suppose, if he really wants to buy, it would be best to sell to him? He's quite right when he says no one is going to want the house as it is, isn't he? I don't think Florence and I have any illusions about the house. Who would want to live here? We don't. In fact, neither Florence nor I is particularly attached to the place.'

'He may not find it so easy to pull it down, though,' said Juliet, 'for all his talk of planning permission.'

'It's not listed,' Damaris pointed out 'It's not special.'

'All the same, you'd be surprised how many people can object to an old house being demolished. Though I'm sure Newman's got friends in the right places. He'll get his planning permission for the houses.'

'You think we should sell to him, then?'

The sisters gazed at Juliet in a way which reminded Meredith of a pair of trusting dogs. She thought she wouldn't want Juliet's job, this responsibility. The Oakleys' future depended on her advice and decision.

'I think I should have a good talk with him first and get him to make a firm offer,' Juliet said. 'Leave it with me.'

They were clearly glad to do so. Damaris made a movement with her hands as if pushing aside the whole problem. 'Would you care for a glass of wine?'

She meant sherry. Both her visitors accepted, individually of the opinion that a restorative was what the sisters needed.

'We have,' said Damaris, when the sherry had been poured, 'had rather an unpleasant morning and it hasn't all been the fault of Mr Newman.'

Florence sipped her sherry and dabbed at her mouth with the handkerchief scrunched in her thin fist. 'Awful,' she muttered. 'Awful news.'

'My sister means the police have now told us Jan died from arsenic poisoning.' Damaris's voice was taut. 'You know, of course, that is how poor Cora died. Well, not exactly in the same way. She didn't eat it – she breathed it in. But William was held to have used the same poisonous substance.' She paused. 'It seems as though someone has gone out of his way to be wicked. Murder is evil enough, but to choose that means. So much malice. Someone hates us.'

Though this echoed her own feelings, Meredith protested, 'No, surely not.'

'What else can we think? The police want to know where the poison came from. We can offer no suggestion. Jan ate breakfast here. It was simple, cornflakes and toast. He had butter and marmalade on the toast, sugar and milk on the cornflakes. The police took away the marmalade and sugar. In fact, they took every open bag and pot in the store cupboard. Jam, salt, salad cream, everything, even some cod liver oil capsules. We – that was distressing.'

Hastily Meredith said, 'He came to tea with me in the afternoon and I'd made chocolate cake. The police have taken that, too. They have to check everything.'

'So he was telling the truth?' Damaris asked in mild surprise. 'He said he'd been to see you. I'm afraid Florence and I were inclined to disbelieve anything he said.'

'I was trying to help,' Meredith confessed. 'I don't think I did much good.'

'Thank you for trying, anyway,' said Damaris.

'What about lunch that day?' Juliet dragged them back to the main matter.

Damaris was able to answer that. 'I made up some salad, just some ham and the usual tomato, lettuce, cucumber and some cress. Oh, and cold boiled eggs. For pudding we had baked apples. We do very little in the way of meat and two veg, that kind of meal, because the old gas cooker is so unreliable. We all ate the same and neither Florence nor I has been ill.' She glanced at her sister who sat, head bowed, the half-full sherry glass in her hands. 'It's all a great strain,' she concluded.

'It's no good my saying don't worry,' Juliet told her. 'You're going to worry and nothing can be done about that. But don't read anything into the police taking food from the kitchen. Above all, don't give any kind of verbal agreement to Dudley Newman. I don't say he's dishonest, he's got a good reputation. But he is a businessman and it would be in his interest to get the land cheap. Just refer him to me.'

'We're very grateful to you, Juliet my dear.' Damaris reached out her hand. 'Thank you for coming and thank you, too, Meredith. Tell Alan we're sorry he isn't to be the one dealing with this. Do you know who will be?'

'It's going to be a London man, Superintendent Minchin,' Meredith told her.

'London?' Damaris raised her eyebrows. 'They must think us very important.'

Outside the house, Juliet paused by her car, keys in hand.

'Meredith? You're not in a hurry, are you? I'd like to take another look round the grounds in view of Newman's offer.'

They set off across the back lawn. 'He'll get five or six houses in here easily,' Meredith said. 'Even more, possibly, although not if he's going for the more expensive homes. He must see it as a profitable scheme for himself. Not that I'd have thought Dudley Newman short of cash, but no matter how much he's made, I expect he'd like to make more. I wonder how much he wants to carry through this scheme.'

'Enough to kill someone who might appear in the way of it?' Juliet asked.

'I didn't say that.'

'You were thinking it. So was I.'

They walked on in silence. Eventually Meredith said, 'It's the arsenic, isn't it? Where would Newman or anyone else, come to that, get such a thing? How would he administer it? Can we show that he ever met Jan?'

'We don't know what Jan was up to, that's the trouble,' Juliet pointed out. 'How do we know he wasn't trying to cut some deal with Newman and they fell out?' She stopped and took off her spectacles. Her eyes were a pale china blue and she'd accentuated the lids with eyeliner although otherwise she wore little make-up, only a touch of pale pink lipstick. The magenta fingernails seemed in quirky contradiction to her otherwise plain style. She took out the spectacle case, extracted the yellow lint cleaning square and began to polish up the lenses.

'You've never thought of contact lenses?' Meredith asked.

'Can't get on with them. Make my eyes water. I suppose if I persevered I'd be all right. I don't mind wearing specs. It helps a bit in business. I like to think they make me look intelligent and you know what Dorothy Parker said: "men seldom make passes at girls who wear glasses"!'

'Is it true?' Meredith grinned.

'No, actually. Some men seem to find the specs quite a turn-on.' Juliet replaced the spectacles on her nose. 'Hello, there's Ron Gladstone.' She raised a hand and waved. 'He looks a bit down in the dumps. I expect he's worried about

259

the Oakleys and he probably saw Newman's car. He'll know what that means. Poor Ron. He loves this garden.'

The gardener had seen them. For a moment he appeared to hesitate and then he began to walk slowly towards them. He did look, thought Meredith, as if he carried the cares of the world on his shoulders and his normally spruce appearance was distinctly ruffled.

'Good morning, Ron!' Juliet hailed him.

'Good morning,' returned Ron. 'If that's what it is, which I very much doubt.'

'Mustn't get down-hearted, Ron,' she told him bracingly. 'Do you know Meredith? She's a friend of Superintendent Markby. You've come across him, haven't you?'

Ron indicated he had. 'He called here after that fellow died. I showed him the garden.'

'He'll have appreciated that,' Meredith told him.

Ron cheered up slightly. 'Yes, I think he did.' He relapsed into gloom. 'You saw that builder fellow, Newman, was here?' His voice rose on a note of despair. 'He wants to put bricks all over this.' Ron swept out an arm to encompass his garden.

'If he does it,' said Meredith, 'which isn't settled, he's talking of just five or six houses and he'd want the surroundings landscaped. He'd probably try and save some of the grounds as they are, certainly the nice old trees. In fact, he may *have* to spare the older trees. It should be possible to get a preservation order on them.'

This crumb of comfort did little to brighten Ron's manner which remained resolutely depressed. He put his hands in his pockets and stared from one to the other of them. 'I haven't seen the police since Markby was here. Any news?'

'A London man is taking over,' Juliet told him.

Ron received this with a 'Huh!' Alan would agree with that, thought Meredith.

'And,' said Juliet, 'we know Jan was poisoned with arsenic. Hard to believe, isn't it? Would—'

She broke off. Both she and Meredith stared at Ron with dismay. His face had turned a greenish-pale on which his red moustache stood out like a wound. He took his hands from his pockets, swayed slightly, and asked in a hoarse tone, 'Come again?'

'Arsenic. What's up, Ron? Are you all right?'

Ron shook his head as if to clear it. 'No,' he mumbled. 'Not all right. All bloody wrong. Oh, hell.'

Meredith stepped forward and touched his elbow. 'Ron, do you know something? Because if you do, you must speak out.'

'That's it,' he replied miserably. 'Should've spoke out before. I mean, normally, I wouldn't forget a thing like that. But what with one thing and another it did slip my mind. Then, well, he died and I thought first of all it'd be drink and drugs. I said as much to Markby. Then I heard it was poison, but I had in mind some modern stuff.' He stopped and made an effort to pull himself together. 'I'll show you where I found it,' he said. 'This way.'

He set off briskly and they followed behind.

'Where are we going, Ron?' called Juliet.

'The old potting shed!' came in reply.

'Something nasty in the woodshed?' whispered Juliet to Meredith.

'I've got a feeling,' Meredith replied, 'that it might prove very nasty indeed.'

'Yes, it was!' said Ron tetchily, overhearing. 'Only it's not there now, is it?'

Chapter Twenty

There was a strange atmosphere at Regional HQ, almost a suppressed excitement, in anticipation of the arrival of the men from the Met. Markby, buried memories of school cadet corps aroused, thought there was a whiff of kit inspection about the whole thing. Pearce, who disapproved of the arrangement and faced working directly with the newcomers, stomped around looking grim. Ginny Holding tidied her desk. Sergeant Prescott looked apprehensive. One or two of the younger officers clearly hoped for a chance to shine and find themselves transferred to metropolitan glory. Markby did his best to assume the attitude of a man above all this, but suspected he wasn't being very successful. All his staff treated him with a kindly consideration which, though it was well meant, only served to irritate him more.

'Thank you, Ginny, no, I don't want any more coffee.'

'It's just after eleven, sir,' said Holding.

'I have a wristwatch, thank you, and there's a clock on the wall.'

'They haven't rung to say they've been held up.'

'Why should they be held up? Are there any special traffic problems today?'

'We've put a desk for Superintendent Minchin in the old filing room.'

'I know. I'm sure he'll appreciate it.'

'It's a bit cramped . . .'

'Ginny!' Markby bit back his words and managed to utter in milder if strangled tones, 'I appreciate all this but can't we all relax? No doubt Superintendent Minchin and Inspector Hayes—'

There was a clatter of footsteps outside in the corridor and the sound of an unknown voice, loud, assertive, redolent with unfamiliar vowels.

'I think he's here, sir,' exclaimed Ginny Holding and rushed out.

'What have I got here?' growled Markby, left alone. 'A spare copper from the Met or a ruddy pop star?'

Whatever his private reservations about Minchin, Markby had to admit the man made an impressive entrance. He stood almost six feet four and was solidly built to match. Markby suspected regular sessions at the gym. Despite that, Markby decided with ignoble satisfaction, in later life Minchin would fight a losing battle with weight. Right now he was heavy but fit. He appeared much the same age as Markby, possibly even a year or two younger. His complexion was reddish giving him almost a rustic look and his blond hair clipped short. His features were regular, handsome in a pugnacious way, short straight nose, thin lips, straight brows over small blue eyes. He looked, and Markby feared he would prove to be, an awkward customer. He wore a pale grey suit, turquoise shirt and red tie. Not a man, all in all, to blend in with the crowd.

Trailing in the rear of this glory came Inspector Hayes. As small and wiry as his boss was large and beefy, Hayes was a true child of the inner-city, sharp-eyed, pale-faced, thin-featured. They made, Markby had to admit, a formidable pair.

He had risen to welcome them. They shook hands and exchanged the usual banalities.

'I've arranged a temporary letting for you,' Markby said, 'unless you'd prefer one of the local hotels. You'd get more privacy in the cottage, but it's up to you.'

'Fair enough.' Minchin showed little interest in the domestic arrangements made for him and cut straight to business. 'Have I got an office?'

'Holding will show you.' Markby disliked the man's brusqueness but was determined to remain scrupulously polite. He didn't want Minchin reporting back that the local superintendent had proved difficult.

I am not difficult, Markby told himself virtuously. I am not a difficult person. No one could say that.

Hayes, in the corner of the room, had been studying everything around him with a flickering gaze. Markby felt an instinctive tingle between the shoulderblades. *Watch Hayes*, it said. *That's the tricky one of the two*. He wondered whether Minchin and Hayes worked regularly together.

'I'd be glad to see the file on this case as soon as possible,' said Minchin. 'We'll try not to be in the way.' Minchin, too, was playing it carefully by the rules until he saw how the land lay.

'Of course. As yet we haven't found the source of the arsenic—'

'Got any factories around?' interrupted Minchin.

'Surprising what they use in the industrial chemicals line.'

'We're not an industrial area,' said Markby. 'We do have some places dealing in agricultural supplies—'

At that moment, there was the sound of some commotion outside. Ginny Holding could be heard saying, 'It's not convenient just now, I'm afraid. Mr Markby's busy. Can I help?'

Three other voices, it seemed, chimed in at once. One was male and vaguely familiar, the other two female and one of those very familiar indeed.

'Hang on a second,' said Markby. 'Let me just find out what all that's about.'

He strode out briskly into the corridor. Holding was dealing as well as she could with a party consisting of Ron Gladstone, Juliet Painter and Meredith. Since Meredith would only have come to HQ if the matter was important enough to warrant it, Markby demanded, 'What's happened?'

'Oh, Alan,' she said in relief. 'Ron's got something to tell you.'

'It's about the arsenic,' burst out Juliet.

'It was there and now it's bloody gone,' declared Ron.

Markby was aware of a large presence at his shoulder.

'Someone come in to make a statement?' asked Minchin. 'Inspector!' Hayes scuttled up. 'Best find this office we've been given and see what these people have got to say.'

Holding, after a questioning glance at Markby, offered to lead the way. They set off, Holding in front, Minchin and Hayes behind, Ron, Juliet and Meredith bringing up the rear. Meredith turned her head to pull a quizzical face at Markby, standing in the doorway of his office.

Dave Pearce, attracted by the rumpus, had emerged from

his room into the corridor. Markby grabbed his arm. 'For God's sake, Dave, get down there and sit in on that.'

The former filing room was, as Holding had feared, rather small even for two people. Filled with six people, it suggested one of those torture devices called Little Ease, in which the victim could neither sit, lie nor stand with any degree of comfort.

Minchin, presumably in order to establish his rank, had claimed the chair behind the desk. Hayes stood at his elbow. Two more chairs had been found and offered to Juliet and Meredith who sat facing him. This left no more space for chairs. Ron Gladstone and Dave Pearce were left standing.

'This won't do,' said Meredith firmly, getting to her feet.

'What won't, madam?' asked Minchin giving her a suspicious look.

'The person giving the information ought to have a chair, surely? I can stand. Sit down, Ron.'

'Perhaps you can leave the arrangements to us, miss?' Hayes spoke for the first time. His voice was reedy.

But their visitors proved impervious to official reproach and were busily rearranging themselves. Ron uttered a protest about 'a gentleman not sitting when a lady stood', but was outvoted by the combined voice of the two ladies present.

'You've had a nasty shock, Ron,' said Juliet. 'Of course you must sit down.'

'When you've all finished playing musical chairs . . .' said Minchin unpleasantly.

Eventually, Juliet and Ron sat facing Minchin and Hayes. Meredith and Pearce stood behind. This shuffling around and changing of places occupied some five minutes and then it was discovered there were no official statement forms in the drawers of the desk and Pearce had to go out and bring some back. He also brought another chair which was promptly claimed by Hayes, to Ron's disapproval. ('Leaving a lady standing. It was never the thing in my day!') Somehow or other Hayes found a corner for his chair and settled himself there with a copy of a statement form and a pen.

When some kind of order reigned, Minchin put his forearms on the desk and clasped his hands. He nodded to Hayes who got ready.

'Right, then. My name is Superintendent Minchin and I've come down from London to take over the investigation into the death of Jan Oakley.'

Meredith looked down at the floor. Unbidden, into her head had come a scrap of the sort of dialogue once attributed to constables. *As I was proceeding in a northerly direction, I observed the accused . . .*

When she raised her head, Minchin's small sharp blue eyes were fixed on her even more suspiciously. She felt he'd read her mind. Any temptation to find him funny disappeared. He wasn't funny. He would make, she decided, a bad enemy.

'This is Inspector Hayes,' Minchin went on. He looked at Pearce, inviting him to identify himself.

'I've met all three of the people here already,' said Pearce woodenly. 'They know who I am. Inspector Pearce.'

'So perhaps you'll favour me with your names?' Minchin invited the visitors.

Juliet spoke first. 'I'm Juliet Painter. I act in an advisory capacity to Damaris and Florence Oakley in the matter of the sale of their house.'

Pearce contributed an explanation. 'The house is

Fourways, where the murder occurred.'

'You're an estate agent?' Minchin said in a flat voice, ignoring Pearce.

Oh dear, thought Meredith.

Juliet bounced on her chair. 'I am not an estate agent! I am a property consultant. I do not buy and sell properties. I advise people who wish to do so.'

Clearly unimpressed, Minchin said, 'Sounds much the same sort of thing to me.'

'Well, it isn't!' snapped Juliet. She drew a deep breath. 'Perhaps you should know that my brother, Dr Geoffrey Painter, is the poisons expert who identified the arsenic in the body.'

There was a silence. Minchin said, 'In the body of Jan Oakley?'

'Yes, who else?' snapped Juliet.

Minchin's stony gaze moved on to Ron Gladstone. 'You're the gentleman who wishes to make a statement? Your name is?'

'It's not a statement, it's information,' said Ron. 'My name's Ron Gladstone. I'm the gardener at Fourways.'

Minchin tightened the clasp of his broad hands but otherwise gave no reaction. He turned his gaze at last on Meredith.

'Meredith Mitchell,' she said. 'I was the first person to meet Jan Oakley. I met him on a train and took him to Fourways. I was visiting the house with Juliet this morning when we met Ron and – and as a result we came here.'

'Right,' said Minchin.

'You should also know that I share a home with Superintendent Markby.'

'Blimey,' murmured Hayes. 'No wonder they sent for someone outside the area.'

Minchin gave him a quick warning glance. 'Now, Mr Gladstone,' he said, 'you understand I haven't yet had time to study the file. I've just arrived. But if you've got some information, perhaps you would care to let us know what it is? Inspector Pearce can slot it into place, I'm sure.'

Ron leaned forward. 'It's about the arsenic. You see, I didn't know he died of arsenic. I knew he was poisoned, but I didn't know, until these two ladies told me this morning, that it was arsenic.' He paused to check that Minchin had followed so far.

'Go on,' said Minchin. 'I'll stop you if I don't get it.'

Ron cleared his throat. 'I have to go back to the day after he arrived.'

'He being?'

'Jan Oakley. Or that's what he called himself,' said Ron. 'We only had his word for it, that's what I say.'

'I saw his passport,' said Juliet. 'It was the first thing I asked for. He was called Jan Oakley all right.'

'There must be more than one lot of Oakleys around!' argued Ron.

'Not in Poland, I shouldn't think,' said Meredith.

'Can we stick to the point?' This from Minchin whose expression suggested an animal trainer whose lions were getting out of hand. Any minute now he'd take drastic disciplinary action.

'Right,' said Ron. 'There's an old potting shed in the grounds. It'd been locked up for donkey's years. I'd never been inside it, but when Miss Oakley told me they were going to sell the house, I thought I'd better take a look. Clear it out, you know.'

He paused and waited for some comment. When none came, he was forced to go on, his face reddening, his rooster appearance becoming increasingly marked.

'The door was locked with a padlock and I hadn't got a key so I had to unscrew the whole hasp. I got the door open and went in. You never saw such a mess. It was a real museum. Stuff had been put in there I reckon forty years ago or more and was still there. Well, most of it *is* still there,' added Ron, 'because what with one thing and another, I was interrupted and never got back to the job.' He cleared his throat. 'I started to take a look round. There were a lot of old bottles and tins, gardening stuff, fertiliser, weed-killer, that sort of thing. All the old-fashioned chemicals. You can't buy most of them now. Right at the back on one shelf I found a dark glass bottle, all dusty. The cap had rusted so I couldn't turn it, but I reckon from the weight it was half-full. The label had turned brown but I could see it was a fancy thing. They took a lot of trouble over everything in those days, even a label. You should see some of the old tools . . .'

Minchin shifted his bulk slightly and drew a deep breath.

Ron hurried on. 'I had a closer squint at the label and could make it out. I remember it pretty well.' He swallowed, his Adam's apple bobbing above the knot of his tie, and straightened his spine. '*Universal Rat and Mouse Poison,*' he declaimed. '*Guaranteed to free your home from vermin. Internationally acclaimed medal-winner.*' Abruptly his voice subsided to a stifled croak. '*Warning: Poisonous. Contains purest quality arsenic.*'

'What?' Minchin, Hayes and Pearce all spoke together.

'Now, I know what you're going to say . . .' began Ron.

'Do you, indeed?' growled Minchin.

'You'll say I should have gone straight up to the house and told Miss Oakley. But just at that very minute, I heard someone coming. It was a heavy step, not one of the ladies. So I put the bottle back on the shelf and went out to see who it was. It was him.'

'Who?' snapped Minchin.

'Jan. It was the first I'd heard or seen of him. I was suspicious. I thought he was a trespasser. We get them. I told Mr Markby – people just walk in like it was a public park. Anyway, after I'd finished sorting him out, I shut the door of the shed because I'd decided to carry on clearing it out later.'

'Did you lock it up?'

'Well, no,' admitted the unhappy Ron. 'I told you, I'd unscrewed the hasp. I just forgot the arsenic.'

'Forgot it?' asked Minchin in clear disbelief.

'Well, I had a lot on my mind!' countered Ron. 'What with the ladies selling up and my garden going to be built on, more than likely, and then this Jan turning up . . . It's not as though I expected anyone to go in the shed, is it? It'd been locked up for fifty years, I reckon. Only the ladies lived in the house, no kids likely to go ferreting about where they shouldn't be. Why should the ladies go in there? Neither of them did any gardening. I thought I'd be going back in there myself sooner than I did. Events overtook me, as you might say.'

Minchin looked as though he might say a great deal, but kept his peace.

'So,' continued Ron, 'the next time I thought about it was when Mrs Painter came.'

Minchin unclasped his hands and pointed at Juliet.

'No!' Ron shook his head furiously. 'That's Miss Painter, Dr Painter's sister. This was Mrs Painter, his wife.'

'Gawd, is she in on it too?' muttered Hayes.

'She's a county councillor,' said Ron, as if this explained matters. 'She'd heard about this Jan fellow and she came over to have a word with him, but he wasn't there. She was looking for him in the garden when she found me. I told her, I thought he was up to no good. She said they were all well aware of it and I wasn't to worry. Then she left. Of course, the minute she left – you know how it is – I remembered the arsenic and I wished I had told her about it, because being on the council, she'd know what to do with it.'

'Hang on.' Minchin raised a hand. 'Did this meeting with Mrs Painter take place in or near the potting shed?'

'No, it was over by the stableblock. I keep my tools there. If it'd been near the shed, I'd have remembered the arsenic.'

'This stableblock is where, in relation to the shed?' Minchin demanded.

'Other end of the property, near the house.' Ron stopped to review his story so far and observed, 'I know it sounds strange, but that's how it was. You see, I'd been so worried about Miss Oakley and her sister. I was trying to keep on eye on that Jan. I worked extra hours so I could watch him. I even went in on the Saturday he died. Normally I don't work Saturdays. Now, the next thing that happened was, he was dead. I didn't hear about it until the Monday morning when I turned up to do the garden as usual. I don't garden on a Sunday. The Good Book says you shouldn't work on the seventh day. I'm not a church-going man, but I was brought up properly. We all had to go to Sunday School, my dad saw to that. He said it instilled proper principles. If there was more Sunday School now, there'd be less of this juvenile crime. Children have to be told what's right.'

'This isn't a debate about juvenile crime,' said Hayes in his thin voice. 'Who told you Jan Oakley was dead?'

Ron stared at him resentfully. 'Miss Oakley told me. She said he'd been taken very ill on Saturday night and the ambulance took him to the hospital, but he'd died. I said I was sorry to hear it. That's true because I was sorry that she'd had the worry of it. But I wasn't sorry to hear he was out of it. He was a trouble-maker.'

'Ron . . .' murmured Meredith. It would be best if Ron just stuck to his account of the arsenic and avoided comments of that nature.

Minchin had heard her and glared. 'I don't think Mr Gladstone needs you to prompt him, Miss Mitchell! Perhaps you and Miss Painter would kindly wait in the corridor while Mr Gladstone concludes his statement?'

There was more upheaval while Ron's two ejected supporters took their resentful departure.

'I thought,' said Ron pathetically, when they'd gone, 'it'd be drink and drugs because it nearly always is, these days, isn't it? The papers are full of it. I thought perhaps he'd been swallowing those Ecstasy pills.' He looked appealingly at Pearce as if he hoped replacement support might come from this familiar quarter.

'He had some?' asked Minchin.

'I don't know,' said Ron, sounding affronted, 'but I've read about them. I thought it'd be the sort of thing he'd do, taking drugs and drinking. I wasn't surprised he died. Of course, later on, I heard he'd been poisoned but I still thought it would be accidental. He'd eaten something he oughtn't.' Ron's whole figure seemed to deflate. 'Then this morning, Miss Painter and Miss Mitchell told me it was arsenic. The fact was, I'd just been in the shed. I'd remembered the arsenic and I'd decided to telephone Mrs Painter about it, so as not to worry the Oakley ladies. Since Mrs Painter is on the council, she'd know what to do. But when I went to the shed, it wasn't there. I came out wondering what to do and saw Miss Painter. It was a terrible shock,' he concluded.

Minchin looked at Pearce. 'Inspector,' he said, 'could you arrange for Mr Gladstone to sign his statement? Give him a copy.'

'No problem,' said Pearce. 'Come on, Ron.'

'Just a sec,' said Minchin, raising a massive hand. 'Bring those two women back, would you?'

Pearce opened the door. Juliet and Meredith appeared with suspicious alacrity.

'I want you here,' said Minchin to them, 'because I want you to hear me say I'd prefer you didn't chat about this to anyone, all right, Mr Gladstone?' Ron nodded. 'Right, you two?' Minchin added to the two women in less than gallant tones.

'We wouldn't dream of it,' said Meredith starchily.

'Can't I tell my brother?' asked Juliet. 'He's been wondering about the source of the arsenic.'

'Why don't you let me tell him?' asked Minchin. He slapped both palms on the desk. 'Thank you all,' he said. 'Very much.'

They were dismissed.

'I understand,' said Meredith, determined to be polite – after all, these were newcomers, strangers to the area – 'that you and the inspector are going to be staying in my cottage. I mean, it's empty. I don't live in it now. It's fully furnished and equipped. I hope you'll be comfortable.'

'*Your* cottage?' said Minchin heavily. 'Now why doesn't that surprise me?'

Pearce, the moment he was free, called by Markby's office to give an account of the interview.

'Thought you'd like to be kept abreast of events, sir, as they say.'

'Absolutely, Dave. You'll report everything to Superintendent Minchin first, naturally. He's in charge of this. But I,' said Markby in a steely voice, 'am responsible for this outfit and I need to know what everyone in it is doing.'

Dave Pearce, not displeased at being cast in the role of mole, made his way to the canteen to get some lunch.

Sergeant Prescott was already there, demolishing the last of his sausage and chips. A lively murmur of conversation which had been going on in the room ceased abruptly as Pearce entered and then resumed.

Pearce dropped his packet of cheese and tomato sandwiches on the table by Prescott. 'Mind if I join you, Steve?'

'No, sir.' Prescott pushed aside his coffee cup. 'You just missed them.'

'Missed who?'

'The men from the Met.' Prescott gave Pearce a furtive look.

'Why didn't they stay?' asked Pearce. 'Didn't like the look of the grub?'

'Think they judged the place a bit full,' Prescott told him.

'They probably wanted to talk. Mr Minchin asked me how to find Fourways. He said he needed to see the layout for himself. I offered to drive them out there but they reckoned they'd like to go on their own.' Prescott flushed and with some hesitation asked, 'What are they like?'

Pearce broke open the triangular plastic sandwich box and extracted a dry-looking wedge of brown bread. He prised the two pieces apart and looked less than impressed with the small amount of cheese and unripe tomato within. 'I used to bring my own,' he said. 'I reckon I'm going to start doing that again. This is rubbish.'

'I didn't mean the sandwich, sir, I meant—'

'I know what you meant, Steve. I'm sure Superintendent Minchin and DI Hayes will go through the evidence like a dose of salts and solve our case before we've got time to work out what they're doing. Show us rural plods how it's done.'

Prescott cleared his throat. 'I don't know if I ought to mention this, sir, but they've already got themselves a couple of nicknames.'

'That was quick,' said Pearce, who knew that the canteen liked to pin its own labels on any newcomers, especially if, like Minchin and Hayes, they stood out from the crowd.

'They, um, they're calling them Flash Harry and The Ferret.'

Pearce burst into laughter and nearly choked on his sandwich.

'Thought it'd cheer you up a bit,' said Prescott comfortably.

'It's a consolation, Steve,' said Pearce. 'Thanks for telling me.'

He wondered whether it would be out of order to pass that bit of information on to Markby and decided that, sadly, it probably would.

Chapter Twenty-One

The afternoon had turned very warm. Within the grounds of Fourways the heat was trapped, absorbed and reflected by the high stone boundary wall, the walls of the outbuildings and by the house itself. The old place slumbered in a dark mustard-coloured sleep against the background of trees and rolling countryside. Puffs of white cloud hung motionless above it, testimony to the lack of breeze. The impression was of an oil painting. It was there but somehow not real.

Minchin and Hayes stood just inside the entrance by the castellated yew hedge and surveyed it all in silence. They seemed awed by the sight.

Hayes rallied first. 'Not bad, is it, being a country copper? Driving round the countryside, calling at a few places like this one. Beats trying to find your way in and out of a high-rise housing estate without being duffed up and coming back to find your car tyres slashed.'

'That place, Bamford, is bigger than I thought it would be.' Minchin squinted appraisingly at Fourways. 'I expect they've got their drunks, druggies and hooligans.'

'Amateurs,' said Hayes bitterly, dismissing Bamford's criminal element. 'They want to have to deal with real hard cases.'

Minchin had turned his attention to the yew hedge. 'Fancy bit of work, this. What do you reckon to the old boy? Think he was genuine?'

Hayes shrugged. 'If I'd found a bottle of arsenic I wouldn't just stick it back on the shelf and forget about it. But then, perhaps if you live round here, you don't worry about things so much. One day must be much like another. People get a bit lax about things. He didn't like the dead man, did he?'

'Seems no one did.'

'Going to interview the old girls?'

'Not today. I want to get a general impression of the layout. We'll find this potting shed and the stableblock, and take it from there. Soon enough tomorrow to tackle the owners.'

At the mention of owning such a property, Hayes's attention was redirected to the house itself. 'Rum-looking place, isn't it? Like the background for a horror film, all funny shapes, pointed windows like a church and what's that turret doing stuck up there?'

'It's a folly,' opined Minchin. 'That's what they did in the old days when they had more money than they could spend. They built follies.'

'What do you reckon it's all worth?'

'Enough to kill for,' said Minchin briefly. 'Come on.'

Hayes extracted a cigarette from a crushed packet and lit up. They set off side by side in silence. Methodically they toured the outer perimeters of the property and then took it section by section. They found the potting shed and hunted their way through the contents, taking a side of the building each.

'OK?' asked Minchin.

'OK,' said Hayes. 'Provided none of 'em thinks of making

a bomb. Seen those sacks of fertiliser?'

They moved on to the stables. In the old tackroom they observed signs of Ron's occupation, his camping stove and kettle, mug, jar of coffee, folded copy of the day's newspaper.

'Got himself a nice comfy little spot here,' said Hayes. 'Just what would he do to hang on to it?'

Minchin took a seat on the bench. 'We know when the gardener found the arsenic. We don't know when it went missing. The shed was unlocked. Anyone could've gone in there.' He began ticking off names on his massive fingers. 'We know Gladstone was in there. Either of the old ladies up at the house could've gone in there. The dead bloke could've gone in there, come to that. Then there's this woman, Mrs Painter. She could've gone in there when she was looking for the gardener. Either of those two other women, Juliet Painter and Meredith Mitchell, could've gone in there. There are no gates to this place. Anyone passing by could've walked in and looked around to see if there was anything he could nick.'

'Well, that bleedin' narrows it down,' said Hayes sarcastically.

'Doesn't it just?' Minchin gave a thin smile and leaned his head back against the wall. His eyes studied the interior of the tackroom, taking in the harness pegs. 'Yes,' he said softly. 'Someone would kill for this place.'

There was a scrape of footstep outside. They exchanged glances. Hayes stubbed out his cigarette on the floor and ground the butt into the dust with the sole of his shoe.

'Who's there?' asked an uncertain, elderly female voice.

'It's all right, madam,' called back Minchin. 'It's the police.'

The tackroom door creaked and Damaris Oakley appeared in the opening. She was wearing another of her late father's hats, a yellowed panama, and an old-fashioned linen dress with a tucked bodice. On her feet she had well-worn canvas shoes which had split at both toecaps.

'I don't believe,' she said reproachfully, 'that I know you.'

Minchin handed over his warrant card and introduced the inspector. 'We've come down from London, madam, to give a hand.'

'Oh yes, of course. Alan said you would be coming. Why are you in here?' Damaris had studied the card carefully and now returned it. 'I'm Damaris Oakley.'

'Just looking around, Miss Oakley.'

'The other police, our local force, have already done that,' she told him. 'Do you wish to speak to me or to my sister? My sister's taking a nap. She's found all this a great strain.'

'We don't need to trouble either of you just now,' Minchin said. 'One of us will call tomorrow when we've had a chance to bone up on the details. The inspector and I only arrived today.'

She gazed at them with a return of her uncertain manner. 'Don't misunderstand me, but I really can't see why they sent you all the way from London.'

'Ours not to question why,' said Minchin in tones which were a little too placatory.

Damaris gave him a quelling look. 'Quite. Though I for one certainly hope there won't be any more dying.'

The two London men look at her, startled. 'You expect another death?' Minchin asked.

'No, of course I don't. I didn't expect the first one. One doesn't,' said Damaris with asperity. 'I was referring to the verse you quoted. It is, of course, "theirs" not "ours", as you probably know. *Theirs not to question why, Theirs but to do or die.* The Charge of the Light Brigade. My father was very fond of quoting Tennyson.' She paused and reflected. 'Now I see things in that poem I never saw when I read it as a girl. Someone should have asked why, shouldn't he? Doing and dying doesn't help anyone. We shall look forward to seeing you again, Superintendent.'

She departed.

'Is she bonkers or what?' asked Hayes.

'No . . .' An appreciative smile spread over Minchin's face. 'She's a canny old bird.'

'Think she'd murder someone?'

'What? Oh yes,' said Minchin. 'If she decided on it, she'd do it. She might even see it as her duty, if he was a threat. That generation is very keen on duty. Well, let's get back to that pub we passed on the way here and see if we're not too late to get something to eat.'

They drew into the car park of The Feathers a few minutes later and climbed out of the car to subject the pub to the kind of scrutiny they'd given Fourways.

'Quite a nice old place,' said Hayes approvingly. 'Say what you like about the country, they've got some decent pubs.'

They approached the building. As the day was warm, some drinkers had established themselves outside at trestle tables. They appeared to be members of a ramblers' club, judging by their stout boots. Minchin and Hayes threaded their way through them to reach the door and stepped inside.

As if possessed of extra-sensory perception, Dolores Forbes materialised immediately in front of them, arms folded.

'More cops,' she said belligerently. 'As if I haven't had enough of answering questions. At least the other bloke came before we opened. What do you two want?'

'Just a spot of lunch, darling,' replied Minchin, taking this reception in his stride.

Dolores mellowed and unfolded her arms, giving them a better view of her magnificent bosom. 'That's all right, then. Why don't you go over there in the corner, give yourselves a bit of privacy? I'll fetch a menu. The special today is chilli con carne.'

'No bangers and mash?' asked Hayes wistfully.

'Course I can do you bangers and mash!' Dolores told him. 'Darren!'

Their attention was directed to the subdued individual behind the bar.

'Give these gents a drink on the house!'

At this Darren looked as if he couldn't believe his ears. He blinked nervously, 'Yes, Dolores.'

Dolores smiled benignly on Minchin. 'Be with you in a jiff.'

'She's a bit of all right,' commented Hayes as they settled themselves in the corner as directed, having been served with a couple of pints by Darren, who still looked in a state of shock.

'Chatty type,' said Minchin. 'Let's see what she's got to say about that house.' He jerked his head in the general direction of Fourways.

Their food arrived promptly and they set about it. First things first. Only when they'd eaten, and declined lemon meringue pudding, did Minchin turn to official matters. He betook himself to the bar where Dolores now presided. Darren had been demoted to some kitchen duty.

'Lovely grub,' said Minchin. 'We'll have another couple of pints. Have one yourself, whatever you drink.'

'Thanks,' said Dolores. 'I'll have a rum and Coke. Sure you won't have the lemon meringue? I made it myself.'

'I'm tempted, believe me,' lied Minchin with impressive sincerity. 'But I've got to watch the old figure.' He patted his stomach.

'Go on,' said Dolores, 'fine-looking bloke like you? You don't have to worry. I like a man with a bit of meat on his bones myself.'

Perhaps unfortunately Darren chose that moment to reappear in all his weediness. 'Dolores? The bakery's on the phone about those baguettes you sent back.'

'Well, deal with it, Darren!' she ordered tetchily, and he scurried away.

'My former husband,' continued Dolores to Minchin, 'was a big bloke. He used to work out at the gym. We didn't last long as a married couple, me and Charlie. He was a Londoner. I always say Londoners have got style. Not like this lot,' she concluded resentfully as one of the ramblers ventured to approach the bar.

Whilst the rambler was being served with a round of shandies, Minchin glanced up at the plate screwed to the oak lintel above the bar. It stated the name of the licensee of this establishment to be Dolores Bernadette Forbes. The only Charlie Forbes he knew of had been a bank-robber and was currently serving time in Wormwood Scrubs.

'Right,' he said, sipping his pint and exchanging a look with Hayes who was still at the corner table and had lit up. He was already surrounded by a haze of blue smoke.

Dolores had returned. 'You want to know about him, don't you, the bloke who was poisoned? He wasn't poisoned here, you know!' Her normal combative manner returned.

'Course not,' said Minchin easily and Dolores relaxed. 'He ate here, did he?'

'Every evening, cheapest thing on the menu. He didn't pay for it. The old girls were picking up the bill. He was a real sponger. I couldn't stand him. I know the type, see. Pity he got himself murdered, of course. Still, he probably asked for it.'

'Yeah, well . . .' mumbled Minchin.

Dolores, in full flow now, leaned on the bar with the result that Minchin now found himself staring down her cleavage. He closed his eyes briefly.

'The other copper who was here asked whether I'd seen that Oakley talking to anyone. I told him I hadn't. Well, only Superintendent Markby and his ladyfriend. But after he'd left, I remembered.'

Minchin froze with his pint halfway to his mouth. 'Yes?'

'See, the other copper asked if I'd seen Oakley talking to anyone in the pub, here.' Dolores indicated their surroundings. 'That's what put me off. Because it wasn't inside the pub, it was outside, in the car park. It was on the Thursday evening. I remember because that was the first evening this year it had been hot enough for us to have much trade outside at the tables. So I was nipping back and forth in and out of the pub and that's how I saw him. I thought he'd left, Oakley, and I was surprised to see him in the car park out there, talking to a bloke who'd got out of a car. Now I knew that feller – it was Dudley Newman. He's a builder, got a lot of money and a big house. Anyway, Newman hadn't been in the pub or I'd have noticed. So I watched and after a bit of chit-chat, Oakley went on his way but Newman, he got back in his car and drove off. So,' said Dolores triumphantly, 'that means he hadn't come out here to have a drink. He'd come out here to see that Oakley, right? And what could they have to talk about? Monkey business, if you ask me.'

'Very likely, Dolores, and thanks,' Minchin raised his glass. 'Cheers!'

Dave Pearce, meanwhile, was locked in eye-contact with an Alsatian. Since Sergeant Steve Prescott had told him the newcomers had left for Fourways, he'd decided to spend his time checking out Kenny Joss. He'd made his way to Kenny's home and been directed to the garage. It was a large affair, easily housing two vehicles, and apparently fitted out as a workshop as well. A sign above the door read *K. Joss. Taxi Service*. A telephone number followed. Sounds of work, the scrape of metal against metal, a low tuneless whistling, indicated Kenny was inside. But between them stood the Alsatian.

It was the long-haired sort, dark brown with bright eyes. Its mouth, half-open to pant in the hot sunshine, displayed the tips of a sharp set of teeth. Dave moved a step forward. The Alsatian barked.

'All right,' said Dave to it. 'Have it your own way.' He raised his voice. 'Mr Joss?'

The sound of tinkering ceased. Kenny Joss put his head through the doorway. 'Hello,' he said. 'Don't mind the dog. He's just a big softie.'

'I'd appreciate it,' said Pearce, 'if you'd move him out of the way, all the same. Police,' he added.

'I know you're the police,' said Kenny. 'Here, Bruce, go and sit down, go on.'

Bruce wagged his tail and strolled to the corner of the garage where a dirty scrap of blanket had been spread on the ground. He subsided on to it and put his nose on his paws, keeping his bright gaze fixed on Pearce.

'What do you want, then?' asked Kenny, wiping his hands on a greasy rag.

'It's in connection with our investigations into the death of Jan Oakley,' Pearce began and was interrupted.

'I don't know nothing about that.'

'You visited the house on the day he died,' countered Pearce.

'So what if I did? It was business, not what I'd call a visit. I took the two old women shopping. I take them every Saturday. Took 'em, brought 'em back. End of story. What's more, I've already told one of your blokes this. He wanted to know what time I'd arrived and what time I got back. I told him. He wrote it down.'

Pearce had dealt with members of the Joss clan before and their invariable reaction to any hint of impropriety was instant and blanket denial. He therefore took no notice of any of Kenny's protestations.

'Did you go in the house?'

'Not when I called for them, no, I didn't. I had a word with Ron in the garden and then I went round to the kitchen door because that's usually open. I stuck my head through and whistled.'

'Whistled?' Pearce looked startled.

'Just to attract attention, you know. Then I called out, "Anyone at home? Taxi's here," or words to that effect. They

288

know me. I rag them a bit. They don't mind. They're nice old girls.'

'What happened next?' Pearce doubted the Oakleys appreciated being whistled up like a sheepdog.

'Nothing happened next,' said Kenny irritably. 'They came into the kitchen. They were all ready to leave, dressed up, both got funny hats on. They followed me to the taxi and I drove them into town. I arranged what time to pick them up and where. It was the usual place, outside The Crown. That's it.'

Pearce frowned. 'Did you see if they locked the kitchen door when they left? It's got an old-fashioned lock as I remember.'

'Couldn't say. They were behind me. I doubt it. They weren't ones for locking up. Used to being there on their own. I used to tell them to be more careful.'

'Did you see Jan Oakley?'

Kenny hesitated. 'No, not when I picked them up.'

'You saw him later?'

A certain unease had entered Kenny's manner and Pearce didn't miss it. 'When you returned to the house, was he there?'

'Yeah, he was there,' admitted Kenny. 'I didn't speak to him. I just sort of glimpsed him.'

'Where?'

'Going out the door.'

'Which door?'

'The kitchen door.'

Pearce felt his head begin to swim. 'Let's start this again,' he said. 'Talk me through what you did when you brought the Oakleys home.'

Kenny cleared his throat. The Alsatian pricked its ears

and transferred its scrutiny from Pearce to its master. Yes, thought Pearce, something's worrying our Kenny and both the dog and I know it!

'I drove up to the house,' Kenny began carefully, 'and I parked out front by that fountain thing. It hasn't got any water in it but I suppose it's a fountain. You know it?' Pearce nodded and Kenny went on, 'I always park there. I helped them out of the car. They went ahead of me indoors—'

'Through the kitchen door again?'

Kenny shook his head. 'No, they opened up the front door and went in that way. But I used the kitchen door.'

'You went in?'

'Of course I went in.' Kenny sounded more annoyed than defensive. 'I always carry their bags in. They're old folk. Anyway, it's all part of the service. People expect a bit of help from a taxi-driver.'

And the taxi-driver expects a tip, thought Pearce, but only said, 'Go on, then.'

'Right. I got their bags out of the boot and took them round to the kitchen. I put a couple of perishables in the fridge for them and left the rest on the table.'

'And you saw Jan Oakley. Was he in the kitchen?'

The dog pricked its ears again. Peace mentally thanked it. It was better than a lie detector was that dog, and doing its master no favours at all.

'He came out the kitchen door as I went in,' said Kenny. 'He just brushed past me. I said hello and he said something similar. That was it. We didn't what you'd call speak, and that's the truth.'

That wasn't quite it. There was something wrong here but Pearce couldn't work out what it was. He asked, 'What about the two women? Did you see them again? For them to pay you?'

'They've got an account,' said Kenny. 'I tot it up and they pay me once a month. They're regulars of mine.'

'So you just went off and didn't see them again?'

The dog whined softly in its throat. 'I saw them to say goodbye,' Kenny said. 'They were in the hallway, I went through there and just said I'd see them the next week. Then I left.'

'Thank you, Mr Joss,' said Pearce. Kenny looked relieved but his relief was shortlived. 'No doubt we'll be in touch again,' Pearce added.

'Feel free,' said Kenny, plainly disgruntled. He turned to stride back into his garage but at the entrance paused and looked back. 'Here!' he called out.

Pearce, about to get in his car, looked up.

'Instead of bothering me,' Kenny called, 'why don't you go bothering Dudley Newman?'

'Newman, the builder?' Newman was a well-known local figure but this was the first time Pearce had heard his name mentioned in connection with the case. He was curious. 'What's he got to do with it?'

'How should I know? But I saw that Jan bloke in town one lunchtime, chatting to Newman in a pub. It wasn't The Crown, it was, let's see . . .' Kenny frowned, 'I think it was The George. Don't ask me exactly which day it was though I fancy it was the Friday.' He nodded to Pearce and disappeared inside the garage.

The Josses didn't normally give out information to the police on a point of principle. That Kenny had done so now indicated how rattled he was. Pearce was being diverted to other quarry. Whether profitably or not, was another matter.

'Good dog!' said Pearce to the Alsatian.

James Holland sat in his study working on a sermon for the forthcoming Sunday. He wasn't getting on very well. Despite frequent reference to a well-thumbed sermon crib and much scratching of his head and bushy beard, his notes hadn't progressed beyond a single sheet. From time to time, his gaze wandered wistfully to *Superbike* magazine, lying on a chair nearby. A tap at the French windows caught his attention. He looked up, saw who his visitor was and put down his pen with relief.

'It's open!' he called, but got up anyway to usher her in.

Juliet Painter stepped over the sill. 'Bad moment, James?' She indicated the unfinished sermon notes.

'Good moment,' said the vicar. 'I'm suffering from writer's block. I was about to stop and make a cup of coffee. Now I've got a visitor, I can upgrade that to gooseberry wine as made by a parishioner. Very good it is, too, I can promise you. Care for a glass?' He walked to his modest drinks' cabinet and opened the door.

Juliet had seen *Superbike* lying on the chair and hid a grin. 'Love a glass of gooseberry firewater, James.'

'What can I do for you?' he asked when they were comfortably settled with a glass apiece. 'Or is this just a social call?'

'Part social, part business,' she admitted. 'You'll guess what's brought me. It's this wretched affair of Jan's murder and what to do about the Oakleys. Have you seen them recently?'

He nodded. 'I called round yesterday evening. I thought

they were bearing up very well, everything considered. They're very grateful for your help and support.'

She grimaced. 'Yes, I know they are. It's something of a burden. If I'd known, when I agreed to help them hunt for a flat and dispose of Fourways, that I'd end up being interrogated by the police . . .'

'We none of us knew,' said Father Holland. 'How could we?'

Juliet was thoughtful, searching for her words. 'It's – unpleasant. There's a nastiness to it all. Murder is nasty by its very nature but this is – wicked.'

'Murder is wicked,' said the vicar. 'But I know what you mean. I like to read whodunnits, but this is real. It happened in our community. It happened to someone we'd met. It took place at a house we know well and involves people we'd wish to protect and shield from any kind of stress. That's the difference between fiction and reality.' He brightened. 'That's it! That'll do for the theme of my sermon. I'll talk to the congregation about that.'

'Sorry I shan't be there to hear you,' said Juliet. 'My churchgoing has slipped a bit. I go along at Christmas and Easter.' She sipped her wine. 'Gosh, this is powerful stuff! Who made it?'

'Mrs Harmer, my housekeeper, to tell you the truth. Keep it quiet. She's coy about it. Her father was a leading light of the temperance movement in the town.'

'Secret vice, eh?' Juliet managed a brief grin. 'There's been a development, James.'

'I had heard,' he said, 'that a couple of super-detectives from London were expected.'

'They're here and I've seen them. I don't know how good

they are at their jobs. One looks like a prosperous bank-robber and the other looks like a Dickensian pickpocket.' Juliet spoke with a ferocity which the vicar guessed indicated some personal contact with the gentlemen in question.

'Been grilling you?' he asked, chuckling. 'Wish 'em luck!' He raised his glass to the absent Met men.

'I'm not supposed to tell you about this,' said Juliet. 'If I do, can you keep it quiet?'

'If you're not supposed to tell me, perhaps you shouldn't?'

'I want to. Get it off my chest.'

'Ah,' he said. 'Then consider your problem safe under the seal of the confessional.'

'Fair enough. It's only a temporary ban on talking about it, anyway. You knew that Jan was done in with arsenic?' He nodded and she went on, 'Now we know where it came from. Ron Gladstone had found an old bottle of rat poison in a locked shed. He meant to get rid of it but forgot and when he remembered and went to find it, it'd gone. Meredith and I took him over to Regional HQ to tell the cops and we ran straight into Minchin and Hayes. That's the two London men. Poor Ron was in a terrible state,' her tone became indignant, 'and that man Minchin was no help at all!'

There was silence during which Father Holland finished his gooseberry wine, poured out another for himself and topped up his visitor's glass. 'Shed was kept locked, you say?' he asked.

'Was locked prior to Ron's discovery of the arsenic. He left it unlocked afterwards. He's been very stupid about it and he knows it. The thing is, who took it?'

James Holland said slowly, 'Anyone could've taken it. Who knew it was there? That's the real question.'

294

'Only Ron that we know of. But Ron didn't move it. Ron didn't use it to poison Jan, either. If he had, he would have kept quiet about the arsenic. You see?' Juliet grew agitated. 'You see what this has done? We're suspecting one another. We're all scratching round for alibis. Worst of all, we've all got guilty consciences because we didn't like Jan. Did you meet him, James?'

'Pam asked me to talk to him. As it happened I ran into him in town shortly afterwards.' The vicar frowned. 'He was standing in front of an estate agent's window, studying all the cards with house details.'

Juliet scowled. 'I can guess what he was doing. He was trying to work out how much Fourways was worth. I don't believe a word of what he said to Meredith.' Seeing the vicar's bushy eyebrows twitch, she added, 'Meredith invited him along to tea. It was my idea. I thought she could talk him into dropping his claim on Fourways. He told her he had. But I don't believe it, not for one minute. How did you know it was Jan?'

'Ah, because Damaris described him to me with extraordinary accuracy. Most people give you age, height and colouring when they describe someone. Damaris was very insistent that Jan had what she called an aura. I thought she was overdoing it but funnily enough, when I saw him, I understood what she meant. Good-looking bloke, mind you.'

'I didn't think so,' said Juliet firmly.

'Oh? Well, I knew I'd found my man, so I introduced myself. He was a bit startled.'

'People are, when they meet you, James,' said Juliet, grinning. 'You weren't wearing your biker's leathers, were you?'

'Sadly, no. I was wearing pretty much what I'm wearing now,' Father Holland indicated his well-worn corduroy trousers and sagging Aran sweater. 'Jan was very chatty. He told me how much he had longed to come to England and see the family home. He enthused about beautiful Bamford. I like Bamford,' said the vicar, 'but beautiful it ain't. However, I suppose he was being polite. He seemed a harmless enough chap. But then, over the years I've met all kinds of harmless-looking fellows who've turned out to be every kind of rogue. I stressed to him that his cousins, as he called them, were in very reduced circumstances. I was hoping he'd take the hint and not trespass on their hospitality for much longer. He said he was very sorry to see them living as they do, though he did seem worried about the "poor old house". He did, I have to confess, seem more interested in the house than in its inhabitants.'

'See?' said Juliet moodily, twisting the end of her long braid of hair round her finger. 'He came to England to make money by hook or by crook. He didn't just give up the idea, no matter what he told Meredith.' She sighed. 'I wish Pam had got hold of him. Pam at full steam is pretty frightening.'

'Yes,' said the vicar reminiscently. 'She is.'

Juliet leaned back in the battered leather-covered armchair. 'You've got to stand up to Pam, it's the only way. I know she keeps trying to throw us together, James, but whilst I see you as a dear and valued friend, I don't see myself as your wife. I thought you'd like to know that.'

He spread his hands in a rueful gesture. 'What can I say?'

'Don't say anything. I'm just telling you for the record.' She stopped twisting her hair and put her head on one side. 'Besides, I've long ago guessed where your heart lies.'

Father Holland looked startled and what could be seen of his features between thatch of black hair and beard, turned dusky pink.

'It's Meredith, isn't it?' said the ruthless Juliet. 'You've been sweet on her for ages. Ever since she first turned up in our neck of the woods. Don't panic, James. I won't tell anyone. It's like your seal of the confessional. I may not reveal it.'

'Thank you,' he said after a moment. 'But how did you guess? Or am I that obvious? Because if I am, other people will guess it too. I shouldn't like that to happen.'

'Poor James. I only guessed because I know you so well. Besides, I decided that since you had absolutely no romantic interest in me, there had to be someone else.'

He smiled. 'I remain in the tender care of Mrs Harmer, then.'

As if on cue there came a distant crash from the kitchen. It was followed by a patter of footsteps and the vicar's redoubtable housekeeper appeared in the doorway.

'Excuse me, I'm sure,' she said, staring hard at Juliet and then at the bottle of gooseberry wine. 'I come to say, Vicar, that lunch will be ready in fifteen minutes. Is the young lady staying? I expect the shepherd's pie will stretch to two. Don't know about the rice pudding. It's what's left from yesterday. Just a little dishful.'

'I have to go,' said Juliet. 'Thank you, anyway, Mrs Harmer.' Ostentatiously she set down her empty glass. Mrs Harmer reddened and withdrew.

Juliet grimaced. 'I'll come over and cook you supper tonight, if you like. I can do better than shepherd's pie and left-over rice pud. I make a very good spaghetti bolognese.'

'You're on!' said the vicar with feeling.

'Great. I'll bring the ingredients with me. Around seven?'

'I'll provide the wine.' He hauled himself from his chair. 'I know you're worried about the Oakleys but it will work itself out, either with the help of these London detectives or without them. Don't be tempted to underestimate them, will you? That would be a serious error.'

'You bet it'll work itself out,' said Juliet. 'Meredith and I are on the case!'

Chapter Twenty-Two

'I can't think why you see the need to talk to me, Inspector,' said Dudley Newman. He had risen from his chair behind his desk but not left it. He indicated a facing chair to his visitor, but didn't offer to shake Dave Pearce's hand. The small room was cluttered with filing cabinets and strewn with papers and loose files. Various pieces of correspondence and copies of estimates were pinned to a cork board. It looked untidy but it wasn't. It was kept that way to impress on a visitor that Newman was a successful man whose time was precious.

Pearce had gained entry to the builder's inner sanctum after some argument with a secretary. To claims that Mr Newman was busy, he'd replied that he was also busy. He'd met a suggestion that he make an appointment by asking if there was some reason Mr Newman might not wish to see him. The secretary had grown flustered, bad-tempered, indignant. But she buzzed him through after a brief exchange with her boss.

So here was Newman himself, large, outwardly imperturbable, but beneath the surface annoyed. If he showed any emotion, he seemed reproachful. He wanted the police officer to feel he was the one being unreasonable. But Pearce, though young in years, had been a policeman for too long. Inconvenient it might be for Newman to have him here. Like Rhett Butler, Pearce didn't give a damn.

'We're talking to everyone who met Jan Oakley during the short time he was in the country before he died.' Pearce met the builder's eye. 'And you had a chat to him, didn't you? In a pub one lunchtime? We have a witness.'

'I'd like to know who it is!' Newman snapped. He paused, perhaps hoping Pearce would oblige with a name. Pearce said nothing. Newman hunched his shoulders and slapped his palms on his desk. 'Yes, I had a word with him. I'll be frank with you. There's no reason why I shouldn't be. I – ' Newman emphasised the pronoun. '*I* have nothing to hide.'

Pearce still waited. Sometimes one learnt more by waiting than by asking. Ask Newman a question and he'd answer it – no more. Leave him to fill the silence and he might be tempted to reveal a lot more. But he was surprised by Newman's next words.

'You married, Inspector?'

'Yes,' Pearce admitted.

'I expect you and your wife will be buying your first home.'

'What's this got to do with it?' asked Pearce, niggled.

Newman ignored his visitor's irritation. 'You found it difficult, I dare say, to find a suitable place. Young professional couples do, around here. You want to put your money in solid bricks and mortar. You want a place that looks good. You're thinking about a family in a few years' time so you want the space. You probably run two cars and want a double garage. Above all, you want to feel sure that when the time comes for you to sell and move on, you'll find a buyer quickly and he'll be prepared to pay the sort of price you'll be asking for your property. Am I right?'

'What are you trying to do? Sell me a house?' demanded Pearce.

Newman leaned across the desk and shook a finger at him. 'No. You've got a house. I'm thinking of selling houses to people like you who *haven't* got a house. People with two incomes who want a place with character and style but modern, easy upkeep. You don't want a big garden. You haven't got time for it. You want somewhere new, because new means nothing should need doing to the place for years. That's the kind of house I want to build on the land where Fourways stands at present. I'm not interested in building starter homes. I'm looking at people who can pay a bit more for something better. Besides, starter home developments have got themselves poor publicity in the past and getting planning permission isn't so easy as it once was. But getting permission to build a small number of quality homes which will add to the neighbourhood, not detract from it – now we're talking.'

'We're talking,' said Pearce patiently. 'But not about Jan Oakley.'

Newman leaned back and chuckled. 'Don't throw you off the scent, do I?'

'Were you trying to?' Pearce asked him.

Newman shook his head. 'No, and as it happens, we *are* talking about him. I was trying to explain to you why I felt I needed to speak to Jan Oakley. I've had my eye on Fourways for some time. I knew that the time was nearing when the old ladies would either die or move out. Either way, that big piece of ground would be coming on the market, so I made my plans. I thought – we all thought, didn't we? – that there was no other family. To say I was surprised when I heard some cousin or other had turned up from abroad somewhere, is hardly adequate. I was bloody annoyed. He could throw a spanner in the works. I've been waiting a long time for this opportunity and I didn't mean to let it slip. I still don't. I didn't want to phone the house or write to him. I didn't want the old women knowing what I was about.'

Newman noticed the dry look on his visitor's face. 'Well,' he said comfortably, 'No need to worry them, was there?'

'Go on,' said Pearce.

'Right. I found out that he ate every evening at The Feathers, but that didn't suit me. It's too near the house and Dolores Forbes might tell one of the Oakley sisters of my interest. In fact, knowing Dolores, she'd certainly pass it on if she saw me sitting there chatting to him. So I went up there one evening and waited in the car park until he showed up. I got out of the car and called him over, told him who I was and arranged to meet him the next day in The George. That was the Thursday evening. Friday lunchtime, he turned up as arranged and I bought him lunch.' It was Newman's turn to give a dry smile. 'I had him sussed out straight away! He was the sort who never puts his hand in his pocket. I paid for the food and all the beer. He never even suggested he buy me a pint.'

'Why should he?' asked Pearce. 'You'd invited him to be there.'

'Fair enough. But he wasn't a spender. He was a con man – I'd put my last penny on it. I told him my interest in

Fourways, and asked him what his was. He had some plan or other up his sleeve, I was sure of that. He wasn't visiting the old girls just to show family solidarity. His interest was money. He told me there was a will. It'd been made years ago by his great-grandfather, and it entitled him to a half share in Fourways. He was planning to put it before the English courts, he said. If he did, it would hold up the sale. However, if I were prepared to pay him a suitable amount, he'd withdraw that threat. Forget about the will. Let the sale go ahead.'

Pearce snorted derisively.

Newman nodded agreement. 'Too true. I wasn't born yesterday. If there really *was* a will and it really gave him a half share in Fourways, he wouldn't be trying to cut a deal with me. Or if it did exist, I couldn't trust him to hold to any agreement we made. But I decided pretty quickly that either there was no will, or it would be thrown out by a British court. I suggested as much to him. He didn't argue. He saw I'd seen through that ploy so he didn't waste any more time on it. Just changed his tune and came up with a new idea. That, more than anything, convinced me he was a crook.'

Dudley Newman eyed Pearce and smiled. 'Perhaps you think I'm a bit of a sharp operator. Perhaps I am. But there's a big difference between that and being a twister. Oakley was a twister. I'm an honest man. I don't lie. I don't cheat. I look out for my own interest, first and foremost, but that's not illegal.'

Pearce, listening to this with growing distaste though he knew the man was right, responded, 'All right. What did you agree with him in the end?'

'Nothing. He said, if that was the way I felt about it, we'd nothing further to discuss. He would withdraw his objections to the sale and let it go ahead, anyway. He was sure his cousins would act fairly by him. What he meant was, he could bamboozle them into parting with a share of the resulting windfall.'

'And you were prepared to let him do that? Badger those two old women into parting with money they could ill afford? Even though this claim of his was probably entirely imaginary? Even though you'd judged him a con man?' Pearce's voice was sharp. He didn't need to pretend he approved of Newman's attitude. Newman knew he didn't. Knew and didn't care. As he'd said, it wasn't illegal.

'Not my responsibility, Inspector,' said Newman, almost gently. 'None of my business.' He eased himself back into his chair which creaked protestingly. 'As it happens, any misgivings I might have had were taken care of when I found out that Juliet Painter was advising the Oakley sisters. Juliet has a shrewd business brain. She'd look after their interests, I was sure of that.'

'Convenient for you, that,' said Pearce. 'Salve your conscience.'

Newman might have taken this as an insult. Instead he took it seriously. 'If I'd listened to what you'd call my conscience, I wouldn't be sitting here today, head of my own successful business, having done as well as I have. If a man's got a tender conscience, he should enter the church, become a social worker.' Newman's look became malicious. 'Join the police?'

Pearce got to his feet. 'Thanks for your time,' he said abruptly.

'My pleasure, Inspector. I'm always ready to support the police.'

When Pearce got back to HQ he made his way, with some reluctance, to the temporary office assigned to Minchin. He found the superintendent there, alone, shuffling papers and wrestling with a drawer in the elderly desk with which he'd been provided. Pearce wondered uneasily where Hayes was.

The drawer shot out and cracked Minchin's knee. He swore and, rubbing the afflicted area, abandoned what he was doing to turn his attention to Pearce. 'Hello, Dave. Come to report?' Despite the pain he was in and his obvious dissatisfaction with his accommodation, his tone was relaxed and cheery.

Pearce wasn't impressed by fake camaraderie. In fact, he resented it. He wasn't one of Minchin's men. He was someone who'd been assigned to Minchin, much against his will, and Minchin knew it. The use of a first name cut no ice. Stiffly, he said, 'Yes, sir.'

Minchin's broad face showed no reaction to the implied rebuke. 'Let's have it then.' He nodded at the empty chair.

Pearce sat down. 'I've been talking to a couple of people. One of them was Kenny Joss, who runs a taxi service and drove the Oakley women to and from town on a shopping expedition on the Saturday afternoon. He'll be in the file. The other was a local builder called Newman.'

'What?' Minchin asked sharply, his bonhomie vanishing. 'Dudley Newman?'

'Yes.' Pearce had no idea how Minchin knew about the builder. 'Joss saw him talking to Jan Oakley in a pub in town, The George.'

'Bloody hell!' Minchin said vehemently. 'Why didn't you check with me before you went haring off to see this Newman?'

'You weren't here,' said Pearce, reddening. 'And I wasn't aware you wanted the investigation held up.'

Minchin glowered at him. 'No one's holding up investigations. As it happens, Mickey Hayes has just gone off to see this Newman cove. So that's two visits from us Newman will have in one day and a right fool Mickey will look when he turns up only to be told you've just left.'

Pearce did his best to disguise his pleasure at the thought of Hayes being made to look foolish. 'How did you get on to Newman, Mr Minchin?' he asked curiously.

'Woman at the pub near the house, Mrs Forbes, saw Newman talking to Oakley one evening in the car park,' Minchin told him briefly, still simmering with resentment.

'Oh, right, that ties in with what Newman told me, then,' Pearce said complacently. 'I'll get it all written up for you. Basically, Newman wants the land the house stands on and he was worried Oakley would throw a spanner in the works. He wanted to suss him out. He reckoned Oakley was a bit of a con man but on the whole, he didn't have to worry about him, after all. He put him down as a small-time chiseler.'

'Oh, did he?' growled Minchin. 'So, what about the other bloke you saw – Joss?'

'Oh, Kenny. We'd interviewed him before, it's on file. He told me the same yarn only . . .' Pearce paused and scratched the top of his head.

'Well?' Minchin asked impatiently. 'Were you satisfied with Joss's replies or not?'

'Not,' Pearce said without hesitation. 'But I couldn't put a finger on what was wrong. Perhaps nothing was. It could have been he just didn't like talking to the police. Several members of his family have got form.'

Minchin showed interest. 'Like?'

'Oh, like drunk and disorderly, assault, handling stolen goods, poaching, street-trading without a licence. All small-time stuff. Kenny hasn't any record though. Kenny's clean.'

'Possibly. Then he's got nothing to worry about. But he *was* worried, you reckon. What made you so sure?'

'The dog,' said Pearce. He explained.

Minchin listened, rubbing his chin thoughtfully, his sharp gaze fixed on Pearce's face as he spoke. When Pearce came to the end, he fancied Minchin's expression had changed slightly and his manner mellowed.

Minchin said quietly, 'That's good.' The praise was unexpected and Pearce felt absurdly pleased.

'I think,' Minchin said, 'Mickey Hayes will pay a visit to Kenny Joss. He knows you. He knows how to deal with you – no criticism implied. But he knows what to expect from you, right?'

'Yes, I suppose he does,' admitted Pearce.

'But he doesn't,' Minchin smiled slowly and unpleasantly, 'know what to expect from Mickey.' After a moment's silence, he added, 'But then, none of you knows what to expect from either of us, do you?'

'No, sir,' Pearce said.

Minchin stared at him for a moment. Then he said briskly, 'Well, you'll want to go along to Mr Markby's office and fill him in on latest developments, I expect.'

To his dismay Pearce felt himself reddening again.

'Don't worry about it,' Minchin said bluntly. 'If I were Markby, I'd be doing the same, making sure I got to hear what was going on. I've no objection to you telling him. Just so long as you don't tell him things you haven't told me, get it?'

'Yes, sir.' Pearce was on his way to the door when Minchin spoke again.

'You know why we're here?'

'Yes,' Pearce said unwillingly, turning. 'Because Mr Markby has a personal involvement with Fourways.'

'Not only Mr Markby. You're all too close, all of you. Even your poison expert and his family are involved, Mr Markby's ladyfriend . . . the whole thing's bordering on the incestuous. Don't look so ruddy shocked, Dave. You know what I mean. And you should know that's dangerous because you all see what you expect to see. You look at two respectable women in their eighties, bit on the posh side for all they're skint. Old local family. Ladies, eh? Not women. Ladies. You respect them. You feel sorry for them. You treat them with kid gloves. Before you say anything, neither Mickey Hayes nor I are going to upset them needlessly. But we've got no preconceptions, right? To us, they're just two material witnesses. It would even be fair to say, they're a couple of suspects.'

'I don't – ' Pearce began and broke off. More carefully, he said, 'I think it's unlikely.'

'Unlikely things happen all the time, Dave. How long have you been a bloody copper?'

Stung, Pearce said, 'We're not rustics. We're not a bunch of village idiots.'

'Perish the thought, Dave. I can see you're a bright boy. If

308

you're ever interested in transferring to the Met, you let me know.'

'You're not thinking of it?' Tessa, Pearce's still fairly new wife, asked, appalled.

'Transferring to the Met? Not likely. Still, you should have seen his face when he heard I'd beaten them to Newman!' Pearce said with satisfaction.

'You be careful, Dave. I mean, watch out for Newman. He'll still be here when Minchin has gone. Dudley Newman's got a lot of influence hereabouts.' She began carefully slicing a purple object which Pearce was unable to identify but suspected he was later to eat.

'I am investigating a murder!' he told her. 'They may have taken Mr Markby off this case but I'm still on it and I'm not going to be pushed around. What are we having to eat, anyway? What's that?' He pointed at the purple vegetable.

'Honestly, Dave, you must be the only person left in the country who can't tell an aubergine when he sees one.'

'I'm not a cook, am I?' Pearce defended himself. 'And my dad never grew anything like that in his garden.'

'Your dad didn't – doesn't – live in a nice hot climate. Anyway, the only things he grows are carrots. It's a wonder your whole family hasn't turned orange. You can, you know, if you eat too many carrots. I read it in a magazine. I'm making moussaka. We had it the last time we went to the Greek restaurant and you said you liked it.'

'I did like it. I didn't know that was in it.'

'Well, now you do.' Tessa tipped the aubergine slices into a colander and shook salt over them. She placed a plate on top of them and weighted that with a can of soup. Pearce watched all this, opened his mouth, thought better of it and closed it again.

'What are they like?' asked Tessa. 'These two London men?'

'Sharp. Minchin is a bully and Hayes is a weasel.' He told her the nicknames the canteen had bestowed on the pair.

Tessa giggled. 'You tell Mr Markby that?'

'No. I might if things get really bad. I'm sort of saving it up.'

'It's still my show and I'm still in charge at Regional HQ, even if I have been relegated to the sidelines in this case,' said Alan Markby grumpily.

'Don't let it get you down,' advised Meredith. She suppressed a sigh. There were no words of comfort she could offer that she hadn't already spoken. Alan had taken up his position. He wasn't going to let it go. But hadn't he said that to her recently in another context? He didn't let things go. Though she knew it was useless, she repeated, 'You mustn't take it to heart so much. It's no reflection on you. It's entirely due to circumstances.'

A fine set of platitudes, she thought, as she heard herself roll them out. It wasn't surprising they weren't having the desired effect. She was beginning to suspect nothing would. He was entrenched now in the role of a man hard done by. She was genuinely sympathetic but on the other hand, she didn't see why she should bear the brunt of what was developing into an out-and-out sulk. This, she told herself, is all part and parcel of sharing your life with someone, sharing a roof. Once I could have slipped away now, gone back to my own home and returned here when he was feeling more cheerful.

'Look here,' she said more forcefully, 'it's no use letting it blight your life!' (And mine!) 'You can't do anything about it and you're just going to have to put up with it. It isn't the end of the world, for goodness sake.'

He leaned towards her, chin jutting, eyes a-gleam with outrage. 'It's an insult to my officers. The last thing we need is advice from the Met. You've seen Minchin and Hayes. Talk about fish out of water. But I've got Dave Pearce in there keeping an eye on things and reporting back to me. If Minchin thinks he's going to conduct a Met-style operation in Bamford, he's got another thing coming. We don't conduct investigations here by hanging round seedy pubs talking to dubious grasses.' Markby ignored the fact that Minchin's visit to The Feathers had yielded more than Pearce's earlier one had done. He concluded his highly unfair description of Metropolitan Police methods with, 'And tomorrow morning he wants to call round and talk to you.'

'What, here?' Meredith was taken aback.

'I warned you he'd want to talk to you.' Was she imagining it or did he sound distinctly smug? 'It's either here or you can come in and have a heart-to-heart with him in the interview room.'

'So you suggested he came here?'

'No, as a matter of fact, he suggested he came here. You'd prefer it, wouldn't you?'

'I don't know,' said Meredith. 'I talked to Jan here and look what happened.'

'Just don't serve Minchin any of your chocolate cakes.

All right!' Markby held up placatory hands. 'It was a joke.'

'Glad to see you've still got your sense of humour!' she retorted.

The doorbell rang the following morning at ten-thirty sharp. Meredith opened it. On the doorstep stood a hulking figure in a pale-grey suit teamed today with a lime-green shirt and yellow tie with squiggles on it. 'Doug Minchin, you remember me?' His tone was affable but his small sharp eyes as cold as ever.

'Of course I remember you,' said Meredith. 'How could I forget? Come in.' She peered past him. 'No Inspector Hayes?'

Minchin manoeuvred his bulk into the hall. 'He's checking out a few things for me.' As he spoke, he was looking around him in frank appraisal.

Jan had done the same thing but somehow, Meredith minded more this time. Alan was not much concerned about the appearance of his home. For him it had always been a place where he kept his belongings and slept. Since she'd moved in she'd made minor improvements but the whole place still looked as if it had been furnished by the Salvation Army. Jan's opinion hadn't mattered, but Minchin's did. It was bad enough that Alan felt displaced by Minchin, without Minchin going away and telling everyone in London that she and Alan lived in a rundown house with rundown furnishings and an I-don't-care look to it.

'Are you comfortable in my cottage?' she asked with some asperity.

'Very nice,' said Minchin. He sat down uninvited in the stronger-looking of the two mismatched easy chairs.

'We're planning to sell both houses, mine and this one,

and buy a bigger place.' Meredith found herself speaking defensively.

'How are property prices?' asked Minchin unexpectedly.

'Around here? Quite high. That is, for anywhere decent.'

'A place like Fourways, then, where the murder took place, that would fetch a good price?'

Meredith eyed Minchin with greater respect. This wasn't a man who wasted time on idle conversation. 'Fourways is in a dreadful state and it probably wouldn't attract anyone.' She hesitated. 'A local builder, Dudley Newman, is interested in the land. He wants to build several houses on it.'

Minchin leaned back, pursed his thin lips and said, 'Yeah, I've heard about him.' He glanced round the room. 'This where you and Jan Oakley had your tea-party?'

'Yes,' said Meredith, 'though I'd hardly call it that. It wasn't my idea. I invited him just to help out.'

'Whose idea was it?' Minchin turned his hard gaze on her.

Uncomfortably, she said, 'Juliet Painter's. She thought I might be able to influence him. She only thought that,' Meredith added hastily, 'because I'm a Foreign Office official.'

'Are you, indeed?' said Minchin deflatingly. 'And was he influenced by you?'

'Not a bit,' she said, trying to ignore the sarcasm in his voice. 'I suggested to him that his cousins were poor and that to try and get money from them was unfair. He said he'd no intention of doing any such thing. I'm not quoting exactly but that was the gist of it.'

'I've read the file,' said Minchin. 'I sat up till one this morning studying it, in fact. It seems he was very keen to get his hands on a share of any money from the sale of the house. He was talking legal action. Some story about a will.'

'None of us has seen this will,' Meredith said. 'Or at least, not the copy of the original made at the time it was drawn up and which Jan reckons he found among the family papers. Some people have seen what he claimed was a certified translation. I didn't even see that.'

'Probably the so-called original doesn't exist.' Minchin's voice was off-hand. 'The thing is, he came here and he told you he'd changed his mind. Did you believe him?'

'No,' she said frankly. 'But once he'd said it, it left me nothing more to say to him. I told you, he wasn't influenced by me. He outmanoeuvred me.'

Minchin rubbed his chin with his thumbnail. 'Did you like him?'

'No,' said Meredith forcefully. 'No one did. He was a creep.'

Minchin stared at her. 'Let his hand wander to your knee, by any chance?'

Aware that her face gave her away, Meredith was forced to admit, 'He got the wrong idea and I told him to go. He went.'

If Minchin dared to make one even faintly facetious remark . . . but he didn't.

'This Jan didn't make himself any friends. Bet you a pound to a penny he was as much a loner at home in Poland as he was here. You never know with loners.' Minchin's tone had become reminiscent. 'They tend to have hobbies and I don't just mean stamp-collecting. They often see themselves as rejected by the world, so the world is wrong. Sometimes they get the idea to put it right in a big way, all by themselves. All of them, or nearly all, believe they're entitled to something better. Sometimes they get the notion that this "something better" is out there, almost within reach, but they're stopped from getting their hands on it by a conspiracy of other people. See what I'm getting at?'

'Yes, I do,' said Meredith.

'We had a fax from the Polish Embassy this morning. He's got no police record. Seems he spent a blameless life grooming horses down on some stud farm.'

'Grooming? He told me he was a vet.'

'Well, he would, wouldn't he?' returned Minchin.

Meredith reflected. 'Alan said much the same. He thought Jan was lying about his job, but had done it to impress me, the idiot!' She tucked a loose swathe of brown hair behind one ear. 'But it ties in with what you were saying. You're suggesting Jan felt under-valued. He thought he ought to be more important, ought to be doing something more distinguished than clean up after horses. When he found out about the English branch of the family, he thought his chance had come.'

'Perhaps it had,' said Minchin. 'Perhaps it had come. Opportunity knocks only once. It had knocked for our boy Jan.'

Meredith didn't quite know how to respond. She was getting the impression that Minchin had formed some theory and wondered if he was about to divulge it. But was Minchin really taking her into his confidence? Or simply, by a show of doing so, inviting confidences from her? She decided on the latter. He was a skilled interviewer and had been neatly leading her along the road he wanted to travel. Not so easily, Superintendent Minchin!

'We don't know what Jan thought and we'll never know,' she said firmly.

She suspected Minchin knew she'd guessed his purpose and had headed him off. He said nothing for a moment, then leaned back and laced his thick fingers. 'You don't like me and Mickey Hayes being here.'

He'd caught her off-guard. She felt her face burn. 'Alan could have run this show perfectly well.'

'Of course he could. But no officer, no matter how senior or how reliable, should ever be put in a position where personal involvement can cause a conflict of interests – not if it can be avoided. There was a time, you know, when the police force used to move coppers out of their home areas, just to avoid that sort of thing.'

There was a prolonged ring on the doorbell. Meredith leapt up. 'Excuse me a minute!' She hurried out of the room, grateful for the diversion.

She wasn't prepared, however, to find Juliet Painter on the doorstep.

'Meredith!' declared Juliet, hurtling past her uninvited. 'I telephoned Fourways early to see how Damaris and Florence were this morning and do you know? That dreadful Minchin and the unspeakable Hayes have already been out there sneaking round the grounds and prying in the outbuildings—'

'Mr Minchin,' said Meredith loudly, 'is here at the moment.' She pointed in the direction of the sitting room.

They stared at one another. 'Damn!' said Juliet. Both knew there was no way Minchin hadn't overheard. Juliet grasped the nettle. She walked into the sitting room spine ramrod straight, long braid of hair swinging, eyes sparkling behind her spectacle lenses.

'Good morning, Miss Painter,' said Minchin, stony-faced. 'I was hoping to call on you today sometime. Your sister-in-law, too.'

'Why were you creeping around Fourways' garden without telling the owners you were there?' demanded Juliet, standing over him, arms akimbo. 'You should have called at the house first. You frightened Damaris. Ron had gone home and she didn't know who was in the stables.'

It seemed to Meredith she caught the merest flash of amusement in Minchin's eyes. She hoped Juliet hadn't seen it. Then, looking at the man again, she decided she must have been mistaken. Minchin took himself seriously. He was probably one of the last of the old-style male chauvinists still lurking in the police force. He wouldn't find it entertaining to be harangued by Juliet.

'I think Miss Oakley coped pretty well,' he said. 'I'll be calling on her again, too, and her sister.'

Juliet sat down in Meredith's vacated chair. 'Look,' she said to Minchin, ignoring Meredith's telegraphed warnings, 'they're very frail. I don't want them badgered. Even before this happened it was a stressful time for them. I mean, selling up their family home and having to move into a flat. I wish I could get you to understand that!' she concluded in exasperation.

'Now then,' said Minchin, jabbing a finger in her direction. 'As it happens, Miss Painter, I do understand that. I had the selfsame problem with my old mother.'

'Oh?' Juliet was momentarily taken aback. 'Well, then, you should know that they need to be treated with every consideration.'

'You leave that to me,' said Minchin disagreeably.

'You stick to being their estate agent.'

'I am *not* an estate agent!' Juliet's combative manner returned. 'I've told you, I'm a property consultant.'

'Fancy name for it, I suppose,' said Minchin. 'They'll be having university degrees in it next.'

'As it happens,' snapped Juliet, 'I do have a degree and it's in Law.'

'Well, well,' returned Minchin with heavy humour. 'I shall have to watch my ps and qs!' He lumbered to his feet. 'I'll leave you girls for the time being. Thank you for giving me your time, Miss Mitchell.'

'It's all right if I go back to work tomorrow? You won't want to see me again?' she asked.

'Oh, I know where to find you,' said Minchin. He turned to Juliet. 'I'll pop over and see you and Mrs Pamela Painter this afternoon, if that's all right, Miss Painter? I understand you're staying at your brother's home? I'd like a chance to talk to him, as well, seeing as he's the poisons expert. But I can catch him at his place of work.' Minchin glanced at his wristwatch. 'Might nip over there now.'

'He is an infuriating man,' declared Juliet, when Minchin had left. She sighed and added more soberly, 'I didn't handle that very well, did I?'

'Shouldn't let it worry you,' advised Meredith.

'Poor Alan, fancy having that man foisted on him. Was he unpleasant when you were here with him alone?'

'Unpleasant? No, but it was a bit nerve-wracking. You'll need your wits about you when he comes to talk to you and Pam.'

'It must be bad enough to have to sit and look at that shirt,' said Juliet unkindly. 'It was awful. He must be colour-blind.

Do you think he's got a wife? Look, if you're free now, can you come with me to see Damaris and Florence? They need support.'

'You just missed Inspector Hayes,' said Damaris to Meredith and Juliet. 'What a pity. Still, I can't say Florence and I weren't heartily glad to see him leave.'

'Hayes was here?' Meredith exclaimed. 'Minchin didn't say anything about that when he was at my place.' She frowned. 'I wonder why Minchin took me and sent Hayes to tackle you.'

'I imagine,' said Damaris, 'because he thought Inspector Hayes would unsettle us.'

Juliet asked indignantly, 'Did he try and bully you? If he did, I'm taking this to the police complaints' committee.'

'Oh, no, my dear. To be fair to the man, he was polite enough in an off-hand sort of way,' Damaris told her. 'When I said unsettle us, I mean that Mr Minchin rightly divined that we'd never dealt with anyone like Inspector Hayes. I suppose it was quite shrewd of him to send him, really.' Damaris reflected. 'I think he must be a heavy smoker, his fingers are badly stained, but he didn't ask if he might smoke in here.'

'He lit a cigarette as soon as he got outside,' said Florence. 'I saw him through the window. Ron Gladstone said he left cigarette ends all over the floor of the old tackroom. Ron was very annoyed.'

It was chilly in this room. Meredith glanced at the unlit gasfire. Damaris noticed and asked, 'Would you like it on?'

Meredith shook her head and assured her it wasn't necessary on her account.

Juliet, slumped back in her chair, arms folded and a frown on her face, was unaware of physical circumstances. She was lost in her thoughts. She roused herself enough to ask, 'Sorry? Missed that.'

'I asked, Juliet dear, whether you were cold. Meredith says she's all right but I can light the fire. Florence and I don't notice it. We're used to it. I mean, we're accustomed to a low level of heating. The house has always been cold. When we were children, the water used to freeze in the basin in the nursery. We had to crack the ice on the surface before we could wash.'

This fragment from a spartan childhood passed by Juliet unheeded. She sat up with a start. 'We're got to get rid of Minchin and Hayes!'

'We can't,' said Meredith. 'I'd like to, just as you would. But they're here and we've got to watch out for them.'

Juliet leaned forward, her long braid of hair hanging over one shoulder. She pushed her spectacles up the bridge of her nose with a forefinger. They all waited.

'They're here,' said Juliet, 'until this is solved. Then they'll go. So we'll solve it and it'll be goodbye, Doug Minchin!'

'You have a way of simplifying things,' Meredith told her crossly, 'when they aren't simple.'

'It seems perfectly straightforward to me.' Juliet's attention was now fully on Meredith. 'Oh, come on, Meredith. You're the one with the experience in these matters.'

'All right, all right!' Now they were all three looking at her expectantly. Meredith drew a deep breath. 'We know where the arsenic came from. What we need to know is how Jan came to swallow it.'

'And who slipped it to him,' said Juliet.

'If we know how he came to take it, we maybe able to work out who gave it to him.' Meredith looked across the room to Damaris. 'Could you bear to go through the events of that Saturday again?'

Damaris glanced at her sister. 'If it would help, I could. But I don't know—'

Florence said quietly, 'It's all right. If you must, you must.'

'Well,' began Damaris, 'Jan was perfectly all right in the morning. He was all right at lunchtime. In the afternoon he went to see you, Meredith. He came back very pleased with himself.'

'He did?' asked Meredith, startled. 'I threw him out. He – um – misbehaved.'

'I'm not surprised to hear it. Behaving badly was Jan's special gift,' Damaris told her with asperity. 'He broke into my grandfather's desk in the study and went through the papers we keep in there. Ron saw him through the window and told Alan about it. As far as we can make out, he read the copies of our wills – not that we'd ever have changed them in his favour! But Jan being Jan, he'd probably persuaded himself that he could talk us round. He had sort of – faith – in himself.'

Damaris considered the matter. 'I really think he lived in a world of his own, you know. This business of the will and his right to a share in the house . . . You may have asked him to leave, Meredith, but I dare say, in his own mind, he'd decided the visit was a roaring success. Ron Gladstone keeps saying he thought Jan mentally unstable. "Potty" is Ron's word for it. I have to say I wonder if Ron isn't right.'

'If it helps,' Meredith told her, 'Superintendent Minchin

thinks much the same way. Anyway, he was all right during the day, and I agree, he was perfectly all right when he was visiting me. He certainly wasn't ill. So we need to concentrate on the late afternoon and evening. I understand you both went shopping in the afternoon?'

'Yes, that's our usual occupation on a Saturday afternoon. Kenny Joss brought us back in his taxi. Jan was here—' Damaris paused and frowned. 'We didn't see him at first. We didn't see him until Kenny had left. We were in the kitchen and he came in. We told him we were going to make our evening meal and he went off to watch the early evening news on the television, in here.' Damaris pointed at the television set in the corner. 'Later he went out, to The Feathers to get himself something to eat. That was the arrangement. Florence and I sat in here until he came back and then we went to bed. He was still in here when we went upstairs.'

They were coming to the difficult bit. Meredith and Juliet could see Damaris bracing herself. Florence sat very still, her eyes fixed on her thin hands, clasped in her lap.

'I don't know exactly what woke me. It must have been a noise made by Jan. There was a crash, something falling. I came downstairs and found him in the hall. He'd knocked over the telephone table. I realise now he was dying. I think I knew it then. I called the ambulance, but I knew it was no good. Chiefly I was worried that Florence might hear and come down. I was more worried about her than about Jan. That sounds unkind but it's true.'

'I wonder,' Meredith ventured, 'if we might walk it through.'

'Walk?' Damaris looked puzzled but then grasped her

meaning. 'Oh, yes, stage a reconstruction . . . Well, through here in the hall, then.'

'I'll stay here, if you don't mind.' Florence's voice was barely audible. 'I wasn't there. I didn't see. I can't help.'

In the gloomy hall Damaris stood by the telephone table and pointed to the floor. 'He was lying here. His head was here and his feet about there. I was halfway down the stairs at least before I saw him.'

'His feet were pointing towards the kitchen door?' Meredith looked down the long narrow hallway to the door at the far end.

'Yes. The kitchen door was open. There was a broken tumbler and spilled water near it. He must have fetched himself a drink but he dropped it.' Damaris waved a hand vaguely. 'I suppose he wanted to telephone for help.'

Meredith frowned. 'Telephone himself? He didn't call out to you to help him?'

Damaris shook her head in a bewildered way. 'I suppose he thought I mightn't hear him. It'd be quicker to call for help directly himself. The ambulance came quite quickly and took him away. I went upstairs to tell Florence he'd been taken ill.'

'What about the broken tumbler?'

'Oh, that. I picked that up, of course. I couldn't leave broken glass lying around. I'm not sure now when I picked it up. Whether it was while I was waiting for the ambulance or afterwards, when I went to the kitchen to make us a cup of tea, for the shock.'

Juliet asked, 'When you came downstairs, how many lights were on?'

Damaris said promptly, 'The hall light, the sitting-room light and the kitchen.'

'So he'd been in all three places.' Meredith fell silent. 'He was watching television in the sitting room. He went to the kitchen for a glass of water . . .'

Damaris began, 'There was . . .' and broke off.

Juliet reached out and touched her arm. 'What is it? What have you remembered?'

'It isn't important.' Damaris looked a little embarrassed. 'But you're right, I had forgotten. When I went to fill the kettle to make tea, there was a knife lying in the sink. I was surprised because Florence and I had washed up our supper things and we don't usually miss anything.'

'You are sure,' Juliet asked her, 'that it was left over from your supper?'

'Oh, I think so. It had savoury spread on the blade. We had some on toast.'

'The savoury spread?' Meredith asked quickly.

Damaris sighed and shook her head. 'It was one of the things the police took away. It must have been all right or they'd have said so. Anyway, Florrie and I ate it and we were all right.' She looked anxiously from one to the other of them. 'Do you think I should have told the police? It's such a small detail.'

'It might be worth mentioning the next time you see either Minchin or Hayes,' Meredith told her. 'Best to tell them everything, just to keep on the right side of them.'

'Well, it doesn't help us,' said Juliet crossly. 'If he didn't take the arsenic in some way here, he didn't take it at The Feathers and he didn't take it at your place, Meredith, where on earth *did* he take it?'

Meredith said thoughtfully, 'Where – and how?'

Without warning, Damaris chanted in a soft sing-song, 'Their names are What and Why and When, and How and Where and Who?'

Meredith felt a prickle run up her spine, it sounded so eerie. Damaris looked from one to the other of them and seeing their startled faces, flushed. 'Kipling,' she explained awkwardly.

'He's not going to help us, either,' muttered Juliet.

Chapter Twenty-Three

'Vicar's round the back of the house somewhere,' said Mrs Harmer. 'He's tinkering with that contraption of his.'

Knowing that Minchin's plan was to talk to Meredith that morning, Alan Markby had betaken himself to the vicarage. James Holland was the one person left, he reflected grumpily as he pressed the big old bellpush, with whom he could discuss the Oakleys without appearing to trespass on Minchin's turf. His assault on the bellpush had triggered a jangling response in the depths of the house. Markby studied the frontage of the building while he waited for someone to answer the call.

Like Fourways, the vicarage had been built in an age when a gentleman and his family required space in order to pursue a gracious lifestyle and could afford the necessary domestic staff to support the same. Both the vicarage and Fourways had survived into an age in which lifestyles had changed beyond recognition, servants had all but disappeared, and ease of maintenance was the watchword.

Now there was only Mrs Harmer, who reigned from breakfast-time to mid-afternoon, and that because the vicar was a bachelor. She kept tidy in an erratic but sufficient way that part of the house in which he lived: one reception room (the smallest) functioning as both sitting and dining room, kitchen, study, bedroom and bathroom. Four more bedrooms, Markby knew, were closed up and empty, home only to spiders. In the disused drawing room, dustsheets covered old-fashioned furniture inherited by the present vicar from his predecessor who'd died in harness. In addition, up in the attics were the tiny rooms where long-vanished maids had slept.

What to do with the vicarage was a regular subject of discussion at parish meetings. There was a movement afoot to sell it off and buy a small modern house for the priest. Opposition came in the shape of another party which feared selling it off would herald unwelcome change in the centre of the town. It had been suggested that the unused part of the house be turned into a self-contained flat in which some suitable person, a curate for example, could be lodged. Unfortunately, there was no curate and in any case, the cost of transforming the rooms was held to be too high.

'Right,' said Markby. 'I'll go and find him.'

'He gets covered in oil and stuff.' Mrs Harmer's pinafored figure bristled with righteous resentment and it wasn't all directed at the vicar. She didn't like being brought from work to answer the door, not even for a senior police officer.

'He comes in my kitchen to wash his hands and makes the soap all dirty and the towel. I've said to him I don't know how many times, it's not right, a man of God riding round on the devil's machine.'

'Devil's machine?' queried Markby.

'Motorbike!' snapped Mrs Harmer as if he were being deliberately awkward. 'No good ever came of motorbikes. He needs to get himself a little car. I keep telling him.'

'Everyone needs a hobby,' said Markby in a misjudged attempt to calm her.

'Hobby?' Mrs Harmer took a yellow duster from her apron pocket and shook it so violently it snapped like a whiplash. Dust flew out of it. 'Hobbies are for people who have nothing else to do. I never had time for no hobbies.'

'Oh? Someone told me you make homemade wines,' Markby remarked innocently.

She turned turkey-red and stuffed the duster back in her apron. 'Oh, did they, indeed? Well, sometimes I make a few bottles but only when I've got the soft fruit to spare . . . so as it doesn't go to waste. That's no more a hobby than bottling fruit or making chutney with it, or freezing it like everyone does these days. I thought,' said Mrs Harmer fiercely, 'you came to see the vicar? Not take up my time chatting about hobbies.' She pointed majestically to the corner of the building. 'You can go round the back and then straight down the path to the garage.'

The door was slammed in his face.

Markby made his way down the path through the overgrown vicarage garden. Here the parallel with Fourways was even more obvious and poignant. The grounds were extensive but there was no Ron Gladstone here to tend them, even in part. Where once there would have been lawns and flowerbeds there was now only rough grass. Behind a brick wall had lain a vegetable garden, but that was now a wasteland of broken glasshouses, collapsed cucumber frames and rampant weeds. There was even the remains of a tennis court. Its asphalt surface was pitted and cracked, allowing thistles to take root.

He found James Holland busy, as he'd been warned, with

his motorcycle. It had been wheeled out of the prefabricated garage, which leaned precariously to one side, and stood propped up in a patch of sunlight. The vicar's burly figure bent over it as he ministered to its needs as tenderly as a mother over the crib of a newborn babe.

'Mrs Harmer doesn't get any mellower with age,' Markby said to him, by way of greeting, as he neared.

'Hello there, Alan. No, she doesn't, but she has a kind heart. What's more, she's looked after the vicarage for years. She's been here far longer than I have. She cared for my predecessor for thirty years.'

'Good God. How old is she?'

'That's a secret,' said the vicar with a grin. 'No one's allowed to know that.'

'I mistakenly let slip that I knew one of her other secrets. I mentioned the wine-making,' Markby admitted.

James Holland gave a guffaw. 'You won't be forgiven!' He straightened up and wiped his hands on a filthy rag. 'Is this a social visit, or am I subject to police enquiries?'

'Not from me,' Markby said. 'Our biggest case at the moment, Jan Oakley's murder, is in the hands of others. I've been sidelined.'

James Holland scratched his nose thoughtfully. When he took his hand away, a black streak ran across the bridge of it. 'Juliet was telling me about Minchin and Hayes. She seems to have taken against them. What are they really like?'

'Extremely capable,' said Markby. 'And I begin to suspect Doug Minchin of not being without a sense of humour, though he works hard at hiding it. He's what Mrs Harmer would probably call "deep". He favours bright shirts and the hard man approach.' Markby smiled. 'He operates like a conjurer.

330

He gets you looking one way when actually you should be looking the other.'

'You don't resent him, then?' James twitched a bushy eyebrow.

'Of course I do – did. No, not the man. I resent being told I can't run an investigation. But then, my basic responsibility is to see that someone runs it efficiently and as I say, Doug Minchin is certainly doing that.' Markby paused. 'I do resent that I can't visit the Oakley sisters. I've been visiting them on and off since I was about eight years old. Now it would look as if I were straying on Minchin's turf. How are they? That's what I really came to ask you about.'

Father Holland heaved a sigh. 'Inwardly? They're devastated. Outwardly, they're coping well. They've had years of training in adversity of one sort and another. They're the sort who, a hundred years ago, made cracking good missionaries. You know, getting themselves paddled up the Limpopo in a canoe, parasol in one hand and Bible in the other, scorning wild animals, disease, heat and hostile locals. All the same, it hardly seems fair that they should have been landed with this.'

'They've had training in dealing with disaster, all right,' said Markby. 'I'm not just talking about the legacy of Cora Oakley's death. There was the loss of their brother. There were the years of dealing with an irascible old invalid of a father. Edward Oakley was an unhappy man. His son, Arthur, had been his pride and joy. His daughters were no substitute. Then he became wheelchair-bound and suffered a lot of pain from arthritis. He died of an overdose, you know.'

James Holland was so startled, he dropped a spanner which hit part of his cherished bike with a clunk. He was distracted momentarily to check that no damage had been done before replying.

'I didn't know,' he said. 'How did it happen?'

'Secrets,' said Markby. He took a seat on a nearby garden bench and stretched out his legs. The sun was warm on his face and in this time-locked wilderness it would be easy to forget the world outside and its troubles. 'That whole generation,' he observed, 'knows how to keep its secrets. Not like our modern age with its chat-shows full of people telling the world about their most intimate problems.'

A blackbird flew out of the foliage overhead and landed a short distance away, uttering short clucks of unease.

'The fledglings are hidden somewhere,' said the vicar. 'A second brood. They flew the nest about a week ago but the parent bird isn't yet ready to bring them out into the open. Natures keeps its secrets, too.'

Markby nodded but pursued his theme, undeflected. 'Mrs Harmer hides her age and her wine-making. Other old folk hide the truth about runaway wives or husbands, illegitimacy, disreputable occupations – anything, really, that they deem not to be respectable. The Oakley women never speak of Cora and William. Or never did until now, when they've been forced to. In the same way they never speak of their father's fatal overdose. It was suicide, of course. He was on all kinds of medication including sleeping pills. His daughters kept the medicines and doled out his ration of pills every day and in the case of the sleeping pills, every night. They were a conscientious pair of nurses but he outwitted them. He pretended to take the sleeping pills but hoarded them away until he had enough. That evening, before he went to bed, he had a couple of glasses of whisky which was unusual. He wasn't a drinker. He probably wanted to help the pills along. He went to sleep and never awoke.

'The doctor was at first inclined to write out a death certificate as due to natural causes. The old gentleman was, after all, in his mid-eighties. But at the last minute, he changed his mind because he was interested to know the actual cause of the old man's demise. He'd always considered the old chap's heart and lungs to be sound. His appetite was good. The arthritis in itself wouldn't have killed him. Postmortem turned up the presence of the overdose. The doctor then recalled that on various occasions, Mr Oakley had expressed the wish to die since life no longer held anything for him. The whole thing was dealt with, with as little fuss as possible. The poor old fellow had chosen the time of his own exit from the stage. Nevertheless, his daughters took it badly. Suicide is something they'd consider a sin. Perhaps they thought it implied that everything they'd done for him had been as nothing, their love and devotion were rejected and scorned. Possibly, even worse, to them it represented throwing in the towel. Giving up. Trying to explain to them about depression would have been a complete waste of time.'

'Hm,' said James Holland. 'We can only hope that this present business is cleared up soon. Damaris and Florence have certainly suffered more than enough.' After a moment, he asked, 'Have you told Minchin about the old man's suicide?'

'No,' Markby said. 'It must have been twenty-five years ago or more. As you say, they've suffered enough without raking that up.' He saw James Holland's gaze fixed on him.

'Why,' the vicar asked quietly, 'have you chosen to tell me?'

Markby got to his feet and dusted off his trousers. 'You visit the sisters. I thought you might be interested. When you go next, please give them my very best regards and explain, would you, why I can't come in person just yet? I'll see you again soon, no doubt.'

He nodded his farewell and walked quickly out of the garden. The vicar, thoughtful, watched him go.

Later that sunny spring afternoon, as promised, Superintendent Minchin appeared at the Painters' home. He was ushered inside briskly by Pam and directed to an armchair. Opposite him, Pam Painter and Juliet took up positions on the sofa so that they presented a united front. If this deterred Minchin, he certainly didn't show it.

'This has been a disgraceful business from start to finish,' Pam began in her forthright way. 'And I'm glad to have the chance to tell you so.'

'Murder usually is,' said Minchin.

The wind temporarily taken from her sails, Pam glared at him. Juliet, however, took up the attack.

'Why are you wasting your time talking to us? You should be out there,' she flung a pointing hand at the window, 'finding out who *killed* him, for goodness sake. *We* didn't!'

'Mrs Painter.' Minchin ignored Juliet to her manifest annoyance, and concentrated his attention on Pam. 'I understand you went to Fourways to speak to Jan Oakley.'

'Yes, I did, but I didn't find him,' Pam retorted. 'And before you ask, I'm very sorry I didn't find him because I'd have sent him on his way with a flea in his ear! Attempting to bamboozle and manipulate those two old women, it was disgraceful. That's what I meant just now.'

'I see,' said Minchin. 'You don't think *his* murder is disgraceful?'

'Of course it is!' Pam could barely contain herself. 'I'm not going to argue for anyone breaking the law. I'm on the police committee. I organised a Neighbourhood Watch scheme when we moved in here. But because someone's murdered it doesn't mean he's an innocent victim. Jan Oakley wasn't innocent, Superintendent. He was a crook.'

'And don't say there wasn't any evidence of that,' added Juliet, 'because his entire behaviour while he was here – even his coming here in the first place – pointed to it.'

'He had no police record in Poland,' Minchin said.

Juliet leaned forward. 'Because he hadn't got the opportunity in Poland he'd got here! As soon as he saw Fourways, he must have thought his boat had come in! Meredith took him there on his arrival and she said his eyes shone, really shone.'

'All right, then,' said Minchin equably, 'so he was a nasty little twister intent on conning money out of a pair of old women. But someone killed him.'

'Damaris and Florence didn't,' Juliet said promptly. 'I didn't, nor did Pam as we've just said. You can't suspect poor Ron Gladstone – he's in a terrible state over it. If you ask me, it has got something to do with Poland. You'll probably find he was into drug smuggling or even something to do with those horses.'

'Which horses?' asked Minchin, startled.

'He worked on a stud farm, didn't he? Poland exports horses, top quality stock. There's a lot of money in the bloodstock trade. He could have been part of some syndicate working some kind of fiddle.'

335

'Evidence,' said Minchin bleakly.

Juliet struck her knees with her clenched fists. 'I haven't got any evidence, of course I haven't! That's *your* job – finding evidence. All I want you to do is show some kind of lateral thinking. Instead, you seem to be completely tunnel-visioned. You just see the Oakleys and those of us who are their friends. It seems quite clear to me you should be looking elsewhere.'

'It's quite clear to me you'd like me to look elsewhere,' said Minchin.

Pam drew in a sharp breath. 'I don't like the implication of that, Superintendent. We're trying to help you.'

Minchin rolled his eyes. 'When you went to Fourways to find Oakley, did you look round the place for him, once you'd established he wasn't in the house?'

'If you mean, did I look round the garden, yes, I did. I didn't go to the house. I wanted to get him on his own, you see. But I didn't get him at all. I eventually found Ron Gladstone.'

'And while looking around the garden, did you check out the stone potting shed?'

'Oh, I see,' said Pam. She was silent for a second or two. 'I didn't check it out thoroughly. I looked through the door but no one was there.'

'Hey!' exclaimed Juliet. 'Are you accusing Pam of taking the arsenic?'

Minchin held up a broad hand as if he was stopping traffic. Juliet bit her lip, fuming. 'Did the interior of the potting shed look tidy?' he asked Pam.

She looked puzzled. 'I can't remember. I wasn't worrying about how tidy it was, only whether Jan was in there, and he wasn't. There was a lot of stuff lying around, some of it antique.'

'And how long did it look as if it had been lying there? For years, undisturbed?'

Pam frowned and then brightened. 'As a matter of fact, it looked as if someone had moved some stuff in one corner quite recently. There were fresh-looking scrape marks on the earth floor – and there was a box pulled out as if someone had wanted to stand on it to reach a shelf—' She broke off in dismay and put her hand to her mouth.

'Because, you see,' said Minchin patiently, 'I'm trying to find out when the arsenic was taken. If someone had been in that shed, hunting among things on the shelf, before you looked in there, then it could have been taken very early on. You went out there to find Oakley as soon as you heard about his arrival, right? So someone began to make his or her plans almost at once.'

He had succeeded in silencing his companions for the moment. He watched them as they digested the idea. Suddenly he struck the arms of his chair with the flat of his hands. 'Right, ladies. I don't think there's anything more to be gained by my sitting here.' In a bewildering change of subject, he added, 'These houses of yours are new. Built on farmland, were they?'

Cautiously, Pam said, 'Yes, they were as it happens.'

'Local estate agents must have been pleased.' He glanced at Juliet.

'I wouldn't know,' she said through gritted teeth. 'I'm not an estate agent.'

'I see there's still a bit of woodland beyond the estate.' Minchin nodded vaguely in the direction.

'Oh that,' Pam said. 'That's Bailey's Coppice. It's privately owned but there is access for walkers. We get quite a few bird-watchers and nature-lovers down there.'

'Then perhaps I shouldn't miss the chance to take a look at it,' said Minchin. He turned his gaze on Juliet. 'Would you come with me and show me where this access is, Miss Painter?'

Startled, Juliet and Pam exchanged glances. 'Well,' Juliet said after a moment, 'I suppose so. I'll fetch my wellies. It might be a bit damp underfoot.'

Bailey's Coppice was cool, dark and mysterious. There was no sign of either bird-watchers or nature enthusiasts when Minchin and Juliet reached the wooden stile set in the drystone walls surrounding the woodland. Beyond it a narrow beaten path twisted its way between tangled undergrowth and spindly native woodland jostling for space.

'It looks,' said Minchin, 'as though some people can't be bothered with the stile here.' He pointed to where an area of surrounding wall had collapsed.

'You mean the damage done to the wall? That's more likely people after the stone than ramblers or twitchers. Our local stone is expensive to buy now and quarrying is restricted. So if people, generally townies, want a bit of Cotswold stone to make a rockery or a nice little garden wall, they think nothing of coming out and pinching it. The sad thing is, they're probably respectable people who don't think of it as stealing. Because the stone is local and this is the countryside they seem to assume it's in the public domain. If they see a little bit of wall that's in poor repair, they think, Oh, it's abandoned, no one wants it. So they help themselves to a few stones. Or they take one or two from the top and think it doesn't matter. But of course it matters. Because then more of the wall crumbles and when the owner gets round to repairing it, the stones aren't there and instead of a small gap he's faced with a gaping great hole.'

Juliet had clambered over the stile as she spoke and dropped down on to the muddy path. 'Mind out for brambles!' she warned Minchin, following behind her.

'Any of these stone pilferers ever been caught?' Minchin called from behind her.

'Oh yes. Geoff, my brother, was coming along here one day and he came across a couple loading stone into the boot of their car. They were middle-aged and nicely dressed and terribly offended when he asked what the hell they thought they were doing. He told them he had made a note of the car registration and would phone the police as soon as he got home, which would be in five minutes' time. So then they got abusive. The wife was worse than the husband, Geoff said, and she was such a nice sensible-looking woman. Anyway, he made them unload it and watched them drive off. But he suspected that as soon as he was out of sight they nipped back for it. He asked them, when they were arguing, if they would go to the house of the wall's owner and steal things from that. They went ballistic. He thought the bloke was going to dot him on the nose. So then he asked, suppose someone went to this chap's house, wherever it was, and pinched bits of *his* garden wall?'

'They'd assumed it was there for the taking,' Minchin said. 'People make assumptions, don't they? Because they don't understand or because outward appearances suggest something which isn't true.'

'They're daft if they think they can break down walls,'

snapped Juliet. 'Oh, there's a dead bird here. It looks like a spotted woodpecker but something's bitten off the head.'

Minchin moved up to stand beside her and pushed the sad little carcass with his toe. 'There again,' he said, 'it's easy to make assumptions about people, especially if they come from a different background.'

Juliet gave him a suspicious look. 'Are you getting at me, by any chance?'

'Well, you seem to assume you know how I look at this case. You seem to think I'm not capable of seeing anything unless it's under my nose like this dead bird – and even then probably have to have it pointed out to me.'

There was a silence in which twigs cracked in the depths of the coppice and some large bird crashed noisily out of the overhead branches.

'Pigeon,' said Minchin without looking up. 'My grandad used to take me out shooting them. He was a countryman. Kent. Nice county, Kent.'

'Oh, all right,' Juliet conceded. 'I'm sorry if I sounded rude. But you're not awfully polite yourself, are you? You know for a fact I'm not an estate agent.'

A smile spread over Doug Minchin's face. 'Course I do,' he said. 'But watching your reaction whenever I suggest it makes it worth it, every time.'

She gasped and gaped at him. Then she rallied and began, 'Well, of all the damn cheek!'

'See?' grinned Minchin. 'You've got beautiful eyes, you know. Why do you wear those damn-awful granny specs?'

Meredith spent much of the journey to work the following morning concocting a version of events which would stave off Adrian's enquiries. He should be able to understand that she couldn't discuss the personalities in the case with him. She would simply say there had been a death. She had been slightly acquainted with the deceased and the investigating officer had wanted to talk to her. He had done so. The matter was closed.

She didn't think this would really satisfy Adrian and knew he would add her unwillingness to confide in him to the list of things he held against her. She didn't know quite why he appeared to dislike her so much. She put it down as one of life's mysteries. He wasn't a person, in any case, whose favour she sought. It didn't matter. Except, of course, that she shared an office with him. Meredith sighed.

But life is full of surprises. When Meredith marched briskly into the office, ready to reel off her prepared account, she was stopped in her tracks by an unfamiliar sight.

At Adrian's desk sat a young woman with long black hair and a frown on her face as she sorted through the contents of what appeared to be Adrian's in-tray.

Meredith cleared her throat. The other woman looked up.

'Hello,' she said. 'I'm Polly Patel. I've replaced Adrian.'

'When?' Meredith heard herself say.

'As from yesterday, but you weren't in then, so you wouldn't know.'

Meredith set down her briefcase and extended a hand. Polly shook it. 'Er, what happened to Adrian?'

Polly grinned. 'Nobody really knows. There's a rumour, of course. They say he was discovered snorting a line in the gents' loo. He's been relegated to something routine and harmless until they decide what to do about him.' She raised her eyebrows. 'Sorry if he was a friend of yours.'

341

'He wasn't,' said Meredith with feeling. 'Quite the reverse. I'm very glad to see you, Polly.' She went to the window and stared out for a moment at the pavement below. 'You know,' she said, 'I was wondering how I could get rid of him and in the end, I hadn't to do anything. He did it himself.'

'There you are, then,' said Polly cheerfully. 'Why worry? That's what I always say. Half the time problems sort themselves out. If Adrian was anything like what people have been telling me he was like, he was heading for a fall.'

Meredith turned slowly to face her, hands stuck in her jacket pockets. 'Yes . . . yes, he was.' She contemplated Polly for a moment, then, with sudden movement, grabbed her briefcase.

'Polly, sorry to do this to you, but can you hold the fort alone for another day? I have to go back to Bamford.'

'No problem.' Polly didn't ask why. She'd started work on something and spoke absently.

Meredith hastened out of the office. It was so obvious. It was so damn obvious! Anyone could work it out. She could work it out – well, not all of it. But one bit of it, for sure.

'What,' asked Alan Markby, 'are we doing here?'

He asked this question not in the context of man's place in the universe but of his own presence with Meredith in a lay-by. He had parked his car behind hers and joined her, taking the front passenger seat. Now he peered through the windscreen at a battered transit van parked ahead of them both. 'Not,' he went on, 'that it isn't very nice to see you again so soon, but as I remember, you went off to London this morning on the train and you were not due back until this evening. What's happened?'

'I have to talk to you, Alan, and trying to do it on the phone would've been impossible. You see, I've—'

'There must be other places to talk. What do you suppose he's got in that van?'

'I have no idea,' said Meredith crossly. 'Alan, I've come haring back from London because I need to talk to Minchin, but first I wanted to talk to you. That's why I asked you to come from Regional HQ and meet me here, half a mile away. Then we can go together to Minchin.'

'You talked to Minchin yesterday,' he said, scarcely paying attention, still squinting at the van ahead. 'If you've remembered something, why not just call him up and ask to see him again? Why bring me into it?'

'Because I want to work out with you first what I'm going to say. I'm pretty sure I'm right, you see, but I haven't got the whole thing, in a nutshell. I wish I had. I've got half of it. I thought you might come up with the other half.'

'All right, let's hear your half.'

'It's about the arsenic,' she said. 'I know who took it from the shed.'

'Do you?' He sounded discouraging.

'Yes. It's blindingly obvious. Jan did.'

'And committed suicide with it? I don't think Minchin will buy that. It would get everyone else off the hook, but I think you're going to have to do better than that.'

'If you'd listen? Honestly, Alan, sometimes you're really exasperating.'

'I am?' He looked offended. 'Am I the one who's left her office and brought me from mine to sit here listening to an ingenious explanation for Jan obligingly swallowing arsenic?'

Ahead of them, the van drew away and rejoined the flow of traffic.

'Now I'll never know what he'd got in that van,' Markby said.

'You'll never know what I've worked out if you don't listen. Jan didn't intend to swallow the arsenic. He wasn't out to commit suicide. He was out to commit murder.'

He turned his head to look at her. 'Go on.'

'Right.' She pushed back a troublesome lock of brown hair and got down to the business of explaining her theory. 'This has always been about a will – or wills. Jan came to this country in the first place because he'd come across his great-grandfather's will and he thought he could use it to make himself some money. But when he got here he discovered there was no money, only a rambling great house sitting on a big piece of ground. That wasn't cash in hand but it would become cash in hand if and when it was sold. Right, so far?'

'No one's arguing with that.'

'Somehow he'd found out that Dudley Newman was interested.'

'Newman told him himself,' said Markby. 'He thought Jan might be an obstacle.'

'Did he? Well, Jan had started out by making an obstacle of himself, but he changed his mind when he heard there was a definite buyer in the offing. He wanted the house sold. But he'd realised that Damaris and Florence weren't just going to hand over half of the proceeds to him. They didn't like him. You and I, Pam Painter, Juliet, Laura, anyone who knew the Oakleys, we'd ganged up to prevent him talking the sisters round or pressuring them. But then he did a very simple bit of reasoning. The only Oakleys left in the world were the sisters and himself. If they were to die . . .'

'Ah,' said Markby. 'The wills in the desk.'

'Exactly. If both sisters died, he'd be in a good position to claim the estate, provided they hadn't left it to anyone else. So he took the opportunity to search the desk and he found what he was looking for, the wills. What's more, when he read them, they were just what he'd been hoping for. Each sister left everything to the other. They'd drawn up the wills some years ago when both had been younger. Jan decided quite cold-bloodedly to kill them – and he had the means.'

Meredith paused for comment but Markby said nothing. He was watching her with a thoughtful look on his face.

'The question of who took the arsenic from the potting shed wasn't really so hard to solve. Ron knew it was there but it had slipped his mind. Why had it done that? Because just as he found it, who should turn up but Jan himself, newly arrived. Ron was distracted. He didn't know who this person was and when he found out, the information filled his mind to the exclusion of all else. The shed was left unlocked. Neither Damaris nor Florence would have any reason to go in there. They didn't even know Ron had unscrewed the hasp. It was Jan, prying and poking around everywhere, who went in there and found it. He realised what it was and thought that he might have a need for it if his original plan didn't work out.'

Meredith's enthusiasm wavered. 'I can't prove it, I know. But I'm sure I'm right. Jan meant to poison the Oakleys and he chose to do it by spiking that savoury spread they like so much.'

'Everything in the kitchen cupboard was tested, including that spread.'

'Oh, that jar was all right,' said Meredith. 'It's the other one, the one Jan tampered with we've got to find. He swopped jars, you see. All he had to do was wait until later and then swop them back again.'

'So how did he end up being poisoned himself?'

'Because in the first place, Jan overestimated how much arsenic was required. Didn't Geoff Painter tell you he'd died from a massive dose, far more than would've been necessary? Jan must've realised the arsenic preparation found in the shed was a very old bottle and he may have thought it had lost some of its potency over the years and decided to compensate by being generous with it. Secondly, somehow the exchange of jars got confused. The sisters ate the spread in the cupboard and were none the worse for it. Jan thought they'd eaten the adulterated one. He let them go off to bed, believing they'd be taken ill during the night with what he hoped would appear to be acute gastro-enteritis. I don't think he meant them to die straight away. He planned them to be ill over a period of days. While he waited for the first attack to strike his victims, he fancied a snack. Perhaps it was a sort of gallows humour which made him decide to have some of the spread from the safe jar he'd just replaced in the cupboard. Damaris found a knife smeared with spread in the kitchen sink after she'd called the ambulance. But he'd muddled them up. The sisters ate from the safe jar and Jan ate from the tampered one. We've been looking at everyone, asking who did it. But he did it himself, just like Adrian.'

'Adrian?'

'I'll tell you about that later. What do you think, Alan?'

Markby shifted awkwardly in the cramped space. 'I think the blood supply to my feet has been cut off. I think it's an ingenious theory but only that. It can't be proved. Most of all, I can't see how a man who has hatched such a plan could then be so careless as to muddle up the jars. If he did, where is the adulterated jar of spread now? It ought, by your argument, to have been replaced by Jan in the kitchen cupboard. But the police took the jar from the cupboard and it was fine. If we go to Minchin with this, he'll rightly laugh us out of—'

Markby stopped speaking but still stared at her.

'Alan?' she prompted.

'Kenny Joss . . .' he said slowly. 'Kenny Joss was in that kitchen. Dave Pearce got the feeling he was holding something back. We will talk to Minchin. We'll talk to him right now. Well, come on then, let's go.'

'Your car's parked back there,' she reminded him.

He scrambled out of her car with a muffled curse and ran back to his own. She let him pull out in front of her and lead the way. It seemed more tactful.

Chapter Twenty-Four

'We can bring Joss in,' said Minchin.

He was sitting in Markby's office. Dust particles danced in a shaft of weak sunlight from the window. It fell on the speaker like a spotlight. Minchin hunched on his chair, his arms resting on his thighs and his broad hands loosely clasped. To look at Markby, he peered up beneath his bushy straw-coloured brows. Nevertheless, despite his present truculent appearance, Minchin had been in an usually good mood since he'd returned from his visit to the Painter household the previous afternoon. Perhaps the good humour had made him willing to listen without protest to Meredith's theory. Markby, who'd half expected him to refuse, was both relieved and surprised.

Now Meredith, having argued her case, had left. Minchin had sat silently throughout as she spoke, giving no indication of his inner reaction. Markby thought she'd explained her theory well and persuasively. But as he didn't know how much credibility Minchin was prepared to give it, he'd feared the worst. Now the two senior officers were left together to talk it over, Minchin had broken his silence with his laconic suggestion.

Markby, who'd still been expecting the other man to

begin by expressing his doubts if not dismissing Meredith's ideas completely, knew that his surprise must now be obvious.

'You think it worth questioning Joss again?' he asked, unable to believe Minchin had accepted Meredith's reasoning so easily.

As it turned out, it wasn't Meredith's reasoning which had influenced Minchin.

'You trust Dave Pearce's judgement?' Minchin's small hard blue eyes fixed Markby's face.

'Absolutely.' Dave could be difficult to detach from a pet idea and had brought wooden obstinacy to a fine art, but this wasn't the moment to say so. To express his complete and utter conviction of his subordinate's good sense was Markby's only possible response.

'And I trust Mickey Hayes's.' Minchin matched his display of confidence. 'He talked to Joss after Dave had had a go and told me he also thought Joss was hiding something. I was counting on Mickey getting it out of him. I thought Joss'd be bound to crack, but I was wrong. He only repeated what he'd told Dave Pearce.'

Like Pearce before him, Markby tried not to look too pleased at the thought of Hayes becoming unstuck.

'Mickey reckons, Joss put up a good front but underneath it, he's shit-scared. If we keep working on him, he'll crack eventually.'

Minchin finished on a comfortable note which made Markby a little uneasy. The man from the Met might well be right, but how long was he prepared to wait for Joss to speak up? Though the visitors had not caused the disruption in the office Markby had feared, he was still looking forward to the day they declared their enquiries closed and took themselves off.

'As for the rest of Meredith's ideas . . .' he began.

'Nice of her to come in,' said Minchin easily, 'but she didn't have anything new to tell us, did she? I mean, I'd pretty well worked all that out for myself already and I dare say you had, too.'

This took Markby's breath away for the moment and all he could think was, thank goodness Minchin didn't say this to Meredith's face. He could imagine the probable reaction.

'I'd formed no opinions,' he said at last, hoping he sounded dignified, rather than just pompous.

Minchin shook his massive finger at him. 'Who stands to benefit? *Cui bono*? That's the Latin for it, isn't it? Comprehensive-school boy myself, so I don't have any Latin, but you're a public-school man. You'll know all these phrases. That's what I asked myself. *Cui bono*?'

Again Markby was left bereft of speech, or at least of the ability to make an intelligent reply. How much research had Minchin done on him before coming here?

'Whoever took the poison from the shed, did it because he had murder in mind,' Minchin went on. 'So it was someone who'd benefit from the death of at least one other person. I considered the old ladies. They'd be heartily relieved if Jan dropped dead. But they'd got everyone including their solicitor on their side so really, they were probably capable of seeing off Jan without resorting to lacing his grub with arsenic. On the other hand, when you have two elderly people and one younger relative who's strapped for cash and thinks the old folk are sitting on a pile, well, there you do have a motive,' Minchin concluded appreciatively. 'One of the oldest in the world. The heir who can't wait.'

'He wasn't named in their wills,' said Markby, feeling he ought to lodge at least one objection to this feasible but annoyingly complacent explanation of events.

'No, but he was the only member of the family left, wasn't he? Any court would be sympathetic to his claims. So I reckoned Jan helped himself to the poison but somehow or other, muffed everything when he came to use it. What I haven't worked out yet is quite how – but there Joss could well provide the key.'

Minchin slowly became aware of Markby's stunned expression and had the grace to look a little apologetic. 'Look, I appreciate your girlfriend's input. I wouldn't have wanted to hurt her feelings by saying all this to her, but best leave the detection to the professionals, eh?'

Though Markby had frequently made similar observations to Meredith himself, he knew he couldn't agree now without feeling traitorous, so he contented himself with a nod and returned to the safer subject of Kenny Joss.

'It's your show,' he said carefully to Minchin. 'I would just like to make a suggestion.'

Minchin gave an unexpected grin. 'If I thought this was my show, I'd be a fool. You're the gaffer here and everyone's very keen to let me and Mickey Hayes know it! What's your idea?'

'I know the Joss family. We all do. They're a mix of petty crooks, wheeler-dealer traders and the fairly legit. Kenny, as far as we know, has kept his nose clean. However, the same can't be said of his relatives and if we bring Kenny in for questioning, he'll know the drill. He'll ask for a solicitor straight away and then sit there, refusing to speak a word.'

Minchin rubbed his chin with his thumbnail in the habit he had, and asked, 'They've got a regular solicitor?'

'Oh yes, indeed they have! Bertie Smith. Bertie has represented the Josses for years. They're the type of client in which he specialises, if I can put it like that. He's a familiar face in interview rooms around the county, is Bertie. No client is too seedy. A string of convictions as long as your arm won't prevent Bertie insisting that his client has been framed. Bertie's skill at finding loopholes in the law is unmatched.' Markby spoke with the bitterness born of experience.

'I know the type,' said Minchin in gloomy sympathy.

'I'm sure you do. Under Bertie's guidance, Kenny Joss will keep his secrets as effectively as the Sphinx. So what I'd suggest is that, instead of bringing him in here, we go to him. Yes, I know he's had other visits from the police and has seen them off. But we can turn that to our advantage. He'll be congratulating himself on having outwitted both Dave Pearce and Hayes. Maybe he'll have got a tad complacent? On his home ground, where he thinks he did so well before, we'll stand a much better chance of getting him talking before he decides he ought to phone Bertie. And as we know, the more often someone has to repeat a fabricated story, the greater the chance he'll start to contradict himself or slip up.' Markby smiled apologetically. 'I'm saying "we", but I should, of course, be saying "you". You and Inspector Hayes, I mean.'

Minchin was silent for a moment or two, tapping his broad fingertips on the desk. Then he said, 'Why don't you and I go together? It's unusual, I know that, but it might work. Faced with the two of us, he might just be overawed enough to lose his presence of mind and cough up the truth. How does that sound to you?'

'It sounds good,' Markby said promptly. 'After all, he's lied to Dave Pearce and he's lied to Mickey Hayes. But he hasn't lied to us, not to our faces. It'll make it easier for him to change tack if we can persuade him it's in his interest.'

But Kenny Joss was at work, somewhere in Bamford, driving his taxi. That was clear from the empty garage.

'What do we do?' asked Minchin, staring morosely through the windscreen of Markby's car. 'Go in and ask his wife, or whoever it is he's got manning the phone, to call him up?'

'If we do, the second person she'll call will be Bertie Smith. No.' Markby backed the car into a convenient gateway and turned back the way they'd come. 'I've got a better idea.'

He drove them back into town and turned into the car park of The Crown Hotel.

'Going for a pint?' asked Minchin, raising his eyebrows.

'Going to make a phone call.' Markby took out his mobile phone. 'Hang on, I need Directory Enquiries first. Hello? Yes, Bamford, please, a taxi firm – K. Joss . . . Right . . .' He scribbled the number on a notepad. 'Stage One,' he said to Minchin. 'Now for Stage Two.' He punched in Kenny's number. 'Hello? Yes, we need a taxi to pick us up from The Crown, to go to the railway station. How soon can he get here? . . . Fair enough. We'll wait by the hotel entrance.'

Markby put down the phone. 'Concepta Joss – she's his teenaged daughter not his wife – has called him on their radio link and her dad'll be here in ten minutes.'

'Concepta? Blimey,' commented Minchin.

'The Josses like names that roll off the tongue. Kenny was lucky.'

They wandered round to the front of the hotel and positioned themselves by its pillared porch.

'It don't look so bad, this place,' observed Minchin, glancing up at it.

'It's all right but it isn't home from home. I thought you'd be more comfortable in Meredith's place.'

'Nice little cottage, that. She says you're going to sell up both places and buy a house somewhere. You ought to get something pretty good with the money from both sales in your pockets.'

'It's not so easy, though,' said Markby. 'Good property costs the earth. A lot of people fancy living in this part of the world. That's why Dudley Newman is so anxious to get his hands on Fourways.'

Minchin searched in his pocket before taking his hand out empty and giving a mutter of discontent.

'Given up?' asked Markby sympathetically, recognising the reflex action of the recently reformed smoker.

'Trying to. I was starting to wheeze. Mickey Hayes smokes like a chimney. It doesn't help.'

Markby pointed. 'Here comes our man. Stage Three.'

The taxi drew up and Kenny Joss got out. He looked across the car roof at the two men by the portico and his expression became first puzzled, then wary.

'You call for a taxi?'

'That's right,' Markby said.

He opened the rear door and slid on to the back seat. Minchin walked round to the other door and joined him. Kenny, even more unhappy, clambered back into the driver's seat. He looked into the mirror, seeing their reflected faces.

'You want the railway station, right? That's what our Connie said.'

'Actually, we've changed our minds.' Markby leaned forward and reached his ID over Kenny's shoulder. 'How about we go somewhere private, Kenny?'

Kenny twisted in his seat aggressively. 'Am I being fitted up here or what?'

'We just want to talk, Kenny. Anywhere you like. Here, if you want.'

'We're not going back to my place,' Kenny told him. 'My missus would hit the roof if she found out the fuzz had been there again. "Police coming round all the time, Kenny, what you been up to?" I've been getting enough of that. And I'm not going with you to the nick, neither!' He considered the situation. 'We'll go down by the river, OK? Not that I've got anything to say to you.'

He let in the clutch and they lurched forward.

Markby thought Kenny had chosen the spot cleverly. There was a path along the riverside, a popular stroll in summer and at weekends, but deserted now except for the occasional dog-walker. At intervals there were benches interspersed with wooden tables with fixed seating for the use of summer picnickers. The aspens rustled above their heads and from time to time, out on the water, a spreading ring of concentric circles marked the spot where a trout had surfaced briefly. A pair of swans glided past. On the further bank beyond another line of trees, lay pasture land grazed peacefully by black and white cattle. It was a scene straight from a Constable painting and one in which it was difficult to pile on serious pressure, not when everything around them soothed the eye and lulled the senses.

They settled themselves at one of the picnic tables, Kenny on one side, Minchin and Markby facing him. Looking at the empty space beside Kenny, Markby wondered how long it would be before Kenny suggested it was filled by Bertie Smith. One of the swans, seeing people settling down in an attitude it associated with food, changed direction and paddled closer to the bank. When no lump of sandwich came its way, it paddled away again in clear disgust.

Either letting Kenny choose the place of their talk or the peaceful nature of their surroundings had already resulted in the man looking more relaxed than he had while driving. He was possessed of distinctive looks and probably cut a dashing figure among his associates. His complexion was swarthy and his thick black hair overlong but carefully tended. A regular Jack-the-Lad, thought Markby, and wondered whether, born two hundred years earlier, Kenny might have been a highwayman holding up travellers, rather than driving them about as now. As he watched, Joss leaned his forearms on the table and his dark gaze met Markby's.

'Go on, then,' he invited. 'What do you want to ask?'

'We want to go through Saturday afternoon with you,' Minchin said. 'I'm speaking of the day Jan Oakley died.'

'You've got all that on record. I drove the old girls into town and I brought them back. I've got nothing else to do with it.'

'When you came back with the women—' Minchin began.

Kenny interrupted. 'I went through that with the copper who came to my place. Not the London feller, the local chap. Then the London feller came and took me through the whole bleedin' lot again. I can only tell you what I told them. I carried the shopping round to the kitchen and then I left.'

'And you saw Jan Oakley?' Minchin prompted.

Markby fancied Kenny's confident attitude slipped a degree or two. He clasped his hands, unclasped them, looked from Minchin to Markby and said, 'I saw him as I was taking the shopping into the kitchen. We passed. We exchanged a word or two in greeting, that's all. I never saw him again.'

Very few people saw Jan again, thought Markby. He glanced at Minchin and took up the questioning. 'Kenny, we need to know every single thing Jan did that day. We're questioning you because we think you can help us fill in details which might not seem important to you, but may be to us. Now, when you returned from the shopping trip with the Oakley sisters, you told Inspector Pearce that they entered the house through the front door, whereas they'd left it through the kitchen door at the rear of the premises.'

'Ye-es,' Kenny agreed, his eyes cautious.

'I know that house quite well,' Markby said. 'If the front door is open, the quickest way to reach the kitchen is simply to walk through it and down the hall. The inner kitchen door is at the far end of the entrance hall. But you, so you claim, chose to walk all the way round the outside of the house to reach the outer kitchen door at the back, despite the fact that you were carrying heavy bags and the front door was wide open.'

'They weren't that heavy,' muttered Kenny sullenly.

'I think,' Markby said, 'on your return from the shopping trip, you went to the kitchen through the house. You didn't go round it to the back entrance as you did when you called for the fare. I can check quite easily. Either Damaris or

Florence Oakley will remember.'

There was a silence. Kenny said, 'I may have gone through the house. Perhaps I misremembered. I wasn't paying that much attention. Look, I didn't know it was going to be important, did I?'

'It is important, Kenny. This is a murder investigation. It's not a question of stolen goods or counterfeit designer wear – it's murder. We never close the file on an unsolved murder. It stays open and we stay with it, year in and year out, until we're satisfied. We're not going to leave you alone. We're going to keep coming back and we're going to have this conversation over and over again until we're satisfied. And I,' added Markby, 'am very far from satisfied and I doubt Mr Minchin is.'

Kenny said sulkily, 'I remember now. I went down the hall. I carried the stuff through the front door and to the kitchen that way, through the house.'

'So you didn't meet Jan coming out of the back door, as you told Inspector Pearce.' It was a statement, not a question.

Kenny accepted it as such but sought to split hairs. 'No, well, not exactly. I did see him go out of the kitchen. That's right.'

'Where were you when you saw him?'

'I was – ' Kenny looked from one to the other of them. 'I had nothing to do with his death, right? I didn't touch anything. I didn't do anything.' He waited but whatever kind of reassurance he was hoping for, didn't materialise. 'Bloody hell!' he snapped. 'Why should I kill him? I didn't even know him. I'd heard about him. Dolores told me – that's my cousin, Dolores Forbes at The Feathers. He used to eat there in the evening. She reckoned he was a bad lot and Dolores, she knows a thing or two about that. Her husband, Charlie Forbes – well, it don't matter. The thing is, she reckoned that Jan was up to no good.'

Kenny drew a deep breath and leaned forward, suddenly anxious to tell his story. 'I was carrying a couple of supermarket bags, the old girls' shopping. Damaris and Florrie, they were in the hall, taking off their hats and coats and generally messing about. I squeezed past them and went down the hall to the far end. I hadn't got a hand free to open the kitchen door but it was ajar, so I just gave it a push with my foot. It swung open, but not enough. It's one of those big heavy old doors. I was going to give it another shove when I saw him, that Jan. I could see him through the open crack of the door. He was on the far side of the kitchen, reaching up into the cupboard.'

Kenny paused and added in explanation, 'It's one of those old-style kitchen dressers, if you know the sort of thing. It's got cupboards below, then an open shelf and more cupboards above. It was the upper bit he was reaching into. Nothing odd about that, you'll say. But there was something odd about the way he was doing it. Furtive, that's the word. He'd got something in his hand. He reached up and put it in the cupboard. Then he took something else down. Just at the moment, one of the women said something and he must have heard the voice and thought they were coming. He looked round quick, guilty-like. I nipped back behind the door. When I took another look, he was straightening up. He'd been bending down by the bottom of the dresser, at the back of it. When he stood up, he wasn't holding anything. I reckoned he'd pushed something out of sight behind the dresser.

'Then he went into a sort of cloakroom that opens off the

kitchen. I've been in there and a narrow old staircase starts there and runs up at least as far as the first floor. I don't know how far it goes after that. The old dears don't use it. They don't use the cloakroom really, except to keep Wellington boots in and a pile of old newspapers and junk like that. The only reason I know what's in there is because they asked me to carry a sack of sand in there for them once. It was winter and they wanted it to sprinkle down outside the door – so's they wouldn't slip, you know. Anyway, that's where Jan went and I guess he went upstairs that way. Leastways, he wasn't hanging about in the cloakroom because I checked when I went into the kitchen.

'I put the shopping on the table. A couple of the frozen things I put in the freezer compartment of their fridge. They've got no proper freezer. I keep telling them to buy one. Then I took a quick look behind the dresser and sure enough, there was this little jar.'

Kenny made a round shape with his hands. 'It looked like the stuff you spread in your sandwiches, got a beefy taste.' He jabbed his finger at his interrogators. 'Marmite – that's what it's called. I can't tell you for sure that Jan put it there, because I didn't actually see him do it. So it's no use you trying to get me to say I did. But he held something very like it in his hand before he heard voices and took fright. When I looked again, he didn't have it and he was straightening up, like I say, as if he'd been bending down. Then he took himself off up those back stairs. He didn't want to be found there, red-handed.'

Minchin heaved a sigh. 'So what did you do next?'

Kenny shrugged. 'To tell you the truth – and it is the truth! – I didn't know what to do about it. I went back into the hall and looked for the elder sister, that's Damaris, but she was just on her way upstairs. Florrie was still in the hall, fluttering about. I had to make up my mind quick. I'd rather have told Damaris because she's the one who makes all the decisions, but she wasn't there, so I told Florrie – I call her that. She don't mind. I said something like, she ought to watch out for the foreign chap. He'd been messing around in the kitchen cupboards. It looked to me as if he'd hidden something behind the dresser.'

Kenny gave wry smile. 'She listened, peering up into my face like a little bird. She said, "Did he, Kenny? How very strange. I'll have a look." So I thought that was fair enough. She knew. I didn't really want to worry her so I said something to make her laugh, don't ask me what. Then I left.' Kenny sat back. 'And that's it.'

Markby said, 'Thank you, Kenny. You'd have saved us a lot of time by telling us straight away at the beginning. I think I know why you didn't, but you were wrong. We have to know.'

'Yeah,' said Kenny. 'Well, I'm fond of the old girls.'

Minchin spoke. 'You'd better drive us back to the hotel so's we can pick up our car.'

'Here,' said Kenny, 'is all this on the clock? I mean, I've been sitting here twenty minutes with you at least. More like half an hour. I'm a working man, you know. I don't drive that taxi for my health.'

'So,' said Minchin, as they drove out of Bamford, 'Jan Oakley swopped the jars. He put the contaminated one in the cupboard and hid the safe one behind the dresser when he was disturbed. Then Florence Oakley, tipped off by Kenny

Joss, switched them back again. Is that what we think happened?'

They were driving towards Fourways. Markby had turned the car in that direction without comment and Minchin had been sitting silently beside him until now.

'Funny,' Minchin continued, 'I'd have said the other sister was the more likely one. You know, more a woman of action.'

'Florence couldn't have known for sure that there was anything wrong with the jar in the cupboard,' Markby said. 'But she may have been suspicious enough to swop them back, yes. That's not murder. I'd call that no more than a tragic error of judgement.'

'We can decide what it was when we can prove she did it,' said Minchin sourly. 'Anyhow, assuming she did, when she and her sister ate some of the spread in the evening, they were unaffected. But later, when Jan retrieved the jar behind the dresser, he believed it was the safe jar. He decided to have a snack using it and poisoned himself. So far, so good,' Minchin said. 'But when the police took a jar of spread from the cupboard to test it, there was nothing wrong with it and if there had been a jar behind the dresser, we'd have found it.'

'Things have been overlooked before,' said Markby. 'SOCO isn't infallible. For all we know, it's still there.'

'No, no,' said Minchin, 'that's not my point. Look, this is how it goes, assuming we're right. Jan puts bad jar in cupboard, good jar behind dresser. Kenny sees him and tips off Florence. Florence replaces good jar in cupboard, bad jar behind dresser. Sisters eat from good jar, no problem. Later that evening when they've gone to bed, Jan nips into the kitchen. He puts the good jar (which he thinks is the bad jar) back behind the dresser, right? He puts the bad jar (which he thinks is the good one) in the cupboard. Then he decides to make himself a sandwich with some of it and poisons himself. *So why wasn't the bad jar still in the cupboard where he'd put it, the next morning?'*

'Because,' Markby said, 'someone, either Damaris or Florence, realised what must have happened when he was taken so ill and switched them back again – or at least replaced the good jar in the cupboard for us to find and disposed of the bad jar. We don't know whether Florence told Damaris what Kenny had seen. If she didn't, then Florence is the one who realised Jan had been poisoned by some substance intended for her and her sister. But because he was poisoned as a result of her switching the jars, she panicked. She thought she'd be accused of deliberately poisoning him. She replaced the good jar and I don't know what she did with the other one.'

'You realise,' Minchin said, 'that proving all this will turn on finding the bad jar?'

They had passed The Feathers and the house came into view. Markby turned in the gateway and for some reason, perhaps prompted by distant memory, braked. They sat looking down the drive at Fourways.

'I used to come here as a kid,' he said.

'I'll do the talking when we go in,' offered Minchin quietly. 'I'll go in alone, if you like. You don't want to be asking awkward questions of the old women. I can understand that. That's why I'm here, after all.'

'No, I'll come with you,' Markby told him absently. 'It'll calm them to see me. I was just thinking of when I first saw this place, as a nipper. It looked like something out of a story book to me, especially with that turret up there. I thought an ogre must live here and I wasn't far wrong. Old Mr Oakley was a man of strong personality, a domestic tyrant.'

He contemplated the house, glowing like honey in the evening sunshine. It looked its best at this hour of the day. Its unhappy history was disguised by the warmth which seemed to emanate from it. Even its gargoyle waterspouts looked playful. For good or ill, Fourways had been a landmark for a hundred and fifty years. He was sorry to think its days might be numbered.

Then something very strange happened. As from nowhere, thunder filled the air. A huge clap followed by a roaring, rumbling swell as if some great monster were indeed on the loose. The car shook as if struck by an unseen balled fist. The whole east wing of the house rippled and swayed, then ballooned outward. One side of it vanished in a cloud of smoke and dust, through which could be heard the crash of falling masonry. The cloud grew, enveloping the whole structure until it was completely lost from sight. From out of the swirling mass flew the turret, all in a piece like a giant rocket. It splintered its way through the trees and fell with a mighty rending and cracking on to the old stableblock and more smoke and dust swirled up into the sky. Scarlet streaks of flame spurted up and darted through the whole in a tangle of red, yellow, grey and white like a giant witchball.

Minchin gasped, 'It's bloody blown up!'

But Markby was already calling for help.

PART THREE

Family Secrets

I could a tale unfold, whose lightest word
Would harrow up thy soul . . .

Hamlet, Act I, Scene 5

Chapter Twenty-five

'Both the gas company's investigator and the fire service are satisfied the explosion was due to a slow build-up from a leak,' Alan Markby said. 'We all know how many gas appliances there were in that house – a gasfire in each main room, a gas boiler to heat the bath water, a small gasheater to heat water in the kitchen. None of the appliances had been overhauled in a month of Sundays. The most likely culprit is the old kitchen stove, although the bathroom geyser was also dodgy, it seems. Almost anything could have set it off.'

'But how about the sisters?' Pam Painter asked anxiously.

They were seated on the Painters' patio and awaiting with some trepidation the results of Geoff's culinary efforts at his brand-new barbecue stand. The gathering comprised the Painters themselves and Juliet, Markby and Meredith and Doug Minchin, who was due to return to London the following day. Hayes had already departed. Dr and Mrs Fuller had been invited but had regretfully declined owing to a prior engagement. The good pathologist was attending a performance of Schubert's Trout Quintet at which, it seemed, every instrument was manned by a member of the Fuller clan including Mrs Fuller at the piano and a talented nephew on the double-bass.

369

'Damaris, by a stroke of luck, was outside in the garden,' Markby told them. 'Although she's severely shocked and the blast took her off her feet, resulting in extensive bruising, she's otherwise uninjured, no broken limbs. She's staying with James Holland in the care of Mrs Harmer his housekeeper.'

Meredith shuddered. 'Poor Damaris. James sent Mrs Harmer to look after me when I had flu. I don't mean Mrs Harmer isn't in her element when tending the sick, but her idea of an invalid diet would turn anyone's stomach.'

'James says she's in seventh heaven now she's got Damaris at her mercy,' said Juliet. 'Poor James himself is being neglected. Mrs H. has no time for him.'

For a moment Pam looked as if the interesting possibilities opened up by this scenario might distract her. Regretfully she put her match-making plans for Juliet on hold. 'But Florence? I heard she was badly hurt.'

'Trapped in the wreckage,' Doug Minchin put in unexpectedly. 'They dug her out alive but things don't look good.'

Mutterings from the barbecue took their attention. Rather a lot of smoke seemed to be coming from it. The chef, splendidly attired in a scarlet apron and armed with what looked like an assortment of medieval weapons was making feints and stabs at the enemy in the shape of pork chops and sausages.

Pam whispered, 'We've never had a barbecue before, but when we moved here Geoff got it into his head it would be just the thing for the patio.'

'Won't be long!' cried the chef optimistically as another balloon of black smoke wafted skyward.

'It's not,' continued Pam, 'as if he were a cook normally. He never goes in the kitchen, never has. Now he's got this new toy . . .'

'You've seen her, haven't you, Doug?' asked Alan, taking up the previous subject. 'Meredith's hoping to go to the hospital tomorrow.'

'With Juliet,' said Meredith. 'If Florence is fit to have visitors – and it sounds as though she is.' She looked across to Minchin and raised her eyebrows.

'Surely she's not in a condition to be interviewed?' Juliet, aghast at such an idea, bounced on her chair. 'Geoff!' she added irritably. 'For God's sake, we're all being kippered!'

'Not an interview,' said the imperturbable Minchin, waving away a ribbon of smoke trailing past his nose. He'd exchanged his suit for chinos and navy sweatshirt stretched across his broad shoulders. It all suggested his profession lay less in policework than in pugilism.

'Not as such,' he qualified his statement. 'She asked to see me, as it happens, so I went along. There's nothing wrong with her brain,' he added to Juliet. 'She's perfectly coherent, clear as a bell – OK as far as her mind goes. But you've got to remember, she has broken ribs and a broken ankle. The problem is, broken bones are one thing. A broken spirit is another. If you ask me, she's . . .' Minchin paused, seeking a phrase. 'She's calling it a day, if you know what I mean.'

'Oh, this won't do at all!' cried Pam. 'Obviously she's in shock and depressed. She needs someone to cheer her up. When you and Juliet go tomorrow, Meredith, you must—'

'She hasn't got the strength,' Minchin interrupted. 'Not physically, not mentally.'

'You said her mind was all right,' argued Juliet.

'So it is. But she can't cope with the future, whatever it is. Too much trouble. So she's decided to tidy up the loose ends and call it a day.'

'But for Damaris's sake!' Juliet wasn't giving up.

Minchin said to her, his voice surprisingly gentle, 'No.'

Juliet flushed and sat back in her chair, looking troubled. There was an awkward silence. Geoff turned from his fiery furnace, fork in hand, resembling a slightly harassed devil. He cleared his throat and asked diffidently, 'I suppose it's not in order to ask what she had to say to you?'

Minchin hesitated but Alan Markby said, 'Tell them, Doug. They won't be satisfied until they know.'

Minchin shrugged and turned his attention to Meredith. 'Your ideas tallied with ours.'

'You mean I was right?' Meredith asked politely.

That got her a fishy look. 'Tallied with ours,' repeated Minchin heavily. 'I expect you've heard that Kenny Joss saw Jan apparently hiding something behind the kitchen dresser? And that he told Florence?'

They all nodded. The unattended barbecue spat but this time no one paid it any attention.

'Well, off she went to take a look,' continued Minchin. 'She found a jar of savoury spread, open and half-used. She recognised it, she says, as the one they'd been using because there was a dent in the tin lid. When she looked in the upper cupboard of the dresser, lo and behold, she found another jar, but this one had no dent in the lid. It was open and half the contents had been scooped out making it look like the original jar. She didn't know what Jan was up to but she decided it was no good. She didn't want to worry her sister, so she said nothing and switched the jars back, meaning to throw away later the one she suspected Jan of planting. But she didn't get a chance. Damaris came into the kitchen as she was about to replace the jar with the dented lid (the good jar as we now know it to be). Having been caught with it in her hand, Florence made the excuse that she was about to prepare their tea.

'Jan put in an appearance shortly after that but didn't stay long. He went off to watch telly until it was time for him to go to The Feathers. In order to keep out of his way, the sisters stayed in the kitchen, preventing Florence retrieving the bad jar from behind the cupboard. They didn't move to the sitting room until Jan had left, and by then it was getting late. Well, late by their standards!' Minchin permitted himself a brief grin. 'So Florence decided to leave disposing of the suspect jar until the next day. Unfortunately for Jan, he was unaware of this and when he had returned from The Feathers and was satisfied the sisters had gone to bed, he switched the jars back again. So now the poisoned one was back in the cupboard and Jan had tucked away the good one behind the dresser as he'd done originally. As far as he was concerned, he was satisfied the sisters had eaten the poisoned one. He expected them to become ill. Got a bit too clever and managed to outsmart himself!' Minchin informed them with satisfaction. 'He decided to make himself a snack using what he believed to be the good jar and was hoist with his own petard, as the saying goes. If he'd got the dose right, he might not have died. But he got it wrong. He was a lad with a lot of ideas, was Jan. But he slipped up in putting them into effect. I've met a lot of crooks like that.'

'I don't feel a bit sorry for him!' declared Pam Painter robustly.

'Meredith does,' Juliet accused.

'No, I don't!' Meredith denied indignantly. 'I admit, I did feel a bit sorry for him when he first turned up, but not very sorry, not even then.'

'I never felt sorry for him,' riposted Juliet.

'Excuse me,' Alan said mildly, 'I don't think Doug's finished.'

Everyone looked at Minchin. 'Not quite,' he said. 'But nearly, so you girls can start pulling each other's hair in a minute.' He ignored their reaction to this and went on, 'Well, that's about it, really. The poor old lady was shaken to the core when Jan dropped dead that selfsame night. She guessed what had happened, realised her failure to dispose of the suspect jar had been the cause of it, and thought she'd be accused of poisoning him. She crept downstairs in the early hours when her sister was asleep, switched the jars back again and took the poisoned jar to her room where she hid it at the back of the wardrobe. She didn't know at that stage *what* was in it, naturally.'

'Did she throw it away?' demanded Meredith. 'Can you retrieve it? Have you any idea where it is?'

'Oh yes,' said Minchin. 'It's under a couple of tons of rubble. She couldn't think of any safe way of disposing of it. She was in a complete panic and not thinking clearly at all. She reckoned, if she put it in the dustbin, Damaris might see it. If she buried it in the garden, that gardener of theirs might dig it up. In the end, she left it where it was in the wardrobe and it went up with everything else in the explosion.'

'And the arsenic?' Geoff asked suddenly. 'Have you found that?'

374

Minchin shook his head. 'Probably Jan hid it about the house and it's gone up with the rest.'

Markby said nothing. He was thinking of all those toiletries on Jan's dressing table. Swop the arsenic for the contents of a jar of bath salts, get rid of the empty bottle in a bottle bank in town? That's what I'd do, he thought. Had SOCO checked when they'd made a sweep of the room? I should've thought about that, he told himself angrily. That very first morning when I heard of his death, I should've removed every damn bottle and tin from that bedroom! If I had, I might've sewn this up before Minchin and Hayes set foot in Bamford. But I didn't do it. Winsley was right to send for someone else. I had too much sympathy for the Oakleys. I didn't want to distress them. It made me slapdash.

'Let's hope so,' Geoff was saying grumpily. 'The stuff blown to smithereens and dispersed about the landscape suits me just fine. I don't want Fuller sending me any more body organs, not for a while, anyway.' He brightened, 'All ready here! Who's for a pork chop?' He waited. 'Well, don't all rush at once.'

Guiltily, they proffered their plates.

'Perhaps,' said Pam, poking a blackened sausage, 'Geoff will lose interest in that barbecue soon.'

After the spell of fine weather, the following day was overcast and cool. Meredith parked in the hospital visitors' car park and she and Juliet set out towards the main building in silence. Both were apprehensive as to what they'd find.

As they neared the doors, Juliet murmured, 'Perhaps Doug Minchin is wrong.' But she didn't sound as though she held much hope of this.

'Miss Oakley is in a private room,' the nurse told them brightly.

Both visitors looked at her startled and then at each other as they followed her down the corridor.

'Who's paying for it?' whispered Meredith.

Juliet only shook her head in bewilderment.

'Here we are!' announced the nurse. 'Now, you won't stay long, will you? She'll be pleased to have visitors but she tires very quickly. Ten minutes, all right?'

The room was small but pleasant. Several people seemed to have sent Florence flowers but to Meredith's mind, instead of giving a cheerful aspect to the room, the impression was more of a funeral. Florence lay propped up in bed. The television was on, facing the end of the bed so that she could see it, but she didn't appear to be watching. It was some morning chat show or other featuring a row of people on a virulently hued overstuffed sofa. For all her injuries, Florence looked quite pink and well, her white hair braided into a single plait which hung over her shoulder. With shock, Meredith thought, *This is how Juliet will look when she's old, like this*.

Juliet had gone to the bed and stooped to kiss Florence's brow. 'We've brought you some grapes, Florence, and some fruit juice.'

'How very kind,' Florence said, and it was when she spoke that Meredith knew what Doug Minchin had meant. Florence's voice was polite but detached. Her smile too had a mechanical air about it, as if voice and muscles were all working, but the person behind them wasn't there.

They seated themselves by the bedside, Juliet said earnestly, 'You've got to buck up, Florence. You've got to think of Damaris.'

'Damaris is very capable.' Again that polite detachment. 'She was always so much more sensible than I ever was. I always did foolish things. I always had ideas but never managed to think them through.' For a moment emotion entered her voice but it was a kind of bewilderment, as if Florence spoke about someone else. She turned her head on the pillow and regarded them as if they held the answer.

'We all do silly things from time to time, Florence,' Meredith said. She guessed that Florence was thinking of her actions with the jars of savoury spread which had led to Jan's death.

She was right. Florence said carefully, 'I didn't mean to kill Jan.'

'You didn't kill him – that is, he was responsible. He tampered with the contents of the jar and he made himself the – the sandwich.' Meredith had almost said 'fatal sandwich' but that would have been tactless.

Florence wouldn't have been bothered if she had said it. She looked a little put out as if Meredith had questioned her word. 'I changed the pots,' she said pettishly. 'That's why he died.'

'No, Florence,' Juliet said. 'That's why you and Damaris lived. Don't you see that? You saved Damaris's life and your own. It was a good thing you exchanged the jars.'

Florence's gaze had grown absent. 'You see how silly it all is? I didn't mean to kill *him* but he died, anyway. Isn't it odd how things turn out the same way whether you mean them to or not? If I try and kill someone he dies and if I don't, he still dies. Perhaps that's Fate. Or do I mean predestination? No, I don't think I do. I think I mean what Damaris always calls bad luck.'

'She's confused,' whispered Juliet. 'First she says she didn't mean it, now she's saying she did. I hope Doug Minchin realised how muddled she is.'

But Meredith said quietly, 'No, I don't think she is.'

'Now you're not making sense,' Juliet began, but was interrupted by Florence's low clear voice.

'Have you seen the vicar? I asked him to call.'

'If you sent for James, he'll be on his way,' Juliet promised.

'I want to tell him all about it. It's very important that I tell him.'

'You've told Superintendent Minchin and so you don't have to worry about it any more,' Juliet insisted.

Again Florence looked tetchy. 'No, I didn't. I want to tell the vicar.'

'He'll be here, Florence – oh!' Meredith looked up in relief at the sound of heavy footfall. 'He's here now.'

James Holland's bulky frame filled the doorway. Meredith got to her feet and Juliet followed suit. James approached the bed as quietly as he could and whispered, 'Good morning. How is she?'

'She's got something on her mind,' Meredith said before Juliet could speak. 'She wants to tell you something, I'm sure.'

Juliet looked from the occupant of the bed to Meredith and back again. Then she said gently to Florence, 'As James is here, Meredith and I will go now. But we'll come back tomorrow.'

'That would be very nice,' said Florence in that chillingly blank way.

'What do you make of it?' Juliet asked urgently as they left the hospital building.

'I don't know, but it's not our business. Whatever it is, it's between her and her God. That's why she wants James,' Meredith said firmly.

Juliet looked unhappy but didn't argue.

Meredith asked, 'When are you going back to London? I thought you could come over and have dinner with us, or better still, considering my cooking, we could all go out somewhere.'

'Thanks, but it'll have to wait. I'm going back to London this afternoon, right now. I've called in here to check on Florence which is what I wanted to do.' Juliet hesitated. 'I've got to go because I have a date in Town this evening.'

'Oh?' Meredith wondered whether she was to be told the name of Juliet's swain.

Red in the face, Juliet said, 'I'm going out for a meal with Doug.'

'Doug? You mean Minchin, as in Superintendent Minchin?' Meredith stopped in her tracks in the middle of the car park and stared at her companion.

'You don't have to sound so surprised,' said Juliet huffily. 'Dorothy Parker wasn't entirely right about girls who wear glasses, I told you so. Although,' she added in a burst of honesty, 'Doug doesn't like mine. Still, he'll have to get used to them, won't he?' Juliet considered the point. 'I mean, I don't like his shirts.'

James Holland had taken his seat by the bedside. 'Are you in pain, Florence?'

'No.' She moved her head on the pillow in a negative gesture. 'They gave me pills for that.'

'Good. I was going to come and see you, anyway, but I believe you asked for me. I came over straight away and failed to bring you any flowers or fruit, but you seem pretty well provided for in that line.'

'Yes.' Florence moved one frail hand, nothing but bone and skin, discoloured by dark bruises. 'I need to tell you about him.'

'About Jan?'

'Jan?' For a moment Florence appeared to have forgotten who Jan was. Then she rallied. 'No, not Jan. I mean my father.'

'Ah . . .' said Father Holland. 'I know a little about that. Alan told me. He saved up his sleeping pills and – er – took them all at once.'

'No, he didn't,' said Florence pettishly. 'That's just where you're wrong. He didn't save them up. I did.'

The vicar felt a chill hand touch his spine. 'I think you're a little confused, dear. I expect it's the painkillers.'

'There's no point in your coming,' she said, showing some animation for the first time, 'if you won't listen.'

'I'm listening, Florence. Sorry,' he said contritely.

'He was a very good father when we were young.' Florence turned her head to fix him with a stern look. 'You must believe that. But he changed when Arthur died. Then Mother died and he got worse. Finally, arthritis put him in a wheelchair and he *hated* that. He was all eaten up with hate. He even hated us, Damaris and me, because we lived and Arthur had died. Oh yes,' she raised her thin hand again to stop any interruption on her listener's part. 'He didn't consider two daughters worth one son.'

'You were caring for him! Where would he have been without you?' James couldn't prevent himself saying, deeply shocked.

'Oh, well, that's what daughters did in those days. Unmarried ones like Damaris and me, anyway.' Florence dismissed this as a quibble. 'I thought Damaris and I would never get away, not while we were still young enough to make something of our lives. He wasn't a happy man. We were all unhappy, all three of us, in that house. So I saved up his pills and gave him aspirin instead. He grumbled and said he couldn't understand why he was sleeping so badly. He meant to ask the doctor for stronger pills. That evening, he grumbled so much, I suggested he had a good stiff whisky, to make him sleep. He wasn't much of a drinker but he agreed. I poured him out a jolly good glassful!' Florence sounded satisfied.

'And the sleeping pills?' Father Holland barely dared ask.

'Oh, those. I'd already made sure he'd taken those. I mixed them in his shepherd's pie. He was very fond of shepherd's pie. I never liked it so I didn't have any and Damaris didn't have any, either, because she always reacted badly to anything made with mince.'

'Right,' said the vicar faintly.

'He just went off to sleep,' Florence said. 'And that was that. Or I thought it would be, but then, I don't think things through very well. I told Meredith and Juliet that. Our doctor insisted on a postmortem because Father wasn't ill enough to die. As if that mattered at his age. Still, it turned out all right because he'd grumbled so much to the doctor about how unfair life was, that the coroner decided it must be suicide.' Florence pursed her thin lips. 'He was right about life being unfair. I hadn't thought it through. If I had, I'd have realised that it was already too late for Damaris and me. We'd never leave Fourways. We were stuck there for the rest of our lives. Killing Father was a waste of time, really. It didn't make any difference in the long run.'

Father Holland struggled to rally and sound practical. 'Florence, when you did this, you were under great stress. Obviously your father had become unbearably difficult. It's a pity your doctor hadn't suggested a nursing home for him.'

'He wouldn't have gone into a nursing home!' Florence said in surprise. 'Not while he had a house of his own and us. Anyway, we Oakleys, we don't farm out our problems. We take care of them ourselves. Even,' she added regretfully, 'if we do always seem to make a mess of it.'

She turned her head away from him and gestured towards a stack of magazines which lay on a bedside cabinet on the further side of the bed. 'They've left those for me to read. I was looking at one last night. There is an article about some things called genes. I hadn't known anything about genes before. We all have them. Genes can carry all sorts of things, apparently. Predisposition to some diseases and some people think some kinds of behaviour. Tell me, Vicar . . .' Florence turned her head back and met his appalled gaze with her serene expression. 'Do you think there might be a gene for murder? We Oakleys do seem rather inclined towards it.'

Chapter Twenty-Six

The bay window in the sitting room of the one-bedroom flat looked out over the promenade and the beach and sea beyond. It was late summer now and the promenade was thronged with holidaymakers. In winter, the number of strollers would thin dramatically but there would always be someone walking out there in the fresh ocean air.

'Which is really nice,' said Juliet to Damaris, 'because you'll be able to sit here by your window and watch the world go by. There will always be something to look at, something happening. It's got to be better than living in some place so secluded you don't see anyone but the milkman. From the security point of view it's a good thing, too. Anyone coming to the street door of the building is in full view. The double-glazing is really efficient. No matter how much it blows out there, you'll always be snug in here. I'm sure you'll like it, Damaris.'

'Yes, I dare say I shall,' Damaris said placidly. 'It will be nice to see a bit of life and a few young faces. You chose well for me, Juliet, and I'm very grateful for all your help.'

Juliet looked round the room. Since the gas explosion had taken care of the furniture at Fourways, all but one of the items in here were new. Not that there were many of them: a three-piece suite in chintz, a drop-leaf table and two chairs. The sole survivor from Fourways was a Victorian rolltop desk, very much knocked about.

'They built to last in those days,' said Juliet of this item. 'Just think, all that rubble fell on it and still, when they cleared it away, there the old desk stood. Pity about the crack down one side. Still, it doesn't look too bad.'

Damaris said nothing. Juliet, conscience-stricken, said, 'I'm sorry, I shouldn't have talked about the explosion. You must miss Florence dreadfully.'

Damaris stirred. 'Yes. She was the younger and by rights should have outlived me, but I always knew her health was fragile. Even without the accident, I think she would have predeceased me. I should have found myself alone. I could've wished she'd died at home and not in the hospital, though they were very kind to her and she was comfortable there. More comfortable than she'd have been in Fourways if it had stayed standing. I think,' said Damaris in her practical way, 'the bathroom geyser was to blame. It always had a mind of its own.'

Juliet hesitated, unwilling to appear to pry, but eventually curiosity got the better of her. 'The private room at the hospital must have been expensive.'

'Oh, but Dudley Newman paid for that,' Damaris said. Seeing how startled her visitor looked, she explained, 'I went to him at once, the moment Florence was taken to hospital. I said now the house had collapsed that must suit his purpose. He never wanted the house, only the land. I'd sell him the land and the ruins and he could do what he liked with it. Only, I needed some money straight away – up front, I believe the expression is. I wanted my sister to have the comfort and privacy of a private room and treatment. If he'd meet the costs now, he could deduct whatever it was from whatever he intended to pay me for the land. So that's what he did. He did pay a fair price, didn't he, Juliet? You said so, at the time.'

'Yes, he did, and you're right, the house being in ruins did suit his purpose. I still believe he'd have met opposition if he'd tried to demolish it.'

Damaris looked round the room. 'I did wonder, when I first moved in here, whether, had we not decided to sell up, Jan would have started plotting as he did. Perhaps he'd just have hung around for a bit making a nuisance of himself and then gone back to Poland.'

'No,' said Juliet. 'He'd still have been snooping round looking for your wills and trying to persuade you to change them. He'd still have found the arsenic in the shed. He might still have decided to use it. He was a nasty bit of work, Damaris.'

'I always knew that. Anyway,' added Damaris a little inconsequentially, 'as Fourways fell down, we'd have had to move in any case. If he'd still been alive, it might have fallen on Jan and got rid of him. Instead of that, it fell on Florence. I'm sorry it took my sister with it, but I'm still glad the house has gone, because really it had taken both of us long ago. Swallowed us up.'

A little hesitantly, Juliet asked, 'Did you know the estate Newman plans to build there will be called Fourways Estate? I think he'd like to call the main roadway running through it Oakley Drive, if you don't object and the council don't. Well, they won't if you don't – Pam'll see to that. It would be a nice memorial to Florence, I thought.'

'Arthur,' said Damaris firmly. 'It ought to be called Arthur Oakley Drive after my brother. Florence has a grave but Arthur has no proper resting place. Try and get them to call it after him.'

'I'll do my best. Anyway, it'll be Oakley for a long time to come.'

Damaris gave one of her surprisingly impish grins. 'Goodness, on the map!'

It seemed a good moment to depart on this upbeat note. Juliet tried not to look too obviously at her wristwatch. 'I'll come and see you again, Damaris, so will Meredith and Alan. James, too, when he can get away.'

Damaris gave a sad smile. 'Thank you. You'll come for a few months, but then you'll be too busy. That's as it should be. Your life is really only at its beginning. I shall be content to sit mine out here. I've discovered there is a very good public library.' She got to her feet to show her visitor out. On their way to the door, they passed by the Victorian rolltop desk.

'Grandfather William's,' said Damaris briefly. She tapped the painted initials, now scratched almost illegible. 'Should have left it behind, really. We were never able to shake off his shadow. Here I am, in a new abode, in a new town, in a new part of the country and look, I've lumbered myself with this memento of that dreadful rogue. I must be a glutton for punishment.'

'Funny,' Juliet mused, 'we'll never know if that will really existed or whether that certified translation Jan showed us was just a fake.'

Damaris didn't reply. She was an honest woman and wouldn't have wished to lie to Juliet, of all people. But she'd spent that Sunday, after news of Jan's death had been conveyed to them, searching the turret room. If there was a will, Jan would've kept it by him, she was sure. And she'd found it. He'd slipped it under the cracked linoleum in the corner of the room. It had been in German. She'd learned some German as a girl, so she had been able to read it with a little difficulty and the help of a dictionary. It had been just as Jan had claimed. Whether or not it would have been valid was another matter. Probably not, but to be on the safe side, she had burnt it.

'Drive carefully, dear,' she said to Juliet.

'I'm taking all this over to James,' Meredith said, carefully knotting string round the box containing Geoff Painter's research into the death of Cora Oakley. 'James wanted to look through it before I return it to Geoff.'

'Was it worth looking through?' Alan asked from behind the latest copy of *The Garden* magazine.

'It was fascinating, and making up my mind was difficult. I feel in my bones that William was guilty if only because, had he been innocent, I think he would have had the nerve to brazen out local disapproval. He wouldn't have run away like that. I think Geoff's right and William was lucky. If there had been another witness to back up the housekeeper it would've gone differently. Martha Button gave her evidence so confidently at the outset, but once defence counsel began on her, she went to pieces. She never retracted her claim but defence succeeded in making her look less reliable. If the factory had just reported some arsenic missing . . . But I suppose it was such a tiny amount no one noticed. William was a bad lot, there's no denying that. The evidence of the girl, Daisy Joss, has to be taken with a giant pinch of salt!'

Alan put down his magazine. 'A man may be a bad lot, a gambler, womaniser, a thoroughly rotten husband. It doesn't follow he's murdered. Nor does the fact that Cora apparently believed he'd seduced the nursemaid mean that he really had, no matter what Cora told the housekeeper. Don't forget, there was some evidence that she might have been a dope-addict, given to wild imaginings.'

'No real evidence. The pharmacist was keen to stress he didn't know that was the case, only that it might be so if she carried on taking the laudanum. And isn't that what pompous male authority used to say to any woman who kicked up a fuss? *You're imagining it, my dear!* I can just see Wicked William letting it be known, oh very cleverly through his counsel, that his wife was an addict. Who was there to contradict him? Poor Cora was dead. You can say what you like about the dead.'

'That's why evidence has to be tested. That's where "beyond reasonable doubt" comes in. That's why it's often so damn difficult to nail your man. Mrs Button should have come forward much earlier. Had the original inquest heard her evidence, it might not have reached a verdict of accident. Once they had reached that verdict then it was a question of overturning it. A jury has to be awfully convinced before it overturns the verdict of a previous one.'

'But do you think he did it?' Meredith challenged. 'Never mind the evidence, what do you think?'

'Of William? Did he mess around with arsenic and a do-it-yourself chemistry set? Yes, probably. But I wouldn't hope to get a conviction on the evidence of that housekeeper. So we're back to what a police officer thinks, as against what he can prove. If you really want to know what bothers me, bearing in mind I have no proof . . .

'Go on, anyway,' Meredith urged. She settled back in her chair, her hands loosely holding the box of papers.

'Well, I'd like to know the real reason Mrs Button was dismissed. Two possible reasons were put forward at the trial. That William's guilty conscience was shaken by the sight of her. That William's grieving heart was troubled by the sight of her. But perhaps Mrs Button had an agenda of her own? Possibly she knew more about arsenic as a substance than she let on. She'd have used the stuff to kill vermin all her life. Perhaps she knew at once what the garlic smell meant. At the very least she was quick-witted enough to realise something had been set up in that room, some kind of apparatus. Perhaps she intended to use the knowledge to blackmail her employer. That's why she said nothing at the inquest. After a couple of weeks she went to William and told him she had evidence which could overturn the verdict. William knew that if he paid her once, he'd be in her power for ever. He had to get rid of her. But he couldn't afford to have another suspicious death in the house! What he could do was discredit her in advance. He knew that by dismissing her from her place, anything she later said would look like the words of a vengeful servant. It was a bit of a gamble of course, but we know William was a gambling man.'

He picked up his magazine again. 'On the other hand, perhaps Cora was a laudanum addict who, under the influence of her favoured drug, stumbled out of bed, brought down the lamp and burned herself to death. After all, in the end, that's what a jury decided had happened. William was acquitted. You may think he should have hanged. It might have saved a lot of trouble in the long term if he had! But you wouldn't want to send an innocent man to the gallows, would you, just to save a lot of trouble?'

'No, I suppose not.'

'Only suppose not?' he asked with a grin.

'You know what I mean.' She tapped the lid of the box. 'If nothing else, all this is worth reading because of the reporter's notebooks. He was a chap called Stanley Huxtable.' She smiled. 'They contain a mystery of their own.' At his raised eyebrows, she explained, 'On one page he's sketched a woman in full mourning and beneath it he's written *If you live in Bamford I'll find you*. How do you explain that? It doesn't appear to have anything to do with the trial.'

'Perhaps he fell in love?' Markby suggested from behind his magazine. 'People have fallen in love in stranger places than in a courtroom. Emotions run high during trials. Perhaps Huxtable got carried away.'

She was silent for a while and then said, 'Alan . . .'

He lowered the magazine and looked at her cautiously. She was sitting with the box of papers on her knees, cradling it. She looked uncharacteristically nervous.

She said, 'I've been thinking and I've decided it will be best if I move back into my place in Station Road for a while.'

'Oh,' he said. 'I see.' His voice was bleak.

'No,' she told him quickly. 'I'm not crying off the whole idea of us sharing a home. It's just that it can't be this one, which is your home, nor can it be Station Road, which is mine. I feel like a visitor here. You'd feel the same in my place. We've said we'll look for a house together and we will. When we find it, we'll move in and it'll be *ours* – not yours or mine. We'll start off with a clean slate. I'll leave

Station Road on the market in case I get a buyer. If I do, I may have to rethink – if we've not found a house in the meantime, that is.'

Markby said, 'I thought you didn't fancy returning to Station Road since it was vandalised.'

'I didn't. But now Minchin and Hayes have stayed in the place, I feel differently. They've formed a kind of buffer between me and what happened. I won't ask if you mind because I can see you do. But I just don't – I'm not at ease here.'

'Not at ease here or not at ease here with me?' She could hear anger now in his voice.

'I don't want to quarrel. We'll just have to speed up the house-hunting.'

'I'm getting bloody fed up with this!' he said suddenly. 'Why can't we just get married?'

'All right, when we find a house together, we'll get married.' The words were out before she realised it.

Alan leaned forward. 'What was that? Say it again.'

Meredith cleared her throat. 'When we find a house for us both to live in, I'll marry you.'

'Right!' he said. 'I'll hold you to that!'

Chapter Twenty-Seven

From the *Bamford Gazette*, 1890

There were scenes of near riot at the courthouse following the acquittal of William Price Oakley on a charge of murdering his wife. Oakley himself and the members of the jury which had declared his innocence had to be smuggled out by a side entrance to avoid the mob. The crowd had begun to gather early in anticipation of a Guilty verdict. On hearing they were not to get what they wanted, the mood turned ugly. When a cab with blinds drawn was observed departing the precincts of the courthouse, the cry went up that it contained William Oakley. Several rough fellows in the crowd began to pelt it with cobblestones snatched up from the road. Only when it proved to contain the chief witness for the prosecution, Mrs Martha Button, was it allowed to proceed on its way. A large force of constables then set about restoring order and some arrests took place. At last the mob was persuaded that William Oakley had been spirited away by court officials and it could not lay hands on him. It then dispersed. It is understood that charges of causing an affray are to follow in the case of certain persons.

The court had reached its verdict at mid-morning. By early afternoon Stanley Huxtable was back in Bamford and had submitted his final piece of copy on the Oakley trial. He was now on his way home with the rare prospect of a free afternoon ahead of him.

The disturbance outside the courthouse had been a close shave as far as he was concerned. A missile had taken off his bowler hat and when he stooped to retrieve it, he saw that it'd been struck by half a brick. If that had been targeted an inch lower, he'd be in the infirmary now.

Still, such are the hazards of a reporter's life. It might have laid him low, but it hadn't. Stanley whistled to himself as he made his way down the street, turning over in his mind what he should do with his unexpected free time. He'd just decided that whatever else, that evening he'd treat himself to a proper slap-up meal somewhere, when he stopped in mid-tune, pushed his hat to the back of his head and murmured, 'Hello!'

A female form had emerged from a butcher's shop ahead of him and was making her way at a brisk pace along the pavement. There was probably more than one woman in widow's weeds and veil in Bamford, but not many with a figure as neat as that or with that rapid step. Stanley quickened his own pace.

It's possible to sense when one is being followed. The girl in black went faster still. At a corner she paused and looked back. Stanley could only see the veil. Whether she saw him through it, he couldn't tell, but he was pretty sure she had. She almost ran round the corner and Stanley, now in hot pursuit, darted after her.

There she was, scurrying along, the unwieldy wicker basket on her arm hampering her progress. Her haste almost cost her dear. Without due precaution she stepped off the pavement to cross the street, just as a delivery vanman whistled to his horse and started forward.

'Hey!' yelled Stanley. The girl stopped, realised her peril, made to step back, stumbled against the kerb in her long skirts and was forced to drop her basket to save herself.

As Stanley ran up to her, she was picking herself up, her fingers scrabbling at her veil to pull it back into place. Various parcels lay around her.

'Allow me,' offered Stanley, gathering them up and returning them to the basket which lay on its side. By the time he'd done this the girl had succeeded in repositioning the veil and was shaking dust from her skirts. He had missed seeing her face by a fraction.

'Thank you,' she said icily and stretched out her hand to take the basket now held by Stanley.

Stanley hung on to it. 'I was afraid,' he said, 'you were going to be run down there.'

'It wouldn't have happened,' she retorted, 'if you hadn't been following me.'

'It wouldn't have happened,' said Stanley, 'if you hadn't got that veil over your face and could see where you were going properly.'

'You are very impertinent, Mr Huxtable!' Because he couldn't see her, he had to judge her mood from her voice and attitude. Both were combative.

'Remember me, then?' said Stanley cheerfully.

'Of course I remember you! You followed me and my friend in Oxford. You seem to make a habit of following me. I don't know why.'

'I don't know why, really,' said Stanley honestly. 'Just curiosity, you know. I'm a reporter.'

'So you told us. May I have my basket back?'

'It's heavy,' said the solicitous Stanley, 'and you've had a nasty fright. Let me carry it.'

'We are not going the same way.'

'How do you know? Anyway,' added Stanley, 'I've got the whole afternoon off and I can go anywhere I want.'

She was silent for a while and then said soberly, 'The trial is over, then?'

'It is. I looked for you, but you didn't come again. Why did you come along that one time?'

'Like you, I was curious. A neighbour wanted to go and asked me if I'd accompany her. Was he convicted?'

'Oakley? No, he got off. I thought he would. I had a sort of bet on it.'

'Then you won,' she said in a voice of such concentrated fury that he stepped back and felt himself flush.

Embarrassment was a rare emotion for him. 'Don't get me wrong,' he pleaded. 'It wasn't that sort of bet. It was just with a fellow journalist over whether or not the housekeeper would hold up under cross-questioning. All I won was a pint of ale.'

'I hope you enjoyed it.' She stretched out a gloved hand and gripped the handle of the basket. This time, Stanley relinquished it.

He thought she'd walk off straight away, but she remained standing where she was, apparently lost in thought. Then she said very quietly, to herself rather than to him, 'Father will be upset.'

'Your father being?'

'Inspector Wood,' she told him in an absent-minded way as if she no longer cared whether he stood there or not.

To Stanley's mind, this was a step back, rather than forward, in their relationship. On the other hand, he'd acquired some startling information. 'I know your father quite well,' he said loudly.

'Yes,' she retorted, recalled to his presence. 'You are the person my father refers to as "that wretch, Huxtable". I can see why!'

He chuckled and she asked, sounding both puzzled and piqued, 'You find that amusing?'

'Well, I've been called worse – and by your father. Let me carry your basket, Miss Wood. See, here I am at a loose end, nothing to do.'

'Except bother me? You will not get a story for your newspaper from me, Mr Huxtable.'

Stanley's heart rose. He'd been sure he'd seen no wedding ring on her finger when he'd approached her and her companion in the restaurant. Now she'd not corrected the title he'd given her. She was neither married nor a widow, then. The veil was on some other account. Some old uncle had breathed his last, or . . . An idea struck Stanley. A wild idea, but perhaps not so wild when he recalled her past actions, sitting in the corner of the court with her face against the wall. Sitting in the restaurant in the same way.

'I'm not looking for a story,' he said. 'There's nothing more to write about Oakley. If he'd been found Guilty, I could've written a full page on him. But if I write about him now, he'll set his lawyers on me. He's an innocent man.' He paused. 'You're in mourning?'

'No,' she said, after a moment.

He was sure she'd been debating whether to tell a lie but she was a person who set store by the truth.

She then wrong-footed him completely. 'I understand the reason for your curiosity, Mr Huxtable. Many others share it. They, however, do not pursue me through the streets. My father has described you as persistent. I suspect you'll continue to waylay me whenever I put my nose out of my own door until your curiosity is satisfied. Well, then.'

She set the basket on the ground and lifted her hand to her bonnet. 'I shall satisfy it now and perhaps you'll then leave me in peace!' She turned back the veil.

Stanley had guessed what might lie behind the veil and had steeled himself. But in the event, it wasn't as bad as he'd been prepared for. He, after all, had interviewed the mutilated victims of accidents, industrial and agricultural, and he'd certainly seen worse. It was confined to just one half of her face which was disfigured by stretched, shiny red skin and lack of eyelash or eyebrow. The other side of her face was 'enchanting. *She* was enchanting. The scar tissue didn't matter a damn. He wanted to tell her so, but shrewdly guessed it would be poorly received.

So instead, he said placidly, 'I thought it might be some such reason.'

His lack of reaction surprised her. She stared at him for a moment, then raised her hand to replace the veil.

'No!' Stanley said sharply.

She hesitated, puzzled by the vehemence in his voice, her eyes questioning. 'Why not?'

'Why should you?' he countered.

'People stare!' It burst out, an angry accusation.

'They'd stare at you, anyway, all dressed up like that with a veil.' For a dreadful moment, he feared he'd gone too far and she was going to cry. But she was of tougher material.

'That's hardly your problem, Mr Huxtable. Good day to you.' Now she was angry with him.

'I tell you what,' said Stanley, ignoring both her words and her anger, 'I'll walk with you to your home and then you won't need to drape that curtain in front of your face.'

Now he saw panic in her eyes. 'Oh no, I couldn't do that! I couldn't walk through Bamford—'

'Yes, you can,' insisted Stanley gently. 'Because you'll be with me. And if anyone stares, he'll get a good glare back from me that will change his mind. Come on, now.'

He swept up the basket and offered his other arm to her. After a moment, she took it. They walked on in silence for some way.

She was the first to break it. 'Your work is very interesting, I dare say.'

'Sometimes it is and sometimes it isn't. Nothing much happens in Bamford.' Stanley sighed. 'I end up reporting sheep-stealing or some vagrant pinching washing from back gardens.'

'You wouldn't wish to see Bamford a nest of criminals? My father works very hard to prevent it being so.'

'Oh yes, your father's doing a good job,' he agreed. 'But it doesn't help me. No, of course I don't want Bamford to turn into a sink of iniquity. Just the occasional interesting crime, you know.'

At that she laughed and he looked at her in amazement.

One half of her face had lit up with her smile. The muscles of the other half appeared paralysed. He wondered what had happened to cause the disfigurement.

'Do you know you have a dent in your hat?' she asked.

'Yes. There was a bit of a ruckus at the courthouse and my hat got knocked off.'

'Oh dear, that sounds a dangerous situation.'

'What is danger to a true journalist?' asked Stanley rhetorically, hoping to impress.

It didn't. 'The same as danger to the rest of us, I dare say. Best avoided. My father who is, I assure you, a courageous man, always says, only a fool puts his head over the parapet if he knows he's going to be shot at. Use your head, he says, to think with, not to make a target of.'

Stanley nodded. 'One's parents always give that sort of advice. It makes for a very dull life.'

They'd reached Station Road and stopped before a modest end-of-terrace cottage.

'This is where I live, Mr Huxtable. Thank you for your company and for carrying my shopping.' She held out her gloved hand.

Stanley shook it formally. 'Without wishing to sound forward, Miss Wood . . .'

'Yes?' She raised her eyebrows, a gentle note of mockery in her voice.

'You wouldn't care to go for a walk on Sunday afternoon?'

She shook her head. 'Thank you, but no. I think you are a nice man, Mr Huxtable, but my father definitely doesn't approve of you and I – I am not as brave as you fancy me. Because you do mean me to walk unveiled, don't you?'

'Of course I do. Will you be brave enough one day, do you think?'

She considered the question. 'I don't know. Father would like me to go out and face the world. But it's so easy for both of you to say and so difficult for me to do.'

'I realise you can't be rushed,' Stanley told her. 'Fair enough. If you change your mind, you can leave a note for me at the offices of the *Gazette*.'

'I see Father was right. You really are very determined, Mr Huxtable.'

'Yes,' he agreed. 'I never give up.'

Emily took her basket to the kitchen and put it on the table. Then she sat down herself and pulled her gloves from hands which trembled uncontrollably. She'd always believed herself honest. She hadn't lied either to her father or to Huxtable. But to hide the truth, was that a form of lying? Was it any less despicable? Was the burden of guilt she carried eased because of some semantic difference? Yet what had she hidden? Only a snatch of conversation, a few words overheard and spoken by a man clearly in drink.

It had happened some weeks before Cora Oakley's death. There had been an evening meeting at the Methodist Hall to hear a returned missionary describe his adventures. Emily had been tempted out by the idea of hearing about a world far removed from her quiet existence. Originally her father had agreed to accompany her, though generally he was disrespectful of missionaries. But at the last moment he had been called away professionally and Emily had set out alone.

The meeting had been crowded and when the speaker agreed to answer questions, he was peppered with them from the audience. Tea followed and Emily was asked to lend a hand. All in all, by the time everyone had left, the debris was cleared away and the washed cups stacked in the tiny kitchen, the light had faded. At the corner of the street she parted from her last companion and set off home alone.

From behind windows, gaslight gleamed and here and there flickering candlelight, because not everyone in Bamford had the new-fangled gas. The lamplighter had not reached this part of town on his rounds and there was no street-lighting to combat the dusk. Generally Emily welcomed the dark, because it meant no one paid any heed to her. But she was nervous of passing the various public houses. However, nothing untoward happened until she reached The Crown which was both a hotel and the place where gentlemen drank if they were inclined to do so away from home. It was said that in a discreet back room there, those same gentlemen played cards for high stakes, something viewed with disfavour in the Methodist community.

Emily had almost reached The Crown when suddenly, a side door was thrown open releasing a beam of bright yellow light. Two figures stumbled out, one older, one younger. The younger one held his hat in his hand and she saw his face, a handsome, rakish, moustached face she was sure she'd never forget. Automatically she had darted into a convenient doorway and now the two men began to walk unsteadily towards her. She cowered back into the shadows.

'Take my advice, old man,' urged the elder of the two. 'Make it up to her. Take her on a little trip abroad, eh? Whisk her off to Paris where she can buy herself some new dresses. Or the Alps, good for the lungs.'

'If it were that damned easy, don't you think I'd do it?'

came the angry reply. 'She won't listen to anything I say any more. She's talking of separation, says she has evidence . . . Then what should I damn well do?'

'Got to get a grip on the situation, old man.' This was followed by a drunken hiccup.

'Believe me, I intend to.'

They'd stumbled off into the gloom. Emily had emerged, shaken, and hurried home. She hadn't mentioned it to her father, who was probably home himself by now, and already worried at her being out so late. But when Oakley had come to trial, she knew she had to see him, see for herself if it was the same man.

It had been the same one, standing defiantly in the dock. But she still hadn't mentioned the conversation she'd overheard to her father. Suppose, horror of horrors, she'd ended up having to take the witness stand? Though what could she have said? It had been dark. Defence counsel would say she was mistaken in identifying him. Anyway, a man in drink might babble any old nonsense. She didn't know he was talking of his wife.

So she'd held her peace, telling herself that Justice would find its way to the truth. But it lay upon her conscience together with the knowledge that now she could never tell Father. It was the first and only thing she'd ever hidden from him. No, it *had* been the only thing. Now there was her encounter with Huxtable. That had to be hidden, too. Father had little time for the newspaperman.

'That's what happens when you leave this house, Emily my girl!' she told herself aloud. 'Life gets complicated.'

Undeniably, it also got more interesting.

* * *

Wood made his own way home later that evening, a copy of the *Gazette* in his hand. So, they'd failed. He'd failed. The Home Office had failed. Taylor had failed. Who cared who had failed? The point was, William Oakley walked free. Was the acquittal a surprise? No, Wood had had a bad feeling from the beginning. On the other hand, he had to confess to a spark of obstinate optimism, nestling in the depths of his being.

Emily opened the door. She had been watching from the window for his return and forestalled his greeting with, 'You are upset about the Oakley business, but you mustn't be. You did all you could.'

'Where did you hear the verdict?' he asked in surprise, since she clearly knew it.

'Oh,' she looked a little confused. 'I met someone as I was walking home from the butcher's. Someone who'd heard Mr Oakley had been found Not Guilty, and told me.'

'Well, I'm not going to let it get me down,' Wood told her with a cheeriness he was far from feeling. 'So don't worry about me, my dear. Win some, lose some, eh? What are we to have tonight?' He sniffed the air.

'Boiled hock of bacon with leeks and carrots,' he was told.

'Boiled bacon!' Wood beamed at her. 'My favourite.'

Beneath These Stones

Ann Granger

Twelve-year-old Tammy Franklin has learned too much about death, too quickly. Two years ago she lost her mother to a long, lingering illness and now the body of the woman her father married in an attempt to replace his wife has been found on a railway embankment close to the Franklin farm. This time the death is murder.

As Superintendent Markby, one of the first on the scene, well knows, Tammy now stands to have her father taken from her, for Hugh Franklin is suspect number one in the mind of the inspector to whom Markby has delegated the case. But, despite his need to distance himself from the murder, Markby begins to realise that the truth is destined to be far more complex than he ever envisaged . . .

Praise for Ann Granger's hugely popular bestsellers

'Granger's deft touch raises her above the competition and her finely drawn characters are affecting and believable . . . Something quite special' *Crime Time*

'Ann Granger has brought the traditional English village story up to date, in setting, sophistication and every other aspect of fiction writing . . . sheer unadulterated bliss' *Birmingham Post*

'You'll soon be addicted' *Woman and Home*

0 7472 5643 8

HEADLINE

Running Scared

Ann Granger

Aspiring actress and part-time private investigator
Fran Varady knew there would be maximum disruption when her friend Ganesh decided to modernise
his uncle's newsagents, starting with the washroom.
But she isn't prepared for the nightmare that begins
when an agitated passer-by asks to use it: hours later,
he's found stabbed to death, leaving a message for
Fran to meet him, and a mysterious roll of film hidden
behind the old pipes . . .

Fran realises that whoever wanted the negatives
knows where they were hidden. And, probably,
where they are now. With her police protection more
a hindrance than a help, an old friend, Tig, on the
verge of collapse, and the builders wreaking havoc in
the shop, can Fran find out why someone is prepared
to murder for the negatives – before they find *her*?

'One of crime fiction's most engaging heroines'
Yorksire Post

'Fran's a delight . . . the plot is neat and ingenious, the
characters rounded and touchingly credible, and the
writing of this darkly humorous and generous novel
fluent, supple and a pleasure to read' *Ham and High*

'Ann Granger's skill with character, together with her
sprightly writing, make the most of the story . . . she
is on to another winner' *Birmingham Post*

0 7472 5577 6

HEADLINE